Strange
Devices
of the
Sun
and
Moon

Strange
Devices
of the
Sun
and
Moon

Lisa
Goldstein

TOR
fantasy

A TOM DOHERTY ASSOCIATES BOOK ◆ NEW YORK

STRANGE DEVICES OF THE SUN AND MOON

Copyright © 1993 by Lisa Goldstein

A Tor Book
Published by Tom Doherty Associates, Inc.
175 Fifth Avenue
New York, N.Y. 10010

Edited by David G. Hartwell

Tor® is a registered trademark of Tom Doherty Associates, Inc.

Library of Congress Cataloging-in-Publication Data

Goldstein, Lisa.
    Strange devices of the sun and moon / Lisa Goldstein.
        p.   cm.
    ISBN 0-312-85460-9
        1. Arthurian romances—Adaptations.   2. Arthur, King—Fiction.
    I. Title.
    PS3557.O397S75   1993
    813′.54—dc20   92-21572
                                                                          CIP

Printed in the United States of America

0 9 8 7 6 5 4 3 2

Tempting as it may be to have the reader think I did it all myself, I have to admit that this book would not exist without the help of the following people and institutions: the Main, Moffitt and Bancroft Libraries at the University of California, Berkeley, and their wonderfully helpful staffs; Dave Hartwell, editor extraordinaire; and my agent, Lynn Seligman. My husband, Doug Asherman, went with me to plays and lectures, played madrigals for me on the guitar, cheered me up when things got rough, and listened patiently and with good humor to what must have seemed like an endless series of tedious Elizabethan facts. It is to him, with love and gratitude, that this book is dedicated.

"... A company of ragged knaves,
Sun-bathing beggars, lazy hedge-creepers,
Sleeping face upwards in the fields all night,
Dream'd strange devices of the Sun and Moon ..."

—Thomas Nashe,
Summer's Last Will and Testament

Strange
Devices
of the
Sun
and
Moon

February, 1590

1

The traveler in front rode a horned mount, and had horns on his head as well. He was dressed in green, with soft dark-green boots and a cloak that flowed on behind him. The bells twined in the animal's mane made little sound, something like the wind blowing somewhere far off. Behind him rode the standard-bearers, carrying the old banners stained with dew and rotted with rain, and behind them the queen. He lifted a trumpet to his lips and blew it, and then turned and motioned to the troop behind him. They followed him like a wave.

As they passed through the dark streets their way was lit by a sparkling light, as if the element they moved in was not air but fire. If people had seen them pass by (and no one did, though a few looked directly at them) they would have thought of stars falling to earth. And compared to their lights the stars and the round moon were dull, dimmed by fog and soot and the candles from houses and inns and taverns.

They were going into exile, though none of them mentioned it. Some of the flightier ones had even forgotten it, and now they bent to play with the stones on the city streets, thinking them a sort of toy. "Press on, press on!" a few of them called, and the ones who had picked up the handfuls quickly dropped them.

The company moved through the streets, drawing closer as a defense against the strangeness. Some flew ahead on wings like thin and shining silk, some rode fine horses or birds, some were small enough to be carried. They who spent so much of their lives in a kind of dream now looked around as if awakening, seeing the huge wooden and plaster houses, the streets wider than any meadow path, the faint stars overhead. Some of them laughed in surprise. A few whimpered for a moment, and then forgot why it was they were supposed to be unhappy. "Press on, press on!" came the call from the front of the line, and those at the back took it up. Some of them began to sing.

In the cold London houses people stirred in their beds, thinking they heard something. Alice Wood turned and reached for her husband John, forgetting in her sleep that he was dead and in his grave this past year. "It's the wind," she whispered, though to whom she said it she didn't know. In the taverns the wits fell silent a moment and one or two of them made a move to depart. A young man abroad late found himself singing a song he hadn't heard since childhood. And Paul Hogg raised his eyes from an experiment and thought, they're here. They've come at last.

Before cockcrow and first light the travelers dispersed to houses throughout London. A few of them passed the rest of the night sweeping the hearth or mending old clothes. Others curled up in out-of-the-way corners and went to sleep. The queen waited to thank the horned man for bringing them to their destination. They would be safe in this strange place, she thought. By running brook and standing stone, by all the powers of the World, it would go well for them here.

By the time she woke Alice had forgotten the disturbances of the night. She dressed in her skirt and bodice and ruff, and adjusted a small linen cap over her head. Then she took a moment to glance in her small hand mirror. The face that looked back at her seemed, as always, older than she expected, as though somewhere in her mind she was still young and living with John. How had the years passed so quickly? She saw fine blond hair, too light to show the gray, a wide mouth and high cheekbones and strangely uptilted eyes. "Like a Tartar's," John had said about her eyes, though they were blue instead of brown.

It had snowed lightly the day before, but the morning looked to be unseasonably warm for February. Weak sunlight came in through the two windows at the front of the house. As she opened the door to go to work she noticed the place looked cleaner than usual, freshly swept, and without thinking about it she felt strangely gladdened, lighter than she had in days.

Her house was along the north wall of St. Paul's, on Paternoster Row, and the stall from which she sold her books stood in the walled yard of the cathedral itself. The church, to the scandal of the priests and religious people of London, served as the center and meeting place for nearly everyone in the city. As she headed for her stall she saw evidence of the day's activity beginning. A tailor jostled past her, scraps of cloth hanging from his shoulder. Near her someone was posting a bill advertising employment, one of the large London inns seeking a hostler. Scriveners and lawyers, gallants and gossips were hastening toward the large wooden cathedral. There they would spread out through the aisles and nave, display their wares on the tombs and font, look for clients, ask for and receive the latest news.

Almost all the booksellers and printers in London had their stations in St. Paul's, either against the church itself or in rows leading away from it. Some of them had already started setting up their wares and were calling to the early browsers. "Buy a new book, sir—here's the latest news from France!" "Almanacs, almanacs and prognostications!" "Jigs and ballads here!" "Honest man, here are the books you lack!"

"Good morning!" her neighbor at the next stall, Edward Blount, called to her.

"Morning!" she said, putting her books out on display. She didn't have as many books as Blount—in the harrowing time after her husband's death she had been too busy learning the business to acquire any new titles—but John had left her some popular pamphlets and ballads, and she kept the monopoly which had allowed him to print all the playbills in London. Still, she couldn't help envying Blount his impeccable literary taste, his nose for what was both good and popular.

More booksellers were opening their stalls now. A money-lender walked by, deep in conversation with a client. George Cowper called to her as he passed. "Looks to be a fair day," she said to him.

"Aye, but it'll probably turn foul later," he said. "Care to take your dinner with me?"

"If I'm not too busy."

"Come, you won't be as busy as I will."

"Oh, I'll sell a book or two," she said. She liked George, but she wished he wouldn't keep reminding her that his business was brisker than hers. And as if to spite him she did a good trade all day, with hardly any time at all to rest. The lawyers were in town for the Candlemas term, and she and every other bookseller were kept busy answering questions about the books and news they'd missed while they were out of London. By the time she managed to get away to the stalls on Cheapside Street George had already eaten.

More people thronged the churchyard when she got back. In a month or so it would be warm enough for the playhouses to open, but in late winter those who wanted to see and be seen came to Paul's. She watched as a man urged his horse through the crowd and into the cathedral, which was used as a shortcut for those who didn't want to walk the long way around the walls. Two dogs fought over a scrap of meat, and someone wearing the rags of a beggar took advantage of the diversion to dip his hand into his neighbor's purse. A woman near her cried her wares: "Apples and oranges here! Oranges from Seville!"

A thin man wearing unadorned black doublet and hose and the smallest possible white ruff was waiting for her at her stall. He looked like a Puritan, and her first thought was to tell him she had no theological books. Or he might be a spy from the Privy Council, come to make sure that everything she sold had been authorized and licensed. Whoever he was, she wanted no part of him. "What book do you need?" she asked.

"No book," he said. "Are you Alice Wood?"

"Aye."

"Have you a son?"

"I had a son," she said cautiously. No one had mentioned Arthur to her for so long she had almost grown used to thinking of him as dead.

"And where might he be now?"

"I don't know. Who are you and why do you question me like this?"

He took a half crown from his purse. "I'll give you this for any information you might have."

She looked at the coin. "It looks counterfeit," she said.

"Aye," he said, smiling strangely. He put the coin back in his purse. "Beware the false coin and the false man. Beware the moon, counterfeit of the sun."

"Who are you?"

"One who seeks the truth."

"Then seek it somewhere else or stop talking in riddles," she said, suddenly angry. "If you know something about my son I would like to hear it, and if not go back to Bedlam where you came from. Does he owe you money?"

"Nay. We owe him, and more than money."

Alice watched him as he left the churchyard and thought of Arthur. She had been old when he was born, nearly thirty, and he had been their only child. From the beginning he had been a moody boy, sometimes quiet, sometimes talking about nonsense for hours on end. He had never played with the other children, and despite the fact that his father was a bookseller he had never learned to read. Yet he had only to hear a song once to remember it, and when he was young John used to ask him to sing for the customers who wanted to buy a ballad-sheet. As he grew older he began to leave the churchyard for hours, sometimes for days. Finally he had left and not come back. She used to ask the poets and pamphleteers who came to talk to her and John if they had seen him, but no one had. She thought he must be dead, of some illness, like John, or killed in a brawl.

Near her a young gallant was looking around anxiously, probably trying to find someone to dine with before the day ended and he had to go home hungry. She smelled horse dung and the perfume and sweat of the close-packed crowd. Someone laughed loudly and she followed the sound, hoping for a distraction. As if the thought of the pamphleteers had conjured them up she saw Thomas Nashe and fat Henry Chettle coming toward her, swerving wide to avoid a suspected cutpurse. "Good day, masters," she said, smiling a little to see them.

"Good day, Mistress Wood," Thomas said. "How are my books selling?"

"Well enough."

"Well enough for you, perhaps. You have other books to sell, but I must make up a new pamphlet or poem or play every few months or starve."

"Do you think so? You always do well—"

"It would take a new battle with the Armada, and Queen Elizabeth herself riding to St. Paul's to proclaim victory, for anyone to set foot in this churchyard and buy a book again. Forgive me, but it takes only one bad pamphlet to raise a damp enough to poison the entire place. You wouldn't credit the books they sell here. Richard Harvey's, for one."

"Aye, I saw your attack on him in the new manuscript you gave me. I thought perhaps you might take that out—it could offend the man—"

"Offend him? And what's that to me?"

"He would feel he had to give you an answer—"

"Aye, let him. And I'll answer him in kind. We'll have more sport than an afternoon's bearbaiting."

"But it's such a paltry thing—you would be wasting your talent if you spent it on nothing but the Harveys. There is so much you could write about."

"And I will, too. I could make up a pamphlet about your blue eyes, about that apple Chettle's eating."

"Listen, I must ask you something."

The young man looked as if he were about to go on, as if only her question prevented him from improvising for another hour. "Aye?"

"Have you heard any word of Arthur?"

"Your son? You've asked us before."

"Aye, but a man's been around asking about him."

"What sort of man?"

"A man all dressed in black. He had the look of a Puritan about him."

"A Puritan? You want to stay away from that sort."

"Then you haven't seen Arthur? Or heard any news of him?"

"Nay."

She wondered if he was telling the truth. She liked the young men who visited her, but they seemed very much like the plays they wrote, glorious and fantastical but not really fit for daily life. They all thought, or seemed to think, that they needn't work for a living, that their books and plays would earn them enough to live on, and she wondered where on earth they had gotten this extraordinary idea. Look at Tom Nashe now, she thought, lacking nourishment, prone to illness every few months, sometimes unable even to pay his rent. He looked years younger than he actually was, as if he were a foundling. Even his pale watery hair seemed to proclaim his straits, as if it had once been a more robust color, and he couldn't seem to grow a beard. He had on patched and stained clothes, and his newfangled falling collar, worn in place of a ruff, exposed his stark collarbones, thick as thumbs. But they were all of them too thin, all except Chettle, and he looked as unhealthy as the rest. How did they survive? Whenever she saw one of them she wanted to take him aside and tell him to learn a trade before it was too late.

"Well, we must be going," Thomas said. "Robert Greene forced a bailiff who came to arrest him to eat his citation, wax and all, and we have to see about his bail."

"Did he really?" She had to laugh.

"Do you doubt my word? And served to it him very handsomely too, on a fine pewter plate."

She was still laughing as they left, though in truth she was a little appalled. They all seemed to have this streak of cruelty in their makeup, even among themselves. Would they tell her if they found Arthur? Or would they think it was amusing to keep the news from her?

It was almost dusk, the shadow of the churchyard walls falling across a few of the nearer stalls, before she found time to talk to George. They went to the cookshop on the corner for

supper, and as they sat eating mutton and drinking small beer
she asked him, "Did you see that man in black who came to
speak with me?"

"Nay. I told you—I was busy all day."

"He asked me about my son."

"It's not good for you to think too much of Arthur. You have
said it yourself—he is probably dead."

"The man I talked to thought him still alive. He asked for
news of him."

"Who was he?"

"I never saw him before. I was hoping you knew. And
George—it was so strange—he offered me a coin for information, but the coin looked counterfeit, and when I told him so he
smiled, as if he had set me some sort of test. And his smile—I
didn't like it, not at all."

"Did he threaten you?"

"Threaten? Nay, but he seemed—I don't know—intent on
something. Almost as if he burned with a fever."

"Promise me you'll tell me if he comes back."

"I will. But truly I think he's a harmless madman, like the
unfortunates who come into the churchyard at times. I doubt
he'll be back."

"This news worries me, Alice. It's not good for you to live
alone, without a man. He would not have dared to trouble you
if I had been there."

"I do well enough."

"How are your books selling?"

"Not badly."

"But not well, either. You would have done better to have
sold me your husband's business after he died. I thought that
the best course then and it seems that way to me still."

"And how would I have gotten my livelihood?"

"Why, use the money I would have given you. And the
stationers' fund takes care of widows, you know that."

"And when your money was gone? The stationers would
have given me very little."

"Why do you talk that way, as if I had made you a miserly
offer? I would have been quite generous."

"I did not want to sell the shop, no more than I want to sell it now. John would have wanted me to keep it."

"But you knew so little about bookselling."

"I learn more about it every day. I just bought another manuscript from Thomas Nashe—"

"Nashe? Who is he?"

"A young man my husband knew. His pamphlets sell well."

"But how long and how well can you live on one writer's pamphlets? I cannot understand why you must be so stubborn."

"I enjoy living the way I do."

"But it's wrong, don't you see that? A woman must have a man above her to guide her, just as a country must have a sovereign."

"The country does quite well with a woman to guide it."

"Ah, but she was appointed by God."

"I did not come to supper with you to argue theology, George."

"I only tell you what any man in the churchyard would say."

"I know too well what they would say. Tell me something else, something only George would say. You were my friend, the one I turned to after John's death. Tell me about—oh, the election we're about to have. Who do you think the booksellers will choose as Master of the Stationers' Company?"

After supper George insisted on accompanying her home. The moon, just waning from the full, washed the streets with silver. The churchyard lay empty and silent under its light, the square tower of St. Paul's bulking against the night sky. By a strange trick the tower looked to her to be farther away than the stars, a dark shape cut in the sphere of the night.

George steered her away from a muddy pothole in the road. He really is kind, she thought. And he truly cares about my safety. I wish he understood how hard it is to do what I've chosen to do, to continue the business that John had built up so carefully.

A pleasant smell, as of baking almonds, came from her house. She went inside, and in the pale light from the windows managed to make out that someone had left a cooling pan of marchpane on her sideboard. "I wonder who brought this," she said. "It's very good of them, whoever it was. Have a piece, George?"

"Nay. It's late and I must be going home."

"Maybe I have a suitor."

In the dim light she could not be certain, but it seemed to her that George scowled.

2

In the Saracen's Head in Shoreditch, on the outskirts of London, the night was just beginning. It was a dim place with no windows, lit only by the cooking fire and a few candles. Knives and daggers had scarred the tables and benches. The air stank of smoke and tobacco and stale beer, and the rushes on the floor needed freshening. In one corner a group of men and women sang ballads and madrigals, hitting their pewter cups with knives to keep time. Across the room Robert Greene, freed on borrowed money he could not afford to pay back, was holding forth.

"Nay, I counted it a trifle, an afternoon's fair diversion," he said. He took a sip of beer and wiped his mouth on his sleeve. "The Compter is a spacious inn compared to some of the prisons which have sheltered me." He was older than most of the playwrights, and that combined with his stocky build, his great beard and his mane of red-brown hair made him seem avuncular, a natural authority figure.

"Fleet Prison for me," Thomas Nashe said. He drew on his tobacco-pipe. "I was served a rare vintage there, the last time I was in."

Thomas Kyd looked between the two men as if trying to

decide if they were jesting. He had heard otherwise, that men had died or disappeared in London's prisons, killed by starvation or disease or other prisoners. He was a very serious-looking young man, with a black curly beard and a pale face that, as Tom Nashe had once said, looked like unbaked bread dough. Unlike the other two he had not gone to either Cambridge or Oxford, and he seemed to feel very keenly that he was in some sense their inferior.

There was a fourth man sitting by the three of them, but whether he wanted to take part in their conversation, or was even listening to it, none of the others could say. He had red-gold hair and his eyes were an astonishing green, surrounded by dark, almost black, lashes. They had seen him in the tavern before: he never seemed to drink anything, or indeed to have any money, but by the end of the night he would appear as drunk as the rest of them.

"When were you in Fleet Prison?" Tom Kyd said finally, as if unable to keep silent any longer.

"Many a man of honor has sailed in that fleet," Tom Nashe said, grinning at him. "Do you tell me that the queen has never offered you lodgings in one of her pleasure houses?"

"Well, of course not."

"What, never been to the university and never been to prison? Tell me, Tom, what have you been doing with your life? It's a sad case when our brightest playwrights know nothing at all about the world they portray on stage."

"I know enough," Tom Kyd said. He wondered if Nashe meant what he said about "brightest playwrights" or if he was just talking to hear himself talk. Or if he was having another joke at Kyd's expense. A year ago Nashe had attacked him in print, and Kyd had decided never to return to the tavern, never to drink with such men again. But there was something about the university wits that kept him coming back, like a poor beggar to a fire. Their very profligacy seemed to blaze like a beacon; someday they would be consumed by it. Not he, though, Kyd thought. He was far too prudent.

"But this day I have made a vow," Robert Greene said, "never to return to debtor's prison. You see before you a changed man."

"I remember you have sworn such oaths before, Robin," Tom Nashe said. "There is not a dog under the table that would believe you."

"You would do well to make such a vow yourself, my young friend," Robert said. "Give over your intemperate ways. Quit this foolish rancorous feud you have with Richard Harvey—"

"Harvey?" Tom Nashe said, his beer halfway to his mouth. "That gross-brained idiot? He attacked you first, and in print, too—how can you have forgotten it? He said you were not fit to pass judgment on other writers. And the answer you gave him in your pamphlet was not enough, I fear. It's a matter of honor, Robin."

"I have struck out that part of my pamphlet—it will not go to press the way you saw it. I tell you, I have changed. As of this day I vow never to owe any man money, never to drink immoderately, never to do anything, by word or deed, that would show me not to be one of the most civil of Her Majesty's subjects."

"Never to visit Em of Holywell Street?" Tom Nashe asked.

Robert turned to him angrily. But at that moment the fourth man, who until then had said nothing, spoke up. "You may do all of those things," he said. "I forgive you."

"You!" Tom Nashe said. "And who are you?"

"Do you not know your king?" The light of one of the candles flared up suddenly, and the man's shadow on the wall grew huge.

The shadow stilled Nashe's merriment for a moment. A serving-woman called an order to the tavern's host, sounding loud in the silence, and someone laughed and was hushed.

Then the candle guttered and died, and Tom laughed. "Ho, the king! And are you Elizabeth's son, or Mary's?"

"Mary?"

"Look at this fellow," Nashe said, gesturing at the other two. "There's good sport here." He turned to the young man. "Have you never heard of Bloody Queen Mary, who ruled in our parents' time? Surely you had a mother to tell you stories of the old bad queen."

The young man looked confused. "Aye, I remember—"

"Good, he remembers his mother. A brave start. And your father? But perhaps that's a more difficult question."

"Let him be," Tom Kyd said. "He's lost his wits, can't you tell?"

"My father?" the young man said. "I—I don't—"

Nashe laughed. But Robert Greene had not finished with his earlier conversation, and now he turned to his friend. "Think about what I said, Tom. Don't let your pamphlet be printed as it is now, with the attack on Richard Harvey."

"And why shouldn't I? Do you think I'm afraid of anything the Harveys might say? Let them answer me. They're all of them pompous asses. I remember Kit Marlowe said to me once—"

"Are you still keeping company with that man, known to the world for an arrant atheist?" Robert said.

"Where is he?" Tom Kyd asked. "I haven't seen him in London for several weeks."

"He comes and goes as he pleases."

"But on what errands?"

"Errands? No one knows."

A few streets away, in the tavern at the sign of the Black Boar, Christopher Marlowe sat and listened to an agent of the queen. The currency exchanged at the Boar was intelligence, knowledge true and false, and so the place stayed silent, ill lit, remote from the hustle and bustle of London. At one table sat a soldier who had done good service in France a dozen years ago and who waited to be taken on for any trifling task again; at another Christopher recognized a man who would work for anyone, anywhere, who had once sold state secrets three times over, to the French, Spanish and English. A sour smell, of old beer and false hopes, lingered in the air.

Christopher took out his tobacco-pipe and lifted the candle close to light it. Whenever he saw Robert Poley he always wondered at how suited the man was for his trade. Look at him once and you wouldn't want to look at him again: his features were so ordinary as to turn him almost invisible. Average height, sandy hair, nondescript face; only his eyes, which were a pale, watery blue, made him stand out in a crowd.

"Did you get the book I asked for?" Robert Poley asked.

"Aye." Christopher passed a slender volume to the other man, glancing again at the title: *Being a True History of the Nobility of England, with an Especial Account of the Royal Families.*

"I suppose you read it," Robert said dryly.

Christopher pushed back his long auburn hair—the same fashionable color as the queen's but much thicker, nearly unmanageable—and looked at Robert. His eyes were a light brown, and he wore a gold ring in one ear. "Of course I read it. Books aren't that easy to come by—I couldn't afford to pass this one up. I thought it interesting, if a little dry."

"I don't pay you for your opinions. You are to finish the tasks I give you, no more."

Christopher nodded. He had had to search through the yard at Paul's and beyond to find someone who had the book for sale. When he had looked through it he had seen no publisher on the title page; it had been printed illegally, by someone without a license from the Privy Council. He guessed that Robert was building a case against the publisher, who had stated that Elizabeth had no right to the throne.

Robert's silence on the matter galled him. The other man had once told Christopher that he traded in information, and information had to be hoarded to drive its value upward. To goad him into speaking Christopher said, "The man who sold me the book made some interesting points. He told me—"

"Don't tell me you spoke to him!"

"Of course I spoke to him. If I'm to buy a book I want to know what it's about, after all."

"He's a traitor to the queen. When we find the publisher we'll take this man in for questioning as well. Good God, you could have been overheard—you could have been arrested for treason. Don't do anything like that again."

"If I was arrested for treason you would have spoken up for me."

"Would I?" Robert's eyes glistened in the candlelight. He smiled, revealing a row of rotten teeth. "Don't be too certain. I'm wondering how much I can trust you, after all. The last time I sent you on an errand I heard strange news about you."

"News?"

"Aye, news. My informant told me your opinions are quite unorthodox, and that you show no fear of spreading them abroad. Don't think that because you work for me the Privy Council will protect you. If you're caught I'll be lucky to get away with my neck intact."

Christopher waited. Robert would not have sent for him to read him a lecture, after all. At a neighboring table he heard someone say, whispering, "Five thousand soldiers, and whatever money he can raise . . ." Finally the other man leaned forward.

"There are rumors," Robert said, lowering his voice. As always he gave out no names; he would never say more than "I have heard," or "My informants tell me," or "There are rumors."

"Rumors?"

"You know from this book that some in London are speaking of an heir to the throne. Lately these stories have multiplied. Folks say now that there is a man who has come to save his country in time of need, or some such nonsense."

"Who says this?"

"Many people. I'm surprised you haven't heard them. Once they start on their fantasies, these legends, they will talk of nothing else."

"What sort of legends?"

"How should I know? Dreams and fables—that's your province. But all their talk is of the return of kings. In my opinion their mood is dangerous, very dangerous."

"Do you think there is any truth to it?"

"That a man should walk out of legend—"

"That someone is abroad, speaking to people in the language of the old stories, claiming kinship with the heroes of antiquity."

"Perhaps. If there is he will be brought in and questioned."

"And what am I to do about it?"

"You are to watch for him," Robert said. "You go to taverns, don't you? That's where our informers have seen him."

Christopher nodded. Taverns, he thought. Doubtless the man's a poor drunk who doesn't realize what he's saying. But any errand from Robert Poley was welcome. Writing for the stage, even writing plays as successful as his were, paid very little. He needed the spy-work Robert gave him to stay alive in London.

Robert stood. "Where will you go now?" he asked.

"Taverns," Christopher said, smiling slightly. "I'm anxious to begin work."

"Good. I'll walk with you."

They left the Black Boar together. Robert had never wanted to walk with him before; the other man had always taken care not to be seen with him out-of-doors. Was Robert checking up on him? He hadn't intended to carry out the agent's task that night, to be truthful; instead he planned to go to the Saracen's Head and see if Greene had managed to escape prison once again.

They followed the twisted skein of the streets. The white moon shone above them, too high now to cast much light. Footsteps sounded in the dark street, and Christopher looked back over his shoulder out of habit. Few honest people walked abroad so late at night. He could see no one. "Did you hear that?"

"What?" Robert asked. "I heard nothing."

"Someone behind us."

Robert turned. "Are you certain?"

"Nay. I must have imagined it."

A few moments later the footsteps came again. This time when he looked back Christopher saw a young man slipping into a doorway. "There is someone," he said softly. He put his hand to the dagger at his back. "And I saw him before, watching us at the Black Boar. He's been following us."

Any of his friends would have dismissed his fear as an idle fancy, but Poley lived and breathed in the medium of plots and conspiracies. The agent stopped and stared back into the shadowy street. "Nay, there's no one there," he said. "And it's too dark to see anyone, let alone recognize a man from the Boar."

"I tell you, I saw him," Christopher said. A second man turned into the street and began to run toward them. He stopped at the doorway Christopher had seen and gave a loud cry. Christopher and Robert moved back into the shadows of the street.

The man in the doorway shouted, "You! I thought——" Then they both heard the unmistakable sound of steel being scraped against steel as the second man drew his dagger.

The man in the doorway moved out into the street. He had not drawn his dagger; probably, Christopher thought, he had not gotten over the shock of being challenged by a man he obviously knew.

The other man struck. Finally the first man seemed to rouse himself. He jumped back, but his opponent had managed to cut deeply into his arm. He drew his dagger slowly, as if dazzled.

Now Robert and Christopher could see blood welling from the man's sleeve, a flat black against the white of the cloth. The second man moved forward to attack again and the first tried to parry, slashing out in front of him while his opponent slipped deftly to the right.

The first man turned quickly, but it was too late. The second man's dagger came up under him. He twisted to get away.

The second man thrust the dagger forward, into the other's chest. The first man fell slowly to the ground, a look more of surprise than fear on his face.

His opponent bent over him. Robert and Christopher saw the dying man try to speak. "Who——"

"We should leave," Robert said. "Quickly. The watch will come, and they'll take us to prison before we can explain ourselves——"

"Nay!" Christopher said urgently. "He *was* following us. What did he want? Who is the other man?"

The second man looked up sharply. Had he heard them? The man looked back once at his opponent and then ran off down the street.

Christopher moved as if to follow, but Robert held him back. "It's none of our concern," Robert said. "Let's go."

"Of course it's our concern. Who was he?" But it was already too late; the man had gone. And perhaps Robert was right. The watch would certainly come to take them to prison if they stayed. Last year he had gone to Newgate Prison because a friend of his had killed a man in a duel, and he had no wish to repeat that experience.

"Our business is with the man I mentioned, the one who claims to be king," Robert said. He had composed himself and now looked the way Christopher remembered him, controlled, untouchable by any calamity. But for a moment Christopher had seen a different side of the man, had seen him frightened. Now, watching him, he knew that something subtle had changed between them. Whatever it was, it would not soon be forgotten by either one. He walked home slowly, all thoughts of the Saracen's Head forgotten.

3

That night the folk who had been exiled to London met in Finsbury Field. To the north the field's three great windmills turned, making a doleful sound like a man groaning. During the day laundresses used the place to dry their clothes, and marksmen aimed their arrows at large paper heads painted like Turks, but at night the exiles shared the field only with a few beggars and vagabonds. It was the work of a moment to cast a glamour over these homeless men and women, and so render themselves invisible. But one of the men, driven mad by his long exposure to the elements, swore ever after that he had seen a tiny creature with wings like spiderwebs.

"Spring comes on apace and we are no closer to finding the babe," the queen said.

"He is here in the city, though," a horned man said. "I can feel him."

"Others have been asking for him," another said. "I have heard them."

"We must get to him first," the queen said. "Else all is lost." She looked around her at the open space of the field, trying to find something that reminded her of home. They had no gift for planning; she knew that. And here in this strange place they had become confused, thrown off balance. The people around them knew how to plot great stratagems, how to lay plans that came to fruition years later. She did not like to think of what would happen if they found the babe first.

"A great change is coming," said one who had not spoken before, the smallest of them. She had roused from where she lay, nestled in the brownie's palm, and now she spread her silken wings. Everyone quieted to hear her. "This world and all we have known will pass away. Trees and stone, wind and rain, will be as naught. It will be a world of artifice, of vast gears interlocking in one enormous mechanism."

The windmills sighed, turning. The queen felt as if she had just heard their doom pronounced. "Will there be a place for us?" she asked.

But the smallest one's sister was singing now, and by custom they could not interrupt her. "Change and go, change and go," she sang. "Twirl your partner, change and go."

The smallest one caught her sister's fancy and sang with her. They rose, laughing, and skittered off into the night air like leaves. There would be no more prophecies: already the more giddy of the folk had joined in a circle to play and spin in their ancient dance.

The queen looked up at the moon for comfort, but it was smudged and nearly hidden by the fog. She felt very small and alone, and the time left to them was almost gone.

Alice was wise enough not to look too closely at the gifts of food left by her admirer, at the scrubbed hearth and mended clothes. Over the weeks she had become used to such things, almost dependent on them. The day never seemed long enough for everything she had to do and, unlike most of the stationers, she had no wife to cook and clean for her.

Edward Blount had once suggested she find an apprentice, but none of the men eager to learn the bookseller's trade had seemed willing to take orders from a woman. Often they would ask to speak to her husband when they applied for a job, and while she could let that go, understanding their confusion, she never felt that they would in time come to think of her as an employer. She'd kept the young assistant John had hired, but he was a little simple, unable to learn any but the easiest tasks.

So when she came out into her kitchen and did not see her usual breakfast of bread and beer she felt disappointed. Perhaps, she thought, she had offended in some way. Then she saw something move near the hearth.

It was of medium height and man-shaped, though she would have wagered her soul it was not a man. Fur the color of nutmeg covered everything but its broad seamed face. Its ears were pointed, and it wore a small red cap shaped like a triangle. Its feet— But some ancient superstition kept her from looking at the feet. She was afraid that she would find them hoofed.

The thing was asleep, she saw now, and she stepped back, not wanting to wake it. Almost she made the sign of the cross, the way her mother used to do when she was frightened or startled. It stirred and opened its eyes. They were a clear brown, like cow dung, and somehow strangely comforting. "Ho!" it said. "Wood and rock, what a night we had together in the fields. I met a screech owl coming home—"

Hearing it speak brought her out of her daze. She should run, get help, call George or Edward. But her movement seemed to frighten it, as if it suddenly recalled who and what she was. It curled back toward the hearth, trying to hide. Amazed at the thought that it might be as fearful as she was she stopped and held out her hand. "Are you the one I should thank for the labor done here?"

"No," it said.

The old women in her village had told stories of such a creature, she remembered now. It would come into your home and do your work, milk your cows and churn your butter, but on no account should you thank it. If you did it would leave.

She nodded to it, trying to be matter-of-fact. "Good day to you then," she said, and turned and left. The old women had called the man a brownie. They had been wise, but Alice thought she had a friend who was wiser. She would have to seek out Margery and tell her what happened: it had been too long since her last visit.

As she went from her house to the churchyard she smiled to

think of her friend. Margery wore a ring on every finger, each with a different jewel, and had a drop of stone at her ear, like a man's, and her long black hair was unfettered by any cap. She lived in a crowded cottage out beyond the city walls. Inside the cottage a fine patina of cat fur lay over everything, and the smell of tobacco smoke hung in the air, for Margery also smoked like a man. Aye, certainly Margery would know what to do.

Paul's was filled with people as always, but at noon the crowd emptied out to hear a proclamation read on Cheapside Street. She closed her stall and went over to talk to George. "Care to take your dinner with me?" he asked.

"Of course," she said.

As they walked together she wondered if she should tell George about the brownie. But before she could decide he said, "I have something important to ask you."

"Aye?"

They reached the cookshop and he directed her to one of the tables. She could not remember ever seeing him so solemn.

"I have given much thought to what I am about to say," he said as they sat down. "As I have told you, I do not believe it is right for a woman to live alone. And I care for you, Alice, and will always wish you well. I wonder if—well—if you would marry me."

"Marry?"

"Aye. Is it such a surprise, then? I had thought we were friends."

"Aye, we are. But marriage . . . I had not looked to marry again."

"Truly, I believe you could do no better than to marry me, immodest though it sounds to say it. We have known each other a long time, and I believe our shops would thrive together. You have certain copyrights, and the monopoly on the playbills—Do you think I speak in jest, then?" he asked, for she had started to laugh.

"Oh, George," she said. "My dear, sweet friend George. I am sorry, but you make it sound so much like a trade agreement."

"Aye, and so it is, partly. I don't like to see you struggling for want of knowledge of the stationer's craft. It is as I have said—I care for you. By marrying you I can watch over you, I can see that you have everything you need."

"I'm sorry, George. But I do not think that I am ready to marry."

"You needn't give me an answer so soon. I know you will have to think about it. When you are ready——"

"I have told you—I'm not ready to marry again. But I thank you very much for your concern."

He moved back a little, away from her. Something happened to his face; it seemed to harden slightly, to become less pliant. Was he angry with her? But surely he would want her to speak her mind on something so important.

"I'm like the queen in this," she said. "I do not think I will ever marry again."

"And now you compare yourself to the queen?" he said. "Really, you have got above yourself. Perhaps you would like some jewels for your gown, or ladies-in-waiting?"

"Please—this doesn't become you."

"It's not I who have declared myself England's new sovereign."

"That was but an example."

"A treasonous example. And blasphemous too—only God can appoint a monarch."

"Now you're being foolish. I said only that I am like the queen in this one thing."

"The queen is free to choose in this matter because she has been appointed by God. We who are her subjects cannot judge her actions. You are only a woman, chosen by no one. It's not right for you to remain unmarried."

"If that's all you have to say to me," she said, "then I'll go back to the churchyard. Good day."

By the time she had shouldered her way through the crowd to her station she wondered if she had made the right decision. George had been right; he could teach her much about the stationer's trade. And it was hard being a woman and living alone; George could help her there too.

"Have you had ill news?" Edward Blount said as she opened her stall. "You look melancholy."

"I feel well enough," she said, not quite sure if she lied or not. "Only—George has asked me to marry him."

"And do you want to marry George?"

"I don't know. I don't think so."

"Well, then," he said, as if that settled the matter.

She would have talked longer with him, but at that moment a man came by asking for a copy of Holinshed's *Chronicles* and by the time she had directed him to the right stall Edward was deep in conversation. Could it be as simple as Edward made it seem? She didn't think so; she thought that George might end their friendship because she preferred to live alone, and she was loath to give up one of the few friends she had made in the churchyard. And perhaps it went deeper than that; perhaps she had struck at his pride. Whatever happened she knew she could not go back to the old comfort that had existed between them. She could only go on as best she could, the way she had gone on after John died.

Edward was motioning her over to his stall, and when she came he indicated the man he had been talking to. "This is Walter James," he said. "The new member of our company."

Membership in the Stationers' Company was limited to fifty-three people. She found herself angry that they had never elected a woman; it would have been good to have someone in the churchyard she could open her heart to. But had any woman ever applied for membership? She felt in a foul mood today. Edward had been wrong: the humor that possessed her was not melancholic but choleric.

She nodded to Walter James, not feeling civil enough to speak. He was small and thin, and seemed to be put together out of knobs: nose, chin, Adam's apple, knuckles. His straight brown hair made a sharp angle across his forehead. She thought he was about fifty, her age.

"As I was telling Master Blount, I've changed my profession late in life," he said. "I ran an inn before I learned the bookseller's trade."

She felt surprised; she had never known anyone besides herself to learn a new trade at so late an age. "So you must come to my aid if I falter in my new profession," he said.

Was he having a jest at her expense? No one had ever asked for her help before. But he was smiling winningly at her, and she realized that he had not intended to joke. A flatterer, she thought. She would have to watch out for his cozening ways.

George finished his dinner and headed back to his stall. Now that Alice had gone he felt more puzzled than angry. Why had she refused his suit to her? She would not get a better one, and he knew how hard it was for her to live alone. Did she reject him only because his offer had more of commerce in it than of love? But he felt that great things could come from a marriage of their two stalls. He had never understood why poets and ballad-makers wrote and sang so much about love; he had been in love once, as a youth, and he hadn't liked it. It had made him feel as if he were in the grip of a powerful illness, and since that time he had avoided most strong feeling the way his fellow Londoners avoided the plague.

He would ask her again, he decided. Surely she would not be so self-willed as to refuse him a second time.

A man waited by his stall. "How may I help you?" he asked.

"You should ask, rather, how it is that I may help you," the man said. "I have something I think you will want."

"And what is that?"

"You wish to win a lady's favor. What I have—"

"How do you know that?" George asked. Hearing his private life talked of in this manner threw him off balance, but his surprise quickly gave way to anger. "Who are you?"

"My name is Anthony Drury. How I learned your secrets is of no importance. I—"

"It is of importance to me. I won't have men sniffing around my affairs, listening to conversations that don't concern them."

"I don't come by my information that way. Someday you may be allowed to know how I learned about your desires, but not today. What I have is a way to win her."

"How?" George asked, interested in spite of himself.

"Ah," Anthony said. "It's not so easy. Surely you've seen the new play where a man makes a bargain with the devil. I am no devil, but like him I will not give away my wares for nothing."

"I don't go to plays. And I will not traffic with the devil."

"Good. That shows a serious mind."

"Aye, indeed I have a serious mind. And I am of a mind not to like what I am hearing. Talk of the devil, of information ill-gotten—"

"Nay, wait a moment. Think of your lady, yielding to you, eager to do your bidding. She has refused you once, but no longer. Whatever you command her to do will be done."

"This smells of the spirit world."

"I'm not so foolish, my friend. What I offer you has a sound basis in the theory of medicine. I can make you up a potion that will put her completely under your sway."

"Can this be?"

"Certainly. Each of us is influenced by the four humors, blood, phlegm, yellow bile and black bile. And this influence extends not just to our bodies, but to our minds as well. An excess of some of the humors, a lack of others, and she will dance to any song you choose to play."

"And what do you want in return?"

"In return? Only a trifle. I would like you to discover what became of her son."

This must be Alice's man in black, George thought, realizing it at that moment. He wore a doublet and hose of dark brown today, but like the man Alice spoke of he had the look of someone with an intense purpose about him. "Why?" he asked.

"It is not part of our bargain that you ask questions, nor that I answer them. Only that you tell me if you agree or no."

"I'll have to consider it," George said slowly. "Come back tomorrow for your answer."

"Tomorrow, then. Good day."

George stood at his stall and watched him thoughtfully. Then the crowd moved between him and the strange man, and he turned back to his books.

By evening he was still thinking about the offer. He remembered one thing the man had said clearer than the rest: "She will dance to any song you choose to play." The idea of Alice dancing for him, and the larger idea of her doing his bidding, giving over her willful ways, was intensely pleasing to him. And

what was her son to him in any case? The boy was probably
dead, just as he had said to Alice in the cookshop.

He would agree to the offer, he thought. By the time Anthony
realized that Arthur had disappeared, George and Alice would
be married.

Alice left the churchyard early and made her way slowly home.
The house had been aired out, she saw, but even that failed to
please her. She sat at the stool near the hearth and looked out
her kitchen window. The light fell on the houses opposite,
turning them pink, then red, and finally violet-gray, charcoal
gray, black. The house filled up with darkness.

She was thinking of John. One day he had come home,
thrown his cloak down on the bench and gone straight to bed.
"I feel poorly," he'd said, and that was how it had started, just
those three words. She'd nursed him for a day and a half. The
hard lumps had appeared under his armpits, but there had been
little plague in London that season and she had refused to think
about what the swelling might mean. Plague was something
that happened to other people.

After he died she got up and wandered through their house.
She had not left his bedside for hours, and she was surprised to
see that light still shone outside, that people still went about
their business. His cloak lay where he had dropped it, and it
was only then, realizing that he would never pick it up and
wear it again, never go off singing to work, that she began to
understand what had happened to her. From now on, she
thought, I'll always be alone.

What would John think if he could see her now? Would he
urge her to accept George's offer? She was not even sure he
would have wanted her to continue at his stall, but she had
been unable to think of what else to do with her life, how to fill
up the days and months without him. And how else was she to
get her livelihood?

She and John had grown up in neighboring towns in the
countryside around Cambridge and had met at a harvest festi-
val. She'd known him by sight, of course, but she had never
really been aware of him before then. That day she saw him

throw back his head in laughter and something changed within her; she understood that she wanted that laughter, that energy, for herself, that she could very easily be in love with him. She'd chased him with a determination she'd never given to anything else, and when they married she knew that she loved him more than he loved her. But by the time he died she had the satisfaction of knowing that he'd come to love her deeply, and she knew too that marriage had turned out to be far more than merely possessing another person, an adventure she could not have guessed at observing it from the outside.

John's father had apprenticed him to a blacksmith, but he'd felt the work didn't suit him. Instead he'd spent his time watching the printers in Cambridge, the only place in England besides Oxford and London granted a license from the queen to print books. One day he'd come home and told her to pack. She had just set Arthur in his cot, and the excitement in his voice made her turn around to face him.

"We're going to London," he said. "One of the printers wants to sell his books in the city, and he's agreed to take me on as an apprentice."

That had been—how long ago? If Arthur had been a baby then at least twenty years had passed. So much had changed, so much had stayed the same. John had prospered as a publisher and bookseller: he'd a knack for knowing what subjects would catch the public's fancy, and then he had been granted the monopoly to print playbills. But she had made few friends in the city, most of them other stationers who had only wanted to talk business with her husband. And then Arthur had run off, and John had died . . .

What would John think if he could see her now? "Stop pitying yourself," he would say sternly. "Get up, there's things to be done. You're on your own now, so make the best of it."

She stood. A noise from the doorway made her turn around. She wasn't alone: the brownie came into the room, lighting candles as it went. It moved closer and she nearly backed away, but she could tell that it wanted something from her. "Come," it said. "The revels have begun." It looked eager, expectant.

"What?"

"Come with me. By tree and stone, by wind and rain, you'll not get another chance like this one, no, not if you live as long as my queen."

"Chance?" She felt slow, witless.

"To join us, dance with us."

"I have to—I don't—"

"Of course you do. It's given to few mortals to see our celebrations. You'll curse yourself all your days if you don't come with me now."

He smiled engagingly; he looked a little like Arthur had as a child, before Arthur had grown so strange. (And when had she started thinking of the creature as "he"?) She realized she was smiling too. "You looked unhappy," he said. "It would do you good to get outside these walls, this prison. You can't think clearly, packed in closely like this."

She found she couldn't resist him. She nodded slowly. "I'll come with you."

"Wonderful!" He moved closer, and this time she did back away, afraid. "Hold," he said, and breathed on her left eye.

"What was that?" she asked.

"A change." He took hold of her hand and she allowed herself to be led into the darkened streets. As they passed a cobweb on her wall she thought she saw something glimmering, shining like a jewel, but when she turned to look at it with both eyes it was gone.

The brownie went faster now, hurrying to the revels. She pulled on his hand, unable to keep up with him. On one side, her left side, she could see others rushing along with them, small and large, winged and hoofed. The brownie urged her along impatiently. A few minutes later they stopped, and she recognized a field outside the city walls.

A shining round moon lit the field and she saw the creatures spread out before her. Four squat men rolled casks of wine toward the gathering. Women in white with lighted tapers on their heads joined hands and began dancing in a circle. Now she realized that music played somewhere, that it had been playing as long as she had stood there. It sounded both familiar and unearthly, as though she had been hearing it but not recognizing it her entire life. Faster and faster the women went, fire burning from their hair. The music grew shrill, wild. Alice moved toward them.

The brownie pulled her back to his side. He was strong, she realized with surprise; she would not have guessed his strength by looking at him. "You must only watch," he said, and she remembered a story of a man who had danced with the Fair Folk for a night and returned to his village a hundred years later. "And you must touch neither food nor drink. I'll leave you now."

The brownie joined one of the circles. She closed her left eye and suddenly everyone in the field vanished, leaving only a whisper of the uncanny music. Desolate, she opened her eye again. Someone laughed loudly behind her and caught her arm.

She was pulled along with a group of them, men and women wearing green, their arms as thin as twigs and leaves sprouting where their hair should have been. "No!" she said, panicked, remembering the brownie's warning.

The twig-people laughed and tossed her into the air. "Don't worry," one of them said. "No harm can come to you this night, unless you bring it upon yourself. Brownie told us so."

They passed her along from one to the other, hurrying across the field. One of them pointed out a cottage to the others and they raced toward it, laughing and calling. They opened the door. Someone inside shrieked in terror, and then all the candles were blown out.

"Dirty!" said one of them. "Dirty, dirty!"

"Filthy!"

"Where's water for our baths?"

"Where's milk for our thirst?"

"Where are the coins?"

"Here, here!" said a dozen voices.

Her left eye saw a little in the dark, and she watched as they heaped gold coins on a shabby table. The man and woman of the house backed into a corner as if trying to hide. Three or four of the twig-people followed them and kissed them both on the cheeks and mouth. "Here," someone said to Alice, giving her a coin. "For your labors tonight." They all laughed wildly.

They rushed out the door, overturning stools and benches. Alice put the coin in her pouch and hurried after them. "Robin!" one of them called, running down a hillside. "Robin Goodfellow! Give us a light!" The others raced after him, a few turning cartwheels as they went.

A tall burly figure stood at the bottom of the hill. Matted hair grew from his arms, legs and chest, and he was naked. All the others had been clothed; even Brownie wore small breeches which barely came to his knees. Alice looked away quickly, but before she did so she saw with embarrassment that he was erect. He carried a staff in one hand.

"Give us a light, Robin!"

His staff began to glow softly. "Over there, over there!" several voices said, and Alice saw that they had spotted a solitary traveler walking across the field. Robin's staff grew brighter. A few winged creatures, barely the size of Alice's hand, flew toward the traveler. "Come to us," they called. Their voices sounded like silver bells. "Why do you linger? Come!"

The man looked up. The creatures flew toward him and then away again, toward and away, singing. Their wings were the colors of jewels, sapphire, ruby, agate. The man began to follow.

"Come to us!"

The traveler headed toward Robin's light. As he came closer the light left the staff and floated out over the field. He tried to keep up, dazed. The twig-people, edgy with excitement, formed a circle and began to dance. "We wait for you . . . Come!" the winged creatures sang.

The light and the voices led the man to a river. He tumbled in, splashing, and the light went out. The twig-people laughed loudly and scattered across the field.

"Wait!" Alice said, calling after them. They ran toward a grove of trees and she followed. At the edge of the grove she stopped and peered in, hesitating. Not even moonlight penetrated the darkness of the trees. Something rustled among the leaves. An owl called.

Which way had they gone? She could no longer see them or hear their laughter. The music sounded very faint and far away.

Did they lure her here, then, the way they had lured the traveler? What was she to do now? Perhaps she could wait until sunrise and then try to make her way back to the city. But would the city be the same as she had left it, or had she passed a hundred years with the Fair Folk, like the man in the story? For the first time she noticed how cold the night had grown.

She walked slowly back across the field, feeling every one of her fifty years. She was no longer a young maiden, to dance all night and rise fresh with the dawn. Perhaps she could find the man who had been led astray and together they could make their way toward the city gate. But oh, the look on his face as he had climbed out of the stream! She began to laugh.

Something shone up ahead and she hurried toward it, hoping she was not following Robin's staff. A ring of lights burned on the grass, and in the middle of them sat the queen. She looked up and Alice saw her clearly across the field, her golden hair and gray eyes and the crown of crystals on her head. Alice stood rock-still, captured by the woman's beauty.

The queen nodded to her. The gesture seemed to convey something complex, a carefully scripted ritual between equals. We are both alike, her motion seemed to say. No lengthier ceremony can do us honor. Just so must Queen Elizabeth nod to monarchs when they came visiting.

But no—what was she thinking? Why should the queen think of her as an equal? She looked away and saw two horned men, warriors, standing at the queen's back. At her feet sat a small dumpy woman, her black hair plaited into elf-locks . . . Margery?

"You should not have seen this," said a voice behind her. She turned, startled. It was Brownie.

"I—I know that woman," she said.

"You know Queen Oriana?"

"Nay, the other one. She's a friend of mine." Alice looked back at the two women on the grass. The queen whispered something in Margery's ear and they laughed. What business had Margery with the Queen of Faerie?

"Aye?" Brownie said. He sounded doubtful. "I must take you home."

"Now? But— Let me stay awhile. Please."

"You've seen too much as it is." She stepped back but his motion, too fast for her to follow, brought him before her again. He breathed on her left eye, and the queen and her warriors and the circle of lights vanished. Margery sat alone on the field and laughed to herself.

But as Brownie led her home she thought she saw, out of the corner of that eye, strange lights and bright jewels, and once a creature passed them on wings as fine as silk.

4

Christopher found the note from Robert Poley under his door. Though it said only, "The usual place, this afternoon," the agent had written it in cipher. Christopher thought this typical of Poley's secretive, small-minded ways. But what could the agent want? It had been no hardship to check the taverns, looking for a man who claimed to be king, but he had so far discovered nothing. Surely Robert knew that he would have arranged a meeting if he had any information.

At the sign of the Black Boar Robert handed Christopher a note. A brown stain blotted the top of the paper but it was still readable. "All is in readiness," the note said. "Our king awaits."

Christopher looked up. "Where did you get this?"

"Where? I thought you might know."

"I? I have no idea."

Robert made no answer. That was one of his tricks, Christopher knew: the habit of conversation was so strong in people that they would babble anything to fill the silence. "You're jesting," someone at another table said. It sounded very loud.

Finally Robert said, "It was found on the dead man. The man who was killed that night."

The brown stain, then, was blood. "Why should I know anything at all about that?"

"You were eager to go after his killer. I thought perhaps you knew who he was, knew that he had something to do with this errand I gave you."

He understood now. Robert liked making his agents uncomfortable, and liked it not at all to be made uncomfortable himself. The night Robert had shown his fear still rankled. Probably he had gone back to the dead man to prove his courage, had discovered the note and seen a way to incriminate Christopher. And it didn't help matters that Christopher had been right all along: the dead man had been at the Black Boar, and had been following them before he was killed. "If I knew I certainly would have told you."

"Would you? I wonder."

Christopher paused in the act of lighting his tobacco-pipe. "What do you mean?"

"I mean that I'm beginning to doubt your worth to me. Is it coincidence, do you think, that on the same day I give you an errand we are followed by a man who is tied in some way to that errand? Did you arrange to meet him here, at the Black Boar? Did the two of you plan to kill me where I stood in the street?"

"You were the one who asked to come with me."

"Aye, and if I hadn't gone I'd be dead now, stabbed in the back."

"I swear I know nothing about the dead man, or about this note."

"And what is the word of an intelligencer worth? I am one myself, and I know that I will swear and forswear myself in the service of my queen."

"My word will have to be good enough."

"I'm afraid it isn't. Unless I know I can trust you your usefulness to me is at an end."

Now they were coming to it, Christopher saw. The other man wanted to make Christopher pay for witnessing his cowardice. He felt Robert's dismissal almost physically, as if a net had started to close around him or he were being smothered. How would he survive without the extra money Robert gave him? "You know I have always done you good service."

"Do I? I have had other agents who have sworn the same thing, and who have ended their lives on the rack and the gallows."

"There is absolutely no evidence——"

"Nay, there isn't, is there?" Robert leaned back. "I suppose I'll have to keep you on——that way I'll be able to watch you closely. And if I hear of you asking questions you were not meant to ask, or talking to folks you were forbidden to talk to, I'll give you no further errands. I have my eye on you now."

Christopher did not miss Robert's slight smile. It had all been part of the game, then: Robert had never intended to dismiss him. In his probing the other man had found Christopher's weakness, his dependence on the money Robert offered. "What do I do now?"

"Nothing. Listen in taverns——it's about all you're good for."

"What about the dead man? Who wrote that note?"

"That's not your concern. I have other agents who will learn everything I need to know. Your task is to find that man, the one who claims to be king."

Christopher bade farewell to Robert and went to the Saracen's Head close by. As he walked he remembered his first meeting with Robert Poley, while he was still a student at Cambridge. The terms of his scholarship provided him with a shilling a week, but he quickly found out that that would barely keep him in food and drink. A friend had introduced him to the queen's agent and he'd begun then to make regular trips into France. He'd had to interrupt his studies, but they'd started to bore him anyway. The things he found in books on his own were much more interesting.

On his last trip while at Cambridge Robert sent him to Rheims, where the English Catholics had established a seminary in exile. When he returned he found a story making the rounds that he had converted. The authorities threatened to deny him his degree, and he'd had to go over their heads, to the queen's Privy Council, to get it. He still relished the wording of their letter to the university: ". . . because it was not Her Majesty's pleasure that anyone employed as he had been in matters touching the benefit of his country should be defamed by those who are ignorant in the affairs he went about." He could almost hear Elizabeth's imperious tones in those words, though of course she hadn't written the letter herself.

His walk to the Saracen's Head took only a few minutes, but going from one tavern to the other always made him feel as if he had entered another world. The university wits met here: it was usually loud, boisterous and crowded with people.

At this hour, though, only Tom Kyd sat at one of the tables, slowly drinking his small beer. A group of serving-women sat in the corner, playing cards and taking their supper and beer before the crowds came. "Good evening, Tom," he said, sitting down beside him.

"Oh," Tom said. Christopher remembered something Thomas Nashe once said, that Kyd always looked as if he expected to be hit. "You're back. Evening."

"Aye, I'm back."

"Where do you go? Some of us were wondering about you the other night."

"Here and there."

"I heard someone say they thought you'd gone over to the Catholics."

There was that rumor again. Christopher laughed. "Did you?"

"It's no jesting matter. And there were others who called you an atheist— Doesn't it worry you what people say about you?"

"Why should it?"

"Because— It's not right what they say about us, these men who call themselves wits. And it's dangerous besides. Someday Robert Greene will call you an atheist in the wrong company, and you'll be sent before the Privy Council to answer charges—"

"Robin speaks out of envy at my success, nothing more. And no one will call me before the Privy Council, I promise you."

"And Tom Nashe insulted you in print last year, at the same time he insulted me."

"Aye, and what of it?"

"What of it? Why do you remain friends with that man?"

"I don't know. I've forgotten what he said."

"Sometimes I can think of nothing else. Do you remember

what he wrote about me? Every word was chosen on purpose to hurt. He said I got my plays from reading English Seneca. *English* Seneca, as though I know no Latin! 'English Seneca read by candlelight yields many good sentences, as *Blood is a beggar,* and so forth—' "

"You've memorized it!"

"I suppose I have. He's an evil man."

"He means nothing by it—"

"Don't defend him to me! But he won't be allowed to get away with it. There's still justice, divine retribution—"

"Will it comfort you, then, to know that he's in hell?"

"I'm not talking about hell."

"Then what—"

"There's earthly justice. Wrongs do not go unpunished here on earth. Every man gets his deserts."

Christopher looked at Tom in astonishment. "Look around you, man," he said. "Do you see any evidence that evildoers are punished? Ten thousand people were massacred in Paris on St. Bartholomew's Day and still the Catholics flourish there. Does this seem like divine retribution to you?"

"Even they will get their just punishment."

"Look," Christopher said. There had to be some way to make the other man see reason. "By your lights I'm an unrepentant sinner. I can't remember the last time I went to church. I lied to the authorities at Cambridge—under the terms of my scholarship I should have taken holy orders, but I had no intention of doing so—"

"I don't want to hear your sins, Kit—"

"I have so many questions about the truth of the Scriptures I can't even begin to list them all, I take boys into my bed—"

"Stop, please—"

"And yet I go from one triumph to the next. I was destined to be a cobbler like my father, but I escaped and went to Cambridge instead. I've written some of the most popular plays in London. I've met extraordinary people, I don't want for money—"

"Even you will be punished, Kit. If you don't give over your godless ways—"

"And you will be rewarded?"

"Aye."

The finality in Tom's voice silenced him. Perhaps he should give over trying to question people's beliefs; not one person he knew would willingly change his opinions or come to see the folly of his ways. And now that he thought back he recognized this idea of Tom's running like a pattern through his plays, justice for those wronged, revenge carried out against evildoers. Earthly retribution. Who would have guessed that beneath Tom's habitually dour expression he held such strange beliefs?

And yet he had once held similar irrational ideas. He could not help but feel that a pattern ran through his own life, that someone or something looked out for his welfare. Just as he was contemplating with despair the idea of living out the rest of his days in Canterbury, of becoming a shoemaker like his father, he had gotten away to Cambridge. As soon as he'd realized his scholarship would not support him he'd met up with Robert Poley, the queen's agent. Three years ago *Tamburlaine,* his first play, had been performed to as much acclaim as he had dared to dream about, and he'd been only twenty-three. "I hold the Fates bound fast in iron chains," he had written in *Tamburlaine,* a wildly ambitious student who'd known precious little about fate.

As he grew older, though, he somehow lost his belief in higher powers. Everything he had accomplished had been through his own efforts; there was no need to postulate spirits either benign or malign. Anyone with enough talent and wit could have left Canterbury. If, as he'd said to Tom, he would never be called up before the Privy Council, it was only because he'd begun to cultivate those in power, like Poley and the men who had sent the letter to Cambridge.

He appreciated the irony of it: at the very moment that his play *Dr. Faustus* was being performed on the London stage he had lost his belief in devils, and in God as well. Yet the feeling was not terrifying, as he had thought it would be; instead he felt liberated, free to create what he wanted of his life.

"Now you sound like Robin," he said to Tom.

"I sound like any man who believes in God's justice——"

A loud voice interrupted him. "Who sounds like me?" Christopher looked up to see Robert Greene and Thomas Nashe coming toward them.

"—that is to say anyone in England," Tom said, finishing his thought.

"Listen to this man," Christopher said to the two newcomers. "He counts Nemesis as one of the nine muses."

The others laughed. Tom Kyd turned to him quickly, looking angry and a little hurt. Was he so thin-skinned, then, to resent any small jest at his expense? He should have grown up in Christopher's large contentious family, where arguments begun over dinner frequently carried over for days, the winner being the person who could outshout and outlast everyone else. His father had won most of the quarrels, but when he'd come home from the university for visits he'd surprised the old man a time or two.

"I said only that those who do evil are punished," Tom Kyd said.

"Aye, that's true enough," Robert said as he and Tom Nashe took seats at the table. They carried beer and plates of hot chicken and bacon, and as he smelled the food Christopher realized how hungry he was. He looked around for the host or one of the serving-women but they were all busy, carrying out trays of beer or lighting candles.

One of the serving-women dropped a large stack of pewter plates, silencing all conversation for a moment. Then everyone laughed and the talk resumed. A man called loudly to Tom Nashe from across the room; Tom always boasted that he knew everyone in London. He ignored the man and turned to answer Robert.

"Is it?" Tom said, tearing off a chicken wing and wiping his hand on his breeches. "Then the devil's reserved the hottest corner of hell for you, Robin. You've kept none of the vows you made a month ago. You gamble, you dandle the wenches on Holywell Street—"

"Can you tell me you do none of those things?"

"Certainly I do, but I never repented of them."

"Well, what of it? There's still time to change my ways. And these things are but trifles. Far worse would it be for me to have the taint of atheism on my soul."

He glanced at Christopher as he spoke. The other man smiled a little but made no answer. "Do you believe in God, Kit?" Robert asked, raising his voice. He gazed out over the tavern as if playing to an audience. Or perhaps, Christopher thought, he hoped to find an informer sitting nearby.

Tom Kyd was looking at him, his expression pleading for caution. But why should he have to remain silent, when Robert was free to spread his opinions in any company he chose? He reached over and took a sip of Tom's beer, then pushed his hair back and looked directly at Robert.

"We've had this argument before," he said.

"Aye, and you've proven yourself to be a thorough atheist."

"I'm only trying to make men see reason—"

"And what makes you imagine you see more of it than other people do?"

"Because other people don't see reason at all. They terrify themselves with superstitions, with bugbears and hobgoblins—"

"Hobgoblins," said a scornful voice behind him. "What do you know about hobgoblins?"

He turned around. A red-haired man with eyes the color of young green leaves had come into the tavern.

"Good evening, Your Majesty," Tom Nashe said, as the other man sat with them. "It's true we know very little about hobgoblins. But perhaps Your Monarchship knows more."

"Your Majesty?" Christopher asked, intrigued. Could this be the man Poley sought? Here was good fortune indeed!

"I see you have not yet met my friend, Your Brightness," Tom said. "This is Christopher Marlowe. Kit, the man before you is your king. You may rise, or kneel, or what you will."

"The king?"

"So he told us, the last time he was here."

"Ah. And by whose authority is he king?"

"He would not tell us that. By his own, I think."

"But maybe there are stories about him?" Christopher said. "Stories—or legends?"

"Aye," the man said. "Many stories have been told about my birth. And more will be told when I come into my kingdom. But you were speaking of hobgoblins. Perhaps you would be so good as to tell us about them."

"I—" Tom said. "I know very little."

"Tell us."

"Very well," Tom said. Christopher knew his friend could never resist an audience. "They tell this story in Suffolk, where I was born. Once a brownie captured a young woman, and forced her to get up on his horse, and rode off with her as night was falling. 'Ride not by the old pool,' the woman said, 'lest we should meet with Brownie.' 'Fear not, woman,' he said. 'You've met all the brownies you'll meet tonight.' "

Everyone laughed but the king. "Why did the brownie capture her?" he asked.

"Ah," Tom said. "She was a midwife, you see, and he was taking her to the Queen of Faerie, who was about to be delivered of a child."

The other man nodded graciously, as if satisfied with his answer. His manner reminded Christopher of the only time he had seen Queen Elizabeth, when she had ridden to St. Paul's to proclaim victory over the Spanish Armada. He looked magisterial, used to command. And Tom had responded without thinking to his order. Could there be something in his claim after all? Was that why Poley had been so interested in the man? London had never lacked for rumors about Elizabeth and one or another of her courtiers.

"You've never told me your name, Your Kinghood," Tom said.

"Arthur," the other man said.

"Why— But then you're Mistress Wood's son!"

"Wood?" The man who called himself Arthur looked confused.

"Aye, Alice Wood. She has a stall in the yard of St. Paul's. You know her, Kit, her station's next to your friend Edward Blount."

"Nay, I know no one named Alice Wood," Arthur said.

"She's been looking all over London for you. And there's another man too, she says, who's been asking questions . . .

Come, tomorrow I'll go with you to the churchyard. I know she's been worried about you."

"Alice Wood is not my mother. My mother was a queen." Arthur looked angry, dangerous; his hand strayed toward the dagger at his back.

"If you won't come with me I'll ask her myself if she knows you. Perhaps if you see her—"

"I'll hear no more of this talk," Arthur said, rising and heading for the door.

"Wait!" Christopher said. He followed Arthur out into the street. The moon was hidden and the night had grown very dark; he had to strain to see. Where had the man gone? There was only blackness in front of him. He put his hand out before him but could feel nothing; it was as if the world had vanished. In the strange absence of color his eyes began to play tricks: gold sparkled against the night. The shimmer of gold moved off a little, and he followed.

Tom Nashe's friends had all gone home by the time he left the tavern. He stood and pissed against the tavern wall, thinking of the strange questions Christopher had asked. What was the man playing at?

Tom had heard rumors that Christopher did intelligence work for the queen. Could that be true? Tom prided himself on knowing the latest news, the secrets of the highborn and low, of being on intimate terms with nearly everyone of importance in London. It galled him that there was something he did not know about his friend.

And what of the man who had called himself king? Was he truly Mistress Wood's son? Would it be better not to raise her hopes if he turned out to be just another of London's many lunatics?

"Ho!" a voice said. Tom adjusted his clothes and turned around. Arthur stood behind him. "You—the man who knows so much about brownies. Come with me."

"Why? Where are we going?"

" 'Ride not by the old pool,' " Arthur said. He pitched his voice higher so that it sounded uncannily like a woman's.

" 'Lest we should meet with Brownie.' I'll show you brownies, if you like."

Arthur's natural authority was compelling; Tom wanted nothing more than to go with him. He forced himself to stare the other man down. "Where are they? How comes it that you know them?"

"In Finsbury Field. I've seen them."

Arthur set off and Tom followed him. He felt a little unsteady and looked up at the stars to anchor himself. Good—they were still there. No one walked the streets so late; he heard nothing but the soft pad of Arthur's boots and his own breath. It seemed that something miraculous might happen, that wonders were about to unfold before his eyes.

They reached Finsbury Field moments later. "Look," Arthur said, breathing the word. He pointed.

"Look at what?" Tom said. "I see nothing."

"There. And over there—look! The faeries are dancing. Do you see them?"

"Nay." Tom tried not to feel disappointed. An intense expression had appeared on the other man's face, yearning and desire and more than a little fear. Did he truly believe he saw something? It would be a sorry thing for him if he did. And what would Mistress Wood say if this Bedlamite turned out to be her long-lost son? Perhaps it would be a kindness to let her go on thinking he was dead.

He heard mocking laughter from the fields. Nay, it was a screech owl out hunting, nothing more. But now he could make out faint shapes on the grass, figures clad in white with fire in their hair. Winged creatures, impossibly small, darted around them, and they danced to music that was like nothing he had ever heard.

"Arthur," he said, whispering. "Look." But the other man had gone.

The creatures left off dancing. In a single line they moved through the fields, a strange light shining from their faces. Tom followed as they passed through Moorgate and into the city itself.

He would never be certain how long they led him onwards,

or what way they took him through the city. They wound
through the dark streets like a thread of gold in a tapestry, going
past churches and prisons and taverns, past the shops of cob-
blers and ironmongers and brewers. Into the stately groves and
gardens of the nobles' estates they walked, and not a dog
barked to let its owner know they were there. He saw the
London citizens asleep in their houses, and beggars and vagabonds lying on the cobblestone streets, shivering in the cold; he
saw St. Paul's, closed and desolate in the darkness. At last they
came to the river's edge and the wharves with their boats
moored tight until morning.

He had always loved London, loved its noise and smells and
close-packed lanes, the excitement and vitality he could feel in
his stomach whenever he walked the streets. But now he saw
it in the light cast by the faerie folk, and it seemed the promised
city, the city of heaven. Each turning brought him new sights
sharp enough to pierce his heart.

All the while he walked with the faeries, though, he felt that
they searched for something, something they had once had and
given up, something lost. As dawn lightened the east, streaking
the gray water of the Thames with silver, he saw them slow and
finally stop. The wings of the little ones drooped, and the
horned animal, its head once held up so proudly against the
sky, began to tire. What was it they sought? He wished he could
help them.

In the light of the new day they seemed finally to become
aware of him. One of the women in white turned and pointed,
and then a dozen of them surrounded him, laughing and calling. He backed away toward the shelter of a building but they
followed him. Someone ran her fingers through his hair. He felt
drowsy, wearier than he had ever been in his life. It had been
a long night. He lay against the wall and closed his eyes. Their
laughter was the last thing he heard before he slept.

A fine soft rain was falling the next morning as George went
into the churchyard, and the drizzle had kept the usual throng
of people at home. As he passed Alice's station on the way to
his own he saw that she had not come in to work that day.

Instead the young man who worked for her stood at her stall, laying cloths over the books to keep them from getting wet. She must be at the printshop, then. He felt a strange emptiness at not seeing her; he hadn't realized until then how pleasing he found it to watch her work. When she was his he would find ways of keeping her by his side.

Anthony Drury waited for him at his stall, nodding as if he guessed his thoughts. "What decision have you come to?" he asked.

At his words George felt alert, renewed, all disappointment forgotten. "I'll agree to your terms," he said. "I'll take your potion."

"I don't have it here."

"Where is it, then?"

"At my lodgings. Come."

The man's tone angered George. Why hadn't Anthony simply brought the elixir with him? He thought that the other man meant to draw him deeper into this strange business, and he was reluctant to follow him. His only concern was with Alice: he had no interest in Anthony's obsession with Arthur or his counterfeit coins (if Alice spoke true) or his obscure knowledge.

But he would not get the promised potion unless he went along with him. "Very well," he said.

He closed his stall and followed the other man. They walked together through the empty churchyard, and then Anthony led him out onto Cheapside. Past the Eleanor Cross they went, past a small crowd watching expectantly as a man was tied to a cart and then flogged through the street. Anthony turned left off Cheapside, then right, then left again, and soon George was lost in a maze of dark alleys and passageways. The streets here were muddy from the morning's rainfall, and garbage overran the ditches; he smelled excrement and rotting food. Houses closed together over him, blocking out the sky.

Something moved in the shadows. George turned, afraid, but he could see nothing there. Anthony stopped, though, and made a complex gesture with his left hand. "Come," he said.

"What— What was—"

"It will not trouble us further."

He began walking again, and George followed. The houses to either side of them grew shabbier, meaner. This was a part of London George had never seen. He was about to ask how much farther they had to go when the shape he had seen earlier came forward out of the shadows, making no sound. This time when he looked directly at the thing it did not retreat. He saw a creature the color of sea moss, with a long snout, sharp ears and webbed fingers and toes. It opened its mouth in a snarl, showing uneven pointed teeth.

It turned and moved with a certainty of purpose toward Anthony. For a moment George could not speak, fascinated by the thing's horrible grace. He must have made some kind of noise, because Anthony stopped to look at him. The creature dropped back and crouched on its haunches like a cat, preparing to lunge. Muscles slid over bones as smoothly as water gliding over rocks. For what seemed like a long time Anthony stood and did nothing. Then he drew complex sigils in the air and spoke a few words George did not recognize. The creature hissed and fell back toward the shelter of one of the houses.

"What—" George said.

Anthony made no reply. George realized with amazement that the other man looked shaken, almost haunted. Growing bolder, he said, "I told you before I will not traffic with spirits."

"Not—spirits," Anthony said. His breath came in little gasps. George noticed, shocked, that the symbols Anthony had traced in the air still glowed, silver fading to tarnished green.

"Not spirits! Why, man—"

"The thing you saw is not a spirit, but as natural as you or I. We have performed certain experiments—"

"We?"

"You will meet the others when you're ready. We question the nature of things. What is true and what false." The man's rhetoric seemed to steady him.

"That's too deep for me," George said. As far as he was concerned what he saw with his own eyes was true, and everything else didn't matter. And he knew, with more certainty than he had ever known anything in his life, that the thing he had seen had no part in his everyday world. "But that creature had an unnatural air about it. You'll not tell me—"

"Don't speak of what you don't understand. When the time is right we'll tell you more."

George scowled. He wanted to be out of the filthy maze of streets and back at home before nightfall, and he wondered uneasily if the thing still watched them from the shadows. But he knew he could not find the way back on his own, knew too that he needed Anthony to get what he had been promised. He vowed that when Alice was his he would have no more to do with the other man.

Anthony turned in at the most rundown of the houses. "Here it is," he said, unlocking and opening the door.

Dozens of burning candles lit the room beyond. George got a brief glimpse of what looked like a monstrous mechanical being, with a hundred iron arms snaking out from a central core. Then he heard a high shrill scream, and the green creature fell on Anthony from the rafters. It grabbed hold of his arm and pushed itself up toward his face in a strange fluid motion. George backed away into the street and closed the door.

Another scream came from the room, and then silence. After what seemed like a long time the door opened and Anthony came out, blood streaming from his arm.

"Has it gone?" George asked. "Are you badly hurt?"

"Take it," Anthony said. "Quickly." He held out a small earthenware jar in his unwounded hand.

"I— What do I—"

"Quickly!"

George took the jar and backed away. The other man's eyes shone with a strange light, like a Bedlamite's. Something fell with a loud noise in the house behind him. George turned and ran down the street.

After a few minutes he felt something soft squelch under his feet. He shuddered and slowed to a walk. Where was he? How was he to get back home?

He looked around him, seeking a familiar landmark. Clouds covered the sun, making it look like a dark watchful eye. Something moved in the shadows and he jumped, but it was only a scrap of cloth blown by the wind. The same wind drove the clouds before it and the sun flared out for a brief instant. He saw a broad street in the distance and went toward it cautiously. As he came closer he saw movement and heard the creaking of cart wheels. Hurrying now, he followed the sights and sounds and found himself on Cheapside. He walked quickly toward the crowds of people ahead of him, not wanting to travel alone.

Anthony had deliberately confused him, then, so that he would not remember the way back. But why? Did it have something to do with the mechanical monster in Anthony's house? George had only gotten a quick glimpse of it, but he thought he recognized an alchemist's alembic from a book he'd seen in the churchyard. Did Anthony know the secret of changing base minerals into gold? But surely he would not live in such squalor if he had money.

He made his way slowly down the street. Now that he had leisure to think his mind filled with a tangle of questions. What was the creature? It had seemed bound to Anthony in some way. Had he conjured it and was now unable to rid himself of it?

And what was in the jar Anthony had given him? Did it come from the same place as the creature, and would it bind Alice to the same kind of necromancy? What if the other man had given him the wrong jar? He had had only a short time to find what he wanted, after all. If what he had given George harmed Alice in any way, George thought, the other man would have to face something worse than the green creature.

As he prepared for bed that night the memory of his strange journey began to fade. But he dreamed that the creature, in falling on Anthony, had brushed against him. It felt dank, repulsive, and George's gasp of horror woke him up. He lay still, his heart pounding. He tried not to look at the dark corners of the room where, he was certain, something crouched, waiting for him.

Afternoon light fell through the windows when Alice woke. She rolled over in bed and covered her eyes with her arm. What a night, she thought.

But what, exactly, had happened? Had she truly gone danc-ing in the fields with the faerie folk? Were all the stories from her childhood true?

Every muscle ached as she tried to sit up. If only John were here, she thought. What a tale she would have to tell him. Brownies and winged creatures and Robin Goodfellow, and at the end of it all the brightness of the queen herself.

But she couldn't lie here dreaming. There was work to be done, her stall in the churchyard to tend to. Nay, the young man who sometimes worked for her came in today, God be thanked. Today would have been the day she went to the printshop. But it was still early afternoon; she could go by the shop and then, if there was time, she could pay a visit to Margery.

Margery. Had she truly seen her sitting in the field as if she belonged there, talking to Queen Oriana? Alice knew Margery was wise in the knowledge of herbs and flowers and stones, but how did she come to have business with the Queen of Faerie? Aye, she would certainly go and have a talk with her friend, whether she had the time or not. There were questions she had to ask her.

At the printing house near Paul's Wharf she sought out the proprietor, a plump graying man whose leather apron had turned black across the stomach from bending over the presses, and gave him her order. One of her pamphlets and several of the ballads needed to go back to press, and already some acting companies had given her orders for playbills. He looked over the list and nodded, his free hand moving in the air as he calculated costs. The stationers whose books he printed com-plained loudly and often about his rudeness, but she liked him just for that reason, because he treated her the same way he treated everyone else. If he was curt to the other stationers he was also curt to her.

As he looked over the list she watched his employees at work. In one corner the compositor set up type, and when he had finished the corrector of the press looked over what he had done, reading it backwards like a Mohammedan or Jew. Then another man inked the type, worked the screw on the press and took out the finished pages.

Finally he looked up from the list and named a figure. She countered with a lower one, and he handed the list back to her and made as if to go. She called him back, the ritual familiar to her from her other visits and from the times before that, when she had accompanied John to the shop. Finally they agreed on an amount and she left.

It had rained that morning and the water in the ditches and gutters reflected the damp gray clouds. As she watched the sun came out, striking the water and turning it pale gold. The sudden blaze of color gladdened her, reminded her that spring would be here soon. The trees around her were starting to put out fine green leaves. Winter had lasted too long; they had been packed within the walls of the city like goods in a peddlar's bag. The brownie had done well to bring her outside.

Something moved on the surface of the water, something small and clad in gold. Was she always to be haunted like this, by things barely seen? Jewels hung on tavern signs and in horses' manes, and motes of silver winged past her. The gold reminded her of faerie coins, and she put her hand in the purse at her side. She felt the small coins she carried with her, groats and pennies, and a hard round lump. A piece of coal. So that was why they had laughed!

Margery lived out beyond the city walls, and as Alice passed through Ludgate she looked around her, hoping to find some trace of the faeries' revels. These fields, that stand of trees, the small stream running over stones in the distance—it all looked familiar, or nearly so. But where was the cottage? And where the hill where Robin Goodfellow had stood? And yet, look—faerie rings covered the grass as far as she could see.

At last she came to Margery's small thatched cottage and knocked on the door, but to her intense disappointment no one answered. Just as she was about to go she saw Margery coming up the path, asphodels in her upturned apron.

"Good day," Margery said, opening the door.

Whenever she saw the inside of Margery's house Alice always thought that it looked bigger than she would have expected from the outside. Books and scrolls lay open everywhere, the books bound in cracked leather, in vellum or not bound at all. Vegetables and herbs and stones set in silver hung from beams in the low ceiling, and cobwebs fell from the walls. The floor was littered with the parchment Margery used for her calculations, and a scrying stone covered with dust lay half-hidden in a corner. Alice smelled flowers and cat dung and tobacco. The first time Margery had invited her in Alice had thought, Marry, all she lacks is a stuffed alligator to set herself up as an apothecary.

As they came in a plump ginger cat jumped down from one of the stools and yawned hugely, then curled up on a cushion and went to sleep again. Margery set the flowers in a pewter jug and lit fat candles from the fire. She moved a dish caked with what looked like the remnants of a failed experiment but was probably only her supper, and sat down heavily on the bench she had cleared. Alice brushed tobacco crumbs and fur off a stool and sat near her.

Margery said nothing. How do you ask someone if she'd attended the faeries' revels without her thinking you belonged in Bedlam? But just then Margery brushed back her tangle of black hair, and for a moment her face seemed to shine like the queen's. Alice closed her left eye and the light disappeared. "Did you— Were you— Was that you I saw last night, talking to the Queen of Faerie?"

"Aye," Margery said. She picked up her tobacco-pipe from a pile of books and drew on it. Though Alice hadn't seen her light it a wreath of smoke soon covered her face. If the faerie-light had truly been there it was gone now.

"How long have you known her?"

"Oh, a long time."

Alice had forgotten how difficult conversation with her friend could be. She rarely talked about the thing you most wanted to know but would lead you around it, through overgrown and twisting roads. And by the time you emerged into the light of day you had learned many things, each one stranger than the next, but never what you wanted to know. For the first time Alice wondered what sights Margery saw with her left eye, and if that was why she seemed so distracted so much of the time. When the people of Faerie crowded your vision you had little time for the rest of the world.

"What did you talk about?"

"She asked for my aid in something."

"Your—aid? In what?"

"Ah, that I can't tell you."

"Why not?"

"Because many things are told to me in confidence. But be patient—I think you will learn more of this later."

"When?"

"Soon, I think. Things hurry toward their conclusions."

"Does it have something to do with the brownie in my house?"

Margery laughed. "Do you truly have a brownie? I've always wanted one." She turned to look at the confusion around her. "Aye, it might have something to do with him, after all. Does he bring you luck? Would you like some mulled wine?"

"I would, thank you." Alice looked on as Margery set out tarnished silver goblets and poured wine in a pot to heat it. Then she gave thought to the woman's other question, remembering the number of orders she had left at the printshop just an hour before. "I think he does. My business prospers, anyway. But why did he come to me?"

"Why do they come to anyone? But you must do all you can to keep him."

"How do I do that?"

"Never thank him for his labors. Set aside a bowl of milk for him every night, but give him nothing else, or he may consider his wages paid in full and do no more work. Never offend him in any way."

"Can you tell me anything more about the—these—"

"About the Fair Folk? They have not been in London long. An urgent errand brought them here."

Alice nearly asked Margery what that errand was, but she felt certain the other woman would not tell her. "But what are they?" she asked. "They are not angels . . ."

Margery laughed. "Nay, not angels. But they are very old. The uncovenanted powers, folks call them now."

"Then they are not—not godly—"

"I don't know. I don't know what you mean by godly."

Alice felt a small shock. How could Margery not understand a thing like that? She knew that Margery didn't go to church, and the knowledge worried her. In the small town where Alice had grown up the other woman would have been fined for her lack of attendance, might have even been accused of being a witch. Here, so close to the city, people's businesses kept them too occupied to notice her.

"I mean that it may be unlawful to deal with them," Alice said. "Perhaps I should have nothing to do with them."

"Nothing?"

Alice had forgotten Brownie. She felt her face grow hot under the other woman's shrewd gaze. But had that been all that Margery meant by her question? Or did she know something of the future? Had she guessed how strongly Alice was drawn to the splendor of the queen?

The wine had heated; Margery poured it out and handed her a goblet. It tasted a little odd, and she looked down to see cut tobacco leaves floating on top. And this was the woman to whom the queen had gone for help! But perhaps it was as she had thought: Margery's other sight kept her from noticing the things everyone else considered important.

"I hope you've spoken to no one else about these—these powers. If your talk should come to the ears of the Privy Council—"

"Do you think I've lost my wits? But no one listens to old women—you know that as well as I do."

"We're not so old," Alice said. "But you might be right. I'm rarely called on at the Stationers' Company meetings, and it's only when another printer repeats my suggestions that they're taken seriously. Someone tried to flatter me the other day by asking for my advice. I almost believed him—I wanted so much to be accepted by the rest of the company."

The conversation turned to the gossip in the churchyard. "George has asked me to marry him," Alice said.

"George? That foolish-looking man at Paul's?" Margery had met Alice when she had gone into London looking for a book. Later one of the other stationers had told Alice he thought the book Margery wanted had last been printed over a hundred years ago. Since then Alice had kept aside things she thought would interest Margery.

"Do you truly think he looks foolish? He seems to me just the opposite—a man who can never laugh at anything."

"Aye, and that's what makes him a fool. I hope you told him no."

"I did. I don't think I will ever marry again."

"You can do better for yourself than George."

"Didn't you hear what I said? I will not marry again. I'm too old for marriage, and I've grown too solitary this past year. I'm not suited to live with anyone."

"Ah. But you don't know what fortune has in store for you."

"Are you prophesying for me?" Alice laughed, but her heart seemed to lift a little. To marry again, to put an end to her loneliness . . .

"Do you want me to?"

"God forfend," Alice said.

5

Evening had fallen by the time Alice got back to the churchyard. All over the yard stalls stood in shadow; from the gate she could not even make out her own station. Around her the other stationers were putting their books away for the day, closing their stalls, counting out the money they had made.

When she got to her station she saw that the young man who worked for her had gone. She unlocked her stall, curious to see what he had sold that day. Someone moved toward her from the shadows.

"Good day, Mistress Wood."

It was Tom Nashe. How long had he been waiting for her? His manner seemed urgent; she guessed that he had something to tell her. Suddenly, as if from nowhere, an icy winter's wind blew through the yard, riffling the pages of her books. She shivered. "What is it, Tom?"

"I've found him."

"Found who?"

"Your son. That is to say, I found him once. He's gone again."

"My—son?"

"Aye. Arthur. He sits and talks with us sometimes at the Saracen's Head, but he never told us his name. He has red hair—"

"Aye," she said softly, trying not to hope too much.

"And green eyes, with long lashes. But I fear—"

"What? What do you fear?"

"His wits—"

She had never known Tom to hesitate so much. "His wits are gone," she said.

"Not as bad as that. But he calls himself king, speaks of certain prophecies made at his birth . . . I think his poverty has made him frantic."

"That was always one of his fancies, even when he was a small child. He was a king, and we were to do his bidding." She tried to smile. "Perhaps my husband should not have named him Arthur. But where is he?" She looked around as if Tom might have brought him into the churchyard.

"I'm trying to tell you. I looked for him all day today, but he's gone. I'm afraid he might have left because of something I said. When he told me his name I asked him if he was your son, and he grew angry—I had never seen him so angry. He swore to me he was a king and no son of yours. I said I would bring him with me to the churchyard. I think that's why he's disappeared."

"Then he is alive. But so changed—even when he played at being a king he always knew he was my son. Please let me know if you see him again."

"Of course."

"What tavern does he frequent?"

"The Saracen's Head, in Shoreditch."

"Ah," she said. Arthur, alive—she could barely credit it.

Tom took his leave. She nodded to him absently, but all the while her mind was on Arthur. Perhaps she could get someone to go with her to the Saracen's Head. Her son would know her when he saw her, she felt sure of it.

"Alice Wood?" someone said, and she looked up in alarm. A man dressed in the livery of the queen stood in front of her stall. She had been so deep in thought she had not even seen him approach.

"Aye?" she said warily. What did he want with her so late in the day? All her books had been licensed and recorded in the stationers' registry; he could have checked that for himself.

"I have a warrant summoning you to court."

"A—warrant?"

"Aye. The queen wants to ask you certain questions."

What questions? she nearly asked, but she found that she could guess the answer. If Tom had heard Arthur boast he was a king then others had certainly heard him as well. But where was Arthur now? Did the queen's men have him? "What—does this concern?" she asked cautiously, careful not to give anything away.

The man shrugged. "I don't know." He looked down at the warrant and began to read, ". . . by virtue here of to bring her to Court . . ." He looked up, seeming to realize only at that moment where he was, surrounded by books of every sort. Probably most of the men and women he summoned to court could not read. With a gesture almost of apology, he handed her the warrant and left.

She looked at it, the words blurring before her in her anxiety. Who could she turn to? Not George, certainly, and Margery was too unworldly to be of much help. What had Arthur done that Queen Elizabeth herself should take an interest in her?

She had never been in trouble with the law in her life. She would have to ask Margery for her help, she realized; she had no one else. With a heavy heart, she closed her stall and left the churchyard.

A week later Christopher stood in the queen's Council Chamber, looking around him in satisfaction. Busts of great men stood in the corners and carved gold cherubim flew against the ceiling. Two fireplaces faced each other from across the room, each burning what looked like a small tree. Paintings and tapestries lined one side of the hall. Blocks of light, like gold ingots, came through the tall windows on the other side, and as the courtiers stepped into the sun their clothing blazed with color.

A young man walked by dressed in silk hose, a cloth-of-silver doublet, a velvet jerkin and a monstrous starched lawn ruff, all of it white. His jewelry, pale silver chains and pearl earrings, had been chosen carefully to match, and he wore a large white feather in his hat.

He seemed a marvel of moderation compared to the people surrounding him. Now a woman came into the room wearing a black velvet gown embroidered with gold satin, and sleeves of silk striped in purple and gold. She carried a fan of peacock feathers, and her bosom was bare. She started toward the man in white, but before she could reach him a brindled terrier that had been lying by the fire ran to him and leapt up, its tail whipping back and forth with excitement. It left a muddy paw-print on the man's immaculate jerkin. Christopher tried not to laugh.

There was color everywhere: marigold, popinjay blue, peas porridge tawny, the pale tan called dead Spaniard. Some of the men had even dyed their beards purple or orange, and everyone displayed jewelry: brooches, medallions, rings, rubies, diamonds, pearls. The men padded their round hose and sleeves, and stuffed bombast into their doublets, far beyond what the gallants wore in St. Paul's. Christopher watched it all with interest. Someday he too would be able to dress as fine.

Two women entered the hall, both dressed as if in deliberate contrast to the splendor around them. The taller of them wore a plain petticoat, a skirt of russet and a green bodice, and had covered her hair with an unbleached linen kerchief. The other, he thought, would have looked out of place in nearly any company; she was dressed all in black, with fantastic jewels winking at her fingers and earlobes. She did not seem to have combed her black hair, which hung in tangles to her waist.

The first woman had to be Alice Wood, the bookseller; he could not imagine any profession for the second unless it was that of a cunning woman. And now that he saw her he thought he recognized Mistress Wood from the churchyard. He moved back and leaned against a pillar, careful to keep himself in shadow so that she would not see him.

As he watched the bookseller glanced around her nervously, perhaps in awe at her surroundings, perhaps out of fear. To his surprise he found himself feeling a little in sympathy with her. He had wondered, once or twice, what happened to the information he brought Robert Poley, the drama that emerged from all the unrelated facts. Now for the first time he had come face-to-face with one of those facts, and it made him uncomfortable. She seemed a decent, honest woman, whatever the company she kept. And the world could certainly use more booksellers.

He had dutifully reported to Poley what he had heard in the tavern, that the man claiming to be king was named Arthur, and that Tom Nashe thought he was Mistress Wood's son. To his astonishment and delight Robert had arranged for him to come to court, posing as a secretary to one of the queen's courtiers. "You've met this Arthur," Robert had said. "I want you to decide if the son she talks about is the same man, and how far she's implicated in this plot."

Christopher had nodded. But Robert had not finished; the queen's agent had one more surprise in store.

"That's not all I want you to do," he had said, leaning forward. His face, usually so anonymous, seemed to stand out suddenly in the light of the candles. "I suspect that there is a faction at court, perhaps more than one faction, that seeks to use this man for its own ends. It's been over thirty years since Queen Elizabeth gained the throne, and in that time she has constantly faced conspiracies by one group or another—Catholics, Puritans, Spanish. You're too young to have known another monarch, so you wouldn't remember the chaos that existed before she became queen. We must be vigilant to see that those days do not come again."

Christopher had nodded, but privately he wondered how much of Robert's talk was the agent's own fantasy, bred out of his insecurity. Without conspiracies he would be useless; he needed them, or needed to fabricate them, in order to justify his own existence. Elizabeth had been queen during Christopher's entire life: she had certainly proven over and over again her ability to endure. She'll outlive us all, he thought.

Now he saw Mistress Wood move down the hall, clearly at a loss in such grand company. He could not imagine her as part of any conspiracy. Probably, he thought, there was no plot; probably Arthur was just a hapless drunk who had had the misfortune to speak up in the wrong company.

What on earth could he tell Robert? Sometimes months

would go by before the agent sent him on another errand, and he was loath to give this one up so soon. And how did the other man expect him to discover a conspiracy among all these fine people? Perhaps he should invent something.

The woman with Mistress Wood seemed unimpressed, studying the folks that passed her with undisguised interest. He thought for a moment that she caught his eye, though she could not possibly have found him among the shadows. He saw her nod, as if that one glance had told her all she needed to know.

He forced himself to look away from her, and at that moment he became aware of a murmuring at the other end of the hall. A trumpet sounded, and the Knights of the Garter entered the room. The Lord High Chancellor followed them, walking between two men carrying the royal scepter and the sword of state, and after him came the queen. Everyone bent in a bow or curtsy, and several voices called out, "God save the Queen Elizabeth!" Christopher followed the stream of people moving toward her, trying at the same time to keep Alice Wood and the other woman in sight.

"I thank you, my good people," the queen said. She sat, carefully setting her fine hands on her lap in front of her. She was dressed in a white silk gown embroidered with pearls and flowers. Jewels hung from her neck and waist, and pearls were twined in her red hair. Her face was lined and her teeth bad, but as she looked out over the crowd she seemed to have more strength, more vitality, than anyone among them. She spoke to a man beside her and Christopher suddenly thought he understood the secret of her famous charm: she had the ability to focus on just one person to the exclusion of all else, to make that person feel that he alone existed in all the world.

The man called out a name and the day's business began. He wondered how long it would take them to get to Mistress Wood, and when he would be allowed to go home. A watch dangling from a woman's skirt told him it was four in the afternoon. Already he had grown tired of the proceedings, though Mistress Wood seemed to find them interesting. Perhaps, he thought, she rarely left her home.

Someone near him passed a paper to another man. The

second man looked at what was written there, nodded and passed the note back. Christopher watched them closely, not really sure why he did so. Certainly they had done nothing suspicious. Yet the paper reminded him of the blood-covered note Poley had shown him. And he had nothing better to do, and Robert would want a full account of his day.

With his black hair cut close to his head and his haggard expression, the first man looked like a disgraced king in exile. Christopher studied the face until he was certain he would know it again. The second man was of medium height, a little stocky, with unremarkable brown hair and eyes. Then the first man whispered something and the second man smiled, and all at once Christopher's opinion of him changed. There was nothing unremarkable about that smile. He looked as though he wanted you to like him. Nay, more, as if he couldn't conceive of anyone not liking him. It was a disarming, easy smile, one genuinely pleased with the world.

He wondered who the man could be. He wondered more: how someone could have reached maturity without having lost that openness, that pleasure with the world and everything it contained. So intently did he watch the two of them that he nearly missed hearing the queen's man call out, "Alice Wood!"

He moved to the front of the crowd. Courtiers and supplicants blocked his way, and by the time he reached the queen's throne Alice Wood had already risen from her deep curtsy.

"We've called you here to answer certain questions," a man said, and Alice realized with surprise that this must be the queen's Principal Secretary, Sir Francis Walsingham. Churchyard gossip said that the man had been ill, but she was unprepared for the gauntness of Walsingham's face, the pain visible in his eyes. His color was still dark, though; Queen Elizabeth, or so Alice had heard, called him her "Moor." In contrast to the men and women surrounding him he wore a severely cut doublet and hose and no jewelry but a memorial ring.

"We have witnesses," Walsingham said, "who have heard your son claim to be king. What do you know about this?"

Alice glanced at the queen. Her face with its high fine cheekbones gave nothing away. "Nothing, sir. I have not seen my son for several years."

"How many years?"

"Two years. Nay, three now."

"Three years ago, did he ever claim to be king?"

"Only in jest, as a game. He was a child then."

"This is not a child's game, Mistress Wood," Walsingham said sternly.

"I know that, sir," she said, feeling bold enough to raise her eyes to his.

He returned her gaze; there was no pity in his expression. For the first time during the interview she began to feel afraid. She had no friends here, no one who would champion her cause. The air in the chamber had grown stifling. The crowd smelled of strong sweet perfume; the stench made her feel faint. She thought of the fresh open air of the churchyard to steady herself. "Did you or your husband ever give your son cause to think of himself as a king?"

"Nay, we did not."

"Do you know any reason he might make this outrageous claim?"

Margery stirred beside her. God's blood, what was the woman about to say? It had been a mistake to bring her here, Alice had seen that the minute they had walked into the chamber. She said, quickly, "Nay, I don't."

"Have you ever spoken treason against your lawful queen?"

"Nay!" she said indignantly.

Walsingham gave no indication that he had heard her. "We have witnesses who will testify to your loyalty, or the lack of it. Be careful what you say."

"I have never——" She turned to the queen. "Your Majesty, I——"

"I ask the questions here," the secretary said, forcing her to look away from Elizabeth. "We do not allow suspected traitors to speak to the queen, may she reign in peace for many years to come."

"Aye, she will," Margery said.

"What?" The secretary turned to her, astonished. The stately rhythm of question and answer had been interrupted; for the first time he looked flustered.

"She will reign in peace for many years to come," Margery said. She was at least a head shorter than Walsingham; in her old black clothes she looked like a bedraggled crow come face-to-face with a falcon. Still, it was Walsingham who looked away first.

Queen Elizabeth bent her steady gaze toward the other woman. Alice thought she saw the bare beginning of sympathy touch her regal expression. Surely the queen was on her side in this; surely she would not have her wrongly accused. "Are you certain of that?" Elizabeth asked.

"Aye, Your Majesty."

"Excellent. You may both go."

"But——" Walsingham said.

"They may both go."

"But I have other questions. You can't suppose that they're innocent just because this woman"—the secretary looked at Margery scornfully—"this woman invents a prophecy—"

"And I don't. That's not why I've dismissed them. I believe she's innocent."

Walsingham looked as if only decorum prevented him from arguing with her. "Why should she be guilty?" the queen asked. "You are too suspicious, Francis—in your zeal to protect me you see conspiracies everywhere. I don't know if I believe this woman's prophecy or not. But I can see—as anyone with eyes can see—that she wishes me well, that she wishes the realm well. And the loyalty of these subjects is what we're trying to prove here."

"Very well, Your Majesty," Walsingham said.

"Find her son for me, Francis. Find her son," the queen said impatiently, and dismissed them.

Alice turned to Margery as they left the Council Chamber. She should be grateful, she knew; the other woman had probably saved her life. But she could not help but feel annoyance at Margery's manner, the way she seemed to know more than anyone around her. "What did you—"

"Hush," Margery said. She waited until they had left the

palace before she spoke again. Evening had come while they had spoken with the queen; the air, which had grown hot and stifling in the Council Chamber, was chilly outdoors. "I had to distract them in some way."

"What do you mean?"

"I didn't want them to learn the truth about Arthur."

"The—truth?" Alice felt the ground shift beneath her, grow suddenly unstable. What did this woman know? "What is the truth?"

"Ah—that I don't know. But Walsingham was right and the queen wrong—there are conspiracies here."

"What did you mean when you said you had to distract them? Was your prophecy no more than that?"

"I don't know. Perhaps the queen will reign a dozen more years, perhaps she'll die tomorrow." Alice caught her breath at the treasonous statement. "But the important thing for us is to find Arthur."

"Why? Is he in trouble?"

"Aye, more than you could know. And the queen's search for him is the least of it."

Christopher had listened closely while the queen and her secretary questioned Alice. Toward the end he had begun to grin at the turn the interview had taken, at the audacity of Mistress Wood's friend. When the queen had finished he was more certain than ever that the bookseller was innocent. He turned and headed outside, thinking of what he would say to Poley.

The two men he had noticed earlier, the ones who had passed the note, walked in front of him. For no reason other than curiosity he began to follow them. They headed toward the Thames and he feared that they would hail a boat, but they continued to walk, keeping the river to their right. He stayed a few steps behind, close enough to listen to their conversation but far enough away that they would not suspect him. Spies and playwrights, he thought, were the two types of men to whom it came naturally to eavesdrop.

The darker man said something in a low voice, and his companion made as if to turn. The first man restrained him. Had they seen him? But they continued to talk quietly, the second man punctuating their conversation with laughter.

They went around a corner and Christopher followed. He could see no one in the street in front of him at all; it was as if the two men had vanished. He remembered the night he had tried to follow Arthur and the way the air had seemed to shine before him, remembered too a mad story Tom had told him about journeying through a London greatly changed, magicked. But he knew London held no strange creatures lurking in corners: Tom's babble had been the result of having slept outdoors, nothing more.

Someone knocked into him and he fell to the ground. He looked up into the faces of the two men he had followed.

"Ho!" the stocky one said. "Were you following us?"

"Aye," Christopher said. The word was out of his mouth before he had time to think, knocked out of him along with his breath. But he had wearied of plots and conspiracies and secrets, and the man's openness seemed to demand an answering honesty.

"Why? Are you a spy, then?"

Christopher said nothing. Who were these two men? Would it be safe to confide in them? He put his hand to the back of his head and drew it away quickly; he had hurt himself when he fell.

"Good," the man said. "We're spies too. I'm William Ryder, and this is my brother Geoffrey."

Christopher stood up carefully. He could not imagine any two men who looked less alike. Could they truly be brothers? "Who are you spying for?" he asked.

"Ah," the stocky man—William—said. "We must have a fair exchange of information, after all. Tell us who sent you to court."

"Why? For all I know you're agents of King Philip of Spain."

William laughed, as if Christopher had made a jest that pleased him. "Come," he said. "We were heading home before we spotted you. We'll talk there."

He nodded. Perhaps these men had contacts at court; perhaps he could work for them and so avoid odious Poley altogether. Their clothing certainly seemed rich enough. "I'm sorry about your head," William said as they set off.

They continued to walk along the Thames. Dusk had come; they had only a few stars and the thin rind of the moon to light their way. A few minutes later they began to pass the great manors of the nobility. Could these men live here? Why would they waste their time on spy-work if they did?

Geoffrey stopped in front of one of the largest of the houses. It was one of the ugliest as well, made of thick slabs of gray stone that seemed to weep with moisture from the river. Bulky turrets and towers sprouted off from it at odd angles, and its windows were set almost haphazardly into the walls.

William watched him closely, no doubt hoping to see what he thought of the monstrous structure. "It's the sort of building that reminds you Caligula was an architect," Christopher said.

"You should see our ghost," William said as Geoffrey opened the massive wooden front door. "She's ugly as well." He hesitated. "You're not frightened of ghosts, are you?"

"Nay. I don't believe in them."

Fires had been lit in the rooms beyond but the house kept a chill that seemed to seep from the stones. They went inside. Geoffrey called for servants, and an old man and woman came to build up the fires and ask what they wanted for supper. Christopher noted that the servants called him Sir Geoffrey, and the informality of the brothers, the fact that they had not told him Geoffrey was titled, disturbed him.

"Our father spends most of his time on his estate," William said, leading the way to a table before the largest of the fires. "He keeps us in London to take care of his business. Geoffrey is supposed to be studying at the Inns of Court."

"And you? What are you supposed to be doing?"

William shrugged. "What are younger sons supposed to do?"

"Become involved in intrigue, evidently. You still haven't told me whom you work for."

The servants returned with silver trays of cold meat and fruit and a bottle of wine. The manservant lit a few candles but the room remained dark, oppressive. The two men looked like children dining in the ruins of a giant's house.

William reached for a chicken leg. "Essex," he said, his mouth filled with chicken.

"What?"

"The earl of Essex. We work for him."

"What does Essex have to do with all this?"

"He's about to marry," William said.

Geoffrey raised his head in alarm. "You were told not to mention that to anyone," he said angrily.

"Nay, Geoffrey, the man's honest," William said.

"And how do you know that?"

"He told us so himself. I asked him if he was following us, and he said he was. A dishonest man would have denied it. Can I go on?"

"Oh, surely," Geoffrey said, sitting back wearily. "You've already given away all the secrets of state you know."

Christopher thought quickly. Everyone knew the queen doted on Essex; everyone had heard of her anger when any of her courtiers married. If what William said was true then the queen's court would change soon, maybe change all out of recognition. He wondered what Poley would give to hear this news. But William had trusted him; he would not tell Poley unless he had to.

"Walsingham is very ill," William said. "Well, you saw him today—there's talk he won't last the month. Essex hopes to become the new Principal Secretary. To do that, he has to have his own net of spies in place. We're it."

"Of course there are others as well," Geoffrey said, with another angry glance at his brother.

"Of course," William said.

Christopher barely heard him. Walsingham dead! The Principal Secretary was the man responsible for the queen's web of spies, Poley's superior and ultimately his own as well. What would happen to him when the man died? Should he throw in his lot with these eccentric noblemen?

"Who besides Essex is there for the post?" he asked. He added sugar to the wine and took a sip.

"Lord Burghley hopes to advance his son," William said.

"Robert Cecil," Geoffrey said scornfully. "He's far too young,

and a hunchback besides. The queen likes the men around her
to be whole."

"Aye," William said. "We think she'll follow her heart in this
matter. But Essex's marriage complicates things."

"We have received information," Geoffrey said. "There's a
faction at court which hopes to overthrow the queen. If Essex
can discover who these people are—if we can discover it for
him—his chances are that much greater."

Christopher nodded. The brothers' information matched his
own. He decided to trust them, to tell them what he knew. "I'm
working for Walsingham," he said. "My name's Christopher
Marlowe. I was instructed to find this faction as well. We can
work together, share our information."

William grinned at him, and he realized he had based his
decision on nothing more solid than William's appealing smile.
The realization surprised him; usually he favored men who had
more of beauty about them. William seemed too much like his
house, sturdy, a little wayward, but by no means attractive.

He leaned back and drank more of the brothers' fine wine,
studying the two men before him.

6

The day dawned fair, but by midmorning a pelting rain fell over the churchyard. People threw cloaks over their heads and ran for the safety of Paul's or their homes. In five minutes the yard was deserted.

George caught up with Alice as she was closing her stall. "I'd like to talk with you," he said, calling to her over the pounding of the rain.

She looked at him blankly. No doubt she wondered why he approached her now, when he had avoided her ever since his proposal. But no—she was motioning that she couldn't hear him. He called to her again and she nodded.

"The cookshop?" he asked.

"My house is closer."

He tried not to look surprised. She had never invited him to her house; the rest of the company would have been scandalized. He thought that she wanted to make amends for the abrupt way she had treated him the last time they had talked, and he felt pleased to see it. It made his task that much easier.

They left the yard together, hurrying through the rain. Alice lifted her skirt and petticoat and ran through puddles, laughing. Churchyard gossip said that she had been to court the day before, though no one knew why or what had happened. Some even said she had spoken to the queen.

It had probably gone well for her there, he thought; he had not seen her so free of care since before John died. Almost he wished that she had been put in more danger yesterday, that fear would make her turn to him as she had after the death of her husband. Instead she acted as though the day were a holiday, the rain a gift.

It was not good to be so frivolous, and he turned to tell her so. She laughed again when she saw his face. He could not talk to her now, with the rain drowning out all conversation. When she was his he would be able to teach her moderation.

Alice let him into the house, shaking the rain from her cloak as she entered. "Care for something hot to drink?" she asked.

"Please."

He followed her to the kitchen and sat while she poured wine into a pot and set it over the fire. He looked about him, curious to see how she lived. The room was small but neat, with her few good pewter pieces displayed on wooden shelves. It pleased him to see her so industrious, so modest. He watched her in silence, unable to think of anything except that which was uppermost in his mind, the small earthenware jar like heavy gold in his purse.

At last the wine had warmed enough. Alice added spices and sugar and poured out some for each of them. "Come," she said. "We'll sit at the table, and be at our ease."

She took the goblets into the front room. As he followed her he lifted the jar from his pouch and held it cupped in his hand. His heart beat loudly. How was he to give it to her?

His chance came when she turned away for a moment. He pried the stopper out of the jar and poured the contents into her drink, his hands shaking slightly. The elixir was colorless, he saw, and there was very little of it. Both those things pleased him. He had just enough time to thrust the jar back into his pouch before she sat at the table.

"Good cheer," she said, lifting her goblet.

"Good cheer." He watched closely as she drank. How would it happen? Would it be sudden, or would she come slowly to warm to him, a little more as she took each sip, until finally she agreed to marry him? He hoped it would be sudden, so that he would know if the thing had worked. Nay, better if it happened slowly, so she would suspect nothing.

"Ah, that's good," she said. "And it's good to be out of the rain on a day like this."

"Aye." He thought he saw color coming into her cheeks, red and white mixed, like roses. Was that how it started?

"Is something wrong?" she asked.

"Nay. You look—" But he couldn't tell her how beautiful she looked, not until she had declared her love for him. Once she was his he would never have to hazard his feelings again.

"It's good to see you again, George," she said. "I missed the talks we had together." She looked happy, almost giddy.

He heard a noise from the kitchen. "Ah," she said. "He's back." Who was she talking about? "George, come and look."

He followed her to the kitchen. Something moved by the hearth, and at first he thought she had gotten a dog. Then he saw that it walked upright, and that it was scouring the pot Alice had used for the wine. Brown fur covered its body. Without meaning to he stepped back. "What is it?"

"A brownie."

"Nay." He shook his head. "It's a demon."

The thing by the fire had stopped working. It set down the pot and looked from Alice to George, thoughtfully, as if trying to decide something.

"Brownie, this is George," Alice said softly. "He's a friend."

The brownie shook its head. It seemed to have made up its mind; now it looked regretful, infinitely sad. "Ah, Alice," it said. It reached for a triangular red cap hanging on a hook near the fire. "We could have had such merry times together."

"Wait—" Alice said.

The brownie took no notice of her. It put on the cap and left the kitchen. George shrank back a little as it went past him. Then it opened the front door and was gone without another word. As it walked the rain around it seemed to turn the color of pearls.

"What on earth—" George said.

"I've lost him."

"Alice—"

"Margery told me I must not offend him in any way. But I didn't think he would mind being introduced to you. Now I'll never see him again."

"Alice, what is this talk? Don't you know a demon when you see one? How did it come to you?"

"I don't know." She looked desolate. "Margery said I was not to ask such questions."

Margery. Now he understood, and he did not like what he saw happening to Alice. "Margery is that madwoman who sometimes comes into the churchyard? I wonder how it is she is allowed so near a holy place. Does she take you to her witches' sabbaths?"

"Nay!" She looked shocked. "Margery is not a witch."

"What is she then?"

"A wise woman."

George laughed mirthlessly. "There's little to choose between the two of them, I fear. Perhaps she's too wise to tell you her true profession. Does she take you to a deserted field late at night, then, and have you perform certain rites?"

"George, you know nothing of this! She is—"

"Does she?"

"Nay!"

"But she gave you your familiar."

"Brownie? Brownie's not a familiar, he's—"

"Aye? What was he? Not a man."

"Nay."

"And certainly he was not one of the angels." George laughed a little. "Therefore he was a demon."

"Margery said—"

"Margery! All your talk is of Margery. Why do you listen to that addled old woman?"

"She said that these things are old, far older than we know. That they are—"

"Aye, the demons are old, and subtle, too. Subtle beyond your power to understand, it seems."

"You know nothing of this. I have seen——" She stopped, as if she hadn't wanted to reveal so much.

"What? Seen what?"

"Faerie revels."

"Faerie revels? Is that what they call them now? I would call them witches' sabbaths instead."

"Nay, they weren't—they were beautiful——"

"Aye, so they would seem, to you."

Alice said nothing. Had she changed so much since he'd known her? What errors had she fallen into without his experience to guide her? How could she not see that her eternal soul was in peril?

"It's not good to make these kinds of bargains, Alice. Everything has a price, and you would have had to pay this one in the end." He remembered something Anthony Drury had said to him. "There is a play, about a man who signs a contract with the devil——"

"I made no bargain. Brownie was unlooked for, unsought. I did nothing to deserve him."

"Has Margery so cozened you that you believe this thing a faerie? Or is your innocence only pretense?"

"I can't talk with you in this mood——"

But he understood something suddenly. Aye, she had changed nearly beyond recognition. "What did the two of you do here, alone at night?"

He was unprepared for her reply. She started to laugh; truly, he thought, she was bewitched. "Brownie? You think that Brownie and—and I——"

"Aye, Brownie and you. Why not? Perhaps that's why you did not want to marry me. Why take a husband when you have a demon to do your every bidding?"

Alice was silent for so long that he became aware again of the rain drumming outside the house. "You're serious," she said finally. "I will not have you make these accusations against me."

"What do you do there, at these revels of yours? Conjuring, calling up of the devil? Is it true they make you kiss the devil's arse, as I have heard?"

Alice said nothing but went to her front door and opened it, indicating that he should leave. Too late he remembered the elixir. How was it that she was able to make him so angry, angry enough to drive every other thought out of his mind? The elixir hadn't made her yield to him, that was clear. She was still as willful as ever.

The rain had not let up. He pulled his cloak over his head and went outside.

The next day was cold and overcast, but it looked as if the rain would keep away. The booksellers in the churchyard thumbed through their almanacs and glanced at the sky and talked among themselves in groups of three or four, and at last most of them decided to stay.

When George passed Alice on the way to his stall she deliberately turned away from him. By then his anger had grown to include Anthony Drury. If Anthony's potion had worked he would not have been made to look so foolish. When the other man came back into the churchyard he would not find George as compliant as before.

The people who visited Paul's that cold day were not disposed to linger; they did their business and then went home. By midafternoon George's neighbors began to close their stalls. He had just decided to join them when he saw a man in black doublet and hose heading toward him. Could that be Anthony? Good, it was.

"Did you use the elixir?" Anthony asked him.

"Aye."

"And what happened?"

"You know better than I what happened. I could have given her water to drink for all the good it did me. For all I know I did give her water."

Anthony did not apologize, as George had expected. "Sometimes these things can be difficult," he said. "We can try again, and this time we'll be more careful. It might help if you came with us. Aye, the master said once that it's time for you to meet him."

"Nay, I've done with your tricks. Get someone else to help you."

"Do you still want her?"

The other man's question stopped him. Did he? He didn't know. He still thought her beautiful, still enjoyed imagining her by his side. But her actions horrified and disgusted him. She would have to change utterly for him to accept her again. If she kept to her willful ways it would be best for everyone if she left the Stationers' Company. The ideas she harbored were dangerous, very dangerous.

"Perhaps," he said.

"We'll try one more time," Anthony said. "Come with us—I think that will help. If we don't succeed we'll trouble you no further, and you'll have lost nothing. What do you think?"

George was silent. Would they truly leave him alone if they failed this time? He thought that that might be the best bargain of all.

"And if we can't help you win her, we can aid you in other ways."

"I don't want—"

"We can have her taken out of the Stationers' Company, for example."

"How— How did you know?"

"We know many things. If you join us you'll know these things too."

"I don't want to join you. I don't even know who you are."

"Ah, but you do want to. We know that about you too."

He must have looked surprised because Anthony smiled suddenly, a sharp smile that turned his mouth the shape of a *V*. "Think it over," Anthony said. "I'll be back to get you. Good day." He left before George could answer him.

Was it true that he wanted to join them? As he had told Anthony, he didn't even know who they were. He thought that they meddled in magic, and he wanted no part of that. But as if in answer he remembered Anthony saying that everything they did had a natural explanation. Was that possible? Could you make others do your bidding without damning your soul? The idea was a new one to him, and he turned it over slowly.

Why stop with marrying Alice? He could improve his trade, get popular monopolies like almanacs, be wealthy. Perhaps he could even acquire a coat of arms and become a gentleman. He should not have been so quick to dismiss Anthony; clearly the other man had valuable knowledge.

He almost called after him, asking him to come back. But nay—the man would return. He had said so himself.

Alice watched as George closed up his stall. She had tried to understand his behavior of the day before but had finally given up, come to understand that it was a riddle with no answer. When he had been friendly she had responded eagerly, gladdened to see him again. She had even thought, in her happiness, that he would want to meet Brownie. But then he had become insistent in a strange, forceful way, and finally angry. She knew that he would never speak to her again, but she knew too that she did not want him to, that she had been wrong about him. He had been a friend only as long as she had needed him; when she had gotten over her grief and confusion at John's death, he had changed.

The strange thing was that she didn't miss him at all. All her sorrow went for Brownie, who had left her so unexpectedly. Never to join the faeries at their revels, never to see the queen burning in white on the grass . . . But when she closed her right eye she saw their light, like jewels or swords or stars. She still had that, then. He had not taken that away from her.

7

A few days later Christopher sat at the desk he had been given and looked at the confusion of papers before him. The position Robert Poley had found for him, secretary to one of the queen's courtiers, had proved to be far more tedious than he had imagined when he had first heard of it, in the darkness of the Black Boar. Spread out in front of him were letters to copy, accounts to tally, lists to be arranged into some sort of order. He wondered how Poley expected him to find the time to discover anything.

The courtier he worked for, Sir Philip Potter, was a plump, ineffectual man from the north, come to court to ask Elizabeth for some tax monopoly or other. In all the time he had been in London, according to his accounts, Sir Philip had spent enormous sums of money on gifts, on celebrations arranged for the queen, on food, on the servants he had brought to attend him. And in all that time he had yet to see Elizabeth, or any of the men close to her.

Philip Potter had been lodged in a suite of apartments at the palace. The suite was located a fair distance away from the queen's Privy Chamber, which was, Christopher thought, a good indication of Potter's standing at court. One of Potter's servants had shown him to a room perched under a gable, quite possibly the smallest room in the palace; it contained a bed, a desk and a stool, and nothing more.

Christopher looked at the letter on the stack Potter had given him, dipped his quill in the inkhorn and began to write. "The twenty-eighth of March. My dear friend . . ." His hand smudged the word "friend" and he studied the page for a moment, wondering if he should start over. Nay—best to ignore it and continue as though nothing had happened.

He sighed. His friend Tom Kyd sometimes worked as a scrivener in order to survive in London; he wondered now how the man stood it.

He looked away from the task before him and glanced out the window, at the roofs and chimneys of the city below him. Directly beneath him was a hedge maze, the shrubs only now beginning to put forth leaves. Two men walked through the maze, deep in conversation.

From where he sat Christopher could see the turns leading out of the maze, but the men inside were clearly lost. As they came to the end of a path one man pointed left, but the other, shaking his head, pointed right. The first man insisted. Christopher watched as they went deeper into the maze.

The first man's bulk showed him to be Philip Potter. Christopher did not know the second man, but his fine clothes declared him to be someone very important indeed. If Potter had hoped to impress him he had taken a wrong turn, both literally and figuratively.

Watching the two men below gave Christopher a strange godlike feeling. If God existed it would have been just this way that he had watched another two in another garden. Nay, don't take that path, God would have thought, but it would have been too late, they would have already done it. And rightly, he thought. Who would want to spend all his days in a garden, however pleasant?

He set his quill down and left the room. Potter might be all day getting out of the maze, and with his employer gone he could take a while to explore the palace. Poley would be expecting a report soon.

He went down the great central flight of stairs, passing clerks, maids-of-honor, ushers, pages, musicians. Two men spoke a language he didn't recognize; he thought they might have been ambassadors.

Finally he came to a gallery overlooking a courtyard. Men and women crossed the yard, talking and laughing. He watched as two servants passed a statue, a winged representation of Mercury.

He followed the long gallery with its windows and padded benches on one side, tapestries and displays of gold and silver plate on the other. Finally he came to a door. Guards in royal red and purple tunics moved to bar his way, and he realized he had come to the Presence Chamber. He turned and traced his steps back to the stairs, then continued on in the other direction.

The gallery turned, forming a second side of the courtyard. This time when he went through a doorway no one stopped him. More apartments opened off the corridor here, whole suites of them, far richer than poor Potter's were.

He passed several doors, some wide open, some left teasingly ajar. Voices came from a few of the rooms, a man flattering a woman's hands, another man boasting about his success in hunting the day before. Someone was talking about troop strength. Here's where the real business of the court takes place, he thought; Sir Philip has no idea.

At last he came to the end of the corridor. He had seen nothing that would help him. But surely, he thought, no one would plan a crime of state where he could be overheard so easily. Not for the first time he wondered what it was that Poley expected of him.

Christopher awoke early the next day. Something had roused him, a loud burst of song, a sound that could have been a table being hit like a drum. Could Potter be entertaining guests?

The light coming through the window showed him that it was still early morning. He stood and dressed and left his room, following the noises he had heard. Someone laughed, and then voices were raised in song.

The sounds grew louder as he went. He saw that a door to one of the rooms off the corridor had been left ajar. A group of men and women inside the room sat in a circle, singing merrily. One of them looked up and motioned with his hand to come in.

He stepped inside before he could get a good look at them. Someone closed the door, laughing. The room had no windows, but a pale light continued to come from somewhere. He backed away, toward the door. "Oh, there's no need to fear *us,*" a woman said, grinning, and that set them all to laughing again.

"Who are you?" he asked.

"Ah," said a man. "Who are *you?*"

The men and women laughed as if that had been a great stroke of wit. Christopher looked at the circle, thinking that every one of them had something odd about him. The man who had waved him in, for example: his palm was as long as most men's hands. The woman who had spoken to him had a grin that nearly reached her ears. Another woman nursed a child hidden from him by its swaddling clothes; he wondered a little fearfully what the child might look like. Even sitting down these folks seemed far too short; some of them might have been four feet or less.

"I'm Sir Philip Potter's secretary," he said.

"Aye, that too," the woman said, disconcertingly, he thought. How much did they know?

"Are you courtiers?" he asked.

"Aye," the man said. "We're here to—to—" His invention seemed to fail him.

"To see about our ancestral rights," another woman said.

All around the circle men and women nodded in agreement. "Aye, our ancestral rights." "Aye, that's it."

"What ancestral rights?" Christopher said. "Where are you from?"

"Have a drink," the man said, holding out a bottle shaped like a squat face.

It was far too early to drink; it had to be seven o'clock or even earlier. But before he could decide how to refuse another man snatched the bottle and drank from it, then passed it along in a graceful movement that might almost have been a dance. A pipe began to play somewhere. When the bottle came back to the beginning of the circle the man who had offered it to him held it out again.

"Have a drink," he said.

Were they all mad? The queen would never have allowed these folks in the palace, of that he felt sure. How had they gotten past the guards? And how did they eat? He had not seen them at dinner the day before; he would certainly have remembered them if he had.

"Nay, I thank you," he said, moving toward the door. To his relief no one stopped him. (But why relief? Surely, as the woman said, he had no reason to fear them.) He opened the door and headed back to Potter's apartments.

He had intended to wake early the next day, to listen for the voices again. But the sun shining in through the windows showed him that it was late morning, at the least. He cursed softly; he had probably missed them.

Loud laughter came from beyond the corridor. Someone sang, and there was a great crash that sounded like a table or chest being turned over. Suddenly everything fell silent. He waited for a long moment but could hear nothing. Curious, he rose and went down the corridor to the room he had visited the morning before.

He was in time to see a man come out of the room and close the door behind him. Christopher could not be sure, but he thought the man was the one who had offered him the bottle yesterday. And now, as the other man set off down the corridor, Christopher noticed that he carried the same squat bottle with him, tucked under his arm.

Christopher followed, careful to stay out of sight. They went down the stairs and into the gallery, and then the man turned toward the apartments Christopher had seen before. The man knocked once, paused and knocked again, and the door opened to let him in.

The door closed before he could see inside. He stayed a

while, listening, but he could hear nothing and finally turned to go. Then someone laughed loudly. "I say, 'The weather is fine for April,' " a voice said.

Christopher wondered if he had heard correctly. Had the man given some sort of password? He eased back against the wall near the door and listened cautiously.

"Nay," another man said. "The servant comes with our supper. He pours the wine——"

"Aye. I pour the wine, then return with salad and mutton."

"I say, 'This mutton is excellent.' "

Christopher listened in disbelief. This surpassed even the lunacy of the day before. They seemed to be rehearsing a play, but it was a play so tedious that audiences would rise up in a body and revolt if he tried to put it on the stage.

"Then I say, 'The weather is fine for April.' "

"Aye. And your wife comes into the room, and you say, 'Good evening, my lady.' "

The voices beyond the door continued to trade commonplaces back and forth. They seemed less giddy than the day before; he thought that this time they were engaged in a matter that concerned them deeply. Could it have something to do with what the woman had mentioned, their ancestral rights? He imagined the strange folks quietly acting out some mad ritual, passing the bottle back and forth among them.

The phantom supper ended. A new voice said, very quietly, "Another week, then."

Christopher had heard that voice before. Who was it?

"Aye," said the man who had spoken most often—the leader, probably. "April, with his showers sweet."

These were literate madmen, Christopher thought. The leader could quote Chaucer, at any rate.

"I'm certain this play will not be necessary," the new voice said. Christopher had to strain to hear him. ". . . will revolt against her, or so I've heard."

Against whom? The queen? Had he stumbled on a conspiracy after all? The voice was tantalizingly familiar. Could it be one of the men he had heard the day before? Nay—he was almost certain that it was not.

Christopher searched his memory, trying to put a face or a name to it, and nearly missed hearing the men rise and bid each other good day. They were leaving the meeting, he realized, and he slipped into an empty room just in time to avoid them.

"Did you see that?" a man said from the corridor. "Someone was here, listening."

"Nay—I saw no one. You're too fearful."

"He's probably still here. We should search—"

"Stay and look if you want. I'm leaving. Don't forget your part."

The men's voices diminished as they went down the hallway. They had apparently decided not to stay. By the time Christopher left the room he could see no one.

He hurried back to the stairs, hoping to catch them. Who were they? What had they been doing? And what on earth could he say to Poley?

He was stopped by a group of well-dressed people milling about at the foot of the stairway. Those at the back, near where he stood, were laughing and pointing at something he could not see. He strained to look past the brilliant colors of the court, gold and purple and peacock-blue. A woman in front of him raised a feathered fan, blocking his view entirely.

Then she moved. "Oh, God," Christopher said. Two people stood on the stairs, the woman tall and red-haired and imperious, the man stout and flustered, his clothing nearly coming undone. The man was obviously his supposed employer, Philip Potter. The woman, just as obviously to everyone but poor Sir Philip, was not Queen Elizabeth.

Potter attempted to bow, probably an awkward business for him at best, now made even more difficult by the stairs. His leg came out clumsily in front of him. The crowd laughed again. Philip looked around him uncertainly, and the woman, her voice deeper than Elizabeth's said, "Rise."

Christopher studied her carefully. The actor was a man, he saw now, his face heavily made up, his fine red hair a wig. Probably some courtier or other had planned a masque for an afternoon's entertainment, complete with a queen. The actor had been caught outside the tiring-room and had seen an opportunity for amusement.

Philip attempted to say something. "Not now, my sweet man," the actor said. Surely Potter could not be so witless that he still believed this person Queen Elizabeth. But Potter murmured something in reply, and the actor gave him an answer that seemed to satisfy him. Potter bowed again and continued up the stairs.

What now? The courtiers began to talk excitedly among themselves; probably they had not been so entertained by anything in a long time. Christopher pushed his way through them to the stairs. He thought that the actor had promised Potter an audience, and he had to see to it that the appointment was not kept. If this foolish man met the queen, full of some story about her promises to him, his own employment as Philip's secretary would come to an abrupt end.

He found Potter in his bedroom, gazing into a full-length mirror. He entered without knocking. His reflection appeared in the mirror and Potter looked up quickly, startled. "Who are you?"

"Who? I'm your secretary." He sat, uninvited, at the man's writing table and looked around him. Potter had been as ill served in his furnishings as in everything else. Besides the writing table the room held only an empty row of bookshelves and a bed with a sagging canopy. A faded tapestry hung between two windows, something bloody and classical, Actaeon or Adonis being torn to pieces.

Potter frowned. "Ah, my secretary. I'm going to have to dismiss you soon, you know. Can you find other employment? I'll give you a good reference, of course."

"I—" Christopher said. He felt an odd stirring of pity and admiration for the man, who had taken the time to worry about his secretary at the moment he considered his greatest triumph.

"I'm going home, my business here nearly finished," Potter said. "The queen has as good as promised me the monopoly I asked for."

"That person—" Christopher said, but the other man did not hear him.

"And I'm anxious to get back. I've just received a letter from home—my wife's given birth to a girl. Not an heir, of course, but still a pleasant thing. A very pleasant thing. What do you think I should wear for my audience with the queen?"

"Listen," Christopher said, almost savagely. The more Sir Philip spoke the more Christopher felt bound to protect him. The man would never survive among the wolves of the court. Look at him now, preening about his daughter as though it weren't just any man who could father a child. "That person was not the queen."

"Not the queen?" Potter laughed. "Why, man—"

"He was an actor got up to look like the queen. You've been played for a fool."

"An actor?"

"Aye. You've heard of such things, surely, even in the north."

"But this—this is treachery—"

"Ah, then you've heard of that too. But treachery, like acting, is subtler in the south. No one plotted this, I assure you. The court saw a chance to be entertained, nothing more."

"What—what should I do now?"

"Do what many another courtier has done—keep silent and dress like a gentleman. They'll expect you to be there for your appointment, and they'll expect to hear all about your embarrassment as well. Stay in your rooms for at least a week, until all this is forgotten. And for God's sake, don't go to the masque. You'll give them greater entertainment than the actors will."

"Will the queen hear of this—this incident?"

She had already heard of it, of that Christopher felt certain. But he could not bring himself to say so to this innocent. "Nay—the queen has more important matters on her mind."

"Well, I—I thank you. You've proved invaluable to me."

Once again Christopher felt a grudging admiration for Sir Philip. Anyone else would have been humiliated by what the court had done, but Potter seemed to have come through with all his flustered dignity intact. "One more thing," he said. "Don't wear that doublet again."

"This?" Potter said, looking past his chins to his stomach.

"Aye. Do you know what that color's called?"

"White? Dirty white?"

"In London we call it Isabella. After Queen Isabella, who vowed never to change her petticoats until the Moors were driven from Spain. You don't want people to laugh when they see your clothes—and you don't want to remind Elizabeth of another queen, and a queen of Spain at that."

"Ah. Ah, I see. It's all far more complicated than it looks, isn't it?"

"Aye," Christopher said, and left before the man could call forth more pity from him.

Christopher sat at his desk again later that day, staring absently at the confusion of paper in front of him. He had gone back to the stairs after his talk with Potter, hoping to see the actor again, but the man had disappeared. Someone there told him that the masque would not take place for another week, that the actor playing the queen had been so taken with his costume he had gone wandering through the halls against the advice of the other players.

Were the strange men he had overheard rehearsing a masque? It seemed unlikely. If that was the sort of performance given at the queen's court then he should hasten to offer his services; he could do better in his sleep.

Thoughts of the masque reminded him of the play in his travel bag. He took it out, pushed aside Sir Philip's correspondence and read over what he had written so far. Someone knocked on the door.

He covered the play with a book. "Come," he said.

To his surprise Geoffrey Ryder entered. "How did you find me?" Christopher asked.

"I asked. It wasn't difficult."

Christopher looked at him in amazement. The man hadn't the faintest idea what he was doing; not for the first time he wondered why the earl of Essex had chosen him for this sort of work. Anyone who could reason logically would realize now that Christopher was no mere secretary but a friend of Geoffrey's, who was in turn a friend of Essex's. If enough people became suspicious he might just as well go home.

It couldn't be helped. "Is Will here?" he asked.

"He's in the gallery, talking with some friends." Geoffrey looked around him, then down at the papers on the desk. "They could have given you a larger room, at least. Do you know what Philip Potter is supposed to have done?"

Christopher sighed. "Of course I do. He's my employer, after all. Did you come here only to pass along rumor? I have work to do."

"I wanted to see how you were getting on. To exchange information. We agreed to work together, after all."

"And what information do you have?"

Geoffrey hesitated. "Nothing, to be honest. That's why I came. I hoped you had discovered something."

"The season for gift-giving is past."

"I'm not asking for a gift. We should be working together for our queen. Time grows short and we're no closer to discovering who's behind this conspiracy. In two days it will be April already. April with his showers sweet, they say, but will we enjoy them if the queen is dead?"

Christopher looked at him sharply. Could the voice he had heard have been Geoffrey's? Was that why it had sounded so familiar? And did Geoffrey ask him for information now because he wanted to see if his plot had been found out? The man did not seem the sort to quote poetry.

"What do you know about—" Christopher began, but at that moment someone opened the door behind Geoffrey and came into the room.

"Kit!" Will said. The room seemed almost too small to contain both brothers. "They've made you a scrivener, I hear."

"Aye." Did the whole world know his business? He might just as well have posted a sign at Paul's.

"What's Philip Potter like?"

Now Will would want to hear the whole story behind Potter's disgrace. Geoffrey seemed about to make certain he knew it. "The man's an ass," Geoffrey said. "He met an actor dressed as the queen on the stairs—"

"Oh, I heard all about that downstairs," Will said. "He won't keep his appointment, I hope."

To Christopher's surprise the other man seemed to care about what happened to Potter. None of the courtiers had been at all concerned about poor Sir Philip.

"Come, Will—why shouldn't he?" Geoffrey said. "No one at court could write a more amusing comedy."

"For one thing, if he kept his appointment I would have to leave," Christopher said. "I told him not to go."

"Don't scowl, Geoffrey, the man's right," Will said. "Kit needs a reason to be here. He couldn't very well walk in the door the way we do."

For the second time in as many sentences Will had surprised him. He cared about Potter, true, but he had not lost the unconscious arrogance of the nobility. Looking at him now Christopher could see that he had no idea how offensive he had been; he had as good as said that anyone at court would be able to tell Christopher was no gentleman.

"You were about to say something before Will interrupted," Geoffrey said. "What do I know about what?"

"About a group of people here at court," Christopher said, shrugging off Will's comments. "They're small and seem oddly misshapen. They're petitioning the queen about their ancestral rights."

Will grinned at him. "Their ancestral rights!" he said, delighted. "Is this a story?"

"Nay—they're quite real, I assure you."

"I've never seen them. I'll wager even the queen doesn't know about them. Tell me more."

"That's all I know," Christopher said, looking at Geoffrey. The other man had not betrayed any knowledge of the folks Christopher had seen. Could it be that he truly knew nothing? Or was it only that he was a very good actor?

He did not see Will and Geoffrey for another week, until the afternoon of the masque. Then he caught sight of them a little ahead of him, among the great crowd of people going into the Presence Chamber. He nearly called out, but at that moment he spotted Sir Philip Potter, dressed in what seemed like every color but Isabella.

Christopher moved through the crowd, working his way toward Potter. What did the man think he was doing? The sight of him in the same room with the actor playing the queen would doubtless set the court to laughing again. "Sir Philip," he said.

"Aye?" Philip said amiably. "Who are you?"

They had stopped in the middle of the crowd. He took Sir Philip's arm and steered him to a quiet corner. "I told you not to come here," he said softly.

"You told— Oh, aye. I know you now. But surely they've forgotten everything after all this time. Don't you think so?"

A courtier passed them and pointed out Sir Philip to the woman leaning against his arm. Christopher didn't think they had forgotten a thing. "Remember what I told you," he said fiercely. "Say nothing. Give them no cause for amusement."

Sir Philip stepped back a little, alarm showing in his face. Probably no servant of his had ever given him such forceful advice. He nodded meekly and they went into the Presence Chamber together.

They were among the last to enter. Christopher found two places on a bench at the rear of the chamber, and looked around him after they had settled themselves. The queen sat on a carved wooden chair at the front and to the side of the audience, surrounded by her courtiers and maids-of-honor. A consort played somewhere, the music nearly drowned out by conversation.

Will and Geoffrey sat a few rows ahead of them. Will turned and, on seeing him, smiled his extraordinary smile. Christopher nodded back.

The music of the consort grew louder; folks turned their attention to the stage. A painted mountain stretching nearly to the ceiling was wheeled in. The mountain opened, revealing seven women who stepped down to the stage to dance. The music grew wilder, and the women, dressed in artful rags of black and red, began to dance faster and faster until, quite suddenly, they stopped.

The queen applauded enthusiastically. Sir Philip clapped loudly as well, until Christopher forced his hands to his lap.

Only then did the courtiers begin to applaud, and finally the rest of the audience. Philip grinned at him, wholly caught up in the merriment. What am I to do with you? Christopher thought.

One of the dancers stepped forward to speak. Because he and Philip sat at the back they could barely hear her. Philip strained to see around a group of people in front of him. "Who is she?" he whispered loudly.

"Some vice or other—Falsehood or Slander or Discord. Hush."

"Discord? What is Discord doing there?"

"She's to be vanquished by the Virtues."

"How do you know?"

A few people in front of them turned and looked at Philip. "Everyone knows," Christopher said. "I'll explain it to you later."

There was a puff of smoke and a loud burst of music, and then the mountain was hurriedly wheeled off the stage and a large castle wheeled on. Seven knights issued from the castle. One of the knights came forward and began a speech describing the Heroic Virtues, with himself, Order, as the chief of them. Philip glanced at Christopher admiringly. Had the man never seen a masque before? "Who's that?" Philip whispered.

Christopher frowned. A man wearing an ordinary doublet and hose had followed the knights out of the castle. His dress looked odd among the allegorical costumes of the players; only the mask covering his eyes set him apart from the audience.

The man moved forward and addressed the hall, speaking for a long time on the subject of Discord and Order. Order, behind him, looked angry and upset. Christopher had seen enough of actors to know that this part had not been rehearsed; the man had enlarged his speech beyond what had been written for him. And the verses were poor, not nearly as polished as the speeches that had gone before.

"Who—" Sir Philip said.

"Quiet."

The man began to talk about falseness, the false order imposed on a people by tyranny. Suddenly Christopher understood what was happening: the man was not part of the masque at all. He stood quickly. Several people in front of him began to stand as well, and someone called out something he could not hear.

"We here abolish Discord, and do sing," the man said, "about a new Order, and our new king."

To Christopher's astonishment Arthur stepped out on stage. The man in the mask raised a gun. Several people screamed. The knights seemed stunned, unable to move. The man fumbled with the gun, pushing the cover away from the pan filled with priming powder. Then he leveled it at the queen.

An explosive noise filled the chamber. The queen slumped in her chair. For a long moment no one moved. The assassin smiled oddly beneath his mask; he seemed almost to be waiting for applause. Then several men rushed the stage, and more hurried toward the queen.

Amazingly, no one seemed to be paying any attention to Arthur. The young man stood uncertainly for a moment and then ran off the stage and through the room. Christopher followed, trying to keep him in sight among the crowd.

Arthur forced his way past the people in the Presence Chamber. A few of those he pushed shouted after him, but most seemed more interested in the queen and the capture of the assassin. The crowd thinned as they left the chamber. Arthur hurried along the gallery and out of the palace.

Christopher ran after him. Arthur kept the Thames on his right, heading toward the great manors on the river's edge. Up ahead Christopher could see the gray bulk of the Ryders' house, and he wondered again about Geoffrey's part in the conspiracy. But Arthur did not even glance up as they passed the house. Instead he looked behind him quickly, and when he saw Christopher he put on a burst of speed.

Christopher fell behind when Arthur passed through Ludgate and into London proper. The other man seemed tireless. He was near St. Paul's now, pushing through the crowds that surrounded the churchyard. Christopher strained to keep him in sight. A half a mile later Arthur came to Gracechurch Street and turned left. By the time Christopher turned the corner there was no sign of him.

Excellent, he thought, panting. What would he say to Poley now? Dusk had come; the waxing moon rose in the east. Suddenly he grinned and looked up at the street in front of him. He knew exactly where Arthur was going. He took a deep breath and walked quickly toward the Saracen's Head.

Fifteen minutes later he came to the tavern and went inside. Arthur sat at one of the tables, deep in conversation with Tom Nashe. The man he had chased through London seemed at his ease, not even winded. Tom raised his head as he came in and called, "Kit!"

Arthur looked up. Christopher could see in his face that until that moment he had had no idea who had followed him; he was only now beginning to work out what had happened. Arthur rose, nearly tripping over the bench in his haste.

He moved back against the wall. Christopher stood at the only door to the room; the other man was trapped. Arthur looked around him frantically, seeking an exit. "What—" Tom said.

The air in front of Arthur turned golden. Arthur put a hand out in front of him carefully. He hesitated for a long moment, and then walked through the shining curtain and disappeared.

8

Anthony Drury knocked at a door and waited. They had taken a different, winding route to the house, but George thought it was the same place he and Anthony had visited before. Piles of refuse—horse dung and rotting vegetables—overflowed the gutters and lay along the unpaved paths. The houses presented mean, closed faces toward the street.

Anthony knocked again. This time they heard footsteps, and then a deep voice spoke from behind the door. "What was a month old at Cain's birth that's not five weeks old as yet?"

"The moon," Anthony said.

George felt relieved that Anthony had known the answer; he was not very good at riddles. Then the door opened and he realized that Anthony hadn't answered a riddle at all but had given a correct password. They had been set some sort of test.

By the light of the candles George could see the same strange machine he had glimpsed before. It was pear-shaped, with arms of metal snaking out from it in all directions. Alchemy, he thought, with a quick shock of excitement. He had been right. And then, Will they teach me?

The alembic squatted on the wooden floor. Next to it was a table, and on the table stood bottles and stones and retorts and opened books.

When he looked up he saw that there were two other men
in the room. One stood in the shadows, and George could see
only that he was small and had some sort of stain down the
front of his doublet. But it was the other man who drew
George's attention. He had long flowing white hair and a white
beard, but his bones were sharp and clear and his face seemed
that of a young man. He looked at George with dark brown
eyes under heavy black eyebrows, and seemed to read all of
George's secrets at a glance.

The man turned to Anthony. His voice was deep and powerful, and now George realized that beneath his long gown he
had strong, well-defined muscles. "You say you can vouch for
this man?"

"Aye," Anthony said. "His name is George Cowper. He has
promised to lead us to the woman's son."

"Excellent," the man said, his voice so pleasant and full of
authority that it was several moments before George thought,
But I promised nothing. Anthony never kept his part of the
bargain.

"George, this is Paul Hogg," Anthony said.

"Good day," George said. With anyone else he would have
been tempted to laugh at the absurd name, but here in this
house, in front of this man, he could find nothing amusing
about it. Where Anthony burned with his fanaticism, seemed
always on the verge of winning through to some goal, Paul
Hogg looked as if he lacked nothing, as if he had already
achieved his desire. "Good day," Paul Hogg said. "What have
you told him of our work?"

"Nothing," Anthony said. "I left that for you."

"You've seen the alembic," Paul Hogg said. "Our purpose
here is to discover the secrets of Dame Alchemia. I know the
first eleven steps in the process—I lack only the twelfth, the
final one. See here—" He put his hand on the alembic but did
not open it. "I've performed the first three steps, calcination,
solution and separation. And over the course of a year or so I'll
do the rest, and learn the final step. And then I'll have it, the
lapis philosophorum, Philosopher's Stone. All metals it touches

will become gold, the perfect metal, and all men it touches will live forever."

Live forever, George thought, and the idea was so breathtaking, so fanciful, that he laughed. "Aye, even you, George," Hogg said. "Why not? Once we learn the process, you and I and Anthony will live forever."

He wondered why Hogg had chosen him, someone who had had no training at all in the sciences. But he knew enough not to ask. "What do we do next?" he said.

Hogg did not answer him. Instead he inscribed a circle around the four of them, chanting words George thought might be Latin. Sorcery, George thought, remembering his earlier misgivings. How would this help him win Alice? Why had he come?

He made a move to leave but was stopped by Hogg's strong, confident voice. And after a while he no longer wanted to go, could not remember, in fact, why he had ever moved toward the door. Anthony had assured him that everything they did had a basis in natural philosophy. And surely a man as wise as Hogg would not put his soul in peril.

Then Hogg stood and said three sharp words. The roof blew off; they stood on an empty plain with the wind howling past them. George screamed, or was it the wind screaming around him? The plain seemed to stretch out forever. There were no rocks, no trees, no houses, only the other men to catch and hold the eye. Hogg cursed in several languages.

A black shape lit by flickering fire came toward them. As it came closer George could see it was a horse, but larger than any horse he had ever seen. It walked on its hind legs and its eyes were as white as moons. Fire played around its hooves.

Hogg said something, tried again as the horse came on. The horse's neighing sounded like demonic laughter. "Back!" Hogg said over the rising wind. "Go back, and fetch your master!" The horse wheeled around in a circle, laughing, and then left.

No one spoke or moved. George shivered in terror and looked at Hogg, but the other man paid no attention to him. His jaw was clenched and he stared at the horizon as if he could see something invisible to the others. He looked determined, prepared to stay all day if necessary. The wind grew louder.

The other men looked terrified. Something scuttled near them; something else called out, chittering. Wings flapped near George's eyes and he closed them in fear, but the darkness frightened him more and he opened them again at once. The noises around them grew louder: the shapes were drawing closer. Then he heard the neighing again. The horse had returned.

Something man-shaped rode it this time, keeping its balance effortlessly as the horse danced on two legs. It looked like the thing that had followed Anthony to his lodgings, but whether it was the same or not George couldn't say.

"I asked for your master," Hogg said.

The rider laughed. "Are we yours, then, to order about as you please?" it said. Its voice sounded unpleasant, like water coiling past old roots and rocks. It spoke with difficulty through its many sharp teeth. "Are you to tell us when to come and when to go? We made a bargain, nothing more."

"Aye, a bargain. I was promised gold. Where is your master?"

The horse wheeled again. "Gold!" the rider said. "When will you ask us for something real?"

Hogg said something in a language George didn't recognize. The rider made no move that George could see, but a large purse fell at Hogg's feet. Hogg leapt for it. "It turns to coal unless your part of the bargain is kept," the rider said. Then the shabby room came up around them again.

George looked at the other men in the room, at the alembic, at the table littered with tools. He felt he was in a dream and that at any moment he might wake, that the room around him would vanish a second time and he would find himself safe and in his bed. "What—" he said.

"They are not demons, or anything sent from hell," Hogg said. George had not heard him come up next to him.

George shook his head. How could he be certain of anything Hogg told him?

"It's easy enough to make the distinction," Hogg said, almost as if he had read George's thoughts. "They live in light. Their enemies live in darkness. Their enemies are the children of Cain."

"The children—"

"The woman Alice knows them well. She has had dealings with them, if I'm not mistaken."

George nodded. He could see now how everything fit together, how right he had been to chastise Alice.

"We must stop her. Her and the children of darkness. The folks I called up here will help us. You understand now that it is lawful to trade with them."

"What—what was the bargain you made?"

"I asked for the secrets of alchemy. They will, of course, give nothing away. I promised them a fair exchange."

But even before the man finished speaking George knew what he promised to trade. "Alice's son," he said.

"Aye."

"What do they want with him?"

"I don't know. But I can tell you that her son is a sort of child of Cain himself, that he comes from the darkness. If we give him to them we are doing nothing wrong." Hogg untied the purse he had been given and poured out a handful of shining coins. Gold. "Here," he said. "For your help in this matter."

George took the coins. They were sovereigns, he saw, and felt cool and weighty in his hand. He could expand his business, buy more books and copyrights. He didn't need Alice and her stall at all. And with this gold and the money he would soon be earning he could have any woman he wanted. He would not be balked by her stubbornness again.

"They will turn to coal if the bargain is not fulfilled," Hogg said. "And all that you've bought with them will vanish as well. We must have the boy to trade."

George's heart began to beat faster. He ran his thumb over the coins in his hand. "But Alice herself has not seen her son in years," he said, and then wondered if he should have given away so much. Would Hogg want his gold back if he thought George could not help him?

"Then what you must do," Hogg said, his voice low and soothing, "is have her lose her membership in the Stationers' Company. Without her livelihood she will be forced to go to her son for help. We know that with her husband dead she has no one she can turn to in the churchyard."

He marveled that Hogg's commands should come so near to his own heart's desire. With Alice out of the company he would never be reminded of his failure with her, of her immoral ways, of how she had laughed when he had confronted her.

"There is a reason man has been put above woman," Hogg said. He was whispering now, drawing them into a conspiracy of two and excluding Anthony and the other man. "A woman on her own does not have the logic or the will to resist evil."

"How am I to have her lose her membership?" George asked.

"Ah. I'm sure you'll think of something."

Margery's note had said only, "Come visit me on Sunday." Alice felt her usual exasperation when dealing with her friend; since Margery didn't go to church she assumed that no one else did. When Sunday came Alice went to services at St. Faith's beneath the choir of Paul's, the stationers' church. Then she made her way toward Ludgate and out of London.

Margery surprised her by having a visitor. They both sat under her windows, the sun coming in weakly through the unwashed glass and making them look as if lit by dark stained glass.

The other woman's face was nut-brown and completely round, with a wide, thick, smiling mouth to draw attention away from the fact that she had almost no chin. She seemed to grow fatter as Alice looked downward, her shoulders slightly plump but her stomach and hips padded to the shape of a ball. She looked very much at home in Margery's strange cottage.

"Agnes was telling me a story," Margery said. "I think you'll be interested too. She comes from near your village, Alice."

"Aye," Agnes said. She took one of Margery's apples and she bit into it, and then said nothing more for several seconds. Perhaps she was going over the story in her mind. "I'm a midwife," she said finally. "One night a man came to the door and summoned me to a birth. He was a strange one, I remember. Very short, less than four feet tall, and his hair was long and black and wild. Under it I thought I saw that his ears were pointed, like an animal's. I'd never seen him before.

"I told my husband I'd be out for the night. 'Will you be taking the horse?' he asked me, but the little man said, 'Nay, there's no need.' We went outside and I saw his horse tied to a tree.

"I mounted up behind him. I was younger and lighter in those days—this was near twenty years ago, did I say? Aye, twenty, or a little more. We rode quickly, making good time. I'd tell you where we went, but I couldn't see the way. It was dark, and fog lay like a hand over us. Many times since then I've tried to find the road we took, but I never could. We stopped at a hill, and I'd swear I'd never seen that hill before in my life.

"When we got off the horse the little man came close to me and said, 'Don't be frightened,' and he breathed on my eye. And for some reason I wasn't afraid. Then the hill opened, and we went inside.

"It was— Oh, it was fine. I can't describe it. Walls of gold and silver. Men and women dressed in mail as light as cobwebs, with swords as sharp as diamonds. Music like nothing I'd ever heard. No candles, and you couldn't see the moon or stars overhead, but light came from all around. And from the people's faces, too—but they weren't people, were they? They were of Faerie.

"They were in a long hall, feasting, at a table laid with silk and linen, with crystal goblets and silver plate. Everyone stopped when we came in, and one of the men stood and came over to us. 'Is this the best you could do?' he said to the little man. He had horns, but somehow it was his eyes I looked at. Silver-gray they were, and sharp as sword-points.

"The little man shrugged. I thought he liked me, that he might feel badly about the other man's rudeness, but now I wonder if that was true. They don't have feelings the way we do. He smiled, and when he did his mouth stretched nearly to his ears, but he said nothing.

"This second man motioned to me to follow him out of the hall. Tiny creatures flew past us, and I saw more little men, and women carrying fire on their heads. Tapestries of fine silk hung on the wall, and when I looked at them they seemed to move. I couldn't see much as we hurried past, but I thought I saw small creatures mounted on the backs of birds, fighting with lances the size of needles. And men in silver armor, their faces upturned as dragons spewed fire. But it was hard to think of battles in such a place as that.

"There was a woman in labor in the room I was led to, and when I saw her nothing seemed strange or unusual. I knew what to do, why I had come. The man had left, and I was in a room full of women. I went straight to the birthing stool and helped her. She didn't cry out the way other mothers do, and the birth was an easy one. The child was a boy, and healthy. When it was over I got mugwort from my bag to ease her belly.

"All the time I attended her I knew who she was. She wore no crown, of course, just a light gown made of gossamer. But she was the queen. I could tell by the way the other ladies deferred to her, but even if she'd been alone I'd have known it.

"When it was over the little man came into the room again, and the horned man with him. The little man carried a bundle in his arms. 'Quickly,' he said. 'The mortal woman has just given birth, and she'll sleep for a while now.' The women had moved the queen to the bed, and she lay nursing her son. 'You must give him up, Oriana,' the horned man said. 'For his safety, and for ours.'

"The queen looked at her son one last time, and then gave him to the little man. And the man passed over his bundle, which I saw was a baby, a human boy. When the little man got the queen's baby he took it and ran out of the room. The other one looked at me with his hard eyes and said, 'This should not have been done in front of her.'

" 'She'll forget,' the queen said.

" 'I'll see that she will,' the man said, and he took a step toward me. I knew he was going to breathe on my eye, and I closed them both as tightly as I could. But even so I remembered nothing after that, only waking up in front of my house the next morning, with my husband coming out to look for me."

Agnes seemed to have finished her tale. "The queen," Alice said, remembering. "I saw her too. She's beautiful, isn't she?"

"I didn't bring you both here to compare stories," Margery said sharply. "The queen is not our concern. Think, Alice. The boy. The son."

A new thought, horrible and troubling, struggled to come to light. "Nay," Alice said. "It can't be true—"

"It is," Margery said. "The son, the human baby. That was Arthur."

"Nay!" Alice said again.

"Aye, it was. And the child you raised as yours was of Faerie. A prince of Faerie, the queen's own child."

"He's not—" Alice said. But she could argue no more. All of Arthur's strangeness, his moods, his beautiful singing voice, his lack of concern for anything human, all of this forced itself upon her at once, and she knew that what Margery said was the truth. "And my son? Arthur?" she said.

"They raised him as best they could," Margery said. "They know very little of humans, you see, though they need us. He has been well cared for, at least."

"But why?" She remembered the queen in her circle of lights, the strange kinship she had felt between them, and she wondered how such a fair-seeming creature could have done something so ugly.

"They're fighting a battle," Margery said. "They live long, and they have children seldom, so the queen's son had to be protected above all else. If the child was captured the war would be lost. They gave him to you, to keep him safe."

Alice realized, to her own great surprise, that she cared nothing for kings and queens and battles. She wanted only to see her son; it was a feeling as sudden and as strong as being struck by lightning. She wanted to comfort him, to show him his true, human birthright.

Oriana was not there to feel her anger, but Margery was. "Did you know all this?" she asked. "Did you watch Arthur as he grew, laughing to think that he would soon be taken from me?"

"Nay. I did not guess about Arthur until very recently. I saw that the Fair Folk were moving toward London, leaving their true home in the fields and woods, but I thought they came here for another reason. People in the country are being thrown off their land, you know—the landlords are turning all their cropland to pasture. And so the homeless folk are coming here to find work. I thought that the faeries followed them—they need to be with people in some way we can't understand. And maybe that's why they did come, I don't know. Some of them had left the country years ago, before you and your husband thought of moving to London. No one can guess their true reasons."

"Nay, they came for Arthur. You know that."

"Do I? The world is changing, moving in a direction I cannot predict. The Fair Folk have a part to play in all this, but whether it is large or small I cannot say."

Margery's talk of cropland and changes only made Alice impatient; all her concern was with Arthur. "Didn't Oriana—"

"Oriana tells me very little. When I saw the faerie-light on your child I knew what he was, of course. But it was only when I found Agnes that I realized he was the queen's son."

Agnes looked on avidly, not bothering to hide her interest in the story. The apple lay forgotten in her hand, and one of the cats watched intently, in case she dropped it. Of course, Alice thought sourly. She's waited twenty years for the end of this drama.

"And now that he's grown? What are their plans for him now? Will they give him back?"

Margery seemed to be answering a different question. "They didn't expect Arthur to leave home. They've lost him, you see. And they have to get him back, to win the war."

"The man in black, asking about Arthur! But he was human, I'd swear to it."

"Aye. Both sides recruit humans, when they need them."

"Both . . . Then the others are looking for him too?"

"Aye," Margery said. "And they must not get him. We must find the queen's son first, and trade him for yours."

"How?" Alice said, despairing. "A friend saw him once, but he lost him again. The Saracen's Head, that's all he said. I went there to look for him but no one had heard of him."

"You're not alone in this. I'm with you, and I know more about the faeries than a dozen men in black. We'll find him."

Alice was not so certain. How were they to get Arthur back, two women against the combined might of Faerie? The despair had gone, though; she felt to her own horror that her strongest desire was that Oriana should lose the war.

The Stationers' Company met in a hall east of St. Paul's. Rows of cushioned benches faced the front, where speakers would stand and address the rest of the company. Behind that was a fireplace taking up nearly the entire wall. Once, Alice remembered, the stationers had used it to burn all the copies of a book Archbishop Whitgift had declared immoral. She thought that that was the sorriest thing she had ever seen, all that work and knowledge and thought rising up the chimney in flames.

The stationers had closed their stalls for the meeting, but faint noises from Paul's told them that their absence was hardly noticed: the business of the gallants and usurers and cutpurses went on as usual. Nearly everyone had come to the hall except two men down with the ague. As Alice looked around she noticed, as she noticed at every meeting, that she was the only woman in the room.

Speaker after speaker stood and moved to the front. Elections were coming up; names were proposed for the offices of junior warden, senior warden and master. A stationer rose to warn the company that spies from the Privy Council had been through the churchyard, looking for unlicensed books.

One printer accused another of stealing his copyright; the other claimed he had been given the copyright, but could not prove that it had been by the author. Manuscripts were frequently copied by scriveners and passed from reader to reader, and too often an unscrupulous printer would publish a book from a third-hand copy. The second printer was ordered to give up his copyright and was fined, and the change was entered in the register.

The room grew hot, and Alice, her mind on her son, found it hard to pay attention. "Has anyone other business?" the Mas-

ter of the Company said, and Alice looked up with relief. The
meeting would soon be over.

"Aye," someone said.

The stationers turned to watch as George Cowper made his
way to the front of the room. Someone murmured; George, like
Alice, had never spoken at a meeting before. He stood dwarfed
by the vast fireplace open like a mouth behind him. "I propose
that the company reconsider the membership of one of the
stationers."

The murmurs grew louder. "Who?" the master asked.

"Alice Wood," George said, his voice clear and strong.

Alice had been thinking of other things. She looked up, a
little surprised to hear her name. "Alice?" someone said from
the audience. "For God's sake, man, why?"

George's eyes sought and found Alice in the crowd. "Immoral living," he said. "And necromancy."

9

Tom Nashe blinked as Arthur disappeared before him. Christopher moved quickly, stepping through the curtain of gold after the other man. Tom could not bear to let them go without him. He hesitated only a moment and then followed.

It was dark where he found himself, the way lit by a pale three-quarters moon and scattered stars. He looked around, puzzled. He knew he had been sitting in the tavern for a few hours, but surely night could not have fallen yet. Christopher, ahead of him, was a dark blur against the black, and he could not see Arthur at all.

He hurried after his friend. The way lightened before him, though not by any agency of the moon; it seemed instead that light seeped outward from the rocks and trees. He found himself wandering in a grove of old elms and oaks, following a narrow path covered with leaves and moss and stones. He heard a stream close by, water falling ceaselessly over rocks.

When he looked up from the path he saw that Christopher had disappeared. He ran to catch up with him. The strange light made dappling overlapping shadows of the leaves; he blundered into roots or rocks and nearly went sprawling.

Suddenly it seemed to him as if he were the focus of someone's, or something's, scrutiny, as if everything in the land had turned the vast weight of its attention on him. The force of that gaze was so strong that he had to stop his headlong rush for a moment, to stand and let whatever it was study him. He felt as he had on that strange journey through London: that the inhabitants of this land hunted something, something they had lost.

Then the feeling passed, as if the eyes that probed him so intently had released him, allowed him to go. What was it they searched for? Could it be Arthur?

Someone beckoned to him up ahead, near a bend in the road, and he forgot all his questions and hurried after it. He could barely see it through the trees, a squat misshapen man not even a foot high. But when he came to the bend what he thought was a man resolved itself into an old gnarled stone. He looked at it for a moment and continued on.

The stone—the man—moved at the corner of his vision. He glanced back quickly but saw only stone, nothing more. Something called out to the moon, a lonely, yearning cry. The voice of the stream changed, became a sound like music heard far off.

Farther down the road a hand reached out to him from one of the trees. He quickened his pace. Someone laughed, and an animal padded quickly away from him as he ran.

The laughter came from above him, in the trees. He looked around and saw nothing but branches and twigs swaying in the wind. Then a woman stepped from the trees.

She had long dark-brown hair, and he decided the moment he saw her that that color was his favorite for hair in all the world. Her skin was nut-brown, nearly as dark as her hair, and her fingers long as twigs. She looked at him boldly and motioned to him with those fingers, then ran away down the path. He could do nothing else but follow her.

The path widened. She stopped for a moment and turned as if to make certain of him; he saw to his surprise that her eyes were as blue as berries. She hurried along the path to a meadow. More of the nut-brown women sat by a stream and wove garlands out of the flowers around them.

The women reached for her as she ran to them. They bound her hair in a garland of flowers, laughing and calling to one another. When they had done she turned away from him and studied her reflection in the stream. Had she forgotten him? Or had he misunderstood her—had her gaze been disinterested after all?

He followed her through the meadow. The grass was soft, and greener than any April grass he had ever seen. She turned and laughed as he came up to her.

For once in his life he could think of nothing to say. She took a silver flower from the garland in her hair and held it out to him wordlessly. He reached for it, and as he did so the meadow before him, the stream, the women, all disappeared. In the space of a breath he found himself back at the tavern, holding the flower she had given him.

He returned to the tavern the next day. Christopher and Arthur had not come back with him the night before, and he had spent the rest of the evening waiting for them and studying the flower in his hand. He had never seen another like it; its silver petals curved upward and together like the groin of an old church and then unfurled outward.

He wondered where the others had gone to. More than that, he wanted an explanation for everything that had happened, starting with who Arthur was. Did it have something to do with Kit's intelligence work?

Finally he saw Christopher and another man come into the tavern. The man was stocky, with brown hair and eyes, and he walked with the confident air of the nobility. He looked nothing like the other young men Christopher brought into the tavern from time to time, and Tom wondered who he could be.

But if Kit thought the presence of the other man would keep him from asking questions he would soon learn how wrong he was. Tom was not good at subterfuge, he had no secrets; no one would ever offer him work as one of the queen's agents. The only way he knew to get answers was to ask outright. "What happened to you last night?" he said.

"Good evening," Christopher said pleasantly, going to get some supper and a cup of wine. When he came back he said, "This is my friend Will Ryder. Will, this is Tom Nashe."

"Good evening," Tom said. "Where did you go last night?"

"Where?" Christopher said, sitting and looking up at him. "Nowhere."

Not for the first time Tom thought he would never be able to describe Christopher's expression to his own satisfaction: it was a strange combination of curiosity, arrogance and innocence. And now, watching him, he saw that the other man held the meat he ate with his left hand. That would explain five years of smudged and illegible correspondence, he thought; odd that he had never noticed it before. Kit used the same hand as the devil. It suits him, Tom thought.

"Do you take me for a fool?" Tom said. "I followed you."

"Did you?"

"Aye, I did. I saw the land Arthur led us to, the trees and the meadow, the women sitting by the stream—"

"Tom," Christopher said, holding up his hand. The man beside him, Will Ryder, looked amused. "I went nowhere last night. I tried to find Arthur but he had disappeared. This is too much like your last tale, the one about goblins wandering the streets of London. Let's have a new song, at least."

"Listen," Tom said, furious. "I know what I saw. I saw a strange land, and a path through a wood, and then—"

"You have a good imagination, I'll give you that. Best save it for the stage."

"Did I imagine this, then?" Tom held out the flower the dark woman had given him. It had not lost any of its color since the day before.

"Nay, I suppose not."

"She gave me this. And when I took it I found myself here, in the tavern. Look—it hasn't faded at all since then."

"Since yesterday." Christopher did not trouble to hide the doubt in his voice.

"Aye."

"This is arrant superstition. You—"

"Superstition!" Tom said. He could not remember having been so angry with his friend. "You're a man who thinks religion, the proper worship of God, is superstition. You've closed yourself off to any possibility of the miraculous. It's no wonder you saw nothing last night."

No one said anything for a long moment. Tom thought he might have gone too far. He hadn't meant to become angry, had intended only to ask his friend a few questions. The buzz of conversation in the tavern had not diminished; thank God, he thought, no one had overheard them.

Will Ryder spoke into the silence. "My father," he said, "thinks God sends plagues to punish unbelievers."

Christopher looked at the other man. "Do you blame me for the plague, then?"

"Nay. Nay, but I thought—well, I thought that if he was right, then—then you might reconsider. If your life depended on it."

"Ah. But if I can't believe in God—if I'm incapable of it—don't you think that he would know that? Don't you think he would regard my sudden conversion with suspicion, realizing that I did it only to save my life? If, of course, there is a God." He looked pleased with the paradox.

"Then you truly don't believe in God," Will said. Tom winced; this was not the place for such discussions. But Will did not seem disapproving, as Robert Greene had, but genuinely interested. Tom thought that this man, unlike Greene, would take his friends as he found them.

"Nay," Christopher said.

"Nor in these—these goblins? Not even when you saw them yourself?"

Tom looked at Will sharply. "What do you mean?" Christopher said.

"Those strangely shaped men you told me about a week ago," Will said. "Who were they?"

"What strangely shaped men?" Tom asked.

"Whoever they were, they were not goblins," Christopher said. "They told me they had come to petition the queen."

"Did they?" Will said. "Then why is it no one at court has heard of them, not even the queen?"

"Why? Probably because they were part of the conspiracy against her. Did you expect them to come forward and explain their business, like the Chorus in a play?"

"What conspiracy?" Tom asked.

Christopher and Will fell silent. Tom, feeling desperately that they would not tell him anything, began to pour out his questions all at once. "Does it have to do with Arthur? Why are you so interested in him? Why did you follow him last night?"

Christopher pushed his hair back from his face and took a bite of mutton before he answered. "Because he told us he was a king," he said.

"But what business is that of yours?"

Christopher shrugged. "None, really."

"Is it true that you do intelligence work for the queen?"

Will seemed about to say something. Christopher looked at him and he subsided. Then, "Oh, why not?" he said. "Aye, we'll let everyone in London in on the secret—we'll all be conspirators together. You heard, of course, that someone tried to kill the queen yesterday."

"Aye," Tom said. "But the assassin shot an actor dressed to look like her instead." His friend looked a little surprised, and Tom grinned. He might not be an agent of the queen, but he had his own ways of gathering information.

"Will and I were there," Christopher said, surprising Tom in turn. "Queen Elizabeth had apparently thought it amusing to trade places with an actor in a masque. The thought saved her life. The actor was killed and the man who shot her captured, but he refuses to name his accomplices."

"But surely he can't remain silent forever? Haven't they—"

"Aye, they've tortured him. He's said nothing. But the odd thing—one of several odd things, really—is that he seemed to expect the audience to rise up against the queen. He had no idea how much her subjects love her."

"And the other odd things?"

"Arthur was on the stage with him. The assassin brought him out and introduced him as the new king. I don't know if the plot was Arthur's idea—"

"Arthur? He wouldn't—"

"Wouldn't he? Well, perhaps not. Then he was used by these other men, who intended to put him on the throne but control him the way they might control a puppet."

"How do you know there are other men involved? Perhaps the assassin was acting alone."

Christopher ran his hand through his hair again. His friend had been forthcoming so far, Tom thought; he had been surprised at how much Kit was willing to reveal. Would he continue to be open or would he start to dissemble?

"It's complicated," Christopher said finally. "I saw a man die over this. Believe me, there are others involved, and next time they may succeed in killing the queen. So you see how important it is to find Arthur."

Tom nodded.

"Now that you know," Will said, "will you help us?"

"Of course," Tom said, surprised. No matter how open Kit became he would never in his life think to ask for help. He began to warm to this man. "Of course I will. What can I do?"

"Tell us if you see Arthur," Will said. "Try to keep him in sight if he comes back to the tavern."

He has the most extraordinary smile, Tom thought. "Aye," he said. "But I fear he's gone to this new land—that he's beyond our finding him."

Christopher returned to the palace that night. As he walked he thought over what he had said, feeling faintly surprised that he had told Tom as much as he had. He wondered why he had done so. Did he think he had to match Will's openness with his own? But Will had been right: Tom might prove useful. Always assuming, of course, that Tom stayed in this world and did not follow his fancies to Lubberland, or wherever he thought he had been.

Still, he was glad that he had not mentioned Robert Poley. It was important that no one know the name of the man who had engaged him, and especially important that Will not discover it. Will might tell his brother Geoffrey, and Geoffrey—Geoffrey knew something he shouldn't, of that Christopher felt certain.

People were still awake at the palace, standing and talking in low voices. Candles guttered in iron coronas. He heard his name called by several people, all courtiers he barely knew. There had been fresh gossip since the drama of the day before, and folks were shaken and anxious to share what they heard. Sir Francis Walsingham, the queen's Principal Secretary, was dead. Fortunately for him, he had been told nothing about the danger the queen had faced and so had died peacefully.

Walsingham dead, Christopher thought as he went up the stairs to his room. He was too tired to take it in. But the confusion at court meant that he would not be expected to do any work for a few days; he could find a quiet place and think about what he had learned.

The next day he made his way to the gallery and sat on one of the cushioned benches overlooking the courtyard. Morning light came in through the leaded windows, illuminating each of the courtiers passing in colors as bright as an old manuscript. Did Walsingham's death mean that his work here was finished? He knew almost nothing about Poley's arrangements with the Principal Secretary. But if he discovered the plotters he would certainly be kept on, gratefully rewarded by whoever took over Walsingham's post. He would have to work quickly, though, before someone newly come to power decided he was unnecessary.

Well, then, what did he know? A man had shot someone he believed to be the queen, an assassin who acted for a group of conspirators. Or did he? What if Tom, of all people, had been right, what if the man had acted on his own behalf? What evidence did he have for a conspiracy, after all, besides the fact that Poley had told him there was one?

Of course there was the note he had seen in the Black Boar, and a note implied traffic between two people at least. "All is in readiness," it had said. "Our king awaits." But it had been Poley who had shown him the note.

Nay, that was ridiculous. Why would Poley fabricate a conspiracy? To make himself more useful to the Principal Secretary? The queen faced enough dangers, as he had seen, without having to invent any.

If there was a plot, then, who had taken part in it? The odd folks he had seen his first morning at court had almost certainly had something to do with it. But where were they? He had not seen them since he had followed one of them to that strange meeting. He had gone by their room several times, but they seemed to have left the palace for good. And, as Will had said, no one at court had ever heard of them.

There was always Geoffrey. But Geoffrey had done nothing wrong; his only crime had been to quote Chaucer, and any son of Canterbury could do the same. It was hardly an indictable offense.

And what of Will? If Geoffrey had a part in this wouldn't his brother be guilty as well? Christopher could hardly imagine Will in the shadowy world of intrigue; his straightforward nature would almost certainly prevent it. Yet Will had told him that he worked for Essex. And did he?

Nay, he was starting to suspect everyone. If he kept on this way he'd end by thinking Philip Potter guilty. He looked out the window at the statue in the courtyard. Mercury, the god of trickery.

He stood and went back to the central stairway. A number of people headed toward the Presence Chamber and he followed, fully expecting to be turned back at the door. But the queen's guards, as subject to the confusion in the court as everyone else, let him through without a word.

The stage from the masque was still there, and the wheeled castle; probably no one had had time to take them away. A few of the queen's councilors and their secretaries sat behind a table on the stage and were calling men up one by one to question them.

Christopher took a bench at the back. He saw that the courtiers were being made to state where they had been on the night of the masque, and he wondered what good that would do. If the assassin had acted on the orders of a group then that group had probably been out in the audience, enjoying the acting.

After a while, though, he understood what the queen's councilors had in mind. The conspirators would not have been in the palace but out in the streets, waiting for the signal to rouse the populace in revolt. Anyone who hadn't been at the masque, therefore, would be suspect.

Sir Philip Potter came up to testify. "Aye, I went to the masque," he said. "I was there with my secretary."

"What is your secretary's name?"

"His name," Potter said, looking about him as though the Presence Chamber held clues to the answer. "I know it—nay, don't tell me—"

Christopher winced. A few people laughed. "We'll summon your secretary, then," a councilor said, and someone at his elbow made a note.

"Here—I'll tell you what it was about," Potter said. "That'll prove I was there, wouldn't it?"

"Not necessarily," the councilor said dryly.

Potter, seeming not to have heard him, began to describe the seven dancers and explain what they represented. "We thank you," the councilor said, interrupting him. "You may go now."

Potter left. Christopher did not volunteer to come forward. He knew that Sir Philip was innocent, and he was far more interested in hearing what everyone else had to say. Another courtier climbed to the stage. Christopher recognized him as one of the people who had gathered at the foot of the stairs, watching and laughing while Potter played the fool. "Were you at the masque two days ago, my lord?" the councilor asked.

"Nay, my lord."

The crowd murmured. "Where were you, then?"

"At a dinner with some friends."

"Which friends were these?"

"Nicholas Russell, John Stafford, Richard Dyer, Edward White," the courtier said. The councilor's secretary hurried to write the names down. "We began with the mutton. Then we discussed the weather, as I remember. It was fine for April."

Christopher looked up sharply, understanding everything. The strange circle of men he had overheard had been rehearsing what they would say if their conspiracy failed. They had written an entire play that would prove them to have been elsewhere at the time.

"Very well," the councilor said. "We will summon your friends." The secretary made a note.

*   *   *

Though Potter could not remember his secretary's name it seemed that the queen's councilors knew men with better memories. A man dressed in the livery of the queen came to summon Christopher to the Presence Chamber the next day.

He went with him eagerly. The conspirators he had over-heard would be there, and he was anxious to see them. At the chamber he sat on one of the benches and looked around him.

The man who had testified yesterday sat a few rows back, but Christopher could not see his accomplices anywhere. Could they have been frightened off? Had they decided that their careful scheme would not stand up to the scrutiny of the queen's councilors?

A secretary called his name and he went up to testify. He agreed that he was Sir Philip Potter's secretary, and that he had been with Potter at the masque. The councilors, satisfied, let him go.

He returned to the back of the room, hoping no one would ask him to leave now that his business was done. The conspirators had still not arrived. The councilors questioned another of the courtiers, and then a secretary called out the names Christopher had waited for. "Nicholas Russell, John Stafford, Richard Dyer, Edward White!"

What ordinary names they had proved to have, after all, these strange men who had plotted to overthrow the queen. Christopher looked around him. To his great surprise a body of men had risen and were heading toward the stage. He had never seen them before in his life.

10

Alice's first thought was that George must be mad to make such accusations. But as the talk around her grew louder, as more and more people turned to look at her, she started to feel ashamed. She had done nothing immoral, she knew; the only man she had ever bedded had been John, and after his death she had lived chastely. Nevertheless the feeling, irrational as it was, began to grow.

The stationers turned back to George. The set expressions of one or two of them, their pursed mouths and narrow eyes, made her wonder if they had already made up their minds and were only waiting to hear what George would say next. Even if she could prove her innocence, how could she face them tomorrow in the churchyard? She felt the blood heating her face, and her heart began to beat loudly.

George waited until he had everyone's attention. "We have all seen this woman with a certain Mistress Margery," he said. "A cunning woman, a dealer in the forbidden arts. A witch, in plain words. We have seen them deep in conversation together, Mistress Alice neglecting her work as she and her friend planned certain rituals. I don't need to tell you what those rituals were. On moonless nights—she told me so herself—she would go to a field and summon her master."

"That's not true!" Alice said, angered and horrified as much by George's calm tone as by what he was saying.

"Silence," the Master of the Company said. "You'll have your turn to speak when he finishes."

She wondered if she would. Although George did not go to plays she knew that most of the company did, and she had heard talk about *Dr. Faustus,* the story of the man who had bargained with the devil. They were ready to believe impossible stories, tales of necromancy and evil, and perhaps would not stay to hear her answer. And truly, would her account be any less fantastical? How could she tell it and make them believe?

Less than a month ago she had faced the queen's councilors and had been cleared of all wrongdoing. But that thought, meant to be comforting, did not give her courage. The privy councilors had been interested in getting at the truth; now she thought that the Stationers' Company might be fascinated by George's lies.

"Not true?" George said. He addressed the crowd instead of her, as if her words had no importance. "But she admitted to certain revels, as she called them, that she attended. Attended with her friend, the witch Margery. And it was at these ceremonies that she acquired her familiar."

At this a shiver of apprehension passed through the room. "I have seen it myself," George said calmly. "It is the size of a man, and covered with fur. It has horns and cloven hoofs and a tail, and it lives with her, curled up by her hearth. What they do together is not a fit matter for discussion here, but I'm sure you have all heard similar stories.

"Cornelius Agrippa," George went on, and Alice stared; she would have wagered that George had never heard of Agrippa in his life. Who had he been talking to? "Cornelius Agrippa says"—here he consulted a piece of paper in his hand—" 'Because women be more desirous of secrets and inclined to superstitions, and be more easily beguiled, therefore they'—Agrippa means the devils—'therefore they sooner appear to them, and do great miracles.' Do you see what I mean? Do you see what a danger this woman poses to all of us?

"I'll say one thing more, and then I'll have done with this distasteful subject. The Scriptures tell us that man has authority over woman. I have never questioned the word of God, but it is only recently that I have understood why we have been given this commandment. Women are weaker than men. We have been appointed by God to care for them, to make certain they do not stumble on their path. With no one to guide her a woman is not strong enough to resist evil, sometimes not even rational enough to recognize it. I know that no one here objected when Mistress Wood asked for full membership after her husband died. Our charity then was commendable, but I think that we made a mistake, and it has proven to be a very grave mistake indeed. For a woman without guidance is a threat to us all. Her rottenness can spread throughout the company, corrupting everyone it touches."

No one spoke as he returned to his seat. Alice, who had been planning to rise in her own defense, now felt shame overwhelm her so strongly that she could barely move. She wanted only to get away from the hall and the rest of the stationers, to start over at another trade in another city. She knew she could never face any of these people again.

She did not see Edward Blount stand and walk to the front of the room, and only gradually became aware that he was speaking. "But this is nonsense!" he was saying. "I have worked side by side with Mistress Wood for the past year, and I can testify to her modesty, her piety and her virtue. We have all seen her at our services at St. Faith's. To suggest that such a woman consorts with devils calls for a fancy unmatched by anything I have seen off the stage. Perhaps Master Cowper will turn his imagination in the future to writing plays."

A few people laughed. George, unmoved, said from his seat, "Can you prove that she does not have a familiar? As I said, I have seen it. It does her work for her, her household chores. It was washing a pot when I visited."

Some of the stationers murmured among themselves. Blount said nothing. He could not answer, Alice thought bleakly, because he had never been to her house. None of them had except George, because visiting an unmarried woman was considered immoral. And George, of course, would know that, would know that he alone had been favored with an invitation because she had hoped to renew their friendship.

But Blount's defense had given her courage. If he could not help her she would have to help herself. "I have no familiar," she said, her voice quiet but gaining in power as she continued. "You are all welcome to my house to see for yourself."

George laughed harshly. "Will you trust this woman?" he asked. "A demon can become the size of an acorn, if it so desires. Aye, I'm certain we will find no familiar in her house."

"I wonder that you talk so easily about morality," Blount said. "We have all seen you in conversation with a man who comes into the churchyard, a man asking questions about Mistress Wood's son. He is a counterfeiter, they say, and I have also heard that he dabbles in alchemy."

"He is a scientist," George said. "His researches have nothing to do with the spirit world."

"Can you prove that?" Blount said.

"Master Cowper's morals are not in question here," the master said. "Mistress Wood has yet to reply to his accusations."

Alice stood as Blount moved back to his seat. "I can only say that almost everything Master Cowper had said is false," she said, gratified to hear that her voice sounded strong and certain now. "I have a friend named Margery, but she is no witch. I have never consorted with devils. I have no familiar—"

"You lie!" George said, his calm finally leaving him. "I've seen it myself."

"I have no familiar," she said again. How could she explain Brownie? "I can only repeat my invitation. You are all welcome to my house, to judge for yourself."

"And I can only repeat what I have said about the ways of demons," George said. "Is it so hard to decide what to do here? It is not enough that she lose her membership. She should be burned at the stake."

A number of people began to speak, many of them, to Alice's horror, agreeing with George. Someone called for a witchfinder. The master asked for silence. "It seems to me," he said, "that the state of Mistress Wood's soul is not a fit matter for us

to decide. We meet here to discuss the business of the stationers, and that only. I would like to suggest that we take a vote.
If the majority of the members thinks that we made a mistake
a year ago in voting her into the company, then we will take
away her membership. Further than that we cannot go."

"But I would like everyone to remember," George said, "that
talking to a witch, that even being in the same room with a
witch, is a danger to the soul."

"Very well," the master said. "Enough. Will all those in
favor—"

"I would like to say something first." A man rose, and Alice
saw to her surprise that it was Walter James, the newest member of the company. "The company should know, before it
votes, that I have been to Mistress Wood's house many times.
I have never seen a demon such as the one Master Cowper
mentioned. I have seen a clean, well-appointed home, and a
woman who has never, by word or deed, strayed beyond the
bounds of modesty. My friend Mistress Wood is a great asset to
this company. She is one of the reasons I feel proud to be a
member here."

Another burst of comment swept the room. Alice looked at
James with astonishment. She had not talked to him since their
first meeting at Edward Blount's stall. He was carefully ignoring
her, and she realized that for his plan to work she should act as
if nothing unusual had happened. "Silence," the master said
again. "Why have you said nothing of this before?"

"I did not want to call her honor into question. But now that
she's in danger of losing her membership I think my testimony
can only help her."

"I don't believe you," George said. "I've never seen the two
of you talk together."

"Believe it as you like. It's true."

"And it's still my word against yours."

"And against Edward Blount's. And most importantly, against
Alice Wood's. But come, how many people in this company
truly believe that this woman, someone you have all known for
years, someone you have worked with these past months, is a

witch? Have any of you seen her muttering charms? Have your books become rotten with mold when she passes by?"

A few people were laughing now. "She's a witch!" George said angrily. "I tell you, I have seen——"

"Has anyone else seen this demon?" James said. A few members of the company shook their heads. "I have heard a rumor, which I would hesitate to pass along in other circumstances, that Master Cowper asked for Mistress Wood's hand in marriage. And that she refused him. Can this accusation be caused by hurt pride, by a desire for revenge?"

"That's not true!" George said. "I wouldn't have her. She's immoral, evil."

"And how moral is it to lie?" Alice said. "You asked me to marry you, that day in the cookshop."

"You can prove nothing," George said.

"Ah," Walter James said. "As our esteemed master said, we are not here to prove anything but that Mistress Wood is innocent of these ridiculous charges. Does the company still want to take a vote?"

A few people nodded. But the panic George had tried to cause diminished, lulled away by James's rational voice. Some of the members looked around them, puzzled, as if escaping from a long and evil dream.

"I demand a vote," George said.

"Aye, we should have a vote, if only to lay this matter to rest once and for all," James said. He nodded to the master.

"All in favor," the master said, "say *aye.*"

Only three or four people came out for Alice's dismissal. "All opposed——" the master said.

James and Blount said "Nay!" immediately and loudly. A few of the others joined in, quieter, and then a few more. The *nays* swept through the room like a wave. But still no one would look at her.

The master ended the meeting. Some of the members turned and smiled at her then, and a few of them came over to wish her good day. But no one said anything about the victory she had won. Perhaps they were all embarrassed about the parts they had played.

People were starting to leave by the time Walter James made his way over to her. "I want to thank you," she said. "I don't—I don't know—"

"There's no need," he said.

"But why did you—"

He raised his hand to silence her. "This is not the place to speak of it," he said, so softly no one heard him. Then, louder, he said, "After the fright you received today I think you should see a play. Will you come with me?"

Should she? Other stationers might be able to close their stalls and take holidays, but she needed the trade each day brought. And he must need it too; he hadn't been at the churchyard very long. "Come," he said as if reading her thoughts. "One day won't matter so very much."

First Brownie and now this man: folks were always telling her to shake off her cares and go with them. But why not? She hadn't known much joy since John died.

"With pleasure," she said. He held out his hand and she took it.

When she got outside she found her knees would almost not hold her. Now that her shame had gone she felt terror more than anything else, and a nearly insupportable anger. They had wanted to burn her at the stake. To burn her! It would be ridiculous if it weren't so frightening.

"Are you well enough to walk?" Walter asked.

She nodded, drawing a deep breath to get her strength back. But it was a long way to Shoreditch, outside the city walls, where the Theatre and the Curtain stood. They went along Cheapside, through the crowded market stalls and goldsmiths' shops. She stopped to stare, amazed, at the intricately-worked gold and silver saltcellars and ewers and spoons displayed in the windows.

"What would you like to see?" Walter asked.

She hadn't been to a play in years. As they grew older she and John had not gone out very much, and George had thought plays immoral. She tried to remember titles she had seen on the playbills she printed but they all blurred together, stories of love and war and blood and revenge. She would cheerfully see any one of them.

A coach came toward them, taking up most of the narrow street, and they moved to make room for it. Its wheels creaked; the horses' hooves fell loudly on the cobblestones. She waited until it had passed before she said, "I don't know. You choose."

"Dr. Faustus is very good," he said, and then, "Oh. I'm sorry."

"Nay, don't be."

"The Battle of Alcazar, then. Or *Orlando Furioso.* I've heard talk of both."

"Nay, let's see *Faustus.* Everyone in the churchyard has been to it. I want to know what all the talk is about."

"Are you sure?" he asked, and she nodded. "Very well."

The walk was restoring her perspective, her equanimity. She was not a witch. They were fools to think so. How could she have thought of leaving the company? She would stay, and show them the extent of their folly.

They walked in silence for a while, passing the huge court-yard of the Royal Exchange on their left. Alice saw merchants from all over Europe, dressed in outlandish clothes, crossing the courtyard or hurrying through the pillared arcade. She had a quick sense of vast excitement, as if whole destinies were decided here. It reminded her of something she had forgotten, that London was bigger, and contained stranger sights, than the churchyard of St. Paul's.

They turned left onto Gracechurch Street. "Why did you come to my defense?" she asked.

"How could I not?"

The simple answer warmed her, but it explained nothing. "But you lied for me," she said. "You have never been to my house."

"George is an ass. Any fool could see that he hoped to gain something if you lost your membership in the company. And no one who knows you could believe the things he said for a moment. Even I didn't believe it, and I had only met you once. So my conscience is quite clear. If I hadn't spoken up you might have been in some danger. I have seen crowds like that become enraged in a moment, flaring up like fire on a thatched roof."

"You said George hoped to gain something. What do you think it is?"

He looked at her shrewdly. "I don't know. I would guess it has something to do with that man they talked about, the counterfeiter."

She had been surprised to hear, at the Stationers' Hall, that George had befriended the man in black. Now she wondered if he might also be looking for Arthur, if he worked for Queen Oriana's enemies.

"And perhaps it has something to do with your son," Walter James said, looking at her shrewdly.

She said nothing. The man beside her seemed pleasant, and he had come to her rescue when she had most needed it, but she didn't think she knew enough to confide in him. What if it had all been a trick, if he and George had plotted together to get her to trust him? But nay, she was starting to suspect everyone. Surely Walter wouldn't have defended her so strongly if he had been George's friend.

"How long has your son been missing?"

"Some years now."

"Do you know where he went? Or why folks are looking for him?"

"Nay." She was unused to lying, so she hadn't known what she was going to say until the word was out of her mouth. Thinking it over, though, she realized she had made the right decision. He wouldn't believe her story, for one thing, and for another she didn't want to burden him with her troubles. And if, unlikely as it seemed, he and George did work for the same forces, she would be glad she had said nothing.

They went through Bishopsgate and past the small houses and fields of the suburbs. He was silent until they reached the playhouses, as if he understood he had trespassed too much on her privacy. They came to the Theatre just as the trumpets sounded from the roof to announce the start of the play.

They hurried inside. It cost a penny to stand, twopence to sit, and three to sit on cushions. He paid sixpence for both of them and directed her to a row of benches. She sat and looked around her.

The theater was circular, with the stage projecting out into the center and surrounded on three sides by the audience. Near the stage, almost on it, sat the gallants who had come to see and be seen, and who would comment loudly, not on the action on stage but on who had arrived with whom and what they were wearing. Men and women moved up and down the benches near her, selling apples, nuts, bottled ale, tobacco. Next to her a man was talking loudly to his companion, a woman who smelled overwhelmingly of perfume, about his wife.

The man did not stop talking, and the vendors did not stop hawking their wares, when an actor dressed in black velvet came out to speak the prologue. The city apprentices in their blue coats and flat caps, escaped from work for a day, cheered the beginning of the play enthusiastically, and she missed the opening lines.

When she began to be able to hear she was surprised at how much plays had changed since she and John had gone to see them. The actors no longer spoke in rhyme, but the lines, held together now only by meter, retained all of their poetry and integrity. And soon she found that she preferred blank verse, that she hadn't realized how intrusive the constant rhyme had been.

The actors' lines were better, too, and held an excitement she had never heard before. She watched, fascinated and a little horrified, as Faustus drew his circle and conjured up Mephostophilis, as he made the bargain with the devil that was to cost him so much, as he traveled all over the world with his new powers. She barely noticed the noise of the crowd, the gallants standing in a body and leaving, the two men in front of her who had started to play cards. The day grew hot, and the smells of roasted nuts and sweat and perfume rose around her.

She was aware that, once or twice, Walter glanced over in her direction. She thought he might still be worried that this demonstration of witchcraft would prove too much for her. But though the devils on stage frightened her she managed to show Walter nothing of what she felt until the end, Faustus's last terrified speech. The crowd was finally silent; they heard the stately iambics broken now as Faustus stammered out new bargains, tried hopelessly to find a way to escape his coming damnation:

"Adders and serpents, let me breathe awhile.
Ugly hell, gape not, come not, Lucifer!
I'll burn my books—ah, Mephostophilis!"

Then it was over, and she turned to see Walter sitting next to her, looking as pale as she herself must be.

They stood and pushed with the rest of the crowd to the exits. Walter kept up a steady stream of talk on the way home, as if he realized that she had been shaken more than she would like to admit. "The man who wrote the play—I've seen him in the churchyard," he said. "He comes to talk to Edward Blount. Ned wants to publish a poem of his."

She had met Marlowe once, and she told him about that, and about his friend Thomas Nashe. It was so easy to be with Walter that she felt herself forgetting her cares, George's strange attack and her missing son. They walked to her house on Paternoster Row and he waited as she opened the door.

"I'd ask you in, if only to make sure I have no familiar," she said, "but it's been a long day and I'm tired. Thanks for everything."

"I'll see you tomorrow," he said.

She sat in the kitchen for a long time after he had gone. Despite what she had told him she felt awake, alert, too excited to go to bed. She went over everything that had happened that day—George's speech and Edward's defense, and Walter's, and the play, the crowds of people, the way Walter had looked after her . . .

Walter. Why couldn't she get him out of her mind? Was she so lonely, then, so pathetic, that the simplest kindness from a stranger could unbalance her completely? And surely kindness was all that it had been; he hadn't expected anything more. She had made the same mistake before with George; she had taken what she had thought was kindness and turned it into something larger, a friendship that had not been returned. The world was full of traps for lonely old women.

Was she in love with him then? Nay—he was not the sort of man she could care for. She understood why she had fallen in love with John, who had made her laugh, who had had plans which took in more of the world than their tiny community, who had been handsome and strong. When she thought of Walter she could find nothing attractive about him: he was too short, too dark, his eyes too close together and his chin too large. Yet she knew she would think of him all night. She wanted only to be with him, to listen to his light friendly voice as he talked about inconsequential things. She wished she had thought to invite him in.

How could she face him the next day in the churchyard? She could only think that she must not betray to him what she felt, to save them both from embarrassment.

She stood and began to make herself a light supper. Something white on the sideboard caught her attention, a piece of paper. "Come tomorrow," the note said in Margery's handwriting. "The Fair Folk are moving. They have decided not to wait for your son."

11

Christopher watched in astonishment as the four men made their way toward the stage. If these people were the conspirators then who were the odd folks he had met in the room that early morning?

"Aye, we had dinner together that afternoon," one of the men said. "My wife was there as well."

As he listened to them speak Christopher recognized their voices; they were indeed the men he had overheard rehearsing the play. He had been led astray, had decided that these folks were the same as the lunatics he had visited because a man from one group had belonged to the other as well. The truth had proved to be less fantastic than he had thought; the conspirators were ordinary people and not the madmen he had believed them to be. He had complicated things needlessly, like Robert Poley, or worse, like Tom Nashe with his goblins.

One of the councilors nodded and dismissed the four men, and they stepped off the stage. Their story had been accepted; they would not be asked any further questions. He alone of all the people in the room knew that these men had plotted to bring down the queen, and he could prove nothing against them.

An idea came to him then, a way he could demonstrate their guilt. He studied the conspirators' faces carefully and returned to his room, wondering if Philip Potter could be made to memorize a few lines.

The next day he spoke to the queen's guards and then went to dinner with Potter in the Great Hall. The conspirators' standing at court was slightly higher than Potter's, and so in the usual course of things Sir Philip would not have found seats next to them. But he and Christopher had followed the men closely into the hall and then sat at their table before anyone else could. Christopher ignored the men's hostile looks, and Potter did not seem to notice them at all.

When the men turned away Christopher studied them carefully. Nicholas Russell, John Stafford, Richard Dyer, Edward White: he had paid enough attention when they testified to know which was which. And their leader, who had said his name was John Bridges.

Drums and trumpets sounded, and then the nobility and Knights of the Garter came into the room, followed by Queen Elizabeth and her maids-of-honor. In all the time Christopher had been at the palace he had never seen the queen at dinner; she had the habit of dining privately. He had heard, though, that she wanted to show herself to the court; rumor had it that she was dead, with an impostor on the throne.

The queen sat at a raised dais at the far end of the room, her councilors to either side of her. More trumpets played, and the Yeomen of the Guard, each dressed in scarlet with a gold rose on his back, brought in her dinner. A woman Christopher knew to be a countess served one of the guards a portion of every dish, and after the guard had tasted the food the queen began to eat. Only then did servants pass through the hall with dishes of pork, capon, beef, and venison pie. A consort played a galliard in another room.

Nearly a week after the masque the subject of conversation at every table was the same: the assassination attempt and the capture of the man who had tried to shoot the queen. "I hear," someone at another table said, "that the assassin has died. Succumbed to torture, no doubt."

The comment had been loud enough for the conspirators to overhear. But none of them seemed particularly sad that one of their number had died, or relieved that the man had not lived to betray them. For the first time Christopher wondered if he had made a mistake. But these men were consummate actors, he had seen that. Doubtless they were well schooled in hiding what they felt.

"I wonder if the assassin spoke at all before he died," he said.

The men paid no attention to him. Clearly they, like Will, could tell that he was no gentleman, but unlike Will they seemed to want to keep their distance from one so lowborn. Or could there be another reason for their silence?

"If he said nothing his friends will go unpunished," Sir Philip said. "Who are they, I wonder? They could be anyone, anyone in this room."

Christopher felt a vast relief. Sir Philip had not forgotten his lines. He watched with amusement as Potter added a touch of his own to the drama Christopher had constructed: he turned and surveyed the room, frowning at the thought that such evil might be present.

Well, Sir Philip was not stupid, though there seemed to be a great many things no one had ever told him. He had understood the masque, after all.

"Nay, I think the men will be discovered soon," Christopher said. "Do you remember the note that was delivered to my room by accident?"

"Aye," Sir Philip said, as naturally as if there had truly been such a note.

The other men at the table continued to eat, but Christopher thought he saw a few of them tense, listening for his next words. John Bridges turned slightly to be able to hear him.

"I think the note had something to do with the conspiracy," Christopher said. "I didn't understand it at all when I read it—something about an imaginary dinner in April, and one or two lines about the need for secrecy. The last sentence mentioned a new king, that much I do remember."

"For God's sake, man, who was it from?" Sir Philip asked eagerly. Christopher thought he might be overdoing it a little. "Who was it addressed to?"

"All the names were in cipher. But I'm certain that the queen's men could decipher it, if I took it to them."

"Aye, you should do that, by all means," Sir Philip said.

The plotters had abandoned all pretense of eating. One or two of them stared frankly at Christopher as if trying to memorize his features. "I will," Christopher said, biting into the venison pie. It was very good. "I'll do it this afternoon."

After dinner he and Potter went up the stairs to Potter's room. Christopher sat at the writing table but Sir Philip paced the room anxiously, opening and closing the door again and again to see if the queen's guards had come. "Where are they?" he said. "What if they didn't believe you?"

"They'll be here," Christopher said, sounding more certain than he felt. They had certainly seemed to believe his story that morning. He found himself more worried about where the conspirators were; he had expected them to confront him almost immediately. "Stop opening the door."

Sir Philip closed the door and paced the length of the room again. "Will this be dangerous?"

"Not for you," Christopher said, hoping to reassure him. "I'm the one who has the note, after all. I've told you—you don't have to stay."

"And I've told you that I want to be here," Potter said. "I have to prove myself to the queen."

Christopher realized that he had misunderstood the man. Potter did not fear danger but looked forward to it, hoping to demonstrate his loyalty and cleverness to the queen. Suddenly Christopher felt very old, older than Sir Philip though the man was at least forty. What would it be like to be so innocent?

Someone knocked on the door. Christopher stood. Sir Philip turned, flustered, and ran his hands over his trunk hose. The men entered without waiting for permission. "Give us the note," Nicholas Russell said.

"The note?" Christopher said. What had happened to the queen's guard?

"Aye. Don't play the fool. The note you talked about at dinner. Where is it?"

"I—I gave it to one of the queen's councilors."

"Nay," John Bridges said. "No tricks. You didn't have time for that. Where is it? Is it in this room?"

"Why do you want it?"

Sir Philip edged toward the door, moving surprisingly softly for all his plumpness.

"And no questions, either. You!" he said, calling to Sir Philip. Potter stopped halfway to the door. "Stay here. We'll have to pry the answer out of you, then, the way we might pry an oyster from its shell. And the tool for both tasks is the same—the knife."

He motioned to Richard Dyer. Dyer slipped his dagger from its sheath. "We'll start with you, Sir Philip, since you tried to be so clever," Bridges said. Stafford twisted Potter's arms behind his back. "Didn't you learn anything from your stay at court? You're not good at cleverness, Sir Philip—leave it to other people."

Richard Dyer brought his dagger up to Sir Philip's face. Philip's eyes opened almost comically wide. "Cut one of his cheeks, to begin with," Bridges said.

Philip tried to jerk his head away. Stafford held him tightly. But before Dyer could bring his dagger closer something odd began to happen to the tapestry between the windows; it bulged outward for a fraction of a second and then tore to shreds. An explosive noise echoed back and forth through the room, and then Dyer fell, holding his side.

Two men dressed in the livery of the queen's guard stepped out from behind the tapestry. One of them held a gun. "We arrest you, in the queen's name," he said.

The other guard tore Stafford away from Potter. The first threw down the gun and took out his sword, and began motioning to the remaining conspirators, Bridges, Russell, and White. Bridges and White raised their arms away from their weapons, but Russell ran for the door. Before anyone could stop him he had slipped outside and was gone.

Christopher ran after him. They hurried down the main staircase and into the Great Hall, and then Russell opened a door Christopher had never noticed before.

Suddenly Christopher found himself inside a huge kitchen. The strong heat hit him like a fist. A group of men at the hearth were turning a goat on a spit. Russell shoved past them. Christopher followed, his elbow jostling the goat's stiff outstretched legs. "What—" the cooks shouted after them. "Stop!"

Russell ran through another door and down a dimly lit stone corridor. He opened one final door and they stepped outside. Ahead of them was the hedge maze. Russell ran through the ornamental entrance.

Christopher followed. Russell turned a corner ahead of him, then another. Christopher took both corners after him and looked around quickly, seeing nothing before him but head-high walls of leafy green. Russell had vanished. He stood still a moment, listening for the other man.

A noise came from the right. He followed it and heard the same noise, coming from his left this time. Was that Russell or someone else? But who else would be in the maze? He hurried on.

After a few turns he realized he was lost. Russell was long gone. He looked around him, trying desperately to remember the way out.

Left here, or was it right? It had all looked different from the window in his room, more orderly somehow. He passed a stone bench, a statue. Where was he? He began to turn corners at random—was that the same bench, the same statue? He couldn't remember.

He slowed. It seemed that he had spent his entire life surrounded by these dreadful hedges, that he would never see the horizon again. The green walls closed in on him. A branch snapped somewhere.

The air around him seemed to thicken. He could not concentrate. He forced his way along a path until it ended, and then turned right. Ahead of him, at a fork in the path, he saw the same statue he had seen three turns back.

Suddenly it moved. It was not a statue at all, he saw, but a small man, maybe one of the men he had seen his first morning in the palace. The man pointed left. He had the oddest smile on his face, almost as if he had proven some sort of point, though what it was Christopher could not imagine. He wore a circlet of green leaves in his hair.

Christopher went left. The path turned again. Someone moved on the other side of the hedge, and for a terrible moment he thought that it was the little man again, come back to plague him with false directions. Then he looked through the leaves and saw Nicholas Russell.

Russell stopped and glanced around him, looking lost. He began to head back. Christopher dropped behind a corner, waiting for him.

Could he overpower the other man? Russell did not seem to be aware of him; perhaps he could take him by surprise. He tensed, anticipating the moment when Russell would come into sight. Several seconds passed. Where was he?

Christopher moved carefully around the corner. At first he could not take in what he saw. The little man stood over Russell, tying his hands behind him with what looked like supple branches. He sang as he worked; Christopher could not imagine how he had failed to hear it before. The man looked up and smiled. His eyes were as green as the leaves around him.

He tied one final knot. Before Christopher could say anything the man turned and, more quickly than seemed possible, slipped away from him around a corner.

"Wait!" Christopher called. He took the corner after him, feeling clumsy next to the other man's swift grace. The green path stretched out in a straight line in front of him, but the little man was nowhere to be seen.

He went back to Russell. The conspirator was unconscious, breathing shallowly. The other man could wait; he had to get Russell outside the maze somehow, back to the queen's guard.

Looking up he saw a dying hedge, the roots exposed and withered. He lifted Russell to his feet and broke through the hedge, then—he was past caring—tore through another wall, this one whole.

The afternoon light, unfiltered by green, nearly blinded him for a moment. He had made his way out of the maze, and, incredibly, had found himself fairly close to the palace. He set down his burden with relief and went off to find one of the guard.

Once again the Presence Chamber was crowded with people. Christopher and Will sat near the front and watched as Queen Elizabeth thanked Sir Philip for the service he had done to the state.

"Let all men know that Sir Philip Potter, at great personal risk and undeterred by threats to his person, discovered and exposed a Catholic conspiracy aimed at taking our life and sowing disorder in the land," the queen said.

"It was my pleasure, Your Majesty," Sir Philip said, rising awkwardly from his bow. He seemed more reserved than usual, and Christopher wondered if Potter suspected this Queen Elizabeth to be an impostor as well.

No one would say anything about it during the ceremony, but everyone at court knew that Sir Philip had received his tax monopoly, and a gift of some land as well. There had been a certain amount of carping and ill-mannered jesting at this news, but none of the courtiers could say that Sir Philip did not deserve his good fortune. Potter, displaying the same flustered ignorance he had shown from the beginning, did not seem to notice the insults, and looked at everyone he met with the same expression of surprised joy.

Finally the ceremony ended. "The air's too close in here," Will said. "Let's take a walk outside."

Christopher showed Will the way he had taken following Russell: through the Great Hall, into the kitchen and finally down the corridor that led out-of-doors. "I've never seen this, in all the years I've been at court," Will said. "How did you discover it?"

Christopher said nothing. The hedge maze had a gaping hole in it, he noticed.

"I heard you had something to do with the capture of these conspirators," Will said.

The man was as innocent as Potter sometimes, Christopher thought. He looked around him carefully, making certain they could not be overheard. "Aye," he said. "But if folks should hear of it they'll guess that I was something more than Sir Philip's secretary. I won't be sent out on any errands again. Have you passed on this rumor to anyone else?"

"Nay, I won't."

He didn't, Christopher noticed, exactly answer the question. Still, it couldn't be helped if he had spoken to anyone. They began to walk through the formal plots of the queen's garden.

"The queen said these men were Catholic conspirators," Will said. "What could they have wanted with Arthur? Or was he Catholic as well?"

"Nay, I doubt it. They wanted him because some people in London were willing to follow him, and were eager to see him as a king. Once he took the throne they would have been careful to keep any real power from him."

"But what about those strange men you saw? Didn't they have something to do with Arthur as well?"

Aye, probably they had, he thought. What had happened to the little man he had followed to the conspirators' meeting? And what about the man he had overheard at the meeting, the one who had sounded so familiar? Christopher had heard the voices of all the conspirators and was certain this man had not been among them. And while he was asking questions, who was it who had helped him in the maze? And why had Geoffrey quoted the same line of poetry as one of the conspirators?

He had never told Will any of this, though, and he did not intend to start now. Will would laugh and start to talk about goblins again, and he was as tired of the subject as he had been when Tom had mentioned it. His task here had ended; he had discovered the conspirators and would be well paid for it, and then he would go home. To imagine that the supernatural had anything to do with it was folly.

"What must that be like, I wonder?" Will said.

He had been so deep in thought he hadn't heard the beginning of Will's question. "What must what be like?"

"Believing in something so strongly that you're willing to give your life for it, the way these men believed in the Catholic cause."

"Don't expect me to understand a fanatic. To my mind there's little to choose between one religion and another. They could just as easily have become Mohammedan."

He expected Will to object, the way Robin and Tom did when he made some statement they considered outrageous. But Will would not be drawn into a debate. "What will you do now?" he asked.

"Go home. Work on my play."

"Do you write plays? And poetry as well?"

Christopher nodded.

"Good," Will said. "I'll be your patron when I come into my inheritance. I've always wanted to be a patron."

Christopher laughed. "How do you know they're any good?"

"I don't, really. I don't know anything at all about poetry. You'll have to teach me—you seem to know something about everything." Then, to Christopher's great astonishment and delight, he drew him close and kissed him on the mouth.

There remained one final task before he could go home; he had to say farewell to Sir Philip Potter. The next day he visited the man in his rooms, watching as his servants packed up his belongings. There was a great tear in the tapestry between the windows, Christopher saw; he seemed, all unknowing, to have left a trail of destruction behind him in his short stay at court.

"There you are," Sir Philip said. "I wanted to thank you for all you've done. You were the one who exposed the plotters, not I—don't think I don't know that. I tried to tell the queen that—"

"You didn't!"

"Aye, I did. Why shouldn't I? You deserved the credit as much as I did. But her councilors said that they would take care of everything. And did they?"

"Aye."

"Good. Well, I'll miss you. We had some merry times together."

Christopher smiled. Merry was not a word he would have
chosen.

"I'll never forget seeing those guards come out from behind
the tapestry," Potter said. "Remember how anxious I was for
them to arrive? But why in God's name didn't they tell us they
were here?"

"They didn't trust us."

"What?"

"They didn't trust my story. It sounded too implausible—
they thought it was something you and I had invented to revenge ourselves on the court, on these men."

"Revenge?" Potter said. "Revenge for what?" His face was as
round and guileless as a pocket watch.

Christopher sighed. "They wanted to eavesdrop, to see what
we would do if we were left alone."

"Nay, you're too suspicious. I think they wanted to make a
grand entrance, like the knights of Order overcoming the vices.
And so they did." He looked around him. "I think I'm done
here. Don't forget the letter of recommendation I wrote you.
You were the best secretary I ever had."

12

Alice had spent the night unable to sleep. Why had she sent Walter away? Nay—why should she want him with her? What would the Stationers' Company say if she had spent the night with him? A woman cleared of charges of immoral living could not give in to her whims so easily. It was good that he had gone. But wouldn't it be better to have him here? She could tell him the truth about her son, and he could help her think what to do about Margery's note.

By morning she had decided to go to Margery. The message she had sent had sounded pressing. And by avoiding the churchyard she would be able to avoid Walter, too, to gain one more day in which she could decide what to do about him.

It was snowing as she left the house, an unseasonable snow after a winter of mild weather. She went back to get her woolen cloak and continued on to her assistant's house. He was home, God be thanked, and willing to work for her that day. Then she walked through the falling snow to Margery's cottage.

As she went up the path to her friend's house she saw that Margery had built up the fire; a thin gray thread of smoke drew up from her chimney into the sky. "Come in, come in!" Margery said, opening the door to her before she could knock.

After the cold Margery's house seemed almost hot. The fire sounded loud in the small house. She shook off her cloak with relief.

Margery handed her hot cider and pushed a protesting black and white cat off a stool. Alice sat. "You remember Agnes, don't you?" Margery said.

Alice nodded, trying not to feel annoyed. She had hoped to talk to Margery alone, to ask her pressing questions about her son and Walter. What business did the other woman have here? It was true she had delivered Arthur twenty years ago—but nay, that hadn't been Arthur at all but his counterfeit, the boy she had raised, the Prince of Faerie. Did that old tale give this nosy gossip the right to pry into her affairs?

But Agnes's presence would not stop Alice from telling her news. "I must tell you," she said. "George has had dealings with the man in black, the one who's been asking after Arthur."

Margery frowned. "This is ill news indeed. How did you come to learn of it?"

She told Margery the whole story—how George had denounced her to the Stationers' Company, how Edward Blount and Walter James had risen in her defense, how Blount had mentioned the alchemist and counterfeiter who had spoken with George. Margery looked horrified at the charges that had been brought against her, and Alice wondered if someone had once accused her friend of necromancy as well. She realized, not for the first time, how little she actually knew about the other woman.

Through it all Agnes watched her with undisguised interest. Because of Agnes, Alice passed over the play she had seen with Walter and the sleepless night she had spent afterward. When Agnes was gone she would confide in Margery again.

"What can we do?" Alice asked when she had finished her tale. "If these men are truly counterfeiters perhaps we should tell the authorities, one of the queen's men."

"Nay. We must not allow information about your son to come to the queen."

"Why?"

"Why? Haven't you heard the news? There has already been

one plot against the queen. Someone tried to kill her, and I heard stories that Arthur might have been involved. What—"

"Arthur wouldn't plot against the queen," Alice said quickly. But would he? What did she know about him, after all?

"Maybe not. But Arthur is important to a great many people. Imagine what the queen would do if she heard of a man in her kingdom who had been born into the old race."

"Would she use him in some way?"

"Perhaps. But probably she would have him killed, especially if he made claims to the throne."

"Then what can we do?"

"Do? Just now we can do nothing but wait."

Margery lit her pipe and sat back. Why had her friend sent that urgent note if they could do nothing? Alice wanted to shake her, to force her into action. If the weather cleared she should go back to the churchyard. Why had she come?

"We must wait until evening," Margery said finally, smoke blowing from her mouth. "There will be a battle tonight, in Finsbury Field. As I said, they have decided not to wait for your son."

Did Margery read her thoughts? "Battle? But what does that have to do with us?"

"Arthur may be there. We know that he is drawn by these folk, and rightly, since they are his true heritage. And your son may be there as well."

She felt as if she had been stabbed to the heart. Would Margery never stop surprising her? To see her son, after all these years . . . "And what then?" she asked. "Will they let me speak to him?"

"I don't know. We can only wait and see."

They spoke of inconsequential things after that. Margery showed Agnes through the small cottage, the books and the scrying stone, the herbs that hung in bundles from the ceiling: yarrow, vervain, saxifrage, adder's tongue, hellebore.

They began to talk about illnesses, which herb was best for the cough, and Alice realized that Agnes, as a midwife, must have her own small store of knowledge. She felt irritated, even jealous. Margery had never spoken to her like this about the medicines she used. And surely they could spend the time better; surely they could make some plan, devise some way that she could see her son. She might even be able to steal him away from Oriana and keep him for herself. What would he be like after all these years among the Fair Folk? No matter—he was hers, after all, and not one of them.

Finally Margery set out a small supper, cold chicken and leg of mutton. Alice ate hungrily: she had had nothing since breakfast. But Agnes outdid her, eating everything that was put before her, her wide mouth in constant motion. What good will she be tonight? Alice thought again. Why is she coming with us?

Margery set down food for the cats and the women left the cottage. It was still early, not yet five o'clock. But darkness lay over the streets in front of them, an unnatural blackness caused by the low gray clouds overhead. A light snow still fell.

"This mild winter," Margery said, as they walked through the dirty slush of London's streets. "I wonder if it was caused by the Fair Folks' presence here. And if it snows now because of their displeasure at not finding Arthur."

"I wonder," Agnes said. She had taken an apple from the cottage and was eating it as they went.

Their walk took them halfway across London, from Ludgate in the east to Moorgate in the north, a distance of nearly a mile. As they passed Paul's Alice saw that the stationers had gone home early, and the gallants and lawyers and tailors as well. She had never heard it so quiet. The stores and stalls on Cheapside had closed, and in the smaller streets the houses were unlit, shut tight for the evening. It was almost as if folks anticipated something, as if they knew not to be on the streets this night. Only the waxing moon, shining momentarily through the clouds, showed them their way.

At last they came to Finsbury Field. All of them were panting slightly, and Alice nearly laughed. What good did these three old women think they would do tonight?

Alice saw nothing on the field but old archery targets. She closed her right eye but the field remained, plain, substantial, unchanging. She looked at her friend, puzzled. "Now we wait," Margery said.

The evening grew colder. Alice shivered inside her woolen cloak, and Agnes rubbed her arms and stamped her feet to keep warm. How long would they have to wait? Could Margery be wrong, could they have made the long journey for nothing? She thought of the wearisome walk back to her house and she sighed. Her breath showed silver in the air.

Margery touched her shoulder. "Look," she said. Someone moved across the field.

Alice closed her eye again, but no light emanated from the man walking toward them. "George," Margery whispered. Surprised, Alice opened her eye.

George came closer. Now she could see that he had three other men with him. "Who are they?" she whispered.

"Is that the man in black?" Margery said.

Aye, it was indeed. She marveled that her friend could make him out on such a dark night. But as she started to say so she heard Margery hiss, a long breath drawn in between her teeth. "Paul Hogg," she said.

"Who?"

"An evil man. I wonder what his business is here. And who is the fourth?"

Paul Hogg motioned to the others at that moment, and they headed toward the three women. Alice pulled her cloak closer around her, trying not to feel afraid. Don't be foolish, she thought. Margery's here. But Margery had seemed worried by Hogg as well.

"Well, well," Hogg said. "What brings three old women out on such a cold and desolate night? Or can it be that you have nowhere else to go? Have your fortunes changed so much since I last met you, Margery?"

"There speaks one who knows all about homeless women," Margery said, addressing not Hogg but George. "He won't have told you, George, but his profession, before he became a wonder worker and cozener of the innocent, was turning people off their farms. Oh, he was famous for it—landlords all over England would seek him out if any of their tenants gave them trouble."

"Aye, and what of it?" Hogg said, unperturbed. "It's a livelihood, the same as any other, a service rendered for money. But what of you, harridan? How many of the poor have you gulled, taking their hard-earned pence and promising them fortune, health, happiness? How many folks dying of the plague have you promised to cure? For how many lonely women have you pretended to see love in that dusty scrying ball of yours?"

"What have you told George of this night's errand, Master Hogg? Does he know why he's here, why you seek Alice's child?"

"Does she?" Hogg said, turning to Alice. "Do you know the plans Margery has for your son once he's found? For years she has meddled in things beyond her understanding, trying for some small measure of power. She hopes to find Arthur and exchange him for that power, for knowledge. Do you understand? Whatever she's told you is a lie. She plans to barter with your son's life."

His voice sounded low and deep, almost plausible. Could what he said be true? Was Margery using her? Why had the other woman taken such an interest in her, in Arthur?

The cold wind whistled around them, breaking his spell. Nay—what was she thinking? Margery was her friend; she knew it. George had proved faithless but that didn't mean that all her friends would betray her. "That's not true," she said, and was pleased to hear that her voice sounded steady.

"Alice, why are you here?" George said. "Why do you listen to this woman, this witch? I warned you at the stationers' meeting that you put your soul in peril by talking to her."

Alice nearly laughed. "You warned me? Nay, you did more—you nearly sent me to the stake. But I might ask the same of you—why do you keep company with this man? Surely you, who claim to know all the dangers to the soul—"

"What Master Hogg does is lawful," George said. "Those he keeps company with are the children of light, and no demons. But you, Alice—all your friends are the children of darkness. Hogg told me so himself."

Margery laughed. "And you believed him? George, you're a bigger fool than I took you for."

George opened his mouth to reply. But at that moment the fourth man touched Paul Hogg's shoulder. "There," he said.

They all turned to look. The moon had pierced the clouds, and by its light Alice could see the Fair Folk coming onto the field. Four of the horned men led them, wearing silver mail and carrying silk banners that rippled like water. Behind the men walked Queen Oriana, shining in the moon's light, and even George gasped to look at her. How can he call her a demon? Alice thought. But then she remembered what Oriana had done to her, to Arthur, and she wondered if the queen's fairness hid an ugliness within. Could she and Margery be on the wrong side? Nay—they were not on any side; they were here only to see if Arthur came. Oriana could lose the war for all she cared.

Behind the queen came more horned men, their mail glittering like fish scales in the moonlight. Some of them were mounted, and all bore swords. The winged creatures Alice remembered flew among them, and behind them walked Robin Goodfellow, carrying his staff. And look—there was Brownie. Her heart turned to see him, so unprotected among the other warriors. Would he fight along with the rest of them? But he was made for dancing and merriment, not for battle.

Something moving opposite the queen's folk made them all turn to look. A huge horse came onto the field, its hooves striking fire where it walked. Several of the winged creatures skittered away from it as if blown by the wind. It raised itself on its hind legs and neighed, a sound like someone crying. Now Alice could see a shape clinging to its back, a sea-green creature with a long snout. She shuddered. Did George consort with these folk?

A shadow seemed to trail behind the horse, hiding its followers. The sea-creature put a horned shell to its mouth and blew a shrill note, and the horse charged. Then everything became a shock of motion as the two groups met.

Here a green man, as pliant as if he had no bones, grappled with one of the twig-people. Over and over they rolled, and the twig man laughed as Alice remembered them laughing the night of the revels. They almost appeared to be playing some sort of game or dancing an ancient dance, bending backward and forward in shapes a human could never assume. Then she heard something break and the twig man lay unmoving on the field. The sea-creature flowed forward to lift him but at that moment a horned man cut his way through and stabbed the creature to the heart. The substance that flowed from his wound seemed too watery for blood.

There a huge man, thick as a tree, headed toward the queen and the standard-bearers. He carried a club in one hand and a length of chain in another, and the links of the chain rattled like bones. Robin Goodfellow stepped forward to meet him. The chain whirled out and Robin caught it on his staff. A moving light covered the two of them, white near Robin and a tarnished green over the other man. Robin pulled the chain from the man's hand and with a sound like a snarl the man closed with him, his club raised. The light grew brighter and the man fell back.

More green men took the field, some walking, some riding the tremendous horses. And there were other creatures there as well, shadows covering their shapes: flying, chittering forms that kept to the trees, things that scuttled near the ground. A few oddly shaped people came with them: a squat man with hands as long as forearms, a woman whose grin nearly reached to her pointed ears. They did not join the battle but stood off to the side, laughing and pointing at the knots of fighting.

Finally the train ended with a few who appeared to be human. Why would people fight for these folk? Or were they slaves, taken from among London's population?

Could Oriana's warriors stand up to these? Her band looked small and slight next to them, and it seemed to Alice that they were fewer than their opponents. Already the winged creatures had retreated to the edge of the field. Several of the twig-people moved this way and that, uncertain, and one of them somersaulted away from the battle. As Alice watched a mounted sea-creature bore down on one of the horned men and slashed out with its sword. But the queen stood tall and proud, watching the battle from within the circle of her guard. The moon shone over their standards like the sun playing on leaves.

Alice heard screams and strange cries, the flapping of wings and the pounding of hooves. Through it all she looked for Brownie. Finally she saw him, standing a little back from the fight, as if he felt he did not deserve to be included among such heroes. One of the boneless men moved to engage him in battle and he turned to meet it. Then more of the creatures darted out in front of them, and he was lost to sight.

Alice looked at Margery. Her friend stood still, a look of great concentration on her face. "A pity this battle will be lost as well," she heard Paul Hogg say, not sounding sorry at all. "Or did you three think to change its course somehow?" He laughed.

"Nothing has been decided yet," Margery said. "Don't forget—we have the advantage here. This time the war is fought at night, with the moon nearly full."

"Hear her, Alice," Hogg said. "She admits to it—her friends are night-folk, conceived in darkness."

"Aye, and that's what may save us. Oriana's people are stronger in the dark."

"You still hope!" Hogg said. He laughed again. "I tell you, you've lost. Again. Alice, where is your brownie?"

The fighting had moved to another part of the field; she could not see Brownie anywhere. What had happened to him? And how did this man know about him? But that was easy— George must have told him.

"Didn't you see him fall?" Hogg said. "Only one of the brave warriors to die this night."

His voice was so full of malice that she turned to him angrily. Words she had heard in the churchyard but had never used formed on her tongue. He smiled, his lips like a blade. But just then she heard shouting on the field.

"The dragon! The dragon has come!" one of the standard-bearers called. Others around them took up the cry. The fighting stopped; everyone looked upward expectantly.

In the sky Alice saw not one but two dragons, one of them silver-white and the other a reddish-gold. Which dragon fought for the queen? All around her folks cried out in fear and wonder.

The red dragon spewed fire. On the field the twig-people

scattered in confusion, screaming. "Hold!" one of the horned
men called, but they paid no attention. The silver dragon
moved toward its opponent, jaws open, vast wings spread.
They grappled, claws out. Fire rained down upon the field.

Alice turned to Margery, but the other woman's expression
gave away nothing. Agnes watched the dragons calmly, as if
they were a pageant or fireworks display arranged for her
amusement. Would nothing move this phlegmatic woman to
wonder? But Alice remembered Agnes's comments on the
queen, and she knew the midwife would be very interested in
the outcome.

The dragons backed apart. One of them keened; the other
answered. They flew in close again, their silhouettes framed by
the moon. Their bodies and the moon seemed to form a coin
from a country long fallen to ruin. She thought she saw blood
drop to the field.

The silver dragon had been hurt; its wing hung crookedly
away from its body. Near her someone gasped. But as they
watched the wounded dragon made one final attempt. Its
wings turned in as it flew forward; its neck extended and its
jaws gaped wide. The red dragon backed away but its opponent had opened a long gash down its flank. The red dragon
keened again and flew away.

So the red dragon had lost, Alice thought, surprised at how
little she cared. But the silver dragon was leaving too. Folks
began to drop their weapons and stand as if amazed, the
queen's band on one side, their opponents on the other. Oriana
and her standard-bearers advanced toward the center of the
field. From the other side came a man Alice had never seen, tall
and clad in red mail, with a crown red as fire. Several of his
warriors walked behind him.

"Now they parley," Margery said.

"But who won?" Agnes asked.

"No one. No one has won. Neither side has enough men to
continue the fight."

"But someone has lost," Paul Hogg said. "The queen has lost
her ablest warriors this night. Go back to your cottage and sell

your charms for twopence, Margery. The next time these two
meet will be the last."

"Aye, the last," Margery said. How could she stay so calm?
"The battle will end when Arthur is found."

Arthur! Alice had forgotten him. But Margery had been
wrong; he hadn't come to this battle. Whatever ties he had to
the Fair Folk had loosened, or had been weak to begin with.
She would never see him again, him or her true son.

"Arthur's dead, or lost forever," Hogg said. "And what man
would fight for a woman who cared so little for him she gave
him away at birth?"

"Who would fight for a man who never takes the field,
thinking only about his own safety? See where he comes, your
king. King of the Cowards, they call him."

"But they fight for him just the same."

"They have no choice. He's bound them to him with his arts."

"You lie. Nothing he does is unlawful. And next you'll tell me
that Oriana's people fight out of love."

The king and queen had reached the center of the field and
began to talk in low voices. Alice studied the group around
them, trying to make out the humans who had fought against
Oriana. Was it true that they were bound to the king by necromancy? But now she noticed that they all had stains like
splashes of water down the front of their jerkins. She closed her
right eye and saw the faerie-light on them. Of course, she
thought, remembering the stories from her childhood. They
were water-people, lying in wait at the side of lakes and rivers,
ready to drown travelers walking by. The stains on their clothing gave them away.

Opposite this group the queen stood, straight as a sword and
unyielding, her warriors grouped in a semicircle behind her.
What did they talk about? What terms would the red king force
from Oriana? If her folk left London would Alice ever see Arthur
again?

Whenever people talked about war Alice always thought of
the individual people who would have to die. She was not like
the others in the churchyard in this, she knew; when they had
rung the bells and built the bonfires at the defeat of the Spanish

Armada two years ago she could not share in the exultation of her neighbors. She had thought only, Thank God Arthur will not have to go soldiering.

But the Fair Folk cared nothing for Arthur, she knew that. Margery could not claim that Oriana's people fought out of love; whatever emotions they felt love could not be one of them. They understood nothing about the bond between mother and son. Not one of these finely dressed folk would consider her or her son in their decisions.

Suddenly Alice cried out and ran onto the field. She heard Margery call something after her but she ignored her and made for a small bundle of fur near the queen and king. Brownie lay curled up on the grass, a long gash open on his flank. The blood that matted his fur looked black in the moonlight. As Alice watched he breathed in shallowly. He was alive!

"Margery!" she said loudly. "Margery, help me!"

Margery went to join her. "We must not interrupt the parley," she said, speaking softly.

"The parley be damned. He's alive. We have to help him."

"I will. Quiet now."

Margery opened her purse. Alice had been watching Brownie, willing him to continue breathing, and by the time she looked back at her friend Margery had taken out a cloth dipped in herbs. Where had she wetted the cloth? It didn't matter; what mattered was that she smoothed the cloth over Brownie's fur, that his breathing grew more even, that the wound seemed to close a little. At last he opened his eyes and looked up at them.

"Did we win?" He sat up, a worried look in his soft brown eyes.

"Nay. Lie back," Margery said.

"Queen Oriana—"

"Hush. She rules still."

Brownie fell back, satisfied. "We have to get him to my house," Alice said.

Margery looked up at her friend. "Do you think that's wise?"

"It doesn't matter. Someone has to care for him."

Margery seemed to see the logic of that. She nodded and

braced her shoulder under one of Brownie's arms. Alice took his other arm carefully and they lifted him together. He was surprisingly light.

They sat him down against a tree at the edge of the field. George nodded when he saw them, as if his suspicions had been proven correct. Did he still think that Brownie was a demon? How could he, when he consorted with things far more evil-seeming? Alice thought that George's mind must be a kind of swamp where nothing was clear-edged, where he believed whatever was easiest for him to believe.

"You've found him, I see," Hogg said.

"Aye," Alice said. "And still alive."

"For the moment. I doubt he'll last the night."

Alice turned to Margery, seeking reassurance, and for once her friend gave it to her. "You must not believe anything Paul Hogg says," Margery said firmly. "He's told me many lies over the years, haven't you, Master Hogg?"

"No more than you've told me," Hogg said. He looked distracted, anxious about something, and a moment later Alice saw what it was: the parley had ended. The queen and king bowed to each other elaborately and, Alice thought, a little mockingly. Then both sides retreated, and the work of gathering up the dead for burial began.

A chill wind blew suddenly and Alice shivered. "It's over," Margery said. "Nothing's changed—there are a few more dead on both sides, that's all. It won't end until Arthur is found."

"And she claims that I lie!" Paul Hogg said. "It's clear to me that Oriana's folk lost here. One more battle and your precious queen will be vanquished."

"We'll find Arthur before then."

"Arthur!" Hogg laughed. "Alice, let me tell you your future. Arthur is dead. And when she learns the truth about your son, Margery will forsake you as well. She needs Arthur, doesn't she, to progress beyond her small petty magics. You will grow old alone, with no one to love you. You will die in bed, and so little will you be missed that your body will not be discovered for three days."

How had he known her deepest nightmares, her dread of

growing old and friendless? Was that why she had rescued Brownie, because she knew she could not keep company with humans? He was wrong about Margery, though—her friend had no magic, only wisdom and a strong knowledge of plants and stones. She shook her head, not wanting to bandy words with this odious man any further.

"Good night," Margery said to Hogg. "I know we'll meet again."

"Good night," Hogg said. As he and his men turned to go Alice saw that one of them, the fourth man, had a stain on his jerkin like that of the water-people. She closed her right eye and saw the faerie-light on him, though green and tarnished, the way it had appeared over the man who had fought with Robin Goodfellow. What hold did Hogg have over this creature? How had he made one of the water-people serve him?

Brownie was able to walk by the time they left the field, though the nut-brown color of his face had faded to a pale gray. Agnes did not remark on their new companion; no doubt she had seen stranger sights tonight. They said nothing for most of the long walk home, each woman thinking her own thoughts.

As they reached Cheapside they heard the bellman give his call:

"Remember the clocks,
Look well to your locks,
Fire and your light,
And God give you good night,
For now the bell ringeth,
One o'clock."

Without discussing it they hid in a small alley as he passed. "I wonder what he'd make of us," Agnes said, laughing, as he passed. "Maybe he'd think we were whores."

Alice didn't care. No accusation that anyone could make could be as dreadful as what George had said at the stationers' meeting yesterday. Had it been only yesterday? So much had happened since then: the play, and Walter . . .

She felt a pleasant warmth spread through her at the thought of Walter, and she told herself firmly to forget him. Love did not come to someone her age; the only thing left to her was caring for folks and easing their pain: her strange son, and John in his last illness, and now Brownie . . . It was not much, but it was work that would keep her until she died.

As if to prove that her life held no new joy she said to Margery, "Arthur never came."

"Nay. I'm sorry."

"I wonder why not."

"Who knows? No one can say why these folk do what they do."

"What happens if Oriana loses the war?"

"To your son, you mean? I don't know. He might be taken captive, or—"

"So we must find him." Or killed, Margery had been about to say. She had never been one to spare her friend's feelings.

"Aye." They came up to Paternoster Row and Alice's house. "And soon. Good night."

Alice could barely come awake the next day but she took time to look at Brownie and bind his wound. Then she walked to Paul's; she could not afford three days' absence at the church-yard. As she went through the gate she saw Walter coming from his stall to greet her.

"I looked for you all day yesterday," he said. "Were you ill?"

At his words strong feelings coursed through her like light-ning, excitement and pleasure and desire. Her face grew hot and she wondered if he could see it, and the thought made her color more. Blushing, at her age!

"I went to visit my friend Margery," she said. Damn, but she should not have said that; she must be tired indeed. Now he would tell her she should stop seeing Margery, that she should be careful after the accusations leveled at her the day before.

He said nothing. He was not George, after all. But the trip had been dangerous; if anyone still harbored suspicions that she was a witch this would have confirmed them. She felt glad that he did not pry, that he left her alone to make her own

decisions, and thinking this she remembered again how pleasant his company had been the other day.

"There were strange sights last night," he said. "So they say
in the churchyard, anyway. Dragons, two of them, fighting
against the moon. Did you see them?"

She couldn't think what to reply. But her face must have
given something away, because he said, "Has this anything to
do with you? Or with Margery?"

She wished she could answer him. Not because she wanted
advice about her son, or because she was tired of lying, but just
so that she could stay and talk with him a little longer. "Nay, of
course not," she said, and turned to go.

13

Warmer days came to London. The nobility left for their estates or to follow the queen on her progress but the city seemed as full as ever. The acting companies that had gone on tour returned and joined the ones that had remained in the city, drawing huge crowds, showing five or six plays a week. Beggars and pilgrims, madwomen and thieves came as well, and gypsies in scarves and bells who danced and spat fire and told fortunes. The streets stank of offal left to rot in the sun, and the people stank too, and doused themselves liberally with perfume to cover the smell. Kites and ravens flew overhead.

Tom Nashe made his way through the crowds in St. Paul's churchyard, heading toward Alice's stall. He was driven by a kind of anger; Christopher still refused to discuss what had happened the evening they had followed Arthur, and that left Alice as the only person in London he could talk to.

He was jostled as he walked through the churchyard, and without thinking he put his hand to his hat to keep it from falling. He had recently unearthed the hat from among his old clothing, and had pinned the unfading silver flower to it like a lady's favor. "Good day," Alice said as he came up to her stall.

She always smiled when she saw him, he realized, as if she

expected him to say something witty. He wished he could. "Good day," he said. "I think I have news of Arthur."

She looked at him sharply, not hiding the interest on her face. He began to tell her about the strange land he had come to, the women weaving garlands, the flower he had been given. As he talked he felt a vast relief; he hadn't realized how much he needed to unburden himself to someone who might believe him.

"And did you see Arthur in that land?" she asked.

"Nay. I felt—I felt almost as if someone watched me, studied me, and then passed me over. They were looking for Arthur, I'm certain of it. And it seemed to me that—" He searched for a way to explain it to her. "That the land itself was a sort of door. That Arthur reached out without effort and opened the land like a door, and passed through to—to—I can't think where. To another land, maybe."

"Then he's gone."

"Gone for now. I think he left because too many people want him. He was involved with a plot to kill the queen—"

"I know. Perhaps it's good he's gone—I don't think he understands the danger he's in."

"And now these people are looking for him, for their own reasons, whatever they are—"

He saw Alice hesitate. She knew something, he was certain of it. And she could not bring herself to tell him what it was because she had heard of his reputation: that he liked to gossip, liked rumor, liked to pass a tale back and forth.

She said nothing. "Who is Arthur, that he has such power?" he asked. "That he can travel through that land without being stopped by—by whatever lives there?"

She was not good at dissembling. He could see that she wanted to tell him, and that fear and caution stopped her. He had heard that she had been called before the queen's court, and that she had been nearly ordered to leave the Stationers' Company, and he understood that it would be dangerous for her to discuss these matters.

She could not talk to him, and Kit would not. He felt his need for information almost as a need for nourishment; he was famished for it. He would be discreet, he thought; he would show her that he was worthy of her trust, and she would begin to confide in him. Only that way could he answer to his own satisfaction the question of Arthur.

"I'll tell you if I discover anything," he said.

As he turned to go he saw Christopher across the press of people. Kit nodded to him. He felt almost as if he had received an answer to his vow; here, in front of Alice, he could show how little he discussed Arthur with his friends. He nodded back and stood his ground, waiting until the other man made his way to the stall.

"What have you been doing?" he asked Kit.

"Working. And you?"

Talking to Alice Wood, he thought, but he couldn't say that. "I walked a little," Tom said. "Wrote a letter to Gabriel Harvey." He had, in fact, written the letter a few days ago, and now he grinned to think of it. "I was writing my pamphlet against him and his brother, and I thought to read some poems that he had written, so that I might better take aim against him. And I read one that had six feet to the line, and then suddenly, hey, presto!—it had seven. So I wrapped his poem around a louse and then wrote underneath it, 'This verse has more feet than a louse,' and I sent it to him."

"Why do you so malign that man? I agree with you that he is an ass—"

"An ass? That prating weasel-faced vermin? That cheese-brained idiot—"

"An idiot, then. But surely you have better things to do than to set your pen against Gabriel Harvey. Why do you waste your time—"

"Why? It is a cause of great disquiet to me that he breathes the same air I do, that he and I are both alive at the same time. I will never leave him as long as I am able to lift a pen."

Christopher laughed. "You're back," he said. "I'm glad to see it."

"Back? What do you mean?"

"I mean that for some time you would talk about nothing but the land you claimed to have seen. It was almost as if you were

ill. And now you're well again—you have to be well if you're
back to plaguing the Harveys."

"It wasn't an illness," Tom said. "It's an enchantment.
They've enchanted me."

"You're fortunate I'm not your physician—I can see now I've
misjudged your symptoms completely. You're as sick as ever.
You've even got that silly flower in your hat."

"Aye, and what of it? Where do you think this flower comes
from? Why hasn't it faded in all these weeks?"

"I suppose because it's not a real flower."

"Not a real flower? Look at it, man—"

"Nay, I already know what I would find. You've had it made
by a skilled artificer."

"Why in God's name would I do that?"

"I don't know. Why do you persist in this obsession?"

"You're the one who's obsessed. You're the one who thinks
he knows the answer to every question. Who were those
strange men you saw at the palace? You've never found out,
have you? And yet I'll wager that those men had something to
do with Arthur."

"What if they did? I've finished with the task I was asked to
do. Whoever those men were they had nothing to do with the
conspiracy against the queen."

"You're wrong," Tom said, driven, once again, by the anger
he seemed to feel these days whenever he saw his friend. "You
can't possibly know that."

"Nay—I can't talk to you in this mood," Christopher said. He
spoke calmly, rationally, and Tom found that more infuriating
than anything he might say. "Let me know when you recover.
Good day." He left.

"You're not finished yet!" Tom said, shouting after him. "This
thing didn't end—there's more here than either one of us
knows!" But Christopher was lost in the crowd.

Suddenly he remembered Alice Wood. He had been aware of
her at first, had seen her laugh a little when he talked about
Gabriel Harvey, but in the heat of the argument he had forgotten her entirely. And what of his vow to say nothing to anyone

about Arthur? No wonder she didn't trust him; he wouldn't trust himself, if it came to that.

He took his leave of her, and, feeling friendless and desperately unhappy, he turned to go.

Christopher walked back to his lodgings outside the city walls, thinking of his conversation with Tom. Why should his friend be so certain that his task for the queen hadn't ended? It had indeed ended, and in more senses than Tom knew: Christopher would never have to work for Robert Poley again. He was done with secret errands, done with the whole shadowy world of eavesdroppers and hedge-creepers.

He had gone back to court for his final payment from the queen's councilors, and while there had met a distant cousin of Sir Francis Walsingham's, a young man named Thomas Walsingham. The young man had heard of him and had enjoyed his plays, and had offered to become his patron, freeing him from the necessity of writing a play or two a year. With the money from Thomas Walsingham Christopher had had the leisure to begin a poem. It was almost enough to restore his old belief in the Fates.

But nay—there were no Fates. People made their own destinies. Why did Tom cling to his superstitious ways? Why was he so obsessed with this nonsense? He remembered what Tom had said, that he was under an enchantment. If he thought of himself as enchanted wouldn't the result be the same as if he actually were?

He shook his head. People were stranger than you'd ever guess. Will Ryder, for example. He expected to be liked not because he had lived a privileged life, with folks deferring to his wealth and station, but because he was genuinely likeable. He had read what Christopher had written of the poem and had said, with what seemed like real warmth, that he'd rarely seen better. He'd asked countless questions about the theater, about London, about growing up in Canterbury. And he'd talked about his own life with a straightforwardness Christopher had found unusual.

But he couldn't escape his upbringing, and it showed at odd

moments. A few days ago they had gone to a dinner given by a friend of Will's, and halfway through the meal he had seen Will looking at him with an expression of mingled amusement and superiority. He couldn't understand why until he noticed that everyone else at the table was using strange utensils shaped like small pitchforks, that he alone ate his meat with his hand. "They're called forks," Will had whispered. "An Italian custom." After that Christopher had made it a point to leave his fork untouched, to cover his hands with as much grease as he could.

And Will was young, too, and sheltered in a way Christopher hadn't seen since Cambridge. The world of intrigue was new and exciting to him; his assignment from Essex, he had said ingenuously, was his first. He asked endless questions, and he gave away Essex's secrets with a profligacy Christopher found endearing.

The light began to fade as Christopher walked. He should be thinking about his poem. It would be evening soon, and he had added nothing to the poem since yesterday. Perhaps he was no true poet after all; perhaps he should stay with the stage, with what he knew. He had it in mind to write a play based on the life of Edward II from the *Chronicles,* based too on his discovery that people were much more complicated than they seemed.

But nay—hadn't Will said he liked the poem? He watched as dusk came down over the street before him. Will would be waiting for him at his lodgings. He hurried on before darkness fell.

September, 1592

14

The summer of 1592 was the hottest folks could remember in a long time, and the heat lingered on into September. The Thames dried up, and Alice heard of people who walked from shore to shore on the muddy bottom. At her station in the churchyard, looking out at the sparse crowds, she wondered if the Fair Folk had chosen this way to show their displeasure. Two years had passed since the battle she had witnessed and they had still not found Arthur.

But people had other worries beside the heat, for the summer had also brought the plague. Funeral processions, held late to discourage crowds, passed her house nightly; one had been for her assistant, who had died a week ago. In the neighborhood of Paul's alone she had counted four households with red crosses painted on the doors, a warning that those inside were infected. People with red wands, the sign of someone attending a family stricken with the plague, walked up and down the streets, knocking at doors.

Those who could leave London to visit friends or relatives had done so, and the ones who stayed rarely ventured out of doors. When they did they had identical stricken looks, as though they feared some great disaster were about to crush them, and they carried oranges stuck through with a stick of cinnamon or handkerchiefs drenched in white vinegar for protection.

Thomas Nashe, who knew everything, had told her that 1600 people died each week and warned her to leave London. Then he had followed his own advice and gone away, along with all the other poets who could find patrons in the country. She had stayed on, reasoning that if the plague had not killed her when she had nursed John she might be safe from its attack. But she had other, more complex, motives for staying. Arthur might return, and Brownie needed her help. And Walter was still in London, working at his stall.

Walter. She looked over to where he stood, as lacking in customers as she herself was. They had gone to plays over the years and had shared a few meals at the cookshop, but it was as she had thought—he did not seem interested in deepening their friendship. And with the playhouses closed by the city authorities because of the plague they had not seen much of each other recently. But she still sometimes felt a looseness, an excitement, when she saw him. It seemed to her that she had an illness even worse than the plague, worse because it would not end but lingered on year after year.

Anthony Drury, dressed once again in severe black, came into the churchyard and went over to talk to George. She frowned. George had been seeing much of the man, and she wondered if they still looked for Arthur. She thought that no good could come from George's association with Anthony, but she could not help but notice that his business prospered, that he had bought new copyrights and had hired a great many young men to work at his station. And with his prosperity had come a new authority; folks listened to his opinions more, and he was often called upon to speak at the stationers' meetings. There was even talk of making him an officer in the company. She wondered if he had persisted in his accusations against her. Sometimes when she passed through the churchyard she thought she saw people glance in her direction and then grow quiet, and she felt that some of the stationers had cooled toward her. But perhaps she only imagined it.

Anthony and George left the churchyard together. It might soon be time to leave herself; no one had come by her stall in the past hour. She glanced over at Walter one last time, then packed up her books and went home.

The air in the house was hot and stale. She opened the windows in her front room and then went to the kitchen. Brownie lay by the hearth, his triangular cap pulled down over his face.

He had been weak for months after the battle, but his wound had healed finally under her careful treatment. Afterward, though, he had become sullen, uncommunicative, almost unfriendly. In the mornings she sometimes found her hair plaited into elf-locks, or her butter rancid, or mounds of dust behind her bed. Once he had even turned her sideboard against the wall. She had needed the help of three strong men to turn it back again, hired men, for she had not wanted anyone from the churchyard to see it. He did almost no work, and while she hadn't rescued him to be her servant she could not help but resent him a little for it.

Now he sat up, his red cap dropping to the floor. He made no move to pick it up. She wondered if he expected their roles to reverse so that she became the servant and he the master, and she thought sharply that if that was the case she would throw him out into the streets to fend for himself. She had enough to do on her own.

"Ho," he said, rubbing his eyes. "Home so early?"

She had not heard him speak so much in a long time. To keep him talking she said, "Aye. Trade was bad today. Bad this entire summer, for that matter. Everyone's gone because of the plague."

"Plague?"

She looked at him in amazement. But the Fair Folk didn't become ill, didn't die, as far as she could tell, unless they were killed. The plague that caused her and her neighbors such fear and dread, that nearly ruled her life, meant nothing to him. Once again she thought of how much Brownie was like Arthur, but this time she understood why she made the comparison.

"Aye, the plague. Thousands have died already. You have to have heard something of it."

"Nay. I haven't left the house for a long time."

Perhaps it was the memory of John and how he had died that made her suddenly grow angry. "Nay. You stay in my home and do nothing but sour my beer. Why don't you go back to Oriana? You're certainly well enough."

To her surprise Brownie became angry too. "By wind and rain, did you think I wanted to be here? Did you think it was my idea? I would a thousand times rather be in the woods or fields, dancing with my friends."

"Then why do you stay?"

But Brownie had turned silent again, and she saw that he had given away more than he wanted. She pressed him. "You're not a help to me here. Don't think that I would miss you if you left. Truly it would be easier for me if you went away. George has told the other stationers that you're a demon."

Brownie backed toward the hearth, the way he had done the first night she had seen him. "I can't." He sounded wounded, unhappy.

"Why not?"

"The queen has commanded me to stay."

"Oriana? Why?"

"Because—" He sounded reluctant, but she saw that he wanted to tell her. "To spy on you."

"To spy—"

"Aye. In case Arthur comes back."

She could not help but feel a sense of betrayal. She had thought that Brownie stayed on, however reluctantly, out of loyalty to her, out of gratitude for the care she had given him. Now she saw that other forces operated here: they were all pawns in a larger game. "Go then. I won't be spied on."

"I can't. Queen Oriana won't have me."

She almost laughed. What could she do, throw him out of the house? She was not even certain how he had come to be there the first time. "Well, then," she said. "As long as you're here let's make the best of it. Why are you so unhappy?"

"You showed me to that man, the one with the hard face."

"I know, Brownie. That was a mistake. I won't do it again, I promise you."

"Aye, you will. You'll show me to the other one, the man who comes to your door sometimes."

"Walter? Don't worry about Walter—he won't be back."

"He will, though. You love him."

"How do you know that?" she said, sharper than she had intended. "You folks know nothing about love."

"We know some things. Love is a mystery to us, but we can recognize it in others. Someday you will forget your promise to me. You will be so happy to be with him, so eager to do something wonderful for him, that you will bring him inside and show me to him."

"Nay, Brownie. Trust me, please. That man will never bother you. I promise you this, by my hope of winning Arthur back."

He seemed to relax a little. She smiled at him and went to make herself a small supper, and that night, without saying anything to her, Brownie cleaned the dishes and pans.

Thomas Kyd walked through the deserted streets toward Paul's. Today, he thought, he would buy himself a book. Not a history book to base a play on, and not something written by one of his friends, but a book to read solely for enjoyment.

He smiled a little as he walked, thinking of the luxury he was about to allow himself. He had sold his play *Soliman and Perseda* before the closing of the playhouses, and for very nearly the first time in his life he felt he had enough money for his modest desires.

A woman carrying a basket and a red wand hurried down the street and stopped in front of a door marked with a red cross. The door opened, and a breath of rank contagion came from inside. Tom crossed the street quickly.

He turned to watch as the woman went inside the house, delivering food to those quarantined by the plague. What would it be like to minister to folks who were ill, to have to come in daily contact with the infection? Like living in London during the plague season, he thought, and abruptly his good humor vanished.

He had some money, true, but it would not stretch far enough to take him away from London. If he had a patron he could be out of the city, enjoying the healthy air of the country-side. Lord Strange, for example: Strange's company of actors performed everything he wrote. But no invitation from Strange had been forthcoming, and he could not help but feel a little resentful. How many years did a man have to serve his lord in order to receive favors from him?

A year ago he and Christopher had taken a room together, thinking that they both needed a place to write, but he had not seen Christopher since the plague began. He felt certain that unlike him the other man had found a patron. The thought galled him. How had Kit deserved such good fortune while he was left to struggle against the plague? But nay—it was best not to think of such things.

He glanced up the street and saw Arthur coming toward him.

He raised his hand to hail the man before he realized his mistake. This wasn't Arthur but some poor starving beggar, his clothes torn to rags and nearly falling off his shrunken frame. As he watched the man stumbled and went down.

Tom ran forward. It *was* Arthur, he saw now, but an Arthur strangely changed, with hollow eyes and a haunted expression on his face. What had happened to him in the two years since he'd seen him last? Tom's heart turned to see him looking so frail, so lost. "Arthur," he said, bending over the other man. "Arthur, are you ill? Do you need help?"

Arthur looked up. There was dirt caked in his hair and an open sore on one of his arms. "Where were you?" Tom asked.

"Dead," Arthur said. "I was dead and in heaven, or some place like it. Do they still search for me?"

"Who?"

"Everyone. Everyone wants me. Do you know why?" He looked around anxiously and then whispered to Tom, "Be-cause I'm king."

Tom looked around as well. If anyone heard them they could be arrested for treason. "Listen," he said, shaking Arthur's shoulders to make him pay attention. "Listen, Arthur—you must not say such things. Do you understand?"

"But it's true. They all told me so, in the country I went to—they told me I was king. It was because I'm a king that they wanted to—to—" His eyes clouded for a moment, and he shuddered. "So I opened a door and slipped away from them, to another land, and then to a land beyond that. There are as many countries in that place as there are drops of water."

"Don't say it even if it's true. They'll arrest you if you claim to be king. Do you understand? They're looking for you anyway, I heard—they think you had something to do with the plot against the queen."

Arthur looked up at that. "The queen?"

Tom sighed. What could he do with this man? The queen's men searched for him, and so, he knew, did Christopher and Tom Nashe. Nay, he would not allow this sad lunatic to fall into the hands of Tom and Kit, to be used for God only knew what purposes.

He straightened, and as he did so an idea came to him. He thought for a moment of the book he had been about to buy; he would not be able to afford it now. "Get up," he said, trying not to regret what he was about to do. "Please."

Arthur got to his feet and followed Tom for several yards before stopping and looking at the empty streets around him. "Where am I?" he said, his voice suddenly uncertain. "What country is this?"

Tom turned and stared at him in amazement. "England. London. Do you understand?"

"Oh, aye," Arthur said, sounding reassured. "I'm king here too, you know."

Tom walked faster, not caring now if Arthur followed him or not. They went through side-roads and alleys and came at last to Bishopsgate. Once through the city wall they passed St. Botolph's Church and then turned in at the gate to St. Mary of Bethlehem Hospital.

Tom stood in front of the asylum for a while, studying it: a long low building with two dark wings coming forward on either side. Would this be a good place for Arthur? He shrugged; he had no choice. He took Arthur gently by the hand and led him to the steward's office.

"Ah," the steward said as they came in. "Is he a relative?"

"Nay," Tom said. "A—a friend."

The steward frowned. "Lodging in Bedlam is not cheap."

"I—I'm prepared to pay. He has nowhere else to go, and I thought—well, I can't take care of him—"

"Ah." The steward nodded; apparently they were on more familiar ground here. "Good. Come with me."

Tom followed the other man down a brick corridor. The place was ill lit and smelled of sweat and urine and rotting straw. There were ten barred cells, five to a side, and in front of each of them stood the folks who had paid to view the lunatics. Inside the cells men and women laughed or pointed or shouted vile abuse. A few of them lay bound in chains. A woman stared at Tom with wide eyes as he passed. "I have to get a message to my daughter," she said. "Tell her—"

Tom looked around him in dismay. Surely he could find something better for Arthur than this prison. By what right did he think he could sentence Arthur here for what would probably be the rest of his life?

But what else could he do? He certainly couldn't turn him over to the queen's men; Arthur could be killed for treason if they found him. And he would not allow the poor man to be a pawn in Tom and Kit's intrigues. If Kit wanted Arthur he should have stayed in London and looked for him himself.

Arthur went meekly into the cell, and the steward closed the door and turned the key in the lock.

A few days later George went with Anthony to the house off Cheapside. The day had grown hot, and flies buzzed around the garbage in the streets. George felt weary; he wanted only to go home and rest. He had spent over two years with Paul Hogg, and while Hogg continued to give him coins from a seemingly endless supply he could not help but wish that they made more progress. Two years, and they still hadn't found Arthur.

Where was the boy? George remembered him from the churchyard: a simple dreamy lad, almost a half-wit. How had he managed to elude a man like Hogg, who seemed to have all knowledge at his command? And the Fair Folk searched for him

as well, both the red king and Oriana, and Alice and Margery . . .

George felt the silk lining on his jerkin and looked at the ruby
rings sparkling on his hand. It seemed to him that the more
riches he had the more he needed. His shop had expanded too
quickly, and then the plague had brought an end to a large part
of his trade. He owed money to some of his creditors, and to his
new workers and apprentices as well. When would they find
Arthur, and with him the final step in their search for gold?

A man lay in the street against one of the houses, trying to
take advantage of what little shade the wall offered. His mouth
was open and he panted shallowly. George looked away
quickly. A plague victim, probably, and who knew where the
illness would strike next? But if Hogg found the way to the
Philosopher's Stone he would live forever. The plague could
not touch him. The man said something in a weak voice, begging for alms, probably, and George and Anthony hurried on.

They entered the small house. It had grown more cluttered
since his first visit, more filled with glass and tubing, manuscripts and stones and vials of sulphur and salt and mercury. In
the past two years Hogg had gone through the remaining steps
in the alchemical process, all but the final one. At first George
had watched with great interest as Hogg heated and distilled
and purified, as he hunted for certain minerals by the light of
the moon. The substance in the alembic had grown red-hot,
turned black, become liquid, turned white. Hogg had clearly
reveled in the whole thing, carefully explaining why he sealed
the vessel when he did, why he warmed it with fire, why he
unsealed it again.

As the process dragged on, though, George had grown tired
of it. He wanted only the result, the Philosopher's Stone; how
Hogg got there was unimportant. Now, as he went inside, he
glanced at the alembic in its place on the floor, still unchanged.
He sighed.

Hogg welcomed him, his normally grave face shining with
pleasure. His assistant, the man with the stain on his doublet,
stood behind him in the shadows. "We found him," Hogg said
triumphantly. "We've found Arthur."

At last, George thought. "Where is he?"

"Look."

Hogg led him to the table and pointed to the scrying stone there. At first George could see nothing. Then it seemed as if a mist cleared away, and a picture formed of a beautiful young man with red hair and green eyes. The man burst into wild soundless laughter. "Is he enchanted?" George asked.

"I don't know," Hogg said. "That is what we must discover. Come."

George watched as Hogg traced a circle around the floor. Over the years he had become convinced that most of Hogg's conjuring, his Latin and Greek and other strange tongues, meant very little to the Fair Folk, that they came and went as they pleased. Sometimes they even appeared before Hogg had finished his invocation, breaking into the middle of his long and solemn chants.

Even more ominously, the folk sometimes came without being called at all. The green creature still followed Anthony at times, though it had not attacked him again, and Alice had her demon. And George had finally recognized the man with the water-stain as kin to the people who had fought against Oriana. He wondered if those who meddled with these folk somehow bound them unknowingly. Hogg had assured him that what they did was lawful, and so far George had not seen any evidence to the contrary. But lately, when he walked home, he heard the steps of someone—something—following him.

One of the green men appeared in the middle of Hogg's circle. George stepped back, still not used to the thing's sudden appearances, and the creature laughed, showing sharp crooked teeth. "We have found Arthur in the scrying glass," Hogg said to it. "But we cannot discover his whereabouts."

He indicated the glass on the table, among the litter of instruments. The image of Arthur laughed again, silently, and George shuddered. Now he noticed that the man in the glass seemed ill: he had grown thinner, and his hair was caked with dirt. His green eyes looked enormous in the thin face. What had happened to him?

"His whereabouts?" the creature said. "Oh, that's easy, very easy. Ask me something difficult." It hissed a little as it spoke, its words distorted by the long snout, the pointed teeth.

"Where is he?" Hogg said.

The creature laughed. "In Bedlam."

"Bedlam?" George said, forgetting to keep silent. "But we searched there. We went to all the hospitals."

The thing slowly turned its snout toward him. George tried and failed to meet its gaze. "Aye, Bedlam," it said. "You must go and bring him back for us." It vanished before Hogg could give it permission to go.

George looked at Hogg, hoping for an explanation. But the other man seemed confused, uncertain, and for once he said nothing. In the past two years George had grown used to relying on Hogg for guidance, and for a moment he felt frightened, alone. Then Hogg seemed to rouse himself, and the moment passed. "Come," the other man said firmly. "We'll go to Bedlam."

At the asylum Hogg walked up to the steward's office and knocked on the door, showing no trace of the doubts George had witnessed earlier. He talked with the steward a while and then paid the penny entrance fee for each of them. The steward pointed to the left wing and went back into his office.

George followed Hogg down the dark corridor, looking around him apprehensively. How had Arthur come to this dreadful place? Who had paid for his lodgings? If it had been Alice, wouldn't she miss him when they took him away?

He shook his head. It was not his place to ask such questions; no doubt Hogg knew what he was doing. George hurried after the other man.

Hogg stopped at the last cell. The young man they had seen in the scrying glass sat in the room, leaning against the wall. His clothes were torn and dirty and he seemed even thinner than he had in the glass. He had the look of someone who had been exposed to the elements for a very long time. Despite this, George felt jubilant. They had won; they had found Arthur first.

"Good day, Arthur," Hogg said pleasantly. "We've come to take you home."

Arthur laughed. Had he even heard the other man? It didn't matter: they would trade him to the red king and have done with him. "Come," Hogg said.

At this Arthur turned to him. "Where?" he said. His hand moved up and down by his side, as if to unseen music.

"I'm taking you home."

"Home? Where is that?"

"To your people, the Fair Folk." Hogg's voice was gentler and more persuasive than George had ever heard it.

"Ah." Arthur met the other man's eyes for the first time. "Will it be safe for me there?"

"Aye, very safe," Hogg said.

George looked away, hoping that his face did not betray his thoughts. He had never wondered what the red king wanted with Arthur, but now he felt certain that what the king had in mind would not be safe at all. Battles, probably, and harsh conquests, blood and war.

"Who are my people, then?" Arthur asked, plaintively. "Do you know? I know only that my mother is a queen."

A queen? George thought. What folly was this? Alice was Arthur's mother.

"This is no fit place for you, Your Majesty," Hogg said softly. "You should be at the front of your troops, leading them into battle."

"Aye." Arthur's green eyes seemed to shine in the dark room. "In battle. I fought, you know, when I left. I went to far countries, and men flocked to my banner. Aye."

Which side did he fight on? George wondered, but he thought that it probably didn't matter. The man had never held a lance or ridden a horse in his life.

"I saw many things, many strange sights," Arthur said. "Giants, and folks with tails and paws, and a sword that would fight by itself. And the solitary phoenix, the only one in the world, that dies and is reborn once every thousand years. And everywhere I went folks knew me, they bowed to me and did me honor. So I came home, thinking that I would have honor among my own people as well."

He stopped and looked around him, puzzled, as if coming

out of a dream. What he had claimed for himself was so at odds with his true surroundings that George expected him to veer off into madness again. Instead he looked closely at Hogg and said, "Who are you?"

"A friend," Hogg said.

"Aye? I wonder."

"Why should you wonder, Your Majesty? I'm here to take you to your people, your subjects. They're waiting for you. They need to be shown a true leader."

Arthur seemed to think it over. His hand moved to the music again, up and down, up and down. They could force him, of course, but it would be easier, and attract less attention, if he would agree to go with them. George stepped closer to the bars of the cell. "Come, Your Majesty. Do you remember me? I was a friend of yours, in the churchyard."

"Nay, I won't go there again. Go away, all of you! Alice Wood is not my mother—my mother is a queen!"

Hogg turned to George angrily. "Nay, we won't make you go to the churchyard," George said, as gently as he could. His heart was beating very fast. What if Arthur would not leave now, what if he had ruined everything? Arthur had to agree. "We're here to take you to your true family, not to Alice. Alice has lied to you all these years, do you understand? She's not your mother."

George nodded, satisfied. What did it matter if he hadn't told Arthur the truth? Alice had lied often enough on other subjects; she was a liar. And he would say anything if only Arthur would leave with them. He did not think he could face Hogg if they had been unsuccessful.

"Very well," Arthur said finally. He stood up, bracing himself against the wall as he did so. George wondered how long he had sat there. "I'll come with you."

His tone was that of a monarch commanding his subjects. For a moment George forgot who the other man was and what they planned to do with him, and nearly jumped to do his bidding. Then he looked about him and remembered.

"Good," Hogg said. "I'll get the steward to release you." He went back down the corridor and returned with the steward,

who now held a ring of keys in his hand. Hogg gave him a
number of gold coins and the other man opened the door. Then
he backed away, bowing. Hogg went into the cell and led the
Prince of Faerie outside.

15

In Shoreditch, just a few streets away from Bedlam Hospital, Robert Greene lay dying. A month ago he had dined with Tom Nashe on Rhenish wine and pickled herring, and he thought it was this rather than the plague that made him grow weaker and weaker, until he finally took to his bed. Now he lay in the house of Master and Mistress Isam, a shoemaker and his wife who been kind enough to take him in, and he thought about his life.

He would go to hell unless he repented, there was no question of it. He had deserted his wife and child after running through his wife's dowry, he had fathered a bastard child on Em of Holywell Street, he had sold his play, *Orlando Furioso,* to two companies of actors, first to the Queen's Men and then the Admiral's Men. Well, but what of it? He needed to eat, didn't he?—and the money paid to playwrights would not keep a dog alive. It was not his fault he had been forced into these and other tricks: he had had hard luck, and then he had fallen into bad company . . .

Aye, bad company. He had not seen Tom Nashe for nearly a year, but when they met again they had returned immediately to their old habits, eating and drinking heavily and carousing in the streets. If he went to hell it would be the fault of companions like Tom, Tom and that damned atheist friend of his, Kit Marlowe.

He groaned to think of the last meal he and Tom had shared, and its aftermath. His belly had swollen upward until he felt it would burst. He wished he hadn't gone with Tom. He wished many things, that he hadn't left his wife, hadn't come to London . . . His entire life could have been different, richer, happier— and he would not now be lying in this strange house, dying and about to go to hell.

Hell. He had repented of his life before, but now for the first time he thought he truly understood what it meant to be damned. Terror rose up in him like bile, until it seemed to drive every other feeling out, until he seemed made of fear. "Oh, no end is limited to damned souls," he thought, and the aptness of the quotation pleased him, made him forget his pain for a while, until he remembered it had been written by that un-believer Marlowe. How could the man have known?

There had to be something he could do, some bargain he could strike. If he repented, if he showed that he was sincere about repenting . . .

He called weakly to Mistress Isam. She had been in another room but she heard and came hurrying toward him, wiping her hands on her apron. She had strange notions about poets and playwrights: she thought that they deserved to be honored, and so she had kept him in her house and nursed him through his illness though he owed her at least ten pounds. He was grateful to her for that, and for the enthusiasm with which she talked about his plays and books, but he could not help but feel a little impatient with her. She moved so slowly, and when she started talking it was difficult sometimes to get her to stop. But how could he complain? Without her aid he would be dying on the streets.

"What is it, Master Greene?"

"I need pen and paper. Please."

She brightened. "Of course." No doubt she thought he was about to compose something brilliant. And perhaps he would at that. He smiled at her when she brought him what he'd asked for, sat up painfully and dipped his pen in the ink. If he had to die he would at least leave a legacy for his friends. They could learn where he had been too blind to see.

Feeling noble and full of purpose, he wrote: "To those Gentleman that spend their wits in making plays." And then, "If woeful experience may move you (Gentlemen) to beware . . ."

September gave way to October. The days cooled slightly and the plague abated, and some of those who had fled London returned.

Christopher walked from his lodgings to the river, and then hired a boat to take him to the Ryders' manor. He and Will had gone their separate ways for a few months, had each left London to escape the plague, but on his return he had sensed a distance in Will that had not been there before.

He wondered what had happened between them. He had never met anyone as even-tempered as Will, and yet lately they had had one quarrel after another, usually over something so trifling he could not remember what had started it. And the last time they had met Will had said, "I'm going home. I'm not going to argue with you. You know everything, anyway."

Hadn't that been one of the first things Will had said to him: "You seem to know something about everything"? He'd thought that Will had admired that in him, that that was a good trait, not a bad one. How had that changed? Should he pretend to be as ignorant as Will's foolish friends? Most of them hadn't even been able to graduate from the universities their fathers sent them to.

He wondered, though, if Will objected to something else. Will had said several times that Geoffrey disliked it when he went to visit Christopher, that his brother had threatened to tell their father. "And my father," Will had said, "has warned me often enough about the sin of Sodom."

Will's father had been the one who had said that unbelievers brought the plague upon themselves, Christopher remembered. He thought the man must be a singularly joyless individual. "The sin of Sodom," he said. "I always wondered what the sin of Gomorrah would be. And if I would enjoy it."

Will hadn't laughed. "I'm serious, Kit," he said. "He could disown me if he knew what I've been doing. And Geoffrey might just tell him, out of—out of meanness, perhaps, or perhaps he wants to inherit everything."

"Your brother," Christopher said, remembering a quoted line of poetry, "does not sound like a very pleasant person."

"Nay," Will had said, and Christopher had wondered, as he wondered from time to time around Will, how much the other man knew.

Now, going up the steps to the Ryders' manor, he thought about Geoffrey again. Would the man truly disown his brother? What would happen to Will then? Well, perhaps it would be good for him, show him how everyone else had to live. But what would he do? How would he survive?

He knocked on the door and the elderly servant let him in. Geoffrey came to greet him. "Where's Will?" Christopher asked.

"He's not here," Geoffrey said.

"I didn't ask you if he was here. I asked you where he was."

"Ah. I was getting to that. He's gone to France."

"France?" Christopher felt as if he had walked into a room he believed was solid and felt the floor give way beneath him. "Why?"

For a moment, he saw, Geoffrey had been tempted to give a hurtful answer: "To get away from you," or some such reply. But then Geoffrey's face changed and he saw that the other man was about to tell the truth, or what passed for the truth with him. "He's gone to Rheims. To the Catholic seminary there."

At first Geoffrey's answer made no sense at all, like a line of nonsense in a ballad. He tried to think. "To the— But why?"

"I don't know. Our father," Geoffrey said, moving toward the door to signify that the interview was at an end, "is not pleased."

Thomas Kyd sat in the room he shared with Christopher and stared at the piece of paper in front of him. He had gone to Bedlam earlier that day, intending to make that month's payment for Arthur's lodgings, but the steward told him that someone had come for Arthur, a man claiming to be a relative. The steward had described the man but Tom could not think who he might be. A relative, though: that sounded promising. He hoped that Arthur was safe and well cared for.

Tom sighed and looked around the room. Almost immediately after he and Christopher had taken the room he had begun to regret his decision. Sometimes Kit would come in for a few minutes, scribble something on a piece of paper and then leave. At other times he would stay on from morning to evening, lighting candles against the dark, covering pages and pages. To Tom, writing was a job like any other. He came in for the day and left when the day was done, and he had assumed that Kit would feel the same way. But when he had questioned the other man about it Kit had only laughed.

There were other problems as well. Christopher scattered papers throughout the room, letters and books and manuscripts. Once, on a day when he had felt dull and tired and Christopher had been off somewhere, Tom had sneaked a look at some of the pages. He had paid dearly for his sin, though, for what he had seen had been a poem so beautiful he had been unable to write for a week. And yet after that it seemed as if he couldn't help himself: he read the poem guiltily every chance he got, watching as the story of the love between Hero and Leander took shape before him on the page. He knew that Kit wrote better poetry than he did (though perhaps, if it was not boasting to say it, he liked to think that his own plays were better constructed), but it seemed unfair to have to be reminded of that fact day after day.

The door slammed behind him and he looked around. Christopher stood there, back after an absence of several months. "Care to take a walk with me?" he asked.

That was another problem with sharing a room with Kit: sometimes, on the days he didn't feel like working, his friend would try to talk him into going out into London. "Nay," Tom said, turning back to his work. "Where have you been?"

"Canterbury," Christopher said, and Thomas nearly jumped from his seat. He would have sworn that the other man had been behind him, but somehow he had gone over to his desk by the window. He seemed to move at a different pace than other people, though Tom noticed that when they walked together he went slowly, almost languidly.

"Escaping the plague?"

"Visiting my family. Fighting a duel."

Like Thomas Nashe, Kyd sometimes wondered what his friend did in the time he wasn't working. But unlike Nashe, Kyd thought that he probably didn't want to know. Back in January Christopher had told him a story about being arrested for counterfeiting in the Netherlands, and while Tom hadn't disbelieved him exactly he had thought that for his own peace of mind he had better change the subject. Now he did the same. "The plague's nearly over, they say."

"Aye. Let's go."

"I'm busy here."

"Come, we'll be back in an hour. I promise."

"Nay. I know your hours."

"Two hours, then. You're hungry, aren't you?"

He was. He had known from the first that he wouldn't be able to resist his friend. Sighing, he stood and carefully put away the pages he had written that day. He didn't think that Kit would want to read them, but then Kit probably thought the same of him.

They went out into the street. A cool breeze blew and he walked into it gratefully. His friend had been right: he had needed to get outside for a few hours.

On Cheapside a vagabond in torn and dirty clothing came toward them, a begging bowl held out in his hands. "Masters, please," he said. "A penny, a groat, anything you can spare. I've been turned off my lands, my wife and children are dead of the plague . . ."

Kit moved past him, but Tom fumbled in his purse and dropped a coin in the bowl. "Thank you, master, thank you, kind sir," the vagabond said, and moved on.

Kit turned to Tom in astonishment. "You don't believe that he was truly turned off his lands, do you? Or any of those other lies he told you?"

Tom shrugged. "What if he was?"

"What if he wasn't?"

"He was suffering—"

"Oh, aye. You write plays and you know nothing of disguises."

"—and so at least I've done some good," Tom said, ignoring the other man.

"That's right, I forgot. You believe that goodness is rewarded."

Tom said nothing. He had learned over the years not to argue with his friend. Suddenly he noticed that they had gone past all the stalls and cookshops on Cheapside. "I thought we were going to eat," he said.

"Later."

"Where are you going?"

"Paul's."

"Paul's?" Tom said, hurrying after him. "Why?"

"I heard that Robin's book has come out. The last one. His deathbed confession."

Tom had heard of Robert's book too. Folks whispered that it was filled with scandal, with revelations about poor Robin's life and his last hours. If the book had truly appeared it would be worth postponing his meal for a few hours. He should have known that Kit had had something planned, that he would not be getting back to his work that day. It seemed that something extraordinary and exciting always happened whenever he went out with his friend; he wondered how the man could stand an entire diet of it.

They went inside the churchyard. Tom had never seen so few people there, had never heard it so quiet; the plague still kept most folks indoors. Kit nodded to some of the stationers as they passed but did not talk to any of them; it seemed he would not be moved from his original purpose.

Suddenly, though, he stopped and pointed across the yard. "Is that— Aye, there he is. Look, quickly, it's Gabriel Harvey!"

Tom followed his gaze. A middle-aged man with large quantities of lace at his neck and wrists was making his way slowly through the courtyard. As they watched he adjusted his clothing, patted down his jerkin, smoothed his mustache and then walked off with a satisfied air.

"Doctor Harvey!" Kit said, shouting across the yard.

"What are you doing?" Tom asked, whispering.

"I want to wish him good day. Don't you want to talk to him?"

"Of course not. Why should I involve myself in Tom Nashe's silly feud? I don't even know the man."

"Time you got acquainted, then."

Gabriel Harvey saw them at that moment. "Doctor Harvey!" Kit said again, but the other man seemed as reluctant to meet as Tom was. He turned and almost ran out of the yard.

Kit laughed for a long time. "The terrible Doctor Harvey," he said finally. "I wonder why it is he angers Tom so. Why does he waste his time with that man?"

"One of those trifling feuds that neither one can finish, I suppose. Let's get what we came for and go."

But Kit had one more stop to make, at Edward Blount's stall. There he talked to the publisher about the poem he was writing, assuring the other man that with the playhouses closed due to the plague he would have more time to work on it. Tom listened a little enviously. No one had ever been that interested in his poems. His hunger returned, and while the two men talked he browsed through the books on the neighboring stall.

"Look, Kit," he said. "Nashe's book. *Pierce Penniless*."

"Aye, and we'll take that one too," Kit said, breaking away from his conversation. He took sixpence out of his purse and gave it to a pleasant-looking woman at the stall. Where does he get his money? Tom thought. He had heard rumors of a wealthy patron.

They went by William Wright's stall and picked up *Greene's Groatsworth of Wit*, heard talk of another book called *The Repentance*, bought that one too, and then made their way out of the churchyard. Just as they were leaving Tom Nashe came in through the entrance.

"We just saw your friend Harvey," Kit said. "If you hurry you can catch him."

"Nay," Nashe said, and to Tom Kyd's surprise he looked a

little uneasy. "I don't—I've said everything I had to say to him and his brother Richard in my book. That book," he said, pointing to *Pierce Penniless* in Kit's hand. "I hear he came to London just to write his reply to me. Came in the middle of the plague, while thousands died all around him." He laughed.

"Are you thirsty? Come, let's go to a tavern and look at the books we bought."

"Groatsworth of Wit," Nashe said, noticing it for the first time. "I doubt you'll like that one, Kit."

"Why not?"

"Ah. You'll see for yourself."

They made for a tavern close by that Nashe knew. Tom Kyd thought that this was the first time they had all been together in months, perhaps in years, and that it had taken Robert Greene's death to accomplish it. They had been busy with their work and their patrons, and over the years they had drifted apart. And Kit and Tom Nashe had had some sort of falling out, though he didn't know the details: Kit had told him only that he thought Nashe had lost his wits. Maybe poor Robin would work some good, then, especially if his book made Kit think over his life. *The Repentance:* it seemed a promising title.

They were the only ones in the tavern. Most folk avoided crowded places during the plague and the host approached them a little cautiously, as if afraid they might be infected. Tom Kyd was finally able to order his meal. Nashe leafed through the books they had brought.

" 'First in all your actions set God before your eyes,' " he read in a solemn voice.

"A Puritan!" Kit said. He reached for the book but Tom Nashe moved it away and continued reading.

" '. . . for the fear of the Lord is the beginning of wisdom . . .' "

This time Kit managed to take the book from him. He turned a page and read a little to himself, and Tom Kyd saw his face change. "What is it?" he asked.

" 'Wonder not,' " Kit read, " 'that Greene, who hath said with thee (like the fool in his heart), There is no God, should now give glory unto His greatness—' "

"Is he writing about you?" Tom Kyd asked.

"Aye." His face had grown intent, almost hard. There was no other sound in the room. "Listen. 'Why should thy excellent wit, His gift, be so blinded, that thou shouldst give no glory to the giver?' " He looked down the page. " 'Defer not (with me) till this last point of extremity; for little knowst thou how in the end thou shalt be visited.' Oh, the hypocrite! Oh, the damned wretched hypocrite!"

"He deals as badly with me," Tom Nashe said.

"Did you know about this?" Kit asked.

Nashe nodded. Tom Kyd thought that just once in his life he would like to have heard some piece of news before the other man. "The printer told me a few days ago. Robin was not like this when I dined with him, I assure you."

Kit began to read again. " 'Sweet boy, might I advise thee, be advised, and get not many enemies by bitter words . . .' You are the sweet boy, I take it. Had he lost his wits when he wrote this?"

"Does he mention me?" Tom Kyd asked.

Kit laughed suddenly. "You? Nay, it seems he overlooked you. The only playwright in London, I fear." He looked down the page. "Who is this here? 'An upstart Crow, beautified with our feathers . . . the only Shake-scene in a country.' "

"I think I met him once," Tom Nashe said. "An actor who wanted to write plays. Shake—Shakes something. I can't remember now."

Kit pushed back his thick hair and paged through the book. Tom Nashe picked up *The Repentance*. " 'It is better to die repentant than to live dishonest,' " he read in his Puritan's voice, seeming anxious to fill up the silence.

"Aye, and best of all to do both, it seems," Kit said, looking up from his book.

"How can you mock the dead?" Tom Kyd said.

"Mock him? He mocks me, and from the grave, too, where he's safe from my answer. What did he think I would do when I read this, change my ways? Nay, I'm certain that he didn't think of me at all."

"What will you do?" Tom Nashe said.

"Do? Nothing. What should I do?"

"Harry Chettle saw this through the press after Robin died. I know the man—we can go to him and demand an apology, demand he publish something, I don't know . . ."

Kit looked at him levelly and he stopped. "Why?"

"So that— What he says here is dangerous, Kit. If everyone in London knows your views you could be arrested, or—"

"Nay, nothing will happen to me."

"You don't know that. Come, we'll go to him together—"

"Nay. Let it stand."

"But people will think—"

"Let them. I don't care."

Tom Kyd saw with surprise that Kit meant it, that if he had been angry a moment ago it had passed. He thought that he would never understand the man, not if he knew him for a hundred years.

The talk changed; now Kit and Tom Nashe were going over all that had happened since they had seen each other last. It seemed that Kyd would have to hear the story about counterfeiting in the Netherlands after all.

"But why were you in the Netherlands to begin with?" Tom Nashe asked.

"Someone there wanted to publish some translations I did, a book of Ovid's poetry. I met up with a goldsmith, a man who said he could show me how to make coins. I was curious to see it, and I went with him. And the authorities caught up with us, and I was sent back to England." He laughed.

"But why should you want to make coins?" Tom Kyd asked.

"Why? Think of it, man! If I could make my own money I would never have to bow to a patron again. Or change a scene for an actor who didn't understand what I'd written, or write a pretty dedication that came to nothing . . ."

Was he serious? Tom Kyd knew that his friend often said things only for the effect they had. He tried to keep his face impassive, tried not to let Kit see that his talk had shocked him. But he must have given something away, because Kit turned to him and said, "Well, why shouldn't I? I have as good a right to coin as the queen of England."

* * *

A few days later Tom Kyd sat at his desk and tried to concentrate on the work before him. Christopher was out somewhere—God knew where—and Tom had given in to temptation once more and read what he had added to his poem. But when he'd turned back to his own play it had seemed awkwardly written, each word leaden and colorless.

He sighed and looked around. Kit had left the books he'd bought, balanced precariously on top of a stack of other books and manuscripts, and Tom stood and went over to look at them. He picked up Nashe's *Pierce Penniless* and began to page through it.

Almost at once he came to what Tom had written about Gabriel Harvey's brother Richard. "Thou great baboon, thou pygmy braggart, thou pamphleteer of nothing . . . Off with thy gown and untruss, for I mean to thrash thee mightily."

Were these insults a fit subject for a writer? Apparently so, apparently, as Greene had shown, one could write a book about anything. Kyd read on in amazement, coming to Nashe's words on Richard Harvey's book *The Lamb of God:* "I could not refrain but bequeath it to the privy, leaf by leaf as I read it, it was so ugly, dorbellical and lumpish. Monstrous, monstrous . . . not to be spoken of in a Christian congregation . . ."

Robert Greene had been right: Nashe could only make enemies with these words. Robert had been right about a great many things, Tom Kyd thought; both the men he had mentioned could profit from his words, if only they would listen. But nay, they were too fond of their follies, each of them.

He could not help but wish, though, that Robert had said something about him. It was foolish, he knew, but he saw that this book would be read by all of London, that the playwrights in it would be discussed for years to come. If, God forfend, he should die now of the plague, would any remember him in even ten years' time?

Nay, this was nonsense. Fame meant nothing; it was important only to live a modest, sober, industrious life. In ten years' time these men might be dead of their follies, dead or suffering some other punishment sent by God. Already God had seen fit to take away one of their number. But if he lived properly and safely, taking care to keep away from all their excesses, he would not share their fate.

Satisfied, he went back to his work, and wrote until the light faded.

16

Paul Hogg looked up from his stack of books. Arthur sat slumped against the wall like one of the boneless creatures; Hogg knew that he could stay there for hours, getting up only two or three times a day.

He had spent the last few days talking to the man, asking him questions in a gentle voice and waiting patiently for an answer. The red king had sent messengers to collect Arthur but Hogg had put them off. He thought that he would never get another chance like this one, and he was anxious to learn what Arthur knew.

He turned a page of the book in front of him. "The end of alchemy is in celebration, reconciliation, the marriage of the red man and the white lady . . ." he read.

What did that mean? He understood, of course, that writers on alchemy could not speak clearly about what they knew, that this knowledge had to be kept secret, hidden from the multitudes. Still, he wished that the books could be a little more forthcoming. Most alchemists thought the words referred to sulphur and quicksilver, but he had tried those substances in his last experiment and nothing had happened. The red man was blood, perhaps, and the white lady was then—what? Milk?

Nay, it was ridiculous. It had been nearly a year since he had performed the eleventh alchemical step, and he had stalled there, with no idea how to proceed. He had asked Arthur, but the other man hadn't seemed to know.

Perhaps Arthur was what George believed him to be, a lunatic, the half-mad son of Alice Wood in the churchyard. But the more he spoke to Arthur the more certain he became that the man's silence hid knowledge, perhaps a vast knowledge.

How could he take that knowledge away from him? Maybe he had asked the wrong questions; maybe he had been too elusive, like the books he read. What if Arthur only waited for an honest, forthright question—what if the secret of wisdom lay in openness, in revealing, not concealing?

Reveal, not conceal, he thought. It went against everything he knew. He decided to try it anyway: he had a few days, at best, before the king would force him to surrender Arthur.

He moved to the floor and sat next to the other man. "Do you know how to change lead into gold?" he asked in a low voice.

Arthur laughed but said nothing. The music seemed to play in his head again; he moved his hand in time to it, up and down.

A man who searched for the secrets of the alchemists learned patience, if nothing else. "Do you know how to make the Philosopher's Stone?" Hogg asked.

"Aye."

"Aye?" His heart beat faster; he had been right. "How?"

Arthur looked directly at Hogg, his green eyes wide. "I can change lead into gold. Any king can."

"Here," Hogg said, trying not to sound too eager. He went to the table and brought back a piece of lead. "Change that to gold," he said, giving it to Arthur.

Arthur took the lead and let it drop to the floor. He looked at Hogg again. "When will I see my family?"

"Soon, Your Majesty," Hogg said. One of his guesses about Arthur was that the man was not a lunatic at all but a true son of Faerie, a child of either Oriana or the king. The guess made him happy; he might have knowledge few other people had. It was not the need for wealth that made him search for the

Philosopher's Stone; he had more than enough. If he wanted, he could move from this mean house to one of the manors by the riverside. It was knowledge, the idea that Nature had yielded up one more of her secrets. He needed the Stone to live forever, and he needed to live forever to learn everything there was to learn.

"Who were your parents?" he asked, hoping to take advantage of Arthur's sudden willingness to answer questions.

"My father was a king. My mother was a queen."

"King of what?"

Arthur said nothing. Hogg looked at the wall, thinking of his next question. When he turned back he saw that the lump of lead was now shining gold.

George woke, gasping. He had dreamed of something moving in his house, something stealthy and unwholesome. Now, as he lay still, he thought he could smell the odor of stagnant pools, of hot decaying marshland. He tried not to move.

A silver ewer clattered to the floor. George clenched his teeth, trying not to cry out. "George," a voice said. George could hear the thing's difficulty in speaking though the pointed snout, the crooked teeth.

George said nothing. "George," the creature said again. "You must see to it that Paul Hogg gives us Arthur. He must not be allowed to keep him."

"Tell him yourself," George said, and then cursed himself for replying. Now it would know where he was. But what could they do to him, after all? Hogg had called them the creatures of light; the night must limit their powers.

The thing did not answer. George realized that they could not reach Hogg, that the man's protective circles had served some purpose after all. They hoped to get to Hogg through him. "I'll tell him," he said. "Leave me alone, please." He was ashamed to hear his voice tremble.

"Ahhhh," the creature said.

Something else laughed. There were two of them then, two or more. "Please," he said again.

Wild laughter came from the darkness. He heard things being

thrown through the room, stools and candlesticks and pewter plates. His table fell over heavily. What more did they want from him? He had already agreed to help them.

Then there was silence. He lay in the darkness for a long time, too frightened to get up and look at the shambles the creatures had made of his room. Perhaps they were still there, waiting for him. He remembered what they had done to Anthony. The lubber-fiends, he thought, recalling the word from his childhood. They were not demons, not the children of Cain like Oriana's people, but creatures from old stories women would tell by the fire late at night. The lubber-fiends will come for you, his mother had said once, when he had disobeyed her.

He should leave Hogg's service, go back to the churchyard and ply his trade in peace. But would Hogg let him do that? He was in this business too deeply already. And he didn't know the extent of the other man's power: Hogg might call the lubber-fiends down on him, or change all his gold into coal, and then where would he be?

The room began to lighten around him: dawn was coming. He rose and looked around. Books had been torn apart and pages flung across the floor, candles trampled underfoot, their wax ground into the rushes. One of his windows had been broken; he wondered how he had missed the sound of the crash.

He righted the table and began to clean up the room. An hour later a great weariness overtook him and he went back to bed. He sighed as he drifted off toward sleep, comforted by the daylight shining through the window; he would not be going to the churchyard until much later, maybe not at all.

It was evening by the time he awoke. His head felt filled with bombast, his mouth dry. He looked around in confusion. Where was he? Why hadn't he gone to the churchyard?

The setting sun reminded him. Through his window he could see the houses outside grow darker and he felt his terror return. A chance noise in the street set his heart to beating wildly. Shadows pooled in the corners of his room.

He could not stay here, he thought, rising and putting on

fresh clothes. A glance in his looking-glass showed him that his eyes were shadowed and hollow-looking, his mouth drawn. He left the house quickly, seeking company.

He headed toward a tavern on Cheapside, a place frequented by some of the stationers. Alice would not be there; women generally did not enter the tavern alone. He hurried down the streets, looking forward to the glow of firelight and good company. But when he got there he saw that the tavern was almost deserted; fear of the plague had kept most people home. Only Edward Blount and a few other men sat at a table by the wall, talking in low voices.

He joined them, calling to the serving-woman for more beer for everyone. One or two of the men gave him an expression he had come to know well, gratitude and envy and a sort of stupefied puzzlement. He knew what they thought: Why did he thrive while they had to struggle? How had he come by his riches in the middle of a plague year?

As the serving-woman brought the drinks, though, he began to regret his generosity. He was still in debt, still struggling to find ways to pay his creditors. Though Hogg continued to give him gold it seemed as if he would never have enough; he could always think of new ways to spend his money.

"I don't think the plague's ending," one of the men was saying, answering something Edward Blount had said. "I sold two books today. Let's close the churchyard completely—the longer we keep it open the more we risk infection."

"Folks expect us to be there," Edward said. "What else can they do during a plague season but read?"

"Aye, when even the whores are poxed," one of the men said.

A few of the others laughed. George frowned. He did not like to hear women talked of so insolently.

"We should have revoked Mistress Wood's membership when we had the chance," one of the men said, drinking deeply.

Edward looked at him in astonishment. "Do you hold Mistress Wood responsible for the plague?" he asked.

"I don't know," the man said. "We can't know, can we? So it's best not to take any chances."

"Why in God's name would she cause a plague?" Edward asked. "She stands to lose as much by it as anyone else."

Aye, she did, George thought. Hungry and thick-headed from his fitful sleep, a little giddy from the beer, he wondered for the first time if Edward could be right after all. True, he had seen one of the fiends in her house, but they had come to his house as well; they answered to Paul Hogg and they seemed to plague Anthony. Could Hogg be wrong about them? Were they all the children of Cain, or were they something else, something outside Hogg's philosophy? He didn't know. He only knew that he didn't want to spend another night like the last one, that he wished he could be free of them.

A picture of Alice rose in his mind. For the first time in years he saw her without her demon, saw the clean, modestly dressed woman who had first attracted him.

"There's something strange about Mistress Wood, though," the man said. "The queen thought so too, remember? She was called before the court and made to answer questions."

"Aye, two years ago," Edward said. "Whatever questions the queen had were taken care of long ago."

"But what did they ask her? She never said, did she?"

"She never said because it was no one's business," Edward said, angry now. "Because malicious gossips like yourself would be quick to make something evil of it."

"Something about her son, wasn't it?" the other man went on, unperturbed. "Whatever happened to him? What kind of mother would misplace a son like that?"

"Oh, her son's back," George said.

Everyone turned to look at him. What had he done? The words had left his mouth before he'd been aware of them. Had he wanted to clear Alice's name somehow?

All the men at the table began to talk at once. "Where?" "How do you—" "What—"

George thought quickly. He had allowed his doubts to get the better of him, had given in for a moment to sentimentality.

He called for another round of beer to cover his confusion. "I—I saw him on the streets a few days ago."

"Where?" Edward asked.

"Cheapside, I think."

"Did you tell Mistress Wood?"

"Nay, I—I thought he was headed for the churchyard. I didn't want to interrupt their meeting."

"I never saw him there. Are you certain you're telling us everything you know?"

George nodded. He had been foolish, very foolish. Hogg would be furious if he found out what George had done.

Edward looked unconvinced. The other men returned to their drinks, and to talk about the plague, but George could barely follow the conversation.

Why had he thought to question Hogg's knowledge, so much greater than his own? Why should he doubt now, just when they were about to discover the answers they sought? They were close, so close. In a few days they would exchange Arthur for the secrets of the Philosopher's Stone. Riches and eternal life—what could Alice, or anyone else, offer that would better that?

Alice opened her stall and set the books out in neat rows in front of her. Until she had married she had only known how to spell her own name. She had seen her brothers (farmers now, all but the youngest, who had died of smallpox) go off to the small village school, and she had never even thought to wonder what they did there, or what she was missing. Her mother needed help with the household, and she had to learn the arts that would get her a husband: sewing, cooking, cleaning.

When she married John, though, she had been amazed at how many books the man brought home. Her family had had the Geneva Bible and nothing else, and even that had disappeared during the reign of Queen Mary. They had thought books strange, almost foreign, like the tobacco brought from the New World. At first John read aloud to her each night, books of romance and voyages of discovery, plays in which he took each of the parts in turn. Then, over her reluctance, he began to teach her to read.

She had had no idea of the kinds of things to be found in books: recipes, and how to cure wounds, and histories, and old poems. All the knowledge of the world was there; she had only to turn back a cover and she would be transported to some other place and time. Now she found it almost amusing that the stationers had accused her of witchcraft: they themselves practiced a kind of magic no witch could ever equal.

She picked up a book and paged through it. Usually the press of business kept her from looking through her wares, but folk still stayed away from the churchyard and she had time for luxuries like this one. She admired the neat rows of the letters, like a plowed field, the vellum binding, the way the whole thing was stitched together. Her printer may have been rude and surly but he did good work; everyone agreed on that.

A shadow fell over her stall and she looked up. Edward stood there, looking worried. "I talked to George yesterday," he said. "He said he's seen Arthur."

"Arthur! Where?"

"On Cheapside. He said he didn't tell you because he thought Arthur was going to meet you."

"I never saw him."

"Nay. There's something George isn't telling us. I never trusted that man."

"I think—I think he wants Arthur too. He and that friend of his, that man in black. What if they've found him? What will they do to him?"

"If I know George he'll turn him over to the queen. I heard Arthur was involved with that plot, the attempt on her life—"

Alice nodded, not trusting herself to speak. Edward knew George, but he didn't know Oriana and the red king. George could do worse things than give Arthur to Queen Elizabeth.

She looked across the churchyard and watched as George set out his books. Then she turned back to Edward and began to close up her stall. It was time to visit Margery.

* * *

Agnes opened the door to Margery's cottage. After the battle she had stayed on to help Margery with her work. Her husband was dead, she had explained, and she had little to do in the village in any case, since many of the farmers had moved to London. As always the woman annoyed her; Alice's own husband had died as well, but she hadn't run to Margery asking to be taken in. Still, Agnes had proved useful to Margery, assisting at births and bringing a little order to the cottage. And as the plague had worsened she and Margery worked day and night, mixing medicine to bring to those who were stricken.

"George says he's seen Arthur," Alice said.

Margery looked up at that. She had been stirring something in a large pot, and some of it, a brown sticky paste, had found its way into her hair. "Did he say anything else?"

"He doesn't talk to me, you know that. But I'm afraid that they've found him, that they'll—"

"If they've found Arthur you can be sure he's with Hogg, not George," Margery said, talking more to herself than Alice. "I know he would not let Arthur out of his sight. And Hogg has lived in one squalid house or another for as long as I've known him. Still, he might have moved since I last saw him."

She brushed her hair out of her eyes, rubbing in more of the brown liquid as she did so. Then she glanced around the room. The large ginger cat mewed. Margery nodded and went toward it.

The scrying ball lay on the floor near the cat, and Margery picked it up and looked at it critically. Dust and cat fur covered the ball and she took a cloak from a nearby stool and wiped it clean. Then she set it on a table and gazed into it.

The room grew silent. Alice looked at Agnes, puzzled, but the other woman watched Margery with no expression at all on her face. Margery did not dabble in magic, Alice knew that. And yet she had had the scrying ball for as long as Alice could remember. Was it possible that she had been mistaken about her friend, that she had been wrong to defend her against charges of witchcraft?

Suddenly Margery stepped back. Arthur appeared in the glass, but Arthur as Alice had never seen him, dirty, thin, his clothes torn and his beautiful red hair matted. "Where is he?" Alice said impatiently. "And why didn't you use the glass to discover him before?"

"Hush," Margery said. "I used the glass when he first disappeared, but he had gone beyond my power to see him, to—to a country I didn't know. I hadn't known that he'd returned."

Hogg came into view as they watched. They saw him sit next to Arthur and say something. "I wish we could hear them talk," Agnes said.

"He's asking Arthur questions," Margery said. "He's after knowledge, as always."

"But Arthur doesn't know anything!" Alice said.

"He knows more than you may think," Margery said. "He has powers you have never seen, though he's had no way to learn how to use them."

In the glass, Hogg stood and moved out of their view. Arthur nodded his head as if in time to music. "I know that room. Hogg has not moved in years. And look—he studies alchemy." She laughed harshly.

Alice could not see what had so amused her friend. "How do we get him away?"

"I don't know. We'll have to go there and see."

"Now? It's almost evening."

"Aye, and that's why we have to leave now. I'm certain that Arthur is guarded, and his guards will be weaker at night."

"Then it's true what Hogg said—that Oriana's people are the children of darkness, the children of Cain?"

Margery said nothing. "Why do you have to do everything in darkness?" Alice said, determined to get an answer from her friend. "And what kind of magic is it that lets you see Arthur in that glass? I've told the Stationers' Company that you're not a witch, and now I find—"

"What kind of magic? How many kinds are there?"

"White and black, of course," Alice said sharply. Why wouldn't her friend ever answer her questions?

"Ah. And what is the difference between them?"

"White magic comes from God. Everyone knows that. And black magic—"

Margery laughed. "What is magic, Alice? Why is it you can see the Fair Folk?"

"Because—because Brownie breathed on my eye."

"Ah. And why can George see them?"

"I don't know. Because Hogg gave him the sight, I'd guess."

"Nay. Hogg holds as fast to his knowledge as a miser to his gold."

"Someone else gave it to him, then. What does this have to do—"

"No one gave him the sight, Alice. What you call magic is all around us, to be seen by everyone. The world of the Fair Folk and our world are the same—"

"But—"

"And more and more people are coming to see that. London daily becomes more fantastical."

Alice could think of nothing to say. As always Margery's ideas were as outlandish as anything she had ever heard. Agnes nodded slowly, as if she understood all the other woman had said. Maybe she did.

But what did it matter? The important thing was to get Arthur, after all. Margery left food for the cats, stopping to talk softly to the large ginger tom, and then they set off.

Margery led them through Ludgate and past Paul's. A tree stood by the gate to the churchyard, and Margery stopped and placed her hand on the trunk. Alice remembered that the tree had flourished there all summer despite the drought, and saw that even now, in the fall, it had kept most of its leaves. Margery spoke a few muttered words, and Alice felt her uneasiness return.

They went down Cheapside. The sun was setting as they turned left at the Mercers' Hall and left again into a part of London Alice had never seen. Shadows from the houses leaned inward, and a chill wind whistled past them. Garbage filled the streets, and a few rats, made bold by the absence of people, ran from one pile to the next. Was it safe for the three of them to come here? Without discussing it they moved closer, huddling together in the center of the street.

Margery stopped before a house as rundown as its neighbors.

Did she remember which house it was after all these years? And even if she did, what did she plan to do now? Knock politely and ask for Arthur back?

No sound came from inside the house. Margery tried the latch but the door was locked. "Arthur," she said softly. "Open the door."

"His guards won't let him come to the door, surely."

"Quiet. Arthur, open the door. Arthur, do you hear me?"

To her surprise Alice heard footsteps come to the door, and then the sound of a key turning in a lock. The door opened and Arthur stood before her.

Alice barely had time to get over her shock—Arthur, after all these years!—when one of the sea-creatures dropped from the rafters. She cried out and backed into the street, but Arthur only watched the thing incuriously. Margery spoke a few words and made some signs in the air. The creature bared its teeth and padded toward her.

Margery flung her arm in front of her face and shouted to it. Now even Agnes looked worried, her hands twisting in the folds of her dress. The thing hissed and moved closer. Its claw drew blood from Margery's arm. Alice heard herself say something: "Go away! Get out!" but still it came on.

A loud wind blew past them. Margery screamed against it, her clothes blowing out behind her. The creature stopped and hissed angrily. Margery spoke again. The wind howled. Then, in the time it took Alice to blink, the sea-creature disappeared.

The wind died down. Now they could hear Arthur, who must have been shouting over it: "Nay, I won't go with them! Nay, she's not my mother!" The signs that Margery had made in the air still glowed in the evening light, the color of silver.

"Come," Margery said. "We must leave before it returns."

"I won't go with her," Arthur said, quieter now. "She's not my mother."

"Nay, she's not," Margery said. "Your mother is Oriana, Queen of the Fair Folk."

"Queen . . ." Arthur said. Alice could see him struggle with the new idea; although he had somehow known that he wasn't her son he could never have been completely sure. His pleasure at being a queen's son won out over his uncertainty. Alice saw the delight that appeared on his face and felt that something had been taken from her. Why had Margery told him the truth now? Alice had been the one to raise him, after all, not Oriana.

But nay, she had best get used to the idea that she would lose him. Lose him and gain another, her true son. What would he be like?

"When will I see her?" Arthur asked eagerly.

"Soon," Margery said.

"He said that too. But he would never let me go—that thing always guarded the door for him."

"Aye, and we must hurry before it comes back."

But Arthur made no move to go. Perhaps he didn't understand the danger he was in; perhaps he thought that Margery would be no different from Hogg. "He would have given you to the red king, not to Oriana," Margery said. "And the king would have used you in the battle he fights with your mother's people."

Lulled by the promise of learning more secrets Arthur followed Margery as she moved down the street. Probably Hogg had told him nothing at all. Margery began to walk surprisingly quickly for an old woman; no doubt she had spoken the truth when she'd said that the thing might return. As they went she told him the story of his birth, how he had been exchanged for a human baby, Alice's son. He ignored Alice, the faerie-light shining from his face as he listened, enchanted, to the other woman. And when will I get my son back? Alice wondered.

Over the next few weeks Alice thought about visiting Margery, but always the memory of the evening they had rescued Arthur stopped her. Her friend didn't dabble in magic; Alice had known that as certainly as she knew the titles of the books she sold. And yet Margery had used a scrying glass, had spoken words to keep the creature away from them, had possibly even raised the wind she had felt at the end. Nothing was as it seemed to be; her friend was truly a witch and Alice had lied to George and the Stationers' Company. Had Margery sold her soul to the devil like the man in the play?

But still she thought of the other woman a dozen times a day. She missed the talks they had had. And she wanted to see Arthur again; he had looked so thin, so frail, that night he'd come to the door. What kind of mother would let her only child fall into that state? But Arthur was not her son, and no doubt Margery and Agnes, with their knowledge of herbs, could restore him better than she could.

So the weeks passed. Alice waited for a summons from Margery, a message telling her the day they would meet with Oriana, but it never came. Her business prospered: she sold all her copies of Tom Nashe's book and had to order another printing. And then Gabriel Harvey replied to Nashe in his *Four Letters and Certain Sonnets,* and Nashe told her that he was hard at work on an answer to Harvey in a pamphlet called *Strange News.* She wondered that men with so much talent would waste their time on such trifles, but she had to admit that Nashe's book was very funny. When Harvey tried for wit he could not touch him, and Tom knew it.

It was a good season for the stationers. Scandals and gossip swept through the churchyard, a welcome diversion after the grim deaths of the previous summer. All the pamphleteers in London seemed to be engaged in a war of words, but the printers and booksellers were the only winners, and Alice profited as much as any. In December Henry Chettle, who had prepared Greene's *Groatsworth of Wit* for the press, came out with his own book, *Kind Heart's Dream.* In it he apologized to one of the playwrights Greene had insulted, the man Greene had called Shake-scene, but not to Nashe or Marlowe. Alice had recognized Marlowe the day he bought Nashe's book, and she had thought that he did not look like the kind of man who would ask for an apology. And Tom Nashe wrote day and night in order to finish his answer to Harvey and had no time to see Chettle or anyone else.

One day Alice came back from her dinner to find another of the stationers looking through *Pierce Penniless,* chuckling as he read. "You can borrow it if you like," she said. All of the booksellers frequently lent their books to one another.

The man hadn't seen her come up. He set the book down

quickly, then raised one hand to his breast and lowered it. Alice thought he might have been about to cross himself. He turned and backed away, stumbling a little in his eagerness to be gone.

Alice watched him as he went. Her neighbor Edward Blount watched him too, she noticed; she realized he must have seen the whole thing. Suddenly angry, she said, "Does he think it beneath his dignity to speak to a woman?"

"Nay, you know it's not that," Blount said.

"Aye, it's worse than that. They still think I practice witch-craft."

"You should not talk to that woman—"

"Why not? I'll talk to anyone I please. Margery's my friend."

"Then you should not expect the stationers to listen to you. They know that she's a witch, and if you keep company with her they will think the same of you."

"She's not—" Alice started to say.

"Not a witch? Do you truly believe that?"

Alice said nothing. She could not make that claim, not now.

She set Nashe's book back on its pile, feeling melancholy. If it were not for Edward and Walter, she thought, she would have no one to speak to in the churchyard. She knew that George whispered against her, and she thought that his accusations must be having some effect. Folks listened to George; his business had prospered and he had become one of the most influential members of the company.

Now she looked over at Walter's stall. The city authorities had declared the danger from plague over and had reopened the playhouses at the end of December, and she and Walter had braved the cold and the rain to return to the Theatre and the Curtain in Shoreditch. Their talk was limited to the plays they saw and the business of the company, and she sometimes thought that she could learn to regard him as a friend and not as a man she could love. Then he would smile or say something witty, and she would feel herself catch fire again.

Still, she could not help but wonder why he had stuck by her. Perhaps he had some flaw in his character that made him defy the rest of the stationers, the same flaw she herself must have had in order to have stayed so long with Margery. They were two of a kind, then, outcasts among the rest of the company. How had she come to this?

George had his stall a few yards past Walter's. She glanced at him briefly, saw him scowl. Of late he had seemed more and more unhappy; probably he suspected she had had something to do with Arthur's disappearance from Hogg's house. On some days that thought was the only thing that could cheer her.

She saw George close up his stall and leave the churchyard. Going to his counterfeiting friend, no doubt, she thought. His counterfeit friend. She laughed a little, harshly, and turned back to her books.

Anthony Drury had delivered the summons to meet with Hogg earlier that day. Now, as George entered Hogg's cramped room, he saw Anthony sitting at the large table with Hogg. He felt briefly angry. It was bad enough to be humiliated; to have that humiliation conducted in front of Anthony would be even worse. Then he remembered why Hogg had sent for him, and fear drove out all his other thoughts.

"Did you tell anyone that we found Arthur?" Hogg asked.

How had the man known? Perhaps he didn't know; perhaps he was only guessing. George shook his head.

"Come, George," Hogg said. "Lying will not help you here. You boasted to your friends, didn't you?"

Anthony Drury watched them both, his eyes burning eagerly. "I—I told a few men from the churchyard," George said finally. Why had he ever opened his mouth, why had he let his ancient feeling for Alice overcome all his good sense? It didn't pay to be too understanding; it was not good policy. "But they didn't take him—they couldn't—"

"Nay, they couldn't. But someone told Alice, and Alice's friend, that Margery, certainly could. Didn't you think of that?"

"I—"

"You have not been helpful to me at all, George. Nay, you have been worse than that—you have proved to be a hindrance rather than a help. You nearly lost us Arthur in Bedlam, with all your prating about Alice Wood. And now you *have* lost him. What am I to do with you?"

George said nothing. At best, he thought, Hogg would cast him off, would no longer give him money from his supply of gold coins. And he needed those coins to keep his business: he owed too many people money, had spread himself far too thin. Yet he thought he would gladly brave poverty instead of—of those other things, the lubber-fiends or worse.

Anthony grinned. "The pox take you, why are you laughing?" Hogg said, turning to him. George realized that Hogg was genuinely angry now. He had never faced the man's anger, had never seen him lose his careful control, and he felt terrified.

"I'll—I can watch her for you," George said. "I see her every day at the churchyard."

"Do you think she hasn't been watched? Do you think I'm that foolish? She's spied on every minute, she and that demon of hers. She doesn't have Arthur."

"She doesn't— Then where is he?"

"Margery has him. And I don't know where Margery is. She's clever at hiding, I'll give her that."

"Well, then, I could—"

"You could do nothing. Whatever you do will only make matters worse. Go."

George stood still for a minute, wondering if he had heard correctly. Was he to be let off so easily?

"Go! Leave me, both of you. I have work to do."

George left quickly.

After they had gone Paul Hogg stared at the door for a long moment. He had asked that Anthony be present while he questioned George because he had wanted to play the two men off against each other, had wanted to keep them both confused and off balance. Either one might be tempted by the red king's vast power; he knew that he could not let down his guard for a moment in their presence.

Though Anthony, of course, was far more dangerous than George. His desire for knowledge and wealth was too great; he burned with the need for it. He had to be kept on a tight rein, given only so much information and money and no more. Even now, Hogg knew, Anthony sometimes reverted to his former profession of counterfeiter and debased the gold coins Hogg gave him.

George, on the other hand, George might be harmless. Hogg gave him all the gold he desired; his ambitions, so far, had been modest ones. He knew Anthony resented the fact that he favored George, that George prospered while Anthony lived in near-poverty. And Hogg encouraged this resentment, honored George in little ways, so that the two of them would not join forces and study without him.

Not that he truly thought they had the wit to do that. Hogg had met only one other person whose learning he admired, whose talents he envied. Five years ago, when he had first come to London, when he had seen that the Fair Folk were moving and had been moved himself to follow them, he had become acquainted with Margery and had asked to study with her. But she had refused him, saying that she could not accept his methods. He hadn't understood her then and he didn't now: what difference did it make how he achieved his end? She had claimed to be appalled at that.

He should not have lost his temper with George and Anthony, should not have let them see his control slip. And he should not think so much of Margery: she was a woman and suffered from a woman's weaknesses. Her limited thinking would keep her from doing truly great work.

He opened a book on the table in front of him and looked down the page. "It is in the marriage of the red man and the white lady that the Philosopher's Stone is born," he read. What did that mean? Why did all the authors of antiquity understand it, everyone but him?

17

The plague returned that spring. As Tom Kyd walked through the city in mid-May he heard the sound of a loud bell ringing behind him, and he turned to see a death-cart nearly on him. The driver swore and he hurried out of the way, but he was not quick enough to escape the foul odor of death that trailed behind the cart. As it passed he saw the five or six bodies in winding-sheets piled on top of each other. Other than the driver, still ringing his bell, he was the only living soul on the street.

Once again, Tom thought, he had not managed to find a way to leave London. He knew that Christopher had gone to the country with his patron, Thomas Walsingham, and he couldn't help but resent him for it. Kit had sent Walsingham the parts of his poem he had finished and had received an invitation almost immediately. By that time, though, the two writers were no longer sharing the room. Harsh words had been exchanged, the cause of which Tom could no longer remember. It had all grown too much: the other man's mysterious absences, his blasphemous speech, the diversions that seemed to come just when Tom was sitting down to write. Still, Tom wished he could have read the rest of the poem.

He passed a ballad posted on the wall of an inn and paused to read it:

> You, strangers, that inhabit this land,
> Note this same writing, do it understand.
> Conceive it well, for safeguard of your lives,
> Your goods, your children, and your dearest wives.

He could make little of it, only that someone wanted the foreigners out of England. The author of the ballad had even given a date for the strangers to leave: July 9. Tom knew that the large number of people who had come to London had caused a struggle for the jobs that existed, and that some thought the city would be better off without folks coming in from other countries as well. But perhaps the plague would keep the ballad's threat from being fulfilled. Tom hoped so, anyway; he did not like to see men come to blows, except in the controlled spaces of the stage. Once he reached his chamber, though, he put the matter out of his mind and began to work.

A few days later loud knocking interrupted him as he sat at his desk. Before he could get up to open the door two men came in uninvited, one tall and plump, with a heavy blond mustache, the other small and dark, with a face that reminded Tom of a weasel.

"We have orders from the queen's Star Chamber," the shorter one said.

"Aye?" Tom said, standing. He had done nothing wrong, he knew that, and yet he still felt himself grow cold at the other man's words. Anyone might have misunderstood something he had said, or taken his friends' opinions for his own. But he hadn't been to the taverns in several months; he had stopped going about the same time Christopher left.

The tall man picked up Tom's manuscript and looked through it. "Beautiful handwriting," he said. "Look here, Dick."

"Could you—could he put that down?" Tom said.

"Nay," the shorter man—Dick—said. "We have orders, as I told you, from the Star Chamber."

What orders? Tom wondered. Why should the queen send men to look through his plays?

"Did you work on a play called—" Dick looked at a piece of paper in his hand. "Here it is. A play called *Sir Thomas More?*"

"Nay."

"Listen," the tall man said, reading from a paper he had found. " 'And will ye needs bedew my dead-grown joys, And nourish sorrow with eternal tears?' " He looked up at Tom. " 'And nourish sorrow with eternal tears,' " he repeated slowly. Foolishly, Tom found himself wondering if the man liked it.

"Sir Edmund Tillney, the Master of the Revels, had to suppress some of that play," Dick said, ignoring the other man. "He told us six people had a hand in it."

"I didn't write it. I told you."

"The part about riots against foreigners. You've seen the libels posted around the city about the French and Flemish settlers?"

The taller man had finished rooting through his papers and moved to Christopher's old desk. It was hard to listen to Dick and keep an eye on him at the same time. "Aye," Tom said a little belatedly, glad that he could give Dick the answer he wanted.

"The queen wants her new subjects to be happy here. They've suffered enough persecution from the Catholics already. Wouldn't you say so?"

"Aye." Where was all this leading?

"We're to find the folks responsible for posting those ballads. Someone suggested it might have been you."

"Nay, it wasn't—"

"Do you know who it might have been?"

Tom thought. If he could come up with a name, he knew, the men would probably go away. But he could not bring himself to accuse anyone. He shook his head.

"You'll tell us if you hear anything."

"Oh, aye," Tom said.

The taller man lifted a page from the desk. " 'And Jesus Christ which was born of Mary is not counted God with me,' " he said, reading slowly.

God's blood, what was that? Something Christopher had written, or had paid to have copied. Whatever it was it was dangerous, very dangerous. Why had he left it here?

Dick turned to the other man quickly. "Let me see that."

The tall man came over and gave him the manuscript. "What does this mean?" Dick asked. " 'Not counted God with me?' "

Tom's heart beat very fast. He could not seem to gather his thoughts. "I don't know."

"Where is it from?"

"I don't know."

"You don't know," Dick repeated flatly. "Who would know, then? This is your room, isn't it?"

"Aye, but—"

"Then it's your manuscript. Isn't it?"

"Nay. I shared this room with another man."

Dick's eyes narrowed with interest. Tom saw that he had been foolish, very foolish. "Who?" Dick asked.

"Several people, really. I can't remember them all."

It sounded weak to him. The other man must have thought so too, because he said, "You shared a room with them and can't remember their names?"

"Aye. There were many of us."

"But who would have had a manuscript like this one? And why didn't he take it with him when he left?"

"I don't know."

"Look here, John," Dick said to the taller man. "See how fine the handwriting is. You have a fine hand too, Master—" He looked down at his piece of paper again. "—Master Kyd."

"I was a scrivener." Tom said quickly. "No doubt whoever owned this manuscript paid another scrivener to copy it."

"Aye? It looks like your handwriting to me. What do you think, John?"

"Aye, to me too."

"Nay, I—"

"Such things are easy enough to check," Dick said.

Were they? How would they find out something like that? But however they did it they would discover that he was innocent, and that was the important thing.

"Aye," John said. "The rack."

"Nay!" Tom said, backing away. "Nay, I told you it's not mine. Don't— Please—"

"Whose is it, then?"

"I don't—"

"Whose?"

"A man named—named Christopher Marlowe. A playwright."

Both men looked interested at the word "playwright." "And where is this man now?"

"With his patron, Thomas Walsingham." Once the words had been spoken it was easy enough to continue. "In Kent. I don't know exactly where—I haven't seen him for months. Years, really."

Dick picked up Tom's pen and began to write something on his piece of paper. "Kent, did you say?"

Despite himself Tom felt relieved. They would go after Christopher and leave him alone. Kit could explain the doctrinal complexities in the manuscript; he knew how to argue theology, after all. And perhaps no harm would come to him; to hear the man tell it he had been in worse situations than this one. Tom moved toward his desk, eager to return to his work.

"We'll have to take you with us, of course," Dick said.

"What? Where?"

"To Bridewell."

"Bridewell? But—but I've told you everything I know."

"Have you? Torture's best for that, I've heard."

Tom looked toward the window. He could run, escape them, hurry down the London streets and go—where? Where could he hide? But his hesitation gave the bigger man time to seize his arm and turn him roughly, then pinion both arms behind his back. The man tightened his hold, forcing Tom toward the door and outside. Tom nearly cried out in pain.

The streets were empty; nothing moved. London looked like the painted backdrop representing the city of Rome that Tom had once seen in a play. No one was there to watch his humiliation as his captors led him toward the prison; he felt grateful for that, if nothing else. Dogs nosed through the piles of garbage in the streets, and squeaking rats, bold enough now to appear in daylight, scurried on ahead of them.

The two men led him through Ludgate and down Fleet Street for a little while, then turned south, toward the river. Tom had never seen Bridewell and could not help but notice how large it was, covering nearly the same area as Paul's. Once inside his keepers turned him over to a jailer who entered his name in a book and led him into a large common room holding a dozen people. At other prisons, Tom had heard, a bribe to the jailer ensured better lodgings and plentiful food. There was less corruption here, then, but that fact did not work to his benefit. He realized, almost despairing, that that was the kind of thought a criminal would have.

A few prisoners looked up incuriously as he came in, then looked away, staring at nothing. Tom felt revulsion at the sight of them. Cutpurses and horse-thieves, he thought. And what am I? Not a criminal, though, not that. I've done nothing wrong.

The jailer left. Men and women in the blue uniform of inmates passed through the common room on their way to the tasks assigned them. From where he stood Tom could see a large courtyard, where prisoners worked at grinding corn or beating hemp. They won't have me working, then, Tom thought. Nay, I'm here for torture. He shuddered.

He found a place to sit against a wall. The wall was stained and filthy; probably countless people had rubbed against it over the years. No one spoke, either to him or to one another. One man sang a ballad until someone else threatened him with his fist. They all seemed spiritless, content to wait out the months or years they had to serve.

An hour later one of the jailers came to fetch him. Nay, not a jailer—he was too well dressed, and he carried himself like a man of authority. Someone sent from the Star Chamber, then. He went with the man without question, even allowed himself a grudging hope. They've realized the mistake they've made, he thought. They're going to let me go. The man turned a corner and went through a doorway, and Tom followed.

At first he thought that the room held only a table, and he wondered why it should be so lacking in furniture. Then he recognized the rack. He struggled but they were ready for him, both his keeper and the man who tended the machine. They forced him down and tied his legs to the foot of the table and his arms up over his head. Nothing in his life had ever made him feel so helpless, so exposed. The torturer took his place at the head of the table. Tom tried to look at him, hoping to guess by his expression what might be coming next, but they had tied him so that he could see nothing.

"Is this manuscript yours?" the man from the Star Chamber asked from somewhere near his feet.

"Nay, I told you—"

He gasped. A sharp pain traveled along his arms and legs. At first he could not grasp what had happened to him, and then he realized that the torturer had moved the wheel a little.

"Is it yours?"

"Nay." Another turn of the wheel. "It's not! I've said—"

"Whose is it then?"

"I told you—"

The wheel turned again. His body felt on fire. Flames licked at his joints. Each point of agony was a star; he had grown huge, as vast as the crystalline sphere of the heavens.

"—it's Christopher's, not mine," he said. Had they even heard him? It was difficult to speak against the pain, to make his voice carry from such a vast height.

Another turn. Red-hot wires connected each of the stars burning in his joints. "Do you think us fools, then?" the questioner said. "Why should we accept your story as true? How do we know you shared a room with anyone?"

The torturer worked the wheel again. Tom collapsed inward, into a tight shell of pain smaller than a man's hand. He could barely hear the questions. "Whose is it?"

It's Christopher's, he said, or thought he said. Christopher was the one responsible for the pain that coursed through his body, that sang in every joint. The atheist, the blasphemer: they should summon the man and punish him for all his sins, punish him as Tom was being punished. And if they didn't he would see to it himself that the other man suffered. God's justice would be done.

"It's Christopher's!" Tom cried. "He's the one you want, not I!" Then he fainted.

The summons to appear before the Star Chamber did not worry Christopher overmuch. He had been called in front of various authorities in the past and had managed to talk himself out of worse situations. More troublesome, perhaps, was the idea of going to London during the plague season, but that could not be helped. He made his farewells to Thomas Walsingham's household and rode to London with Henry Maunder, the man who had delivered the warrant for his arrest.

They arrived in London by midafternoon, too late for that day's meeting of the Star Chamber. He and Maunder parted company and he was left to his own devices. He wandered through London with no goal in mind and found it deserted, the playhouses closed, Paul's abandoned, the taverns empty.

Hungry now, he made his way toward Cheapside, passing along the way three or four houses with quarantine notices posted on their doors. Best get this business over with and go back to Kent, he thought. London's no place for the living these days.

A few stalls on Cheapside had remained open and he bought a meat pie and a bottle of ale. He had nearly finished eating when he heard whistling somewhere behind him, an eerie sound in the empty street.

He turned. Will Ryder stood there, improbably dressed in a black cloak and tall black hat topped with a black plume. "Will!" he said, embracing the other man.

They stepped back, each regarding the other. Will looked thinner, less stocky, and had golden freckles across the bridge of his nose. His foolish hat had been knocked into the mud of the street.

Will smiled; that at least hadn't changed. He looked very pleased, very certain of his welcome, and at that Christopher remembered where the man had been for almost a year.

"I hear you've turned Papist," he said, and immediately regretted the coldness in his voice.

"Nay," Will said. "I was curious about them, nothing more.

Come, let's not talk theology just yet. Shall we go to my house?"

Christopher followed the other man, his pulse quickening, content for the moment to lay all questions aside. In the cold manor they embraced again, more forcefully now. Christopher undid the other man's cloak. "You've lost your hat," he said softly.

"I know," Will said.

Their lovemaking was hurried, almost desperate, as if each thought the other in danger of disappearing once more. Later they did it again, slowly and languidly, then lay in Will's bed and talked. "Why did you go to Rheims?" Christopher asked.

"I went—because of you, I think."

"Because of me!"

"Aye. You probably don't know how you appeared to me. Here you were, a poet, a playwright, a true spy, not a dabbler like myself—I began to think that there was nothing you hadn't done. And then I remembered the scornful way you spoke of the Catholics, and I thought that there at last was a place you hadn't been. It took me three days in Rheims to discover that you had been there too. I felt that you were mocking me—that even in your absence you mocked me."

"I mocked you? You were the one who told me in such a superior fashion to use those outlandish Italian forks."

"Nay, I didn't!"

"What do you mean, you didn't? Of course you did."

"I don't remember."

"You did. What were they like, the Papists? Do the monks still lie with the nuns as they did when I was there?"

"Nay, don't jeer like that. They're serious about their religion in a way that we've lost, I think. And there's a lot of good in them. We hear about the bad they do, but I wonder—I wonder how many of those stories are true."

"Most of them, I would think."

"I don't think so."

Could Will be right? The other man seemed so certain, and his old superior manner had returned, as if Christopher were an erring pupil. But what did it matter what Will thought of him?

Yet he found to his surprise that he was anxious for Will's good opinion.

"Why did you come back?" he asked.

"My father sent for me. He'd disowned me after I went to Rheims—Geoffrey was quick to tell him what I'd done. But when I came back to England he wrote and asked to see me. He's in London on business. But what brings you to the city? You're the last person I expected to meet."

Christopher told him about the summons from the Star Chamber, what little information Henry Maunder had given him, making light of it so that Will wouldn't worry. Then, realizing only at that moment how good it was to confide in someone, he recounted all that had happened in the months since they had seen each other, his falling out with Thomas Kyd, Robert Greene's death and the final confession he had made.

"And this other man, Chettle—he never apologized?" Will asked.

"Nay. All of London waits to see if I'll repent. You have no idea how trying it can be."

"And will you?"

"Nay," he said.

The light began to fade from the windows. Will's room, invariably cold, grew chilly, and he moved closer to the other man. Will drifted off to sleep; he had always been an easy sleeper. Christopher stayed awake and thought about the Star Chamber meeting tomorrow, worrying over what he might say. A nuisance, but then if it hadn't been for the summons to London he would not have seen Will.

He must have slept, because two thoughts came together in his dreams and woke him, his heart pounding. At least one of the Catholic conspirators had never been found, the man whose voice had sounded familiar. And Will had gone to the Catholics in Rheims.

He lay still and listened to Will's soft, even breathing. He had not known how much he cared for the man. Nay, he was done with mysteries. He had all the answers he needed.

*   *   *

The faces of the judges of the Star Chamber looked grave, impassive, and Christopher took that as a good sign; they hadn't made up their minds to condemn him just yet. Some of them he recognized: Archbishop Whitgift, dressed all in black, and his secretary, Abraham Hartwell; the Cecils, Lord Burghley and his son Robert. Burghley was a portly man who seemed a little pompous; Robert Cecil, the hunchback, was thinner and fragile-looking, with fine cheekbones and a languid courtier's expression. To his left sat the Earl of Derby, and Christopher felt pleased to see him; his son, Lord Strange, patronized the acting company that had performed several of his plays. He didn't recognize the three other men, but they made no move to introduce themselves.

Henry Maunder, the man who had come to arrest him, had said only that blasphemous papers had been found in Thomas Kyd's room, and that Kyd had told the Star Chamber the papers were Christopher's. He could not remember leaving any manuscripts with Kyd but he supposed that that didn't mean he hadn't. He wondered what the Chamber had found, what they had thought important enough to bring him to London in a plague season.

"Do you recognize this manuscript?" Archbishop Whitgift asked.

He took the papers Hartwell held out to him. Someone had written on them: "Vile heretical conceits denying the deity of Jesus Christ our Savior found among the papers of Thos Kyd, prisoner," and another hand had added: "Which he affirmeth he had from Marlowe."

He looked from that to the manuscript itself, and when he did so he nearly laughed in relief. If poor Tom Kyd had known anything at all about theology and been able to argue a little he would not have needed to drag anyone else into this business; the thing was nearly as safe as the Geneva Bible. He had been fortunate, very fortunate, that this was all they had found.

"Aye," he said.

Robert Cecil made a note on a piece of paper in front of him. "Is it yours?" Whitgift asked.

"Aye."

"How do you come to have such a blasphemous manuscript?"

Christopher looked directly at the archbishop. "It isn't blasphemous. It's—"

"Not blasphemous! Why, man, how can you say so? It denies the divinity of our Lord."

"Aye. That's the Arian heresy, which claims that Christ was not divine. But the manuscript itself is called *The Fall of the Late Arian,* and it refutes those claims."

"I didn't see any refutation."

Nay, Christopher thought, you didn't see it because it isn't there. I hadn't paid the scrivener to copy that part out. "Aye," he said. "I know a little about theology; I studied it at Cambridge for six years. I had thought, perhaps presumptuously, that I would try to answer the claims myself."

"And how would you answer them?"

This part was easy; he could do this in his sleep. He marshalled arguments, quoted Scripture, referred to church authorities. At least one of the men he cited, judging by the archbishop's expression, was unknown to Whitgift. He finished with a statement of conventional piety that brought satisfied nods from nearly half the judges. Robert Cecil, he noticed, had covered his entire page with notes.

But Whitgift still looked unconvinced. "And you yourself," the archbishop said. "Do you agree with the claims put forward here?"

"Nay, of course not," Christopher said firmly. But if you ask me what I do believe, he thought, I will have to lie to you.

No one had any further questions. Christopher spoke into the silence. "My lords, some of you in this room may know that I was once an agent for Sir Francis Walsingham. I went to Rheims several times to gather information on the Catholics there. And a few years ago I helped Sir Philip Potter discover the names of those who had plotted against the queen."

A few men looked up at that, interested. Robert Cecil hurriedly made another note. "Aye," Lord Burghley said. "I remember. That was a job well done."

"Still, I can't understand why you copied only half this manuscript," Archbishop Whitgift said. "It seems somehow sinister, wouldn't you say?" He turned to the others in the chamber for confirmation.

"But if he was a student of divinity, after all . . ." one of the men said.

Silence settled over the chamber again. Finally Burghley spoke. "We'll have to discuss this matter among ourselves," he said. "Please wait for us outside."

Christopher went out into the antechamber. The room had become hot and he was sweating lightly, worried, finally, about what the judges would decide. His throat felt dry. He shouldn't have talked for so long; folks didn't like it when you were too clever. He had antagonized Whitgift, that much was clear. The archbishop would probably prefer that no one meddle in divinity, that everyone accept the answers that came down from the clergy. And the idea of copying out a manuscript simply because you were curious about the ideas in it, because it stated something different from the common platitudes mouthed by every clergyman you had ever known—well, Whitgift would not like that at all.

But how much weight did the archbishop's opinion carry? Some of the others seemed to oppose him. Burghley, for example, clearly remembered Walsingham with affection; Christopher had done well to mention the man's name. But he hadn't remembered to remind Derby of his connection with Lord Strange. Well, it couldn't be helped; if they gave him another chance he would say something.

Damn, what was taking them so long? He walked up and down the narrow room anxiously. If they decided he was a heretic what would they do to him? Prison, torture, death at the stake? They had cut off a man's hand for writing blasphemy.

Nay, best not to think about it. He would triumph over these judges as he had won out over others in authority. And perhaps when this was over he would be more careful in his speech. But why shouldn't he be able to speak his mind? It galled him to have to remain silent.

Hartwell, Whitgift's secretary, called him back into the chamber. Whitgift began to speak, and for a moment Christopher thought that he was lost, that they had all come to agree with the man. What would Will think if he didn't come back? "We have been unable to reach a decision," Whitgift said. "We command therefore that you remain in attendance on us, and that you report to us daily to show that you have not left London."

Christopher nodded, not trusting himself to speak. He had not been set free, then, but at least he would not be going to prison. He found he had been holding his breath and he let it out slowly.

"You may go," Hartwell said, and he left the chamber.

In the afternoon he and Will walked around London, trying to find his old companions. The sun shone weakly overhead; he was surprised, after the warmth of the Star Chamber, at how cold the wind felt.

In Paul's he talked to the few booksellers who had remained during the plague. No one knew where Nashe had gone to, but Ned Blount had heard that Kyd had been sent to prison. At that Christopher felt his heart stop for a moment and then start again, loudly and too fast. What had happened to Kyd? Did they torture him? He had not known the dangers he faced when he had argued theology so heedlessly with the men of the Star Chamber.

"Do you do much spy-work?" Will asked at the end of the day, as they walked back to the manor.

"Nay, none at all."

"Why not?"

"I have a patron now, for one thing. I don't need the money."

"But the excitement, the— Didn't you enjoy it?"

Christopher laughed. "It proved a little too exciting for me, finally. But I've been out of the game so long I wouldn't know how to go about getting in again. Walsingham's dead, and I haven't seen Rob—my superior in years."

"But surely they'd take you back. You discovered the Catholic conspirators—"

"Weren't you the one siding with the Catholics?"

"I told you—I found them interesting, no more. I wouldn't want to be ruled by them."

Christopher laughed again. "Nor I. But sometimes I think the Protestants are as bad, or worse." Too late he remembered his promise to be more circumspect in his speech, and he looked around him carefully. But the street was deserted, as every public place in London seemed to be.

When they returned to Will's manor they found a letter waiting from his father. Will read it several times, anxiously. "He wants to meet with me," he said at last, looking up. "Look here—he's set a date. Finally."

"Good."

"Aye. But I'm worried."

"Worried? Why?"

"What if he still wants to disown me?"

"What if he does?"

"What'll I do?"

"You'll do what the rest of us do. Why should it matter what your father thinks?"

"It matters," Will said. He looked troubled.

Christopher thought of his own father, who still, after six years, could not grasp what it was his son did in London. "Why should he disown you? He'll be pleased that you're back from Rheims, that's all."

"Aye. You're probably right."

For the first time in his life Christopher thought he could see what the future held for him. Will would inherit a good portion of his father's estate, and he and Will would live together. "Come live with me and be my love," he had written a long time ago, when he had been too young to know what love was.

The days they spent together seemed almost to exist outside of time; if not for the plague he would have had no worries whatsoever. Sometimes he made an appearance before the Star Chamber but he soon stopped going daily and the judges came not to expect him: doubtless they wanted to do their job and return to the country as soon as they could. In the afternoons he and Will walked through the streets, marveling at the absence of crowds. The usual London sounds had disappeared; they heard only bells rung for funerals and the howling of hungry dogs. They climbed to the top of the tower at Paul's and looked out over the river, sparkling in the weak May sun. They went to plays and discovered a few crowded taverns filled with men who didn't care what happened to them. Several times they saw the huge bonfires lit at night to drive away the corruption of the air.

Once, as they walked back to Will's manor, they heard a Puritan at Eleanor Cross on Cheapside, calling for their repentance.

"There is wrath gone out from the Lord: the plague is begun!" the preacher shouted. A group of people surrounded him, defying the order against crowds.

There was no way around the assembly. He and Will tried to push through but the preacher stopped them. "Hold!" he said. "Are you the sort of men who profane the Lord's Day?"

Christopher hadn't even known that it was Sunday. "Evidently," he said.

They made it to the edge of the crowd, but something caused him to turn back. A man stood there watching him, someone with pale, watery-blue eyes. A man he hadn't seen in over three years. Robert Poley.

18

The cold May wind blew through the churchyard, riffling the pages of books and scattering ballads. Alice weighed down her books and pamphlets with rocks and then looked out over the yard. A lone gallant walked back and forth in front of the tomb of Duke Humphrey, clearly hoping that someone would stop him and offer him a meal. He must be unfortunate indeed, Alice thought, if he's had to stay in London.

She hadn't much pity to spare for him, though. She had sold two books the day before and one so far today. Most of the acting companies had gone to the countryside and wouldn't need the playbills she published every year. If the plague continued, she thought, she would run through her meager savings and have to sell everything she owned to another stationer.

But not to George—nay, not to George, though he seemed to prosper while others failed. One of his young apprentices worked at his stall today, and rumor had it that George had gone to buy a printing press, that he was setting himself up to be a printer as well as publisher and bookseller. According to Edward, George had a ready supply of gold coins, and he was not miserly about treating men to a drink. The stationers whispered stories of counterfeiting among themselves but only Alice knew the truth: that George dabbled in black magic. She could almost laugh at the way things had fallen out: George was guilty of the very crime he had accused her of, but because she had never been acquitted of the crime no one would believe her.

Could she sell to Walter? But Walter had started in the book-selling trade late and fared even worse than she did. And what would it be like to engage in a trade agreement with him? Nay, she couldn't face it. She would have to sell to Edward, then. Edward would be a good choice.

She sighed to think of her books displayed on another stall. Would Edward take as good care of them? Nashe's *Strange News* had come out in February and had sold well for a time, until folks had started to escape to the country. She paged through it now, marveling that the man's invention never seemed to fail, that he had been able to fill page after page with invective against Gabriel Harvey. Would Edward know what to do with a book like this?

She looked through the book, laughing a little as she read. "I say no more but Lord have mercy upon thee, for thou art fallen into his hands that will plague thee . . . His verses run hobbling like a brewer's cart upon the stones . . . This mud-born bubble, this bile upon the brow of the University, this bladder of pride new blown . . ."

She laughed again. Nashe had put her in a good humor, something he always seemed able to do. Her business would not fail: she had come this far on her wits, the only woman ever to do so, and she would survive everything, even the plague. With this new hope it seemed to her that spring, delayed for so long this year, would arrive soon; that it had traveled far, over perilous routes, but that within the next few days all the church-yard would wake to the intoxicating smell of fertile earth and new green leaves. Everything was on the verge of beginning, she felt; and as she thought this she saw, out of the edge of her left eye, a gleam of coruscating silver.

A tiny creature hovered in the churchyard, its wings beating rapidly for balance. As she watched it was joined by another, and then more, perhaps a dozen all together. No one else seemed to see them. They circled and skittered off toward the gate, then returned.

She watched them as they flew. They spun dizzily and arced to the gate again. Without thinking about it she closed her stall and followed them.

Margery stood outside the churchyard gate. Agnes was with her, and Arthur. Her breath caught to see him again. "It's started," Margery said.

"What has?" Alice asked. She had not seen Margery for months, not since they had taken Arthur. Her friend and Agnes seemed no different, but Alice marveled at the changes in Arthur. He looked healthy, his skin clear and his hair bright. The faerie-light shone from his face.

"Come with me," Margery said. "We can't talk about this here, so close to George's stall."

She led them to Cheapside. No one walked the streets but still she spoke quietly, as if she could be overheard. "We meet with Oriana today."

Oriana! Alice felt her heart beat loudly. Did that mean she would finally see her son? But she hesitated, reluctant to go with the other woman. Margery had done something so terrifying that night a half a year ago that even now Alice did not like to think about it. Am I damned if I go with her? she wondered. Is it a choice between my son and my soul?

She shook her head. I've done nothing wrong, she thought. And there's no other way to get my son back. What I want, all I want, is to have him. Oriana can fight her own wars after that.

Several of the winged creatures flew past her and stopped abruptly near Arthur, their wings trembling. Slowly first one and then another circled over his head. They're crowning him, she thought, feeling almost as if she wanted to laugh. Dull-witted Arthur, the child who had never learned to read. It's his coronation today.

She studied him as they made the familiar walk to Finsbury Field. He had grown fatter in Margery's house, and he seemed more sure of himself, striding on ahead toward the field. She noticed that he never looked in her direction. What had Margery told him about her?

Evening fell by the time they reached the field. Of course, Alice thought. Creatures of night. But now she could see Oriana and her train, shining silver against the dark field. It was too late to change her mind.

The queen's people stood around her in a semicircle. The horned men looked at the three women with cold challenge in their eyes and moved their lances forward. Then they noticed Arthur and sank as one to their knees. "Welcome, my king," one said.

Arthur looked foolishly pleased. Oriana held out her hand. "You must tell them to rise, my son," she said.

Arthur took her hand. "Rise," he said. He could not keep a note of triumph out of his voice.

"I am pleased to see you back," Oriana said, as the men around her came to their feet. "The war has gone badly for us."

"Aye," Arthur said. It all seemed too much for him. Alice wondered if Oriana would blame her for his slowness. Margery motioned to him and he added quickly, "My queen."

Oriana seemed pleased at that. "But now I have no doubt that we will conquer. Now that you are here with us."

Arthur grinned. "I thank you for your help in this matter," Oriana said to Margery. She motioned to her guard and turned to go.

"What about my son?" Alice said, coming forward. Margery waved at her to stay back but Alice ignored her. Had it all been a trick, then, to get Arthur from her? What did they care if she got her son or not? Oriana had never even embraced Arthur, her own child.

But the queen turned back. "Aye, of course," she said easily, as if Alice's son were a parcel she had misplaced. "Come, my boy."

A boy stepped between two of the horned men. Surely this child could not be over twenty! Alice thought. He smiled at her, the expression of someone who hopes to please. She held her hand out to him and tried to smile back, but all the while she could not help but feel that a mistake had been made.

He did not resemble either her or John. He was slight, with long dark-brown hair. A light seemed to shine in his brown eyes, like a candle behind a closed curtain. Now she saw that he must be older than she had first thought, but that a kind of innocence had made him look almost boyish. There must be so much that he didn't know, she thought, so much they hadn't told him. What had it been like to grow up among the Fair Folk?

"Come," she said. She embraced him, not out of any motherly feeling but out of a certain spite toward Oriana. He responded slowly, as if he had never seen such a thing before.

Margery turned to go. As they left Alice saw Oriana and Arthur deep in conversation, Arthur laughing and nodding eagerly. She felt as if a blade had pierced her heart. Nay, she thought, almost going back to say it. This isn't my child. Arthur's my son, my true son! Then she felt Margery's hand on her shoulder, and she allowed the other woman to lead her back to the city.

There was, first of all, the problem of what to call him. By asking the child questions she found that the Fair Folk had never given him a name, calling him "Boy" whenever they needed him, which hadn't been often. For the most part they seemed to have treated him as unwanted baggage, carrying him with them from place to place.

She remembered that John, who had loved the old stories, had insisted on Arthur as the name for their baby, and at that thought she realized that John had never seen his true son. Her heart hardened further against Oriana. Very well, she thought. I'll call him Arthur, as John would have wanted. It was our name before it was hers, after all. But Arthur had too much of majesty about it, brought back too many memories of the Prince of Faerie, and she soon shortened it to Art.

The nickname was a liberty the old Arthur would never have allowed, but this child was almost pathetically eager to please. He was not disappointed that Alice could not light a room by simply walking into it, the way Oriana apparently had; instead he seemed to think that setting a candle alight was magic as good as anything the queen could do. When they talked it soon became clear that neither of them understood the other: he did not know what a coach was, or a book, or a church. She, on the other hand, could not follow his tales of the queen's court, which seemed filled with intrigue and complicated in the extreme.

She realized from his stories that he must have been a very observant child. John would have loved this boy, she thought. For her part she could only try to prepare him for the society of men and women, and she felt herself growing wearier and wearier under the magnitude of her task. She was not a young woman, to raise someone as childlike as this boy seemed to be.

Brownie helped, of course. She had thought that Brownie would return to Oriana now that they had found Arthur, but he had stayed on, and for that she was grateful. Her son had known Brownie from his time among the Fair Folk, and now Brownie kept him company when she went to work, showing him how to do simple household chores and telling him stories. She thought that perhaps the boy might have gotten a better introduction to human society than that, but it could not be helped.

It was only when she saw the two of them together that she noticed the faerie-light shining from her son's face, and it increased her feeling that a mistake must have been made. But why not? she thought. Surely Art had lived long enough among the Fair Folk to become a little like them. The thought made her even more determined to teach him his place in the real world.

She told the stationers that Art was the son of her sister, now dead of the plague. She was sorry for the lie, but she knew how quickly families changed in times of infection, and that it would not surprise anyone in a month or so if she started to call him her son. A few of the booksellers worried that he had brought the plague with him, but when they both remained healthy the objections ceased. Probably folks thought she had kept the illness away by black magic.

19

Christopher turned away, pretending that he hadn't seen the other man. It seemed to him that Robert Poley, of all people, had no place in the timeless holiday of the past week. But Robert came toward them, calling his name. "Do you know him?" Will asked.

"Aye. Let's go before he catches up to us."

"Christopher!" Robert said, shouting. He had been one of the few of Christopher's acquaintances never to call him Kit. "Wait!"

Christopher waited. He might as well stop and talk. What did he care what Poley said? He was done with spying.

"Good day," Robert said, looking at Will. Christopher knew that look; he was trying to remember if he should know Will, if the other man was someone of consequence. "How have you been?"

"Well," Christopher said. As always around Robert he felt impatient, annoyed with the man's subtleties. "And you?"

"Oh, doing well, doing well." Robert looked off into the distance, abstracted. "We haven't seen each other for—years, isn't that so? Three years."

Christopher nodded. For a few months after his work in the

queen's court he had wondered why Robert hadn't contacted him again. Perhaps, he'd thought, Robert had lost his place during the shift of power following Walsingham's death, or had been envious that it was Christopher who had discovered the conspirators. Finally, though, he had decided that it didn't matter. He had his patron, and would never need to work for Robert again.

The other man seemed surprised to see him still in London, looking fit and prosperous. No one had told him about the patron, then. "What are you doing now?" Robert asked.

"Working for someone else," Christopher said. Immediately he felt childish; he had responded to an old desire to wound Robert, had reduced himself to the other man's level. Still he couldn't help but feel gratified at the expression on Robert's face, a strange mixture of resentment and curiosity. After Walsingham had died the field was wide open; he could have been working for anyone.

"Are you?" Robert looked at Will again, as if to say, Should we discuss these delicate matters in front of him?

Christopher nodded. Now it was his turn to keep silent, to hoard information. He felt sure that it tormented Robert not to know who his employer was, who Will was.

Robert looked at the ravens wheeling in the sky above London. "We should have a talk, you and I. Catch up on what we've missed. A great deal has changed since that dotard Walsingham died."

Why not? Christopher thought. Now that he was free of Robert he could listen to the other man rationally, without anger. And he might learn something; Robert's sources of information, he knew, were very good. "When?"

Will moved slightly. "Nay, don't go," he said softly. "Tell him you're busy."

Did Will want to spend all his time with him? To his surprise Christopher began to feel hedged in, impatient. What made Will think he had such a claim on him?

"I'm not that busy," he said to Will. "You're meeting with your father the day after tomorrow. I could go then."

Will looked defeated. Christopher turned back to Robert. "The usual place?" he asked.

"Usual——? Nay, you have been away a long time. There's a new place now, in Deptford. A widow's house, very private. No one listening over your shoulder. I'll tell you how to get there."

Two days later Christopher and Will walked to the river, where Will would get a boat to take him to his father's estate. The sun had not yet risen; his father, Will explained, liked to begin the day early. Heavy fog lay on the river.

"Listen, Kit," Will said. "Are you certain you want to meet with this man?"

"Of course I am," Christopher said impatiently. "Why shouldn't I be?"

"I don't know. I——I don't trust him. He looks——I don't know——untrustworthy. Devious."

"Aye, he is untrustworthy. But I know that in advance, and that's what makes me safe from him. Don't worry about me."

"Well, but be careful. Promise me you'll be careful."

Christopher was saved from answering by the cry of the waterman. "Westward ho!" the man called from his boat, his voice muffled.

The boat came toward them out of the gloom. It looked black, like a mourning barge. They said their farewells, and Christopher watched as Will stepped inside. Will seemed to grow insubstantial, blending with the pearl and gray and black of the river. The waterman pushed off. Fog curled over them.

He watched until they were lost to sight, and then hailed a boat to take him east, toward Deptford.

Christopher had never seen Robert Poley so affable, so expansive. They sat at a table in the widow's house in Deptford, and Robert regaled him with story after story, tale after tale. His accounts were like those Christopher had sometimes heard in the Black Boar, tales of journeys taken, information exchanged, men betrayed. But he felt certain that Robert's stories, unlike the others he had heard, were true.

The widow came in and set their dinner on the table. Robert

stopped halfway through an account of how he had exposed a spy selling information to the Spanish ambassador and began to eat, motioning to Christopher to join him. "Well met," Robert said with satisfaction, adding sugar to his wine and taking a sip. "Well met indeed. It's been far too long."

"Aye," Christopher said. He had prepared himself for everything but this strange new mood of Robert's, and he could not help but wonder what the other man wanted. The name of the man Christopher worked for, probably, but the answer was so ordinary, so lacking in drama, that Christopher hesitated to give it to him. He found himself wanting to match Robert's stories with his own.

"I hear you acquitted yourself well at court," Robert said. "That was well done, very well done. Though I wish I had heard the story from you."

Christopher looked at him in surprise. He had thought, when weeks went by and he hadn't heard from Robert, that the man hadn't wanted to see him. And by that time he had found a patron, and there had been no reason to seek the agent out. Did Robert think that they were friends?

He began to tell him about his adventures at the queen's court: the men he had overheard rehearsing the play, the actor who had been killed instead of the queen during the masque, his chase through the hedge maze after one of the conspirators. "I waited for him to turn the corner, wondering if I'd be able overpower him, but in the end I didn't have to. There was another man in the maze."

"Another man!" Robert said, his pale blue eyes intent. "Who?"

"I don't know." Suddenly he thought he understood something, and the realization was so strong that he wondered how he'd missed it for three years. "He was one of your men, wasn't he? You had more than one agent at the palace, didn't you?"

"More than one agent?" In the space of a breath the Robert he had known was back, secretive, impassive, closed in on himself like a fortress. "Nay—one was enough, certainly. Why would I want more?"

"I don't know. You didn't trust me, perhaps."

"Of course I trusted you—"

"Nay, you didn't. You told me so often enough. Perhaps you sent this man to spy on me."

"To spy—"

"Aye." It was a relief to be able to tell Robert what he thought, to no longer have to depend on the man for employment. "You told me my opinions were unorthodox. You said you doubted my worth to you—"

"Do you think I have so many men, then, that I can spare one to do nothing but watch you? And who would watch this watcher—another man, I suppose? Nay, you're being foolish. And how can you suppose I would have hired this strange-looking man, barely four feet tall? Who would have trusted such an outlandish fellow?"

It seemed to Christopher that everything stopped suddenly, that the entire motion of the world came to a halt with Robert's last sentence. He felt very cold. "I didn't tell you he was four feet tall."

Robert hesitated only a moment. "Of course you did. How would I know it if you didn't tell me?"

"Nay, I'm certain I didn't." He spoke slowly, putting his guesses together as he talked. "You knew because he was one of your agents, as I said. All those strange folk at the palace, the ones who told me they were petitioning for their ancestral rights, all of them were yours. And that voice I overheard, the one that sounded so familiar—that was your voice, I'm certain of it."

"What are you talking about? What voice?"

"The one plotting to kill the queen."

"Plotting— Nay, you have lost your wits. And why in God's name would I hire you to discover this conspiracy if I was a part of it?"

"Don't change the subject. Who were they? Were they searching for Arthur too?"

Robert's eyes widened; his guess had been correct. He pressed on. "Good. There were two conspiracies at the palace, then—the one I discovered and the one involving these other folks. Both of them wanted to overthrow the queen and set Arthur in her place; both were looking for Arthur to use him in some way. You were part of this second group, hurrying to find him before the first one did. But you used the first group, too, didn't you?—in case they got to him before you did. You encouraged them to think that the populace would rise up in revolt against the queen despite all evidence to the contrary. And if they got too close you knew you could always expose them. But nay—you couldn't expose them yourself because they trusted you, they thought you were one of them. If the queen didn't believe you you'd have to start all over again. So you hired me to do it. But Arthur got away from you, didn't he?"

"Aye," Robert said. He was breathing heavily. "Where did he go?"

"What?" Whatever Christopher had been expecting it hadn't been this.

"Where is he?"

"I don't know."

"I'm certain you do. You know too much about this business to be as innocent as you pretend. Cecil swears you're not working for him, and Essex has no idea what he's doing most of the time. So you have to be working for these people. But which side? Oriana or the red king?"

"The—red king? Who is he?"

"Oriana then. How close are you? Do you know where he is?"

"Which one do you work for?"

"The red king, of course. He pays me very well, far better than Oriana would."

"Wait. Wait a moment. You work for this—this red king? Was it in the service of this man that you encouraged the plotters to kill the queen? They nearly did kill her, you know. It was only luck that saved her."

"Let's abandon the pretense that you know nothing, shall we? You don't care what happens to the queen. You've as good as told me you work for the Fair Folk."

The Fair Folk. First Tom and now Robert: this lunacy seemed to be a disease sweeping London like the plague. But Robert, unlike Tom, was a practical man, far too canny to believe in goblins. What was the agent hiding? Who were these people he had mentioned, Oriana and the red king? How far was he sunk in treason against his queen?

He was not done with spying after all. He would have to discover more. How much did Robert think he knew? What would he be willing to barter for information?

Christopher ran his hand through his hair. "The murdered man, the one who was killed the night we left the Black Boar," he said cautiously. "Who was he? Which side did he work for?"

"He worked for the Catholics, actually. For John Bridges and his men," Robert said.

Christopher tried not to let the other man see his exaltation. The gamble had worked; for the first time since he'd known him Robert had parted with information.

"He'd discovered the other plot, the folk working for the red king," Robert went on. "He made the mistake of telling me about it. I had to have him killed."

"That's why you were so anxious to leave that night. You didn't want me to see that you knew him, and knew his assassin as well."

"Of course." Robert looked at him condescendingly, as though he were a slow pupil who had finally come to understand that day's lesson. "But then I changed my mind—I decided I needed you at the court after all. So I forged the note I showed you—"

"You forged— Did you forge the blood as well?"

Robert showed his rotting teeth. It took Christopher a moment to realize that the other man was smiling. "Nay—the blood was real enough," he said. "I didn't know if you would believe me—I had to pretend to be angry at you that day to keep you from suspecting anything. But you did believe it, didn't you? Enough to go to court and do the work I needed you to do. Though you needed the red king's men to help you every so often."

"Aye," Christopher said. He sat back, astonished. He had never left the maze he had entered at court, he realized; he had been wandering through its twists and turns for three years. And the end of it all was the same as the beginning, this smiling man here before him. Robert had had a hand in everything. He said slowly, "Do you know—did you know a man named Geoffrey Ryder?"

"Aye," Robert said pleasantly. "Since we're being so open with each other I may as well tell you—I lied to you a moment ago. I did indeed have more than one agent at court. Geoffrey was the other one. How did you know?"

"You quoted Chaucer to him once. You heard one of the plotters speak a line from *Canterbury Tales* and you repeated it to him, probably without even realizing it. And he repeated it to me. That's why, I guess, he and Will asked me if I was a spy the first time we met—Geoffrey had heard about me from you and he said something to his brother. Or—" The next question proved much harder to ask. "Or was Will working for you too?"

"Will? He was Essex's man, wasn't he? Not very suited for this kind of work, I always thought."

Christopher let out his breath in relief. He did not think he could stand more of Robert's double-dealing.

"Now it's your turn to answer questions," Robert said. "I never give away knowledge for nothing. Who are you working for?"

What would Robert say if he told him the truth, that the man who employed him, Thomas Walsingham, wanted not information but a poem? Oh, he would have to be careful, very careful.

"I haven't done much at all since I left your service," Christopher said slowly. "I know some of the old men, followers of Sir Francis, but I've been out of the game for a while."

Robert watched him shrewdly.

"To tell you the truth, I miss it," Christopher said. "Does this—this red king have anything to offer me? Who is he?"

"I told you," Robert said. "He's king of the Fair Folk. Nay, why are you smiling?"

"The Fair Folk. It's—well, it's hard to believe, that's all."

"I assure you it's true. Probably he would have a place for you, if you're interested. That is, if you're telling me the truth. How do I know you're not working for Oriana?"

"I suppose my word will have to be good enough. I can only tell you I've never heard of her in my life."

"Ah. And so we're back where we started." Robert called out a word Christopher didn't catch. Something sharp pressed against his neck.

One of the little men moved into his sight, still holding the sword to his throat. The man grinned widely. How had he gotten into the room without Christopher hearing him?

"Your clothes are too fine," Robert said. Christopher turned back to him. "Who's paying you? I don't believe you're as much out of the game as you pretend."

"I—I have a patron now. Thomas Walsingham. A cousin of Sir Francis."

"I know who he is. Why didn't you mention him earlier? And why do you need work from me if this man pays you so well?"

Christopher thought quickly. What could he say? That he hadn't said anything because he suspected Robert of treason?

"You work for Oriana, don't you?" Robert said. "Is that what Walsingham hired you to do?"

"Nay!" The sword cut deeper into Christopher's skin and he tried to back away. "Listen. Listen, Robert. You've been deceived. There are no Fair Folk—this is all folly. This man who calls himself the red king convinced you of his powers but it's a lie—it's all lies. He's tricked you."

"Is that what you think?"

"Of course. What proof do you have of anything supernatural? These folks have led you astray, have caused you to betray your queen."

"Proof?" Robert said. "Oh, I have proof enough."

The little man flared, became a spire of flame. Heat radiated from him, scorching the sleeve of Christopher's doublet. Then, just as quickly, he returned to what he had been, a small unearthly man grinning widely from ear to ear.

"There will be a battle soon," Robert said. "A great battle. He would fight in that form, but his enemies can turn to water just as easily. Do you understand? There's your proof, if you need it."

Christopher barely heard him. What had happened? Was it true then, all of it? Did Tom really journey through that strange land he talked about? Was Arthur really a king? Robert had challenged everything he believed in, called into question all he knew. He could not ignore what he had seen, but it was something so far removed from his experience that he could hardly bring himself to take it in.

"Do you believe now?" Robert asked.

"Nay, I saw nothing. Why should I believe you?"

"Nothing! Why, man, he turned into fire before your eyes. How can you say——"

"Did he? I didn't see it."

"What is this folly? Do you only believe things you see with your own eyes?"

"Aye," Christopher said, his voice level.

"Is this something you learned at Cambridge?" Robert said angrily. For a moment no one spoke.

The man blazed outward again, becoming fire. This time Christopher was ready. He stood quickly and drew his dagger, then knocked over the table and placed the dagger at the agent's throat. The flame darkened, solidified, became a man again.

"Call him off," Christopher said harshly. The little man looked from one to the other of them, uncertainty in his eyes. "Do it or I'll kill you."

"I——I will," Robert said. "You heard him. Put away your sword."

The little man returned his sword to a sheath almost as big as he was.

"Good," Christopher said. "Now——" He tried to think, but the wonders Robert had shown him kept crowding into his vision. Things he had denied had proved to be real. What else had he been wrong about? The world had shown itself to be a far stranger place than he had thought.

Robert called out a word he didn't understand. The window opened, and little men slid through like a fall of leaves, grinning and calling to each other. Several held swords out in front of them. Christopher turned, but he was not quick enough. One of the men knocked the dagger from his hand.

"Nay——" Christopher said, backing away.

Robert motioned to the man. Christopher headed for the

door but another man stopped him: Christ, they were fast! He spun to face Robert.

"I can't let you leave," Robert said. He sounded almost regretful. "I don't know what your business is here, or who you work for."

"I told you—I don't—"

Robert signaled to the first man again. Christopher turned toward him quickly, looked wildly between him and Robert. His mouth felt dry. The little man leapt to a bench. His sword came up and pointed toward Christopher's right eye. He looked for his dagger but it was too late. The man thrust the sword forward.

Thomas Kyd knocked loudly on Thomas Nashe's door, knocked again when no one came to answer. Finally the door opened and Nashe looked out at him. Though it was midday he seemed to have just gotten out of bed.

"What half-wit plucks me from my naked bed?" Nashe said, misquoting Kyd's play *The Spanish Tragedy.*

Kyd scowled at him. He had come prepared to offer sympathy, but now he realized, angrily, that Nashe had no feelings of compassion at all, that there was nothing he would not turn into some sort of joke. "Your friend's dead," he said.

"Friend? Who?"

"Kit Marlowe."

Nashe turned pale. "Lord have mercy on us!" he said. "Was it the plague?"

"Nay. He was stabbed."

"Stabbed?"

"Aye. He went to dinner with some friends of his, and there was an argument over who would pay the bill. Kit took a dagger away from one of the men and made as if to stab him, and the man turned his hand and drove the dagger into his right eye."

"Where did you hear this?"

"It's all over town. Where have you been?"

"With a patron." Nashe paused, as if trying to collect his thoughts. "You're out of prison, I see."

"Aye. They let me out a few days ago. They had to—I've done nothing wrong."

Kyd had expected the other man to joke about his time in Bridewell but Nashe said nothing. He looked distracted, at a loss for words. Perhaps the news had affected him more than Kyd had thought possible. Well, it didn't matter. Kyd made his farewells and turned to go.

Nashe spent a restless night. He had not slept well since the brown woman had given him the flower; sometimes he thought he might be haunted by her the rest of his life. And now this dreadful news Tom Kyd had brought kept him awake. Could it be true? He had never known Kit to argue about a bill before; of all of them his friend seemed to have the most money, though where he got it had always been a mystery. At last Nashe passed into a sort of half-sleep, and he began to dream.

It was not like any dream he had ever had. He saw nothing, could only hear a witless, idiotic voice speaking in the darkness, droning on and on. After a time he became aware that he could make out the words.

"Left, right," the voice said. "Day, night. Front, back—have, lack. Right, wrong—short, long."

Through it all he knew that he was dreaming, and he struggled to come awake. "Short, tall," the voice said. "Big, small. False, true—old, new."

The voice seemed to speak to him for hours, tireless. Finally, near dawn, he awoke. An idea had grown in his mind while he slept, planted by something the voice had said. He dressed quickly and went out to find Tom Kyd.

Kyd was not in the room he and Marlowe had once shared. The place had apparently been rented to someone else, a man adding up columns of numbers who demanded to know what he meant by this interruption. Nashe closed the door on him and hurried toward Kyd's lodgings, his suspicions hardening into certainty as he ran.

He took the stairs to Kyd's room two steps at a time. "Tom!"

he said, pounding on the door. "Tom, listen. Kit was murdered—I know it!"

Kyd opened the door. Nashe made as if to go past him, into the room, but Kyd blocked the way. "Listen," Nashe said, breathing hard. "He was murdered—Kit was murdered. Listen to this."

Kyd moved aside reluctantly. Now Nashe noticed that Kyd looked ill, as if something had broken within him at Bridewell. He shuddered to think what they must have done to him there. As he went inside he saw a candle on the desk flicker and go out. Piles of paper were heaped around the candlestick, all of them covered with Kyd's fine spidery writing. The man must have been up for hours. "What do you want?" Kyd asked.

"Listen to this. Here," Nashe said. He took the quill from the desk and handed it to Kyd. "Hold this. Pretend it's the dagger. You're holding it in your right hand, and if someone bent it backwards it would go into your right eye. Like this." He twisted Kyd's wrist, a little too violently, and the other man cried out. Nashe let go. "But Kit is—was left-handed. If he held the dagger in his left hand, like this"—Nashe held the quill himself this time—"it would have gone into his left eye. Do you see?"

Kyd said nothing. "Do you see?" Nashe said again, nearly frantic to make the other man understand.

"Aye," Kyd said. "What of it?"

"What of it?" Nashe asked, incredulous. "Someone's lying. Someone murdered him and made it look like a quarrel. We've got to tell the authorities—"

"Why?"

"To bring his murderer to justice. He was your friend too, wasn't he?" Kyd did not reply. "Wasn't he?"

"He was no friend of mine," Kyd said coldly.

Something on the desk caught Nashe's eye. "He was intemperate and of a cruel heart . . . Never could my Lordship endure his name, or sight . . ." he read.

"What is this?" he asked, almost whispering. He felt suddenly cold.

"Nothing," Kyd said, but he made no move to cover the pages.

"It's about Kit, isn't it?"

"Aye."

"Why?"

"Because— You spoke of justice, but justice has not been done here. I went to prison because of your friend, I was whipped and tortured because of him and his blasphemous opinions. Is that justice? Does it seem to you that justice has been done?"

"But—but he's dead. Isn't that justice enough for you?"

"Nay. I'll never rid myself of the taint of atheism. I've lost my patron because of him—Lord Strange no longer speaks to me. I've had to give up the room I rented for lack of money."

"But what you say here—it isn't even true. 'Intemperate and of a cruel heart'—even you can see that's false."

"Is it? He fought duels, he told me so himself."

"Everyone fights duels."

"Not I."

"Nay, you use more cowardly means. Do you think that blackening his name this way will return you to your lord's favor?"

"I do, aye. And he's beyond caring, I assure you. I have to live. I have to win my patron back, and do it by whatever methods I can."

"But this is monstrous!" Nashe said, horrified. He was about to say more, but suddenly he was visited by a premonition so strong it struck him dumb. Thomas Kyd would not survive the year. He had been so ill-used at Bridewell that his health had broken. They would all be dead, then, all the jolly companions, Robin and Kit and Tom. And he would have to find a way to go on alone.

Kyd said something else, but Nashe didn't hear him. He turned and left, his heart overcome with grief.

A few days later Tom Nashe found himself at the old tavern at the sign of the Saracen's Head. He had gone there for a midday meal, unable to work but unwilling to be alone with his thoughts. The tavern was nearly deserted because of the plague, but there was no one he wanted to talk to anyway. Why had he come? He could not rid himself of old memories; he thought he would give almost anything to hear Kit and Robin argue again.

It was as he had told Kit long ago: he was enchanted. The brown woman had enchanted him. Why else should he be the only one of all of them to survive? He had done nothing to deserve it.

The door opened and Will Ryder came in. He realized, guiltily, that he had given no thought to the boy since Kit had died, and he motioned him over. As Will sat Tom noticed that his usual open expression had gone; he looked like the stunned survivor of a disaster.

"I'm sorry," Tom said softly.

"Aye," Will said. "Aye, so am I. I keep thinking about the poem he was writing, and how no one will ever read the end of it now. I was going to be his patron, did he tell you?"

Should he tell Will what he knew? Would it help him or would it only serve to make him angry? But the need to unburden himself was too great, powerful enough to drive out any other consideration. Slowly at first, and then with more confidence, he repeated what he had told Tom Kyd.

Will listened, saying nothing. At least he would not condemn Kit out of hand, and for that Tom felt grateful. He had had enough of folks in London saying that Kit's death was punishment for his atheism. What about Tom Kyd? he had asked them. What sin had he been punished for? And what of the thousands who had died of the plague? God's judgments, he knew, did not work so neatly.

Will nodded when he had finished. "Aye," he said. "The story I heard never sounded right to me either."

He looked directly at Tom, and Tom, who had elicited hundreds of confidences over the years, knew what was about to happen next: Will would tell him something he had never told anyone else. For the first time in his life he felt he could not bear hearing another confession. But his face, so used to wearing an expression of interest and concern, must have betrayed him, because Will continued to speak.

"Do you know—I knew that man, that Robert Poley. My brother knew him. I'd seen them whispering together often enough, and I knew that he was not to be trusted. I tried to tell Kit not to go with him—"

"It wasn't your fault."

"I know that. I know. But I keep thinking that if I'd tried harder, if I'd told him what I'd seen—"

"No one could ever talk him out of anything, once he'd made up his mind. He was the most stubborn man I ever met."

"Aye, that's true enough." Will almost smiled. "What do we do now? Do we go to the authorities with what you've told me?"

"They wouldn't believe us. Poley had agents of his swear that they were there in Deptford, swear that Kit was killed in self-defense. They've already been pardoned, all of them."

"Then—we're helpless, aren't we? Who can we go to? I don't have the friends at court I once had—I've been away—"

"It has something to do with those men Kit saw at the palace, those misshapen men. And with the land I went to, and with Arthur. We don't need to go to court—if we find these people, these goblins or whatever they are—"

He took off his hat and looked at the unfading flower he had pinned to it. "They gave me this," he said slowly. "What if this is a way to summon them? What if I had it these three years and more and never knew?"

"What are you going to do?"

"I don't know. Shall we try to summon them up, like Faustus calling up Mephostophilis?"

"Nay, don't—"

"Don't worry—they're not demons. I know that much about them." He unpinned the flower and held it in his hand. "Maybe if—if I think about them—"

He fell silent a moment. Nothing happened. "Well, it was worth trying," he said. He moved to pin the flower to his hat again.

"Nay, wait a minute. Who gave you the flower?"

"A woman—a beautiful woman—"

"Think about her. Call her to you. Summon her up in your mind—remember everything you know about her. What did she look like? How did she move? What color were her eyes?"

"Blue," Tom said. He closed his eyes. "Blue as berries."

"Good. And her hair?"

"Brown. Brown and tied up in a garland of flowers."

"And what did she—Tom. Tom, look."

He opened his eyes quickly. There in the dim light of the tavern stood the woman he had carried in his mind for three years. "You wear my favor," she said. He had never heard her voice before; it was clear as a running stream. "I'd forgotten that."

"Aye," Tom said. He could not seem to speak above a whisper.

"Then are you prepared to fight for us?"

"To—to fight?"

"Aye. We are not ready yet, and we try never to fight in the light of the sun, but you have called us to you. We cannot resist a summons by a mortal who wears our favor—the battle must begin now."

"Battle?"

"Come." She turned and began to leave the tavern.

"Wait!" he said, calling after her. The few men in the tavern looked up at him in surprise; no one but he and Will seemed to have seen her. "Wait—at least tell me—"

But she had opened the door and was gone.

20

A week after Art had come to live with her Alice saw Walter making his way toward her station. "Shall we close our stalls?" he asked, smiling. "I haven't sold a book all day."

"What do you want to do?" she said. As always her voice trembled a little when she spoke to him, though she tried to control it. What would he think if he knew her true feelings about him? She thought that she would not be able to face it if he did.

"See a play, I thought."

"We've seen all the companies that stayed in London," she said, more sharply than she intended. "I should know—I publish the playbills."

"What, then? We can't stay in this dismal place."

As if to underscore his words a bell rang out, tolling for another death. She looked up at the tower of Paul's, remembering that she had seen a young man—had it been Tom Nashe's friend?—climb to the top. In all her years in the city she had never seen the view, though it seemed that every visitor to London went there. "We could go to the top of the tower."

He said nothing, and for a moment she feared she had been too forward. Until now they had only gone to playhouses and cookshops together, and perhaps he would not want to disrupt that routine, to change the nature of their friendship. Then he said, "That's an excellent idea. I've always wondered what the city looks like from there."

She closed her stall and led the way into the church. They walked through the huge wooden nave, their footsteps echoing off the high arched ceiling. It seemed strange to hear the church so quiet; usually the halls rang with the sounds of men preaching sermons, lawyers calling for clients, employers looking for folks to hire. Then they went up the stairway to the top.

She was a little winded from the climb, but even so the view took her breath away. London spread out before them like an engraving, small and vital. They could see the stairs leading down to the Thames, and beyond that the sun striking the sails of the boats on the river. To their left was London Bridge, and across the river she could just make out the round building that was the Bear Gardens.

"I should have come here a long time ago," Alice said.

"You've never seen this?"

"Nay."

"And you've lived here—how long?"

"Over twenty years." She laughed. The river below them sparkled and dimmed as the sun moved in and out of the clouds. "But you've been here three years and have never seen it either."

"Aye." They fell silent, watching the ever-changing scene beneath them. He began to speak of his life before coming to London, the inn he had owned, the problems of being an innkeeper. "My wife couldn't stand it," he said. "I would have come to London long ago, probably, if she had lived."

"Your—wife?" she asked, startled.

"Aye. She died in the last great plague, nearly thirty years ago."

"And you never remarried?"

"Nay. And you—what was it like for you when your husband died?"

She had never spoken of John's death to anyone, not even Margery; she had not wanted to trouble folks with her sorrow.

Now it seemed to her that if she started she would not be able to stop, that she would burden Walter with the accumulated weight of four years' unhappiness. But he had probably asked out of politeness, and not because he really wanted an answer. She said, carefully, "It was hard, especially at first."

He turned away from the view in front of him and looked directly at her. "Alice, you are the most vexing person I know."

"What?" she said, surprised. "I—"

"In all the years I've known you you have told me nothing about yourself. Your son has gone missing, but I know that from the other stationers and not from you. Now your sister has died, and you have a new son to care for, but you have said not one word about your sister or your son. I have never heard how it was your husband became a stationer, or what it was like for you to take over his trade, or how you feel about George's accusations against you. If I didn't listen to the other stationers I would almost think you had no life outside of the church-yard."

She had listened to him talk with growing amazement. At the end of it she found she could not speak, did not know where to begin. It had grown hot in the tower, and stuffy from lack of air. "I—"

"Am I prying?"

She shook her head.

"Is it because of George? Because you trusted George, and he betrayed that trust?"

How well he knew her, after all. She nodded, glad for the moment that she did not have to speak.

"Alice, listen. I am not like George. I care about you, more than you know. I think you are brave, very brave, to have done as much as you have on your own, but it is not good for anyone, man or woman, to be too much alone."

She nodded again, thinking that she must be dreaming. For how many years had she imagined he might say something like this? For how many nights had she lain awake, hoping that perhaps the next day, or the next, would bring a declaration of his feelings? She turned to him, intending, finally, to tell him the truth. Then she saw something move outside the tower, and she gasped.

They were in one of the highest places in London, she knew. Nothing human could walk outside the tower. The thing scuttled along from buttress to buttress, using its feet and hands equally. Then it stopped and looked directly at her, opening its pointed snout to show her its teeth. She shuddered and turned away from it, toward the churchyard, and saw a few more of the creatures scurrying among the booksellers. The battle they all had waited for had finally begun.

"What is it?" Walter asked.

He hadn't seen it. She looked out beyond the churchyard walls, and what she saw there made her gasp a second time in alarm. A few of the creatures were headed toward her house, toward Art and Brownie. What did they want with her son? Did they imagine she still had the Prince of Faerie? She could not think. She knew only that she had to stop them before they found Art.

"I—I'm sorry, but I have to go home," she said. "Something—something pressing—"

"What is it? Can I help?"

Of course. He could come with her. All at once her feelings of dread left her, and she began to breathe easier. She turned to ask for his help, and then she remembered the promise she had made to Brownie. She had said she would never bring this man into her house. Walter had spoken of trust, and she could not betray Brownie's trust a second time.

"I— Nay. I wish you could. But this is something I have to do alone."

He nodded slowly. She could see that he did not understand, that he still hoped to do something for her. "I wish you trusted me more, Alice."

"It's not that!" she said, feeling that she could bear any words but those. "I have to do this alone." And she turned and ran down the stairs before he could say anything more.

Tom Nashe hastily pinned the flower to his hat and hurried outside after the brown woman. She had joined a group of women, the ones he had seen by the stream in Arthur's land. They moved quickly down Bishopsgate Street and he ran after them, trying to keep her in sight. Ahead of them he could barely make out a crowd of outlandish figures, horned men and animals, tiny flying creatures, all of them calling to one another excitedly.

The procession continued down Cheapside, toward Paul's. As they turned in at the gate Tom saw Alice Wood run from the tower and pass him on her way out. Did she have dealings with these folk? Her son certainly did. It irked him that someone might know something about London that he didn't.

Then the brown woman motioned toward him again, and he forgot everything but her face, her hands, her hair.

When Alice reached her house she found Margery and Agnes at the door. "Where's Art?" she asked. "Is he in danger?"

"Nay," Margery said. "Brownie's hidden him."

"Brownie? Where?"

"I don't know. Come—they're moving toward Paul's."

"What do they want with Art?"

"The red king wants him. He doesn't know which child is Oriana's true son. And even if Art is not her son he hopes to gain information about her from him."

"How do you know?"

"Never mind that. We must hurry."

Alice nearly followed her, moved by the urgency in Margery's voice. But something made her stop and face the other woman squarely. "Why? What do I care about Oriana's wars?"

"You can do nothing here. And Brownie may be in danger."

Alice sighed. Her life seemed to be bound up with these people whatever she did. She followed Margery back to Paul's.

They were in time to see the red king's creatures pass into the churchyard. The huge horses came first, then the sea-creatures, and after them a group of small misshapen figures who laughed and pointed as they walked. Finally they saw a long line of folks covered by shadow. Alice shivered a little in the afternoon sunlight, remembering what that shadow had hidden in Finsbury Field. The red king was nowhere in sight.

Some of the stationers looked directly at creatures and seemed to see nothing. Others rubbed their eyes, as if their vision troubled them. Though the weather was fine, a sun too bright for June shining on the yard, a few of the booksellers began to pack up their wares and close their stalls.

Oriana's soldiers, some of them mounted on the horned animals, some standing, faced the creatures with their lances ready. Their silver mail seemed light as gossamer. Behind them were the standard-bearers, and then the circle of horned men surrounding the queen. Alice thought she saw Arthur next to Oriana, but in the next moment the guard moved together and hid him from her. Was he ready to fight a battle of this magnitude? She did not believe that he could be.

There must have been some signal she missed, because in the next moment the two sides began to grapple with each other. The sea-creatures climbed over the stationers' stalls, scattering books and papers as they went for Oriana's men. Some scurried up the strong wooden buttresses of the church, or broke windows and ran through the aisles, calling shrilly to each other. As Alice watched one jumped from the roof to land on a horned man, who cried out and fell to the ground. The creature's strong, supple limbs kept him from reaching for his sword.

The booksellers had completely abandoned the churchyard now. Some watched from beneath the pillars, their faces filled with amazement and terror, but most had packed up and gone home. Two of the red king's men rocked a stall back and forth and finally succeeded in toppling it to the ground. They sent up a wild high cry of triumph.

Alice could not see George anywhere. But Walter had come down from the tower and was looking out at the disorder spread before him, standing too far away for her to make out his expression. What on earth would he make of it? Would he think it her doing? She remembered their conversation in the tower and thought that even he would not be anxious to keep company with her after this. Oriana had blighted her life, had taken away two of the people Alice had held dear, Arthur and Walter.

She glanced at the queen, standing surrounded by her guard,

and hoped bitterly that she would lose the war. Look at her, she thought, watching it all from the safety of her protected circle as others go out to die for her. How is she better than the red king? Arthur stood next to her, an abstracted look on his face. Oriana pointed to something, and Arthur nodded.

A brown figure darted out into the midst of the fighting, and Alice held her breath as she watched. She had never known Brownie to hold a sword before, but she saw with a sense of loss that it seemed to suit him, that he fought as well as any of the men alongside him. If the red king defeated Oriana she prayed that Brownie would come through safely. It was only then, her hands clenched hard in supplication and hope, that she remembered that Brownie had hidden Art, that he might be the only one to know where her son was. What if he dies? she thought. How do I get my son back? It seemed impossible to her that Art could have been given to her for so short a time, another of Oriana's cruel tricks.

The fighting closed in around Brownie. Margery was saying something at her side but Alice barely heard her. A sea-creature cut down one of the guards and moved up behind Brownie, and as Alice watched he turned at the last moment and parried its sword. Then he plunged his own sword into the thing's heart. "Look," Margery said again, pointing.

Alice turned away with difficulty. Paul Hogg stood by the churchyard gate, along with George and another man and his assistant, one of the water-people. How long had they been there? Hogg said something to the water spirit and it moved out into the battle. To Alice's horror she saw it going directly for Brownie. Then several of the twig-people, running through the yard, cut them both off from sight.

Perhaps the battle turned then, or perhaps Alice only noticed it at that moment. All over the yard Oriana's people were falling. The sky darkened, casting a kind of twilight over the churchyard. A huge creature carrying a club in one hand and a chain in the other grappled with one of the horned soldiers. The twig-people ran from the field, crying out to one another, and small leathery shapes scuttled after them. The winged creatures fluttered around the tower, not daring to come closer. As Alice watched she saw the light die from Robin Goodfellow's staff.

"Something went wrong—somehow the battle started too soon," Margery said, as if speaking to herself. "They were not made to fight in sunlight."

"But the sun's fading," Alice said. "Won't that help them?"

"Nay, that's the red king's doing. Darkness covering light, that's his weapon. Just as Oriana's weapon is light shining through the darkness."

Who were the creatures of darkness then? Alice thought. George had been wrong; the division between the two was not as sharp as he had thought.

"When will Oriana send Arthur?" Margery asked. "They will follow her son whatever happens."

"Arthur?" Alice said. "Look at him. He's not here to fight. He's here to be admired, to be made much of. After twenty-three years he's found a mother who will let him do as he pleases. Do you think he'd give that up?"

They saw Oriana speak to Arthur. "He might, if you talk to him," Margery said.

"If I—" Alice said, astonished. "Even when he thought he was my child he never listened to me. He's Oriana's son now— let her convince him."

"But she can't. Look at her."

"That's nothing to me. It's not my war."

"Then they will almost certainly lose."

Alice turned toward her friend, away from the field. What did Margery care who won? But before she could ask she saw something that stopped the words in her mouth. Margery held her hands out over the battlefield. Light streamed out from her, and the force of it seemed to raise a wind that blew her thick hair back from her head. The fighting stopped momentarily as both sides turned to see where the radiance came from, and then Oriana's folks raised their voices in a cheer.

When the battle started Tom lost the brown woman in the confusion. He moved anxiously around the edges of the churchyard, hoping that she had not decided to join the fighting. After a few minutes he caught sight of her, standing near the guard of horned men. She turned to him and then looked back at the churchyard.

He remembered what she had asked of him, back at the tavern. She wanted him to fight for her. And it was true that he wore her favor, though he hadn't realized when he had pinned it to his hat what she would require of him. But nay, he thought, shaking his head. What am I thinking? I'm no soldier.

Her eyes sought him out again, and this time she looked beseeching, filled with hope. I have no sword, he thought, but even as he protested his hand reached for the dagger he wore at his back like every other gallant in the city. Would it be enough? Would it protect him against the great horses that were even now moving into the thick of the fighting? Truly I must be bewitched, he thought, moving slowly into the churchyard. A few of the stationers called to him but he ignored them.

Blackness enveloped him almost immediately. He realized that he must have stepped into one of the eddies of shadow that covered the red king's followers. Muffled sounds of fighting came to him, the ring of sword on sword, the neighing of horses, but he could see nothing. Even the solid bulk of Paul's was lost in the darkness. He flailed around with his dagger and backed away a few paces. If he couldn't fight he could at least return to the safety of the church.

Two white eyes peered out at him from the shadows. The eyes looked sickly, like marshlights. Something hissed. He moved toward it, his dagger poised. The eyes disappeared, reappeared to his left. Or were there two of the creatures? He changed his course to counter it. The hissing noise came again, louder.

The eyes vanished again, and he spun around. This time they reappeared to his right, and slightly closer. I'm going to die, he thought. Who is this woman, that she can ask this of me?

He heard the hissing noise again, and something else, the sound of a great wind driving across the churchyard. As he watched the wind swept away the blackness. Nay, it did more than that; it seemed to carry with it its own light, a brilliance that suffused the yard. Now he could see the soft, wrinkled creature that stood before him. It was barely three feet high. He moved toward it and it turned and ran. "Coward!" he called to it, laughing wildly in his relief. "Will you attack only in the dark?" In two steps he was upon it, and he hewed it down. The fluid that came from the thing seemed more like foul water than blood.

The sweep of the light revealed Brownie. He and the water spirit thrust and parried with their swords, first one and then the other gaining the advantage. Alice watched as they moved back and forth across the churchyard, and she remembered that Hogg had spoken to his creature before it had gone out to fight. Had he directed it toward Brownie out of spite? Did he want Brownie dead because he knew of her fondness for him? She had not realized, in all her years, that such malice existed.

The water spirit gained the shelter of one of the stalls and clambered to the top. From its advantage it moved as if to cut Brownie down, but Brownie overturned the stall with one quick motion and the water spirit fell. She saw Brownie stand over it and slash downward with his sword.

But the triumph for Oriana was short-lived. As Alice watched the glowing light seemed to dim. Shadows began to creep back, coiling like oozing water over the churchyard. The wind around Margery grew less fierce and her face looked strained, grim. "What is it?" Alice asked, but Margery did not seem to hear her.

"It's Hogg," Agnes said. "Look—he's fighting back."

The blackness seemed strongest by the churchyard gate, where Paul Hogg stood with George. Alice struggled to see through the gloom but she could make out only that his arms were raised, like Margery's.

"Now," Margery said. Her breath came in gasps, and Alice saw to her horror that sweat ran down her face. "I can't— Arthur. You must—talk to Arthur now. Or they will lose this war."

And why shouldn't they, after what Oriana's done to me? Alice thought. She took away my only child and left me a stranger instead. John never knew his true son. And Walter—

She looked up and saw Walter's eyes on her. What would he think if she went to talk to the queen? Nay. It felt to her as if she had one last chance at happiness, and she'd be damned if she let Oriana take that away too.

But she could not say any of this to Margery, could not break the terrible concentration she saw on her friend's face. She could only watch as the light around them faded to almost nothing. And then another voice came to her out of the darkness. "Aye," it said. "You're right—it's useless to meddle in these affairs. Arthur will not listen to anything you say."

"What—"

"You were never a very good mother to the child," the voice said. "You couldn't teach him anything, couldn't keep him from leaving you finally. Look how quickly he went to Oriana, without even a backward glance. He cares nothing for you. Why should he heed you now?"

Aye, it was true. She felt something almost like relief. The outcome of the battle could not be affected by anything she did. She would not have to speak to Arthur after all. The red king would triumph, of course, but that was nothing to her.

There was even a painful satisfaction in being told that she had been a poor mother to Arthur. All those years of wondering, of thinking that if only she had done things differently her son would not have left—all of them were cancelled out, just like that. She had no more questions, only certainties. She had been a bad mother, and she had paid the price.

"It's Hogg!" Margery said. "He's the one whispering these things to you. Don't listen to him!" She lowered her arms, drained by her effort.

"I don't care!" Alice said. "Don't you understand? I don't care what happens to Oriana. She took my son and I want her to suffer for it."

"I'm not—" Margery said. But all around them folks were raising their eyes, looking to the church's tower. The dragons had come.

The red and silver dragons Alice had seen over Finsbury Field circled for advantage near the tower. As she watched the silver dragon gained the air above the other one and flew down toward it, claws extended. The red dragon cried out and spewed flame.

Fire coursed to the churchyard below, and several of the stationers called out in alarm. The wooden structure of Paul's burned easily; lightning had destroyed the steeple ten years before Alice had come to London. Smoke began to rise from one of the stalls. A stationer ran out from the safety of the pillars and smothered the fire with his cloak.

"I'm not talking about Oriana," Margery said, as if nothing had interrupted their conversation. The yard in front of them grew lighter as the silver dragon harried the red one, keening loudly. "I'm talking about your son. He needs to become independent of both his mothers, so that he may learn how to be a king."

Alice looked at her friend, incredulous. Perhaps the battle with Hogg had been too much for her and she had lost her wits. Or perhaps she was older than Alice thought, and had already reached her dotage. "Arthur is not my son," she said, speaking slowly, as if to a child. "The Prince of Faerie is not my son. He's a changeling. This woman here—" she turned to Agnes—"told me so herself. She was present at his birth."

"There was a woman in the village where I grew up," Agnes said. "She lost her son shortly after he was born. And there was another family killed by the plague, all but a little boy. And the woman raised the boy as if he were her own son, and soon no one remembered that the two of them were not related. There are other ties than those of blood."

"What are you saying?" Alice said slowly. "That Arthur is my son, whether he's related to me or not?"

"I'm not saying anything," Agnes said placidly. "Do you think Arthur is your son?"

Alice looked into the sky to avoid answering. The red dragon had slipped out from the other's deadly embrace and now flew over the tower. Flames shot from its mouth. The silver dragon darted away but the other was too fast for it. Fire scorched its wing, leaving a gaping wound that showed black against the silver.

Noises came from the churchyard. Alice saw that the fighting, which had come to a standstill while the dragons grappled with each other, had begun again. The shadowy tide had returned, creeping forward.

Was Arthur her son? She remembered her thoughts when she had exchanged him for the other boy, her strong feeling that a mistake had been made. And she remembered other things too: how he had sung to her and John in the evenings, his beautiful voice soaring, the light of the fire reflecting in his eyes. He had been happy then, she would stake her life on it. And the way John had carried him on his shoulders through the churchyard, showing him off to the other stationers, as proud as if he'd fathered a whole brood of sons. And how Arthur had taken her by the hand to show her a birds' nest in the rafters at Paul's, his face serious and intent, and how he had watched the birds for hours after that, nearly motionless.

She looked over to where he stood with the queen. He alone shared her memories of the happy time before John had died, the only one in all the world. He was her family, all that was left to her. What would happen to him if Oriana lost? Probably the red king would take him captive; perhaps they would even put him to death.

"Arthur does not even remember you," the voice said in her mind. "Leave him to his fate. What does it matter what happens to him?"

Was that true? Had Arthur forgotten her already? Then she was truly alone; the time with John might not have even existed.

"Don't listen to him," Margery said at her side. "It's Hogg who is saying these things to you."

What did it matter who said them? She felt them to be true, knew that if she went to Arthur he would not recognize her. She could see his vacant, idiot's stare in her mind.

The shadow had coiled forward while she stood there. It seemed that dusk had come to the churchyard, so dark did it appear. She searched for Arthur but could barely see him in the gloom. And yet she thought he looked back at her, and his expression did not seem vacant at all.

"A trick of the light," Hogg said. "Nothing more."

She shook her head to silence him. She could not rid herself of the idea that Arthur wanted something from her. She remembered how he had looked at her as a child when he had met with something out of his experience, half bewildered and half calmly certain that she would know what to do, and it seemed to her that he wore the same expression now. Perhaps Hogg was wrong; perhaps Arthur still cared for her, as much as these folks cared for anyone. It was that thought more than anything else, her curiosity to see what had become of the boy she had raised, that made her start around the edge of the yard toward where he stood with the queen.

She could barely find her way in the mist of shadows. Shapes rose up before her: warriors on horses with their lances ready, luminous dragons breathing flame. Something made her push forward and the figures gave way. She thought they might be tricks of the darkness, one last attempt of the red king to keep her from reaching Arthur. If that was true then the battle must be nearing its end, the king too exhausted to send his creatures against her. And what of Oriana? If the darkness was any indication the queen fared even worse.

Something seemed to light the way ahead of her, a shape as white as a candle. Oriana. She made her way toward the queen, parting the mist before her like a curtain. The horned men moved forward to block her but the queen raised her hand and they fell back.

She had nothing to say to the queen. All of her concern was for Arthur. The child she thought she had known so well stood before her, light shining from his face. She realized how much she had missed him these past years. She had done him wrong by not visiting him at Margery's cottage, had done them both wrong. "Arthur," she said softly.

"Aye," he said. He sounded as confused as a child. "Where am I? What is happening?"

"You are with your mother, your true mother," Alice said. It hurt her to say it, but she forced herself to go on. "She is the Queen of Faerie, and you are its prince."

"Nay," he said. "I've been asleep, and have only woken now.

Or I have been awake until today, and this is my dream." He looked closer at her. "You are my mother, are you not?"

"Aye." Oriana looked at her, and Alice felt gratified to see something like fear in the queen's eyes. "We are both your mothers. One to bear you and one to raise you."

"I thought that she was my mother. I was unhappy, and I thought I would be happy when I found my true family. But things are different here, so strange and terrible—" He gestured helplessly. "I don't belong here either. I don't belong anywhere."

She could not bear the pain in his voice. "Take me home with you," he said. "I want everything the same as it was before."

It cost everything she had to summon the strength to refuse him. She could not speak, only shake her head. "If I took you with me you would be happy for a day, no more," she said finally. "You would always wonder what you had missed, you would go seeking after enchantment the way you did as a child."

"Nay—"

"You are my son, Arthur. You have my strength, and John's. We taught you as best we could, not knowing what you were. You have lived among us, and so it may be that you have learned something of love, and compassion, and understanding. But your place is with these folks now. You are their king."

"King . . ." he said wonderingly. She saw that he had never realized what that word meant before, had not understood the responsibilities that went with it. "And I am to—to lead my people into battle?"

So it had come to this, Alice thought. Arthur had missed the Armada but he would go soldiering anyway. She could not say the word to condemn him to that.

But others could. One of the guards gave him a sword. Another called to the standard-bearer, who took his place at the king's side, carrying aloft the old rotted banners. A mount was found for him, and someone blew the horn, the ancient call to battle. It seemed to Alice that the darkness stopped a little at that sound, that its forward motion might have halted for just a moment.

Alice went to Arthur and took him in an embrace. "Come back safely, my child," she said.

The horn sounded again, and he mounted and rode into battle.

All around the churchyard folks lifted their heads at the notes of the horn. One by one Oriana's soldiers fought free of their attackers and hurried to their king's side. By the time Arthur reached the center of the yard he had gathered a sizable train. "O-ri-a-na!" they called with one voice. Light came from them, driving back the darkness.

Arthur wheeled the horned mount and faced the first of the red king's people. Alice saw that his face had lost the foolish smugness it had acquired the day they gave him to Oriana; instead he looked purposeful, determined. A sea-creature rode up on one of the huge horses, and he engaged it in battle.

The fighting surged back and forth across the churchyard. Alice caught no more than glimpses of it: Arthur rallying those who fought for the queen; Brownie, his brown eyes shining as he followed his king; Tom looking puzzled but fighting on anyway. The dragons flew above them, circling the tower. Dusk had come, but the churchyard still glowed with its own light.

Suddenly she became aware that Hogg had turned away from the battle and was looking at the gate. Margery had grown very still, as if she waited for something. Reluctantly, Alice followed Hogg's gaze. The red king came into the churchyard.

His crown seemed to burn with a dark fire. Each link of his suit of mail flickered like a small flame. A hellish glare came from his eyes. One of the winged creatures cried out and flew helplessly toward him, like a moth to candlelight, and fell to the ground before it reached him.

Will he fight? Alice thought. Has it come to that? But instead of joining the battle the red king went to Paul Hogg and said something to him in a low voice.

A strong heat rose from the red king, and his voice was like flame speaking to wood. Hogg stood his ground, trying not to back away. "You must see to it that your part of the bargain is kept," the king said.

"What do you mean?"

"You promised to bring me Arthur."

"Arthur? But Oriana has him."

"Do you think that's the end of it? If she has him then you must take him from her."

"It was never part of our bargain that I fight for you," Hogg said. Could he hold off the power of the red king? How much protection would his magic circles afford him?

"Aye, it was," the red king said. The last word hissed like rotted wood consumed to ashes. "You and your warriors." He looked at George and Anthony.

"Nay, I will not."

"You will. You will when I tell you what you so desperately need to know."

"And what is that?"

"The true nature of the Philosopher's Stone."

The red king moved closer and whispered in Hogg's ear. Hogg's eyes widened with astonishment. The king stepped back, and in his hand was a glowing sword.

Hogg took the sword from him carefully. It burned against his skin for a moment, then cooled to the temperature of his hand. He studied along its length; it seemed almost made for him. "Come," he said to George and Anthony, and then, without waiting to see if they would follow, he moved into the thick of the fighting.

Someone bellowed in his ear; someone nearly knocked him down with the hilt of a sword. A horse neighed close by. It was far more chaotic than he had expected. He thrust his way through the fighting toward Arthur.

Arthur shone like the sun on water. The light nearly blinded Hogg. One of the horned men stepped out of a knot of soldiers, his sword drawn, and Hogg raised his own weapon to counter him.

It was not like any sword-work Hogg had ever known. Men on both sides jostled them as they fought, and it was hard work to keep his footing in the shifting tide of battle. He moved in to attack but his opponent seemed to be waiting for him; he backed away but the man came after him. Then someone stumbled against the horned man and he went down, knocked off balance. Hogg bent over him and thrust his sword to the man's heart.

He turned and looked for Arthur. As he straightened he felt a sharp pain in his side, fierce as loss. He closed his eyes, overcome with the pain, and when he opened them again he found himself on the ground. Two pairs of boots scuffled near his head.

What had happened? He raised his head with difficulty and saw that he had been wounded. Blood seeped over his doublet.

He tried to see Arthur, but the boy was still hidden by the press of fighting. He closed his eyes again, felt the last of his strength ebb away. The noises around him stilled.

The red king looked out at the battle. He had not moved or changed his expression, but Alice thought that something had happened to displease him. He raised his arm and a giant shape came into the yard, something so huge it battered the gate's lintel to the ground. It was the size of a tree, and it carried a chain in one hand and a club in the other. It headed purposefully toward Arthur, moving quickly, and the red king's soldiers parted to make way for it.

Arthur's mount shied as it caught sight of the thing. In two steps the giant was upon him, the length of chain swinging from its hand. Arthur brought his sword up to meet it. He looked very young. With one thrust of its club the creature knocked the sword from Arthur's hand. Another thrust, and Arthur fell from his mount. He moaned and clutched his side. The giant stood over him, its club upraised.

Without even thinking about what she was doing Alice darted out into the fighting. She snatched Tom's dagger from his hand, and before he had time to react she came up behind the giant and plunged the dagger deep into the sinews of its knee.

It roared and turned to face her. She ran as its club struck downward. It raised the length of chain. Out of the corner of her eye she saw Arthur stand and retrieve his sword, and as the giant bore down upon her Arthur struck. It turned again, and Arthur stabbed it in the stomach.

The giant staggered back. Alice felt the ground shake as it fell. Two of the horned men hurried up to it, their swords lifted. She moved as quickly as she could toward the pillars of the cathedral, not waiting to see what they did with it.

Tom looked around him slowly. The noises of battle were fading, and it seemed as if the sun rose, though surely they had been fighting all day. He picked up the dagger Alice had dropped and noticed that it was covered not with blood but with a sort of pale watery fluid. The sight appalled him.

So did the memory of the exultant mood that had come over him in battle. He had never killed before. Had the brown woman truly bewitched him? Or did he only feel what all soldiers felt in the heat of war? He backed away. Fighting was not for him. Yet was this so very different from the paper battles he fought with Gabriel Harvey?

He stumbled toward one of the side doors of the church. The brown woman stepped out from the shelter of the doorway and came toward him. She put her arms around him and kissed him, her mouth tasting smooth as clear water.

The silver dragon screamed. The red dragon backed away and then, to the horror of the stationers who had stayed to watch, it plunged down and came in toward the churchyard, near the gate. A few stalls toppled as it landed, and the swing of its tail burst one of the stained glass windows.

Seeing it in the sky had not prepared Alice for the size of the thing. It stretched nearly half the length of Paul's, and its scales were as big as dinner plates. The scales reared up into two ridges, almost horns, over its eyes. The eyes were slitted, like a cat's, and a plume of smoke came from its nostrils.

The dragon lowered its snout to the ground as if questing for something. It took the red king in its mouth, carrying him almost gently, and turned and set him on its back. Then it lifted its wings and flew away. The wind of its passage raised the dirt in the yard, blew clothing backward and knocked the stationers' books to the ground.

The silver dragon dove for it as it gained the air. The red dragon feinted to the left and then swooped back over the tower, but the other was too quick for it. The silver dragon flew in close and gripped the red dragon hard with its talons.

The red dragon struggled to get free, its tail lashing back and forth like a whip. Something the size of a child's toy dropped from its back and plummeted to the earth. The stationers watched in horror as the red king fell to the churchyard. No one moved for a long moment. Then, as if he were licked from inside by flame, the king caught fire and burned to ash. The red dragon keened, a sound of such grief it seemed to rend the air in two, and flew off toward the river. The other followed, crying out in triumph.

With the red king dead his soldiers seemed to lose heart. All around the churchyard his creatures dropped their weapons and ran for the gate, those that were not caught and killed by the queen's folk. A few people cheered. Even some of the booksellers cheered, though there was not one of them who had not suffered some loss in the destruction of the yard.

Suddenly Alice noticed that a knot of stationers had gathered around George's stall. Curious, she made her way toward it. As she came closer she heard some of the men murmur in alarm, and one or two of them crossed themselves. A few of the men moved aside for her, as if to acknowledge that she of all people had a right to be present, and finally she stood at the front of the crowd. What she saw there made her gasp aloud.

All the books on George's stall had turned to coal.

21

Anthony Drury pushed George toward the churchyard gate. "Wait—" George said. "What are you—"

"He's dead," Anthony said harshly. "He won't be able to protect us anymore."

Did Anthony mean Hogg or the red king? It didn't seem to matter. George glanced back once at his stall and saw that a crowd of people surrounded it. He thought he could guess what had happened.

"Where are we going?" he asked, hurrying after Anthony.

"I have a friend, a man who worked for the red king. He'll help us."

They left the churchyard, moving quickly. Why did Anthony need help? If all George's books had turned to coal the stationers would very likely hunt him down for a witch, but what had Anthony done?

"Hurry!" Anthony said. "Do you know what happens to counterfeiters?"

George could barely summon the breath to speak, let alone to answer Anthony's question. "They'll cut my ears off," Anthony said. "If I'm lucky. They could kill me if they were angry enough."

Dusk had fallen; that and the strange events of the day kept folks from venturing out-of-doors. Anthony and George ran through the empty streets, blown like embers from a long-dead fire.

"Pray that he's home," Anthony said, slowing to study the houses as they passed. "He does a great deal of business overseas."

Finally he stopped and knocked on a door. Every window in the house was lit; someone, George thought, had stayed up for something. For them? A man carrying a lantern came to the door. In the dim light his pale blue eyes shone like wet stones.

"The red king?" the man asked.

"Dead," Anthony said, pushing his way past him into the house. "It went badly for us, Master Poley. The red king fell, and Hogg is dead as well."

George sat shakily on a stool near the hearth, suddenly overcome with weariness. "Dead," Poley said, pacing back and forth in front of the fire. "Well. Worse than I'd expected, far worse." He seemed to be talking to himself, to have forgotten the presence of the other men.

"They're after George," Anthony said. "They'll be after me soon enough—the magic that protected me is gone, and they'll see how I debased the coins. We have to get away, go—go somewhere—"

"Of course," Poley said. He seemed to rouse himself. "I can arrange that. I'll send you to the Low Countries, there or to France. You'll be caught in the middle of war either way, but it can't be helped."

George raised his head. Did Poley mean exile? He had never bargained for this when he had listened so heedlessly to Anthony, that day in the churchyard. He began to shiver, though the fire at his back was warm. "I don't—I don't want to—"

"Quiet, George," Anthony said. "You have no choice in the matter. Either come with me or be tried as a witch."

George fell back, feeling miserable. "You'll have to stay here for the night," Poley said. Even through his unhappiness George understood that nothing would happen to Poley; he was the sort of man who would be able to start over whatever happened, who could always find a port no matter what the weather. "We'll leave in the morning."

Alice looked around for George, could not find him anywhere. "Imagine," one of the men said to her, "him calling you a witch when he was the witch all along."

She felt too shaky to answer. The light began to fade from the churchyard. She looked around her in alarm, saw that only a handful of Oriana's folk were left. Brownie—Where was Brownie? And where was her son?

"What a sight," one of the stationers said to her, and all the men in the little group turned to hear her reply. She understood that they wanted to talk to her, wanted to make amends for the shabby way they had treated her. But she noticed that none of them attempted an apology.

She pushed her way through the crowd, feeling impatient and angry. She had no time to waste on these people, who, after all, had left her to herself for three long years. Art was still missing, and she needed to find Brownie.

"Alice!" someone called to her from across the churchyard. "Hurry!"

It was Brownie. She ran toward him with relief. As she left the circle of stationers she saw Walter, standing at the edge of the crowd and watching her with an expression she could not make out.

"We must hurry," Brownie said. "They're starting to leave us."

"Who?"

"Queen Oriana and her people. They've had terrible losses here today. I doubt you'll see the Fair Folk ever again."

"Why? Where are they going?"

"I don't know. They're moving away from mortals, away from this world. All the passages are growing dim and hard to find. We must find your son soon, or he will be lost to you."

"But you—you were the one to hide him."

"Aye. But they've cast a glamour over the roads. Soon their lives and yours will be sundered forever."

"I don't understand. How will we find him?"

"Come," Brownie said. "Take my hand."

She reached out hesitantly. His hand felt warm and dry, with only the soft fur on the back to remind her of who he was.

They began to walk. The sun had set, or the Fair Folk had taken their light with them. She could barely see Brownie at her side. After a moment she realized that they had somehow left Paul's, that they should have reached the gate or the walls by now. The air had grown cold. "Where are we?" she said, whispering.

"Hush."

She looked at Brownie and saw that the lines on his face were creased with concentration. Then a glow came up around them, at first so faint she thought she might have imagined it. The light grew stronger. "Did you do that?" she asked, but he did not answer.

Now she could see that they walked through a dense forest, a place of thick leaves and overgrown paths. She had not seen such large trees since she left her village; certainly there was nothing like them near London. Almost immediately they came to a fork in the road, a junction where three paths met. Brownie stopped. He looked from one road to another, and Alice felt afraid to see the puzzled look that appeared on his broad seamed face.

He chose the left-hand path and they continued onward. A screech owl called, and another answered. Something scurried beside them through the drift of leaves. Frogs croaked in the distance.

A long howl came to them from far off and she cried out. Brownie urged her forward. But soon he stopped at another fork in the road, four paths radiating outward, and this time he took even longer to decide what to do. At last he chose one of the middle paths and they went on.

She thought they might have spent the night walking through the forest, but she saw no hint of dawn. Once something brushed past her and she nearly turned back; once she saw the hint of a luminous bird flying far off and away from them, the only bright thing in all those dark woods. And through it all

Brownie had to stop and choose their path perhaps a dozen times, until she thought that they must be hopelessly lost.

Finally he raised his head, as if sniffing the air. They began to hurry, tripping over roots and breaking through hanging branches. Once she thought they might have left the path altogether. The animal's howl came again, closer this time.

Something impossibly bright shone through the dark leaves of the forest. As they drew nearer Alice saw that it was a silver hill, almost perfectly circular. Beside her Brownie breathed a sigh of relief. "We're here," he said. "I'm home."

"Where are we?" Alice asked.

"Oriana's court," he said, and walked forward.

She had no choice but to follow him. They entered through a small door and she looked around her in amazement.

The place was as Agnes had described it in her story. Light came from the walls, from the jewels on the people's fingers and from their faces. In the center of the room stood a long table where the people feasted, and serving-men moved up and down, carrying silver trays filled with food. The music she had heard the night of the revels came to her; though she had forgotten the melody, and had tried countless times to remember it, she recognized it immediately.

But Agnes had not mentioned the empty places at the table, the seats of all the men who had fallen in battle. Surely Oriana could claim fealty over more than this handful, far fewer than the ones Alice had seen the night of the revels. And those who were left seemed to have dwindled somehow, their light less strong, their music sadder. But still they feasted and sang and called for the serving-men to fill up their glasses. Don't they mourn at all? Alice wondered.

Oriana sat at the table's head. Alice looked for her son and for Arthur, and finally saw the King of Faerie at the other end of the table. They had crowned him with a circlet of crystal like the one Oriana wore. He was listening to two men near him and drinking from a goblet made of silver. He looked grave, concerned, but when he glanced up and saw her she thought he smiled.

"You made it back, my brownie," Oriana said. "Come—sit with us. Join our feast."

"Aye," Brownie said. He took an empty place at the long table and motioned to Alice to sit next to him.

"Why did you linger? The roads were nearly closed."

"I know. I had to find Alice, and bring her here."

"Alice?" The queen turned in her direction for the first time, as if only now aware of her presence. "Why?"

"I hid her son here."

"Oh, aye, the boy." Oriana made a dismissive gesture. "Was he so important to you? Important enough to be worth exile?"

Alice looked at Brownie sharply. What did she mean? Had he nearly missed the closing of the roads because he had stayed to look for her? Had he risked his place with Oriana for her?

"Nay, my queen."

Oriana sat back in her chair. She's jealous, Alice thought in astonishment, jealous that Brownie might have preferred me to her. But nay—they don't feel human emotions. Who could know what Oriana thought?

A serving-man came up to them and set his tray before her. She saw apples and pomegranates and other exotic fruit she did not recognize. "Take one," the man whispered, but as she reached for the tray Brownie grasped her hand and held her back. She remembered how strong he was, remembered too what he had said the night of the revels, that she was not to touch either food or drink. The queen watched them with what looked like amusement.

"The boy is hardly important to me at all," Brownie said. "It's Alice I care for. She would be unhappy without her son."

"Would she? Well then, we must give him to her." The queen clapped her hands and someone brought out Alice's son. "Take him and go," she said to Alice. "You will not see us again, I assure you."

Alice moved closer to Brownie. Was she to travel the dark roads alone? How could she possibly find her way back? Her first thought must have been correct: the queen was jealous. Oriana could not understand why Brownie and Arthur cared for her.

"Would you like to go with her, my brownie?" Oriana said. "You may, if you like. But if you leave you will not be able to come back. Already the roads are drowned deep in mystery and confusion."

Brownie looked from Alice to his queen. Finally, slowly, he nodded.

"Nay!" Alice said. "I won't let you do it. Your place is here, with these people. I won't have you go into exile for me."

"I have no choice, Alice," Brownie said. "How will you find your way back alone?"

"I remember the roads you took," Alice said, lying.

Brownie smiled sadly. "Did you think the roads are the same every time?"

"There is another way," Oriana said. "I will give her a guide." The queen clapped her hands again and a cat, black as the forest Alice had come through, walked sinuously through one of the doors.

"I accept," Alice said quickly, before she could change her mind, or Brownie could convince her otherwise.

"Nay, Alice," Brownie said. "You will not be able to see this creature in the dark."

"It's the only way. You can't leave your place here. I'll be safe—truly I will."

Art was watching them with his perpetually astonished look, as if he expected miracles. Did he understand why she had come? She stood and went to the boy's side. Brownie followed her. "Fare well, Alice," he said softly.

She embraced him. At first he tried to pull away, startled, but then he stood calmly, as if waiting for her to finish. He was warm, and she could feel the hard cording of muscles under his fur. He smelled of dirt and sweat and leaves, a wild-animal smell.

She broke away. "Come, Art," she said. The cat went before them, its tail held high, and together they left the court of Faerie.

The darkness of the forest had not lifted. After she had taken a few steps even the light of the faerie hill disappeared, and she reached out to take Art's hand. Brownie had been right: she could barely see the cat in the dark, a shadow among shadows.

It was sleek and whip-thin, unlike Margery's fat contented cats, and it moved with a grace she had never encountered outside of Faerie. Perhaps it was not a true cat at all.

At the first choice of roads she nearly blundered past the cat, but the spark of gold from its eyes warned her to turn back. After that it became easier: she had only to look for the glow of its eyes to tell her which path to take. It seemed patient, turning back several times during the journey to make certain she was following. She had assumed it would share Oriana's dislike of her, but now she wondered if it was on her side after all. Or perhaps she had only imagined the queen's jealousy. She knew that she would never understand these folk, that even Margery did not understand them.

But she had not imagined Brownie's concern for her. She grinned in the dark, remembering it. She had taught him to care for something; Oriana could not take that away from her. And Arthur had changed too, had become stronger, more certain. She laughed, and Art turned to her in puzzlement. But she could not tell him what she had found so amusing. It had been only that afternoon that Hogg had called her a poor mother, and she had agreed with him. But how many mothers could claim to have called up affection in the stony breasts of the Fair Folk?

She went forward with a lighter step, not minding the strange calls and rustling sounds of the forest around them. And the cat didn't seem to heed the noises either; it paused only a moment when the howl of the wolf drifted through the trees.

After a time the forest thinned. To her surprise she saw Aldergate ahead, and from there it was only a short walk to Paul's. She went down Aldergate Street, the stars lighting her path.

A tree stood near the gate to Paul's. Its branches were thick with fruit of all sort, growing indiscriminately among the leaves—apples and oranges, pears and plums—and the stars shone among them, fruit of a different kind. It had to have come from Faerie, she thought, a final sign to mark the place where their country ended and the everyday world began.

She studied it for a long moment. Was this the tree Margery had touched the day they had exchanged Arthur for her son?

And did she only see it plain now, or was it hidden under the faeries' glamour, its true form what Margery had shown her?

Beside her Art stirred with impatience; probably he had become used to miracles. She took one last look and then led him to her house on Paternoster Row.

She was surprised when the cat followed them inside. She built up the fire and sat near the hearth. The cat jumped into her lap and she stroked its smooth fur, getting used to the idea of it. It arched back and looked at her with its rich gold eyes. "Oh, Art," she said, "how will we manage without Brownie?"

22

King Arthur sat amid the green grass of a field in Faerie. He had gone there to be alone, but now he became aware that some of the winged creatures had followed him. They flew around him in circles and then scattered across the field, singing and laughing. He could not bring himself to tell them to leave.

So few of the creatures had returned from the battle, perhaps only half a dozen. A handful of the horned soldiers had survived, and almost none of the twig-people. Some of the Fair Folk had stayed in the world when the roads had closed, either out of choice or because they could not find the way back.

He remembered how he had felt when he had seen his mother—nay, not his mother but Alice—fight her way across the churchyard toward where he stood with Oriana. Darkness had fallen over the battleground, but when she spoke to him it seemed the darkness in his mind had lifted; he knew who he was and what he had to do. He understood then that all his wandering through the world—through many worlds—had been a prologue to this. All the battles he had fought and all the strange sights he had seen had been necessary to teach him to use his power.

He was, as he had thought, a king: to how many children was

it given to realize their childhood fantasy? But with this realization had come a responsibility he had not foreseen. Oriana had not explained it to him because to her it had been obvious; she had been raised as a queen and had never understood that it had been otherwise with him. It had taken Alice, a mortal woman, to show him his task.

Now he looked out over the field and laughed harshly. He had finally taken his place as king over these people, only to find that they had dwindled almost to nothing. After he had fought their battles what was there left for him to do? He could lead the Fair Folk in their revels, perhaps, and sit at the head of the table at their feasts, but nothing more. There had been one last important decision to make, the command to close the roads, but Oriana had taken it upon herself without consulting him.

If she'd asked him, though, he would have said she'd made the right choice. It was true that the Fair Folk needed the people of the world, that they were drawn somehow by their mortality. The people died so early they seemed to shine with life, as if they concentrated hundreds of years in one brief span. But he saw that mortals carried danger with them as well, that within the past few years mortal and immortal had grown far too close. It was possible to lose oneself in serving them. Look at Brownie, pining because he had had to leave Alice. And what had he done in her house, after all, but wash her plates and sweep her hearth! And what of himself? He had felt it too, this pull toward them, as if he could be warmed by the fire of their mortality. Was this love? Was it what Alice had called love?

The winged creatures sang around him. "Change and go, change and go. Twirl your partner, change and go."

Aye, the creatures were right. He remembered his other life, the long talks in smoky taverns, and he knew that the Fair Folk had lost their place in the world. A new day had come, one in which they would dwindle into legends, stories. He felt happy that he would not be in the world to see it.

He stood and went back to the hill. It had been given to him to preside over the twilight of his people, and he would have to do the best he could. "Change and go," the creatures sang,

circling in flight above him. "Change and go. Twirl your partner, change and go."

The task of cleaning up the churchyard took longer than the
stationers expected. Weeks after what some called the great
battle and others a monstrous wind they were still at it, ham-
mering stalls, carting away trash, sorting out the books and
ballads scattered all over the yard. The stationers' fund had
been almost exhausted by the repairs, and in the meetings
some called for higher dues and charitable donations.

Alice worked side by side with her neighbors in the yard. In
the hours left to her in the evenings she tried to take care of her
household tasks. It was in those moments that she found herself
missing Brownie most of all, wishing that he had come back
with her through the maze of roads, and she would stop herself,
angrily. His place is in the queen's court, she would think. Do
you imagine he would willingly leave her to be your servant?
Then she would sigh, and wipe the dust off her hands, and wish
she could teach Art to boil water or wash a dish. What would
become of the boy?

During those weeks she barely saw Walter at all, though once
or twice she thought he had looked up at her from across the
yard. She wanted to talk to him, but always something stopped
her. Had he seen her speak to Oriana? What did he think of her?
The stationers no longer avoided her but their behavior now
was very nearly worse: they treated her with deference, asking
her opinion on every question. Perhaps they still thought she
was a witch, but if so they seemed to want to be on her side,
whatever side that was. But she had no answers to give them;
though she might know more than they did about the great
battle she felt that she understood very much less.

She did not see Margery at all. There was no question in her
mind that Margery was some sort of magician, and that she had
used her art to raise the wind and light over the churchyard.
Sometimes Alice thought that she might lose her immortal soul
if she talked with the woman, but usually she knew that that
was not what kept her from her visits.

The truth was that Margery had terrified her. She had thought she had known the other woman well, she'd had a hundred comfortable conversations with her, but what she had seen in the churchyard still made her shiver to think of it. How could she sit in the woman's crowded house and drink her mulled wine, all the while knowing she was capable of—of that?

A few months after the battle nearly all the booksellers reopened their stalls. Alice, like her neighbors, had lost most of her books in the destruction of the churchyard, and she was straightening up the sparse piles before her when she saw Tom Nashe turn in at the gate. The sight of him cheered her; perhaps he would say something amusing to lift her spirits.

But he looked different somehow, chastened, his usual wildness gone. "Good day, Mistress Wood," he said.

She saw that he carried a sheaf of papers under his arm, and she wondered if it could be a manuscript. "Good day," she said. "Have you been ill?"

"I've had—trouble sleeping. There's a woman—I can see her when I close my eyes. She has long brown hair and berry-blue eyes. Do you think I'll ever meet her again?"

"Nay, Tom," Alice said as gently as she could. "The roads to her country are closed now." She noticed then that the flower he wore pinned to his hat had wilted and turned brown. Poor man, she thought, remembering Brownie. What will he do now?

"I thought as much. Anyway," he said, looking a little more cheerful, "I have a manuscript for you."

"Good. I could do with something lighthearted."

"It's not very lighthearted, I'm afraid. It's about London, about the follies of Londoners."

She took it doubtfully. On almost the first page she saw something she had never expected to see: an apology to Gabriel Harvey. "Nothing is there now so much in my vows as to be at peace with all men, and make submissive amends where I have most displeased . . . Even of Master Doctor Harvey I heartily desire the like, whose fame and reputation I rashly assailed . . . Only with his mild gentle moderation hereunto hath he won me."

She looked up. Tom grinned at her, the old Tom, and for a

moment she thought he had written the entire manuscript as a jest. Then he said, "Are you surprised?"

She nodded. "Gabriel Harvey—after all he's said about you—"

"I've done with fighting."

"Aye," she said. "I understand that only too well."

They spoke a little more, and then Tom said he must be going. "Take care, Tom," she said. She watched him as he left the churchyard. How he had changed; she wouldn't have believed it unless she'd seen it. An apology to Gabriel Harvey! She shook her head.

She paged through his manuscript, keeping one eye out for customers. But no one came; folks still feared the plague, and people had started to whisper about the strange sights in Paul's churchyard. She left her stall and began to look through the other stationers' books, something all the booksellers did two or three times a month.

She was interested to see what had happened to all of George's books and copyrights. When he hadn't come back after the final battle his copyrights had been portioned out at the stationers' meeting. Alice had gotten some of them; most people thought she deserved them.

Now she paged through one of George's books on another stall and then turned her attention to a book near it, a thick volume bound in black leather. It looked familiar; she thought she might have seen something like it in Margery's house. She opened it at random and began to read:

"Not all the things the physician must know are taught in the academies. Now and then he must turn to old women, to Tartars who are called gypsies, to itinerant magicians, to elderly country folk and many others who are frequently held in contempt. From them he will gather his knowledge, since these people have more understanding of such things than all the high colleges."

She closed the book and looked for the author. Paracelsus, the great physician and alchemist. Then she stood a moment, her eyes nearly closed, and thought. If Tom could make his peace with Gabriel Harvey then she could find it within herself to talk to Margery. She went back to her stall, closed it, and walked to Ludgate and Margery's cottage.

Agnes opened the door to her. "Good day, Alice," she said calmly, as if Alice made regular visits to the cottage.

"Good day. I came to talk to—ah, there she is."

Margery turned from where she had been hanging a bunch of herbs by the window. "Alice," she said, sounding pleased.

Once again, unbidden, there came to Alice's mind the picture of Margery in the churchyard, the great light that had swept across the yard, her hair streaming backward from the force of it. Could this small dumpy woman have done all that? Now her hair was tangled in a hundred knots; she looked as if she had not combed it since that day.

"Sit down," Margery said. She rummaged among the confusion on the floor and found her pipe, then came over to join her. "Would you like some wine?"

"I— Nay. Thank you."

Margery moved a pile of books and manuscripts and sat comfortably on a three-legged stool. "Is something wrong?" she asked, drawing on her pipe.

Now that it came to it Alice was unsure how to begin. Surely it would be uncivil to ask the woman if she was a witch, if she practiced the black arts.

"You want to talk about the battle in the churchyard, and about my part in it," Margery said.

Of course, Alice thought. She should have remembered the way Margery seemed to read her thoughts. "Aye," she said, not trusting herself to say anything else.

"I used what I had learned in my studies, nothing more."

"And what studies were those?"

"Do you still think I consort with the devil, in spite of everything you know about me?"

"I don't know. I don't know what to think. You can't tell me that those—that what you did came from God."

"Nay. I told you before, Alice—don't you remember? I tried to explain. There are more than two kinds of magic."

"Aye, I remember. And I disbelieved it as much then as I do now."

"Was Oriana on the side of God or the devil? What about the red king?"

"On—on the devil's side. Both of them."

"Nay, you don't believe that. You fought for Oriana yourself."

"I did, aye. But I've come to believe that my soul may be damned for it. She's a godless creature, I think. It was wrong of her to take my son away."

"Wrong? It seems so to you, but these creatures don't follow your laws. You of all people should know that—you've seen them at their revels. And I cannot think of anything for which you might be damned, unless it be a surfeit of kindness."

"But then—were we right to fight for Oriana?"

Margery drew on her pipe; smoke drifted in the air before her for a moment. Then she looked at her friend shrewdly. "Your mind contains two boxes—right and wrong, good and evil, left and right. And everything you encounter goes into one box or the other."

Alice could not think what to say. Why would Margery never answer her questions?

"Hogg thought the same thing," Margery said. "The red king's people were the children of day, he thought, and Oriana's folk the children of night. But you've seen yourself that the differences are not so clear. The red king commanded creatures made of fire and of water, and so did Oriana. Both can withstand light of the sun and moon.

"But Hogg went beyond that. He persuaded himself that the red king's people were good, and Oriana's evil, so that he could continue to do his work. Yet he never found the last alchemical step, the one he sought for so long. Do you know why?"

Alice shook her head. She was not interested in Hogg's business, but she knew from experience that Margery would continue no matter what she said.

"Who was Arthur's father?" Margery asked.

"His—father?" Alice said, startled. "I—I don't know."

"You do. You know enough about this matter that you can guess the answer."

"I don't know. Was it—nay, it couldn't be—"

Margery nodded.

"The red king?" Alice asked, astonished.

"Aye. He and Oriana were married once."

"But why—"

"They quarreled shortly before Arthur was born. And for years afterward the red king did nothing but feed on his hatred, while Oriana grew cold. What do you know about alchemy?"

Alice shook her head. "Very little."

"Many books will tell you that the final step consists of the marriage between the red man and the white lady. Folks have interpreted this in different ways—the red man is one substance or another, and the white lady some other substance. They are so used to secrets, to things which are hidden, that they don't recognize the bare truth when they see it. The red man is the red king, of course, and the white lady is Oriana."

"And Arthur?"

"Arthur is the fruit of their union. The Philosopher's Stone." She grinned at Alice's expression. "Oh, aye, he can change lead into gold, though he's only just learned how. You didn't know that, did you, when you and John raised him."

Alice said nothing, too amazed to speak. "Hogg never understood that about Arthur," Margery said. "To him one side was good and the other evil, and so the idea of marriage, of reconciliation, never entered his mind. For all his knowledge, for all his wisdom, he was too blind to see what was before him all the time."

"What happens now? Now that the red king's dead?"

"Now the Fair Folk dwindle. The age passes, and their power fades from the world. And my power with it, I'm afraid."

"Your—"

"Aye. As long as the king and queen were alive there was a balance in the world, and I could use that in my magic. And so could Hogg, though he didn't understand where his power came from."

"But you worked for Oriana, against the red king."

"Aye. But for years before that I worked for reconciliation between them. It was only when I saw my cause was lost that

I began to work for Oriana. I feared what the red king might do in his hatred. But I entered her service unwillingly, and I would not have chosen the way things turned out. Too many died in her war, too many good people."

Alice said nothing. What would it be like to lose all your power? To give up that power, however reluctantly, for something you believed in?

"Do you remember what I told you, that day we talked about black and white magic?" Margery said. "I said that magic was all around us, to be seen by everyone. But that's no longer true. I tried for reconciliation, and I failed. But you, I think, will succeed."

"What—what do you mean?"

Margery drew on her pipe. "Have you talked to Walter yet?"

"What?" Alice asked, thrown off balance by the change of subject. "Nay, I—I don't—I haven't spoken to him since that day—"

"Why do you wait so long?"

"I'm not waiting. Walter would as soon talk to a demon as speak to me. To be honest, I think he's afraid of me. All the stationers are afraid of me."

"I shouldn't wait much longer, Alice."

"Don't you listen to anything I say? And why should I speak to him? What would I say?"

"Ah," Margery said. "You'll have to talk to him and find out."

Walter was putting his books away when she returned to the churchyard. Perhaps Margery was right; perhaps she should talk to him. She went up to his stall before she could change her mind.

"Good day, Alice," he said when he saw her.

"Good day," she said.

They stood awkwardly for several moments. Their old ritual, the plays they had seen together, would not serve them this time: most of the acting companies had still not returned to London for fear of the plague, and she and Walter had seen all the ones that had remained. What does he think of me? Alice thought for the hundredth time. And then, Does he wonder the same thing about me?

"I would—I would like to speak with you," she said finally.

He nodded. "Just let me close up here."

After he closed his stall they left the churchyard and began to walk aimlessly. Despite what she had said she could not think of anything to say to him. It seemed to her that they were each several people: the friends who had gone to plays together, the intimates who had spoken so closely to each other in the tower, the woman who had fought for Oriana and the man who had watched the battle with thoughts she could not imagine. Now she could not tell which of those people she would speak to if she attempted conversation, and so she remained silent.

Finally Walter began to talk, hesitantly. "Folks say," he said, "that the man on that horned animal in the battle—the king, I suppose—that he was your son Arthur."

"Aye, he was, in a way."

"In a way? You have not lost your old habit of secrecy, I see."

"Nay," Alice said, protesting. "I'm not being secretive. I— It's a long story, and complex, and I would not want to burden you with it—"

Walter stopped and looked at her. "I care about you, Alice— have you forgotten that I said so? I would like to hear your story. And I think you would like to tell it, more, that you need to talk to someone."

She did not want to tell him. If he knew the truth about her, how she had consorted with the Fair Folk, he would surely never speak to her again. But he seemed kind, willing to listen; he had never looked at her with disapproval the way George had. And she knew that in one thing he was right: she did need to talk to someone, if only to make sense of the story herself.

And so, haltingly at first and then more and more certainly, she began to tell him the whole strange, fantastic tale. Arthur's disappearance, and Brownie, the faerie revels and the birth Agnes had seen, Arthur's capture and the exchange they had, made for her true son Art. They stood in the street near Paul's, and the sun set over the rooftops of London as she spoke, and opposite it the moon began to rise.

She saw that he did not disbelieve her or attempt to judge her but heard her through with a look of amazement on his face. "Who would have thought it?" he said once. "There's more to you than one would think, Alice."

They had begun to walk again. As they came to back to Paul's Alice stopped, her gaze caught by the tree near the gate. Was it the same one she had seen the night she came back from the faeries' court? The myriad fruits that had hung from its branches were no longer there, but perhaps the glamour had gone from it now that the roads had closed for good. She looked up into its weave of interlocking branches, and she thought that she understood something for the first time.

Reconciliation, she thought. Margery had indeed been right; she, and everyone she knew, had attempted to put everything about this strange business into one box or the other. But here in front of her was the truth, this multibranching tree that would carry first the sun and then the moon as fruit among its leaves, this intricate thing growing and changing and dying. All divisions disappeared before her, and she knew then what Margery had tried to teach her.

She turned to Walter, wanting to tell him what she had learned, and found that she could not manage to put it into words. The vision, if that was what it was, began to fade; she wondered if she had realized anything at all. And yet the tree still stood before her, dense, solid, a real thing.

Walter must have seen something in her eyes, because he moved closer and put his arms around her. He asked her a question. The transport of the moment had not yet left her, and so he was forced to ask again.

"Aye," she said, whispering. "Oh, aye."

All the stationers came to St. Faith's for their wedding. Art sat near them, smiling at everything and everyone, and her surly printer took up a spot a little apart from the body of people. Margery was there, and Agnes, both looking a little out of place in the sanctity of the chapel. And Tom Nashe had made it too; she felt glad to see him.

In the middle of the ceremony she became aware that other

guests had entered the chapel. Once or twice she thought she saw a light in the air of the church, and when she closed her right eye the light grew stronger. Not all the Fair Folk had returned when the roads had closed, she guessed.

Afterward the stationers came up to congratulate her, and several of them took her aside for talks in which they could not seem to come to the point. "You know that I—well, I never trusted George—and even when—you understand—" She had watched them go from feeling distrust of her to treating her almost with awe, but it was the idea of her doing something as normal as marrying that made them think of her as one of their own. She found, strangely, that she could not hate them for it, that she could only accept as she had been accepted. Perhaps that made her weak-willed, but if that was true she could not seem to bring herself to care.

When she and Walter opened their gifts, she found that her guess in the chapel had been correct. For someone had given them a knife and spoon made of golden filigree, with glowing jewels set where the strands of gold met. None of her friends could afford such a fine present; it must have been the Fair Folk, thanking her at last.

The next year Art got married, to a strong sensible woman who took him to her family's farm. He proved to have an aptitude for growing things, and the farm prospered. Alice gave them the faeries' gift when they married. They passed it in their turn to their daughter, and their descendants have it to this very day.